TAILORED REALITIES

Fiction by Brandon Sanderson®

TAILORED REALITIES

BRANDON SANDERSON

TOR

Tor Publishing Group

New York

TAILORED REALITIES

Copyright © 2025 by Dragonsteel, LLC
Illustrations copyright © 2025 by Dragonsteel, LLC

Brandon Sanderson®, Mistborn®, The Stormlight Archive®, Reckoners®, and Cosmere® are registered trademarks of Dragonsteel, LLC.

The phrase "The Wheel of Time®" is a trademark of Bandersnatch Group, Inc.

Cover art by Bryan Mark Taylor © Dragonsteel, LLC

Interior art by Ben McSweeney and Jessi Ochse © Dragonsteel, LLC

Illustrations preceding "Brain Dump," "I Hate Dragons," "Probability Approaching Zero," and "Moment Zero" by Jessi Ochse

Illustrations preceding "Snapshot," "Dreamer," "Perfect State," "Defending Elysium," "Firstborn," and "Mitosis" by Ben McSweeney

A Tor Book
Published by Tom Doherty Associates / Tor Publishing Group
120 Broadway
New York, NY 10271

www.torpublishinggroup.com

Tor® is a registered trademark of Macmillan Publishing Group, LLC.

EU Representative: Macmillan Publishers Ireland Ltd, 1st Floor, The Liffey Trust Centre, 117–126 Sheriff Street Upper, Dublin 1, DO1 YC43

The Library of Congress Cataloging-in-Publication Data is available upon request.

ISBN 978-1-250-41048-1 (hardcover)
ISBN 978-1-250-44728-9 (trade signed edition)
ISBN 978-1-250-44729-6 (signed edition)
ISBN 978-1-250-41049-8 (ebook)

Our books may be purchased in bulk for specialty retail/wholesale, literacy, corporate/premium, educational, and subscription box use. Please contact MacmillanSpecialMarkets@macmillan.com.

First Edition: 2025

Printed in the United States of America

10   9   8   7   6   5   4   3   2   1

COPYRIGHT ACKNOWLEDGMENTS

For Ben McSweeney,
    Who illustrates imagination.

TABLE OF CONTENTS

TAILORED REALITIES

SNAPSHOT

One

Anthony Davis—one of only two real people in a city of twenty million—caught the burrito his partner tossed to him. "Which end is the mustard on?" he asked.

"Mustard?" Chaz replied. "Who puts mustard on a burrito?"

"You. What side?"

Chaz grinned, showing perfect white teeth. They were fake. After taking that barstool to the face two years back, he'd gotten one replaced, but had insisted that the dentist make it too perfect to match his other teeth. By this point, he'd had most of the rest replaced as well.

"Mustard is in the end on your left," Chaz said, nodding to the burrito. "How'd you know?"

Davis just grunted, ripping off the corner of the burrito. Beans, cheese, beef. And *mustard*. Chaz clung to this stupid belief that someday his partner would happen upon a mustardy bite and convert. Davis shook his head and tossed the ripped-off chunk of burrito into a dumpster.

The two strolled down the street in plain clothes. The vast city of New Clipperton enveloped them, so authentic that one would never be able to tell it was a Snapshot—a re-creation of a specific day in the real city. Using methods a simple cop like Davis struggled to understand, the entire city had been reproduced.

They were actually in some vast underground complex, but it didn't seem that way to him; he saw a sun overhead and smelled the stench of the alleyway they passed. It all felt real to him. In its way, it *was* real: built from raw matter you could touch, smell, hear, and—as evidenced by the bite Davis took of his burrito—taste.

Damn. He'd missed some of the mustard.

"You ever wonder," Chaz said, talking with his mouth half full, "how much these burritos cost? Like, for real. The energy to create them and stick them in here so we can buy them?"

"They cost tons," Davis said, then took another bite. "And nothing at the same time."

"Huh. Kind of like how you can say things, but have them mean nothing at the same time?"

"The Snapshot Project is a sunk cost, Chaz," Davis said. "The suits already paid for the place, the technology to do this. Everything is already here, and the setup cost was enormous. But we didn't really have much choice."

When the new American government had pulled out of Clipperton, they'd decided not to remove the installation built underneath it. Davis had always assumed that the Americans wanted the place to stay around, in case they decided to return and play with their experiment some more. But they also hadn't wanted to just *give* it away. So New Clipperton—officially an independent city-state—had been granted the "opportunity" to take control of the Snapshot Project. For a very large fee.

Davis took another bite of his burrito. "This whole thing cost us a ton, but that's done. So we might as well use it."

"Yeah, but burritos, man. They make burritos for us. I always wondered if the bean counters would figure, 'Burritos are too frivolous. Let's take them out.'"

"Doesn't work that way. If you're going to use the Snapshot to re-create a day, you have to do it exactly. So our burritos, the graffiti on the wall there, the woman you're leering at—all part of the package. Expensive, but free, all at once."

"She *is* fine though, eh?" Chaz said, turning around and walking backward as he watched the woman.

"Have a little decency, Chaz."

"Why? She's not real. None of them are real."

Davis took another bite of burrito. His taste buds couldn't tell that it wasn't real. Of course, what did it mean to be "real"? The beans and cheese had been modeled on a real burrito in the real city, and it was exact down to the molecular level. It wasn't just some virtual simulation either. If you'd placed this burrito beside one from the real world, even an electron microscope couldn't have detected the difference.

Chaz grunted, biting into his own burrito. "Wonder who bought these in the real city."

It was a good question. This Snapshot had been created overnight, and was an exact replica of a day ten days back: the first of May, 2018. This entire re-creation would be deleted once Chaz and Davis left for the evening. They'd push a button, and everything in here would be reconstituted back to raw matter and energy.

Chaz and Davis were real though—from "in real life," so to speak. Their insertion—while necessary—was also problematic. As Chaz and Davis interacted with the Snapshot, they would cause what were called Deviations: differences between the Snapshot and the way the real May first had played out.

Some things they did—though it was impossible to tell which ones ahead of time—would end up having a ripple effect throughout the Snapshot, making the re-creation happen differently from the real day. The Deviation percentage—as calculated by statisticians—would be a factor in any trials associated with evidence discovered in the Snapshot.

Chaz and Davis usually left that to the bean counters. Sometimes, they'd go the entire day doing things they were sure would ruin their cases—but in the end everything played out fine, and the Deviation percentage was determined to be small. Another time, Davis had locked himself away in a hotel saferoom, determined not to create any Deviations. Unfortunately, by slamming his door, he'd woken up a woman in an adjacent room. She had therefore made it to an interview on time, and that had sent ripples throughout the entire Snapshot, causing a 20 percent Deviation level. That had cost them an entire case.

Nobody had blamed him. Cops in the Snapshot would introduce Deviations; it was the nature of what they did. Still, it haunted him. In here, everyone else was fake, but he and Chaz . . . They were somehow something worse. Flaws in a perfect system. Intruders. Viruses leaving chaos in their wakes.

It doesn't matter, he told himself as he finished the last of the burrito. *Eyes on the mission.* The department shrink told him to focus on what he was doing, on his task at hand. He couldn't function if he fixated on the Deviations.

The two made their way to the corner of Third and Twenty-Second, near rows of little shops. Convenience stores, a liquor shop with bars on the windows. The backs of the stop signs had random stickers from this band or that plastered over them. This wasn't one of the nicer areas of the city; there weren't many of those left.

Davis called up the mission parameters again on his phone, looking them over. "I think we should stand inside," Davis said, gesturing toward the liquor store.

"Makes it hard to chase someone."

"Yeah, but he won't see us. No Deviations."

"Deviations can't be stopped."

He was right. Each day, they'd be interviewed about what they did, and data from their phones—which tracked their location—would be downloaded. Their actions were audited by the bean counters in IA, but the language was always about "minimizing Deviation risk in targets." Never about *eliminating* the Deviations.

Besides, the phone data could be fudged, as Davis well knew, and signals from outside had trouble reaching inside the Snapshot. So really, nobody knew for sure what they did in here.

Still, Chaz didn't argue further as Davis positioned them inside the liquor store, which was open despite the early hour. The place smelled clean, and was well maintained, notwithstanding the unsavory section of town. A bearded Sikh man with a sharp red turban swept the floor by the checkout counter. He regarded them curiously as they set up near the front window.

Davis read the mission parameters again, then checked his watch. A half hour. Not much time. They shouldn't have stopped for breakfast, despite Chaz's complaining.

The shopkeeper continued his sweeping, eyeing them periodically.

"He's going to be trouble," Chaz noted.

"We're just two normal patrons."

"Who didn't buy anything. Now we're staring out the window, one of us checking his watch every fifteen seconds."

"I'm not—"

Davis was interrupted as the shopkeeper finally set his broom aside and came walking over. "I'm going to need you to leave," he said. "I need to close for, um, lunch."

Davis smiled, preparing a lie to placate the man.

Chaz flashed his badge.

It looked normal to Davis. Just a silvery shield with the usual important-looking embossing. Nothing abnormal about it. Except it was a reality badge. To anyone from the Snapshot—to anyone who was a dupe, a fake person—it wouldn't look like a normal police shield at all. Instead, it was certification that the men bearing it were real.

And equally, certification that *you* were *not*.

The Sikh man stared at the badge, eyes widening. Davis always wondered what it was they saw. They got that same far-off look in their eyes, as if they'd stared into something vast. Stunned. Even a little in awe.

Has a dupe of me ever seen one of those? he wondered. *Thinking he was the real me, completely ignorant of the fact that he—and his entire world—was just a Snapshot. Until he saw the badge . . .*

The shopkeeper shook himself and looked at them. "Hey, that's a neat trick. How did you . . . I mean, how'd you make it . . ." He trailed off, looking down at the badge again.

Dupes always recognized it instinctively. Something inside them knew what the badge meant, even if they hadn't ever heard about them. Of course, most *had* heard of them, with the privacy dustups recently. Beyond that, the general public up in the Restored American Union had a fascination with the project; it was becoming a favorite of cinema. You could stream half a dozen cop dramas about detectives working inside a Snapshot—though as far as Davis knew, the only official facility was here in New Clipperton.

The cop dramas never showed what the reality badge looked like. It seemed to be some kind of unwritten rule. It was better in your head.

The shopkeeper whispered something softly in his native tongue. Then he looked up at them again, more somber. Chaz nodded to him.

The shopkeeper took it well. He just . . . wandered off. He pushed out the door of his shop in a daze, leaving it all behind. Why work a retail job when you've just found out you aren't real? Why bother with anything when your entire world is going to end around bedtime?

"Want anything to drink?" Chaz asked cheerfully as he tucked his badge into his front pocket. He nodded to the now-unguarded store shelves.

"You didn't need to do that," Davis said.

"We only have a few minutes left. No time for chitchat. This was the best way."

"He'll introduce Deviations."

"There's no way to stop—"

"Shut it," Davis said, slumping against the window and checking his watch again. *Sometimes I hate you, Chaz.*

Though he envied Chaz at the same time. Davis would be better off if he could simply start viewing everything in here—even the people they passed—as fake. Puppets created from raw matter and animated for a short time.

It was just that . . . they were *exact* reproductions, right down to their brain chemistry. How could you not view them as real people? He and Chaz ate the burritos, treated *them* as real, but were at the same time supposed to pretend the people they met were nothing more than simulacra? Didn't seem right.

Chaz squeezed him on the shoulder. "It's better this way. He'll be able to enjoy what's left of his life, you know?" He dug in his pocket, then dropped a handful of change onto the windowsill. "Here. From the burrito stand."

Chaz wandered off to dig out an India pale ale. Davis stewed, then checked his mission parameters. Again. Two cases today. The one out on the street corner, then another near Warsaw Street at 20:17. Deviation percentage might be high by then, particularly if Chaz was in a mood today, but they could still do some good. Help cases going on in the real world. Get information to the real cops.

And Warsaw Street. 20:17.

Davis finally took the handful of coins and began sifting through them, holding each up to the morning sunlight coming through the window, checking the date. Chaz sauntered back over, then shook his head at Davis. "We could go to a bank, you know. Ask them for an entire *bucket* of coins."

"Wouldn't count," Davis said, frowning at the quarter he was holding. Did he have 2002, Philadelphia mint? He pulled out his phone, scrolling down.

"Wouldn't count?" Chaz asked. "By whose rules?"

"My own rules."

"Then change them."

"Can't," Davis said. Yeah, he'd found a 2002 already. It was 2003 he needed. Hard to find a place that used coins these days. The street vendors, the occasional convenience store.

"You do realize," Chaz said, "how much more difficult you make your life, don't you?"

"Sometimes," Davis admitted. "But I can't cheat, or the collection will lose all meaning. Besides, Hal knows the rules." Davis had gotten an email from his son last week; the kid had almost finished a complete set of the 2000s. There was a soda machine in Hal's school that gave real-money change.

"Let's say you find one in here," Chaz said. "Some little bit of metal that happens to have the right stamp on it, to make you all freaked out or whatever. What would you do? We can't take anything out of the Snapshot."

"Unless it's inside us," Davis said, nodding to Chaz's beer.

"You'd—"

"Eat the coin? Sure. Why not? What are the precinct bean counters going to do? Search my stool?"

Chaz took a long drink of beer. "You're a strange little dude, Davis."

"You're only now figuring this out?"

"I'm slow," Chaz said. "And you, you're like subtly weird, Davis. *Stealth* weird."

Davis's watch buzzed, and he checked the time. Five minutes. He leaned in, watching the building across the street. A bar with some apartments on top.

Chaz reached for the holster under his arm.

"You won't need that," Davis said.

"A man can dream, can't he?" But he did let go of the gun. "What makes this guy special anyway? A thousand murders a year in the city, and this one gets a Snapshot?"

Davis didn't answer. Seriously, couldn't Chaz be bothered to check the news once in a while? Or *at least* read the case notes?

They barely heard the shot across the street. Standing where they were, the little pop could have been almost anything. Someone flinging a bottle at a dumpster, a window breaking, even a door slamming. Davis jumped anyway.

Their perp, Enrique Estevez, hurried out of the building's stairwell a minute later, hands shoved in his pockets. He looked around nervously, then set off down the street. Not quite at a run, but still obviously agitated.

"I'm off," Chaz said.

"Don't let him see you."

Chaz gave him the look that meant, *What, you think it's my first day?* Then he was out the door tailing Estevez, phone in hand.

Davis ducked out a moment later and turned down an alley, following the map on his phone toward Sixth. He would wait at the last point Estevez had been seen on the real day, in case Chaz lost the trail.

Davis called Chaz on the phone. "How's he looking?"

"Nervous," Chaz said over the line. "Street's gone empty. Only a handful of people here. Should I take pictures of anyone, so the IRL cops can seek out witnesses?"

"No," Davis said. "Too suspicious. And what would they witness? That Estevez was on the street? Just tail him."

"Right," Chaz said. "Hold up. He turned toward Eighth."

Davis stopped in place. It was the wrong direction. "You sure?"

"Yeah. Is this a problem?"

"He was seen on Sixth in a few minutes," Davis said. "Is he turning back?"

"No, we're heading east, crossing avenues. Seems determined now. Not looking around as much."

Davis cursed quietly, turning on his heels and heading back along the alleyway at a swift pace. The eyewitness who claimed to have seen Estevez on Sixth was wrong—either that or a Deviation had sent their subject in the wrong direction. If the percentage was that high already, this entire Snapshot would be a wash.

"I'm moving parallel to you," Davis said, trying to keep himself from getting nervous. "You at Eighth yet?"

"Just passed it," Chaz said. "Damn, Davis. He ducked into an alleyway, heading south. It's going to be really hard to follow without looking suspicious."

They couldn't risk that. If Estevez got suspicious, it could create a ton of Deviations in his behavior. That was one type of Deviation they *could* do something about.

"I'm to the south on Twenty-First now," Davis said. "I'll bet I can intercept him."

He stopped on the corner at Eighth Avenue, trying to hide the fact that he was puffing from the short jog. He'd never have passed fitness requirements for IRL fieldwork. Not anymore.

Still, he'd gotten into position fast enough to catch sight of Estevez leaving an alleyway ahead. Estevez turned east along Twenty-First Street, and Davis followed.

"I've got him," Davis said, strolling along, trying to look nonchalant. Just another guy talking on his phone. Nothing to notice or worry about.

Damn. He was already feeling nervous. Stupid. This was a simple chase. He could do this without becoming a wreck.

"Nice work," Chaz said. "I'm heading east on Twenty-Second, parallel to you."

"Roger."

Davis kept pace with Estevez. The perp was a thin man, but taller, more . . . intimidating than his mug shots had made him seem. He'd made a big mistake—not just in murdering a man, but in picking the man to murder. The mayor's nephew.

This was already ramping up to be a big case for the prosecutor, who felt he'd have heavy hitters in the city leaning on him. Unfortunately, their case against the accused wasn't strong. So he'd requested a warrant for a Snapshot.

The city government of New Clipperton had bought the Snapshot Project. Paid the Restored American Union through the nose for it. But what did they know about how it worked? Barely anything. One of those . . . things was trapped somewhere, kept unconscious, electricity buzzing through it and doing this. Re-creating days, in their entirety, from provided raw matter.

Well, you had a small window to get a Snapshot of a specific day made. A few weeks, and that was it. You had to start it up in the morning, insert people right away. If you waited it grew more difficult. Like the doorway in just wouldn't open. And getting data out . . . well, the cops had to carry it out with them. You could usually get secure texts through, but even with those there was interference sometimes.

Privacy watchdogs had lost their minds when they'd found out about the Snapshot Project. Particularly when they'd discovered that originally, the mayor had been using it for personal enjoyment, details redacted.

The resulting flurry of laws and restrictions meant that you needed a court order to re-create a day, and it could only be used for official government business. They could technically send in drones to record what was happening, and the precinct had experimented with that. Might eventually move to it full-time, but for now, old-fashioned detective work seemed most effective. This way you could put a cop on the stand to testify about what he'd seen with his own eyes. Juries responded to that sort of thing.

He was proud of how he stayed on Estevez's tail with no sign of alerting the man. Like a real cop.

Chaz met him at an intersection, and the two kept following as Estevez called someone on the phone. They were too far back to hear anything, but the end result was that they saw when the man knelt down at the edge of the sidewalk and fumbled with something, then stood and darted down another alleyway.

Chaz cursed, speeding up, but Davis caught him by the arm.

"He's getting away!" Chaz said, reaching under his arm for his gun again.

"Let him. This was what we've been waiting for."

"This?" Chaz asked.

Davis walked up to the place where Estevez had knelt: a storm drain on the side of the road. He peered down, then reached in with his phone and took a few pictures. He held it up, scrolling between them until he found a good shot.

A handgun lay in the filth of the drain. "Murder weapon," Davis said, standing up and showing Chaz. "The IRL detectives have been searching for this in all the wrong places." He opened the secure HQ communication app on his phone, then attached the image to a message.

He sent the message to Maria, their HQ liaison. *Murder weapon found,* he wrote. *Storm drain in front of a beauty salon on the north side of Twenty-First, between Tenth and Eleventh Avenues.*

"I hate just letting him go," Chaz said, folding his arms.

"You hate not being able to get into some kind of gunfight," Davis said back.

He waited, worried he'd need to send the message again. You never could be certain what would get out. Fortunately, a few minutes later his watch buzzed, and he glanced at the phone. A line was open, for the time being.

Intel received, Maria sent. *Nice work. Between Tenth and Eleventh? That's far from where you should have been.*

Eyewitness is wrong, Davis sent back. *Estevez went east after the murder, not west.*

Chance of Deviation? Maria sent.

Ask the bean counters, Davis replied. *I'm just reporting what I've found.*

Roger. Sending a team to that gutter IRL. Stay close in case they need follow-up.

Davis showed the phone to Chaz.

"So . . ." Chaz said, looking around. "We have some time. You want to head to Ingred Street?"

"It's noon," Davis said dryly.

"And?"

"And it's a school day."

"Oh. Right. What, then?"

"Well, we had some million-dollar burritos," Davis said, nodding toward a diner. "Shall we have some million-dollar coffee to wash them down?"

Two

David couldn't help wondering how the people in the diner would react to knowing they were dupes. The fat lady behind the counter, going over receipts. The two white guys in flannel and trucker caps, chewing on Reubens and grunting at each other. The mom with a gaggle of kids, hushing them with force-fed fries.

Davis felt he could take the measure of a man or woman by the way they handled the news that they weren't real. It was uncomfortable, intimate, and fascinating to watch. Some got angry, some got morose. Others laughed. You saw something about a person in that moment that they wouldn't ever know—couldn't ever know—about themselves.

His watch buzzed as the waitress arrived with a plate of fries for him and topped off his coffee. Davis had momentary sadistic visions of himself guessing the reactions of the people in the room, then pulling out his badge and showing it around to see if he was right. Trouble was, Chaz might do something like that if he got too bored.

Chaz got back from the restroom as Davis was munching on fries. "Sure," Chaz said, sitting, "you'll put mustard on *those*."

"Mustard belongs on fries."

"Like it belongs on burritos."

"Disgusting."

"You just aren't willing to live, Davis," Chaz said, stealing a fry. "Try new things, you know?"

"Once again, this isn't new," Davis said, checking the message on his phone. "You literally have been trying to get me to eat like you for *three years*."

"It's why I'm a good detective," Chaz said. "Tenacity. What's hottie pants say?"

"Hottie pants? Maria?"

Chaz nodded.

"She's like twenty years older than you."

"And hot. What does she say?"

"They found the gun in real life," Davis said. "It was down there in the storm drain where Estevez threw it. Soaked in ten days' worth of grime, but they rushed it through ballistics and it came back a match for the bullet. We might have to testify." They now had enough evidence to convict Estevez, and the testimony of two hardworking cops would only reinforce that.

Chaz grunted. "Would still feel better if I'd been able to gun that punk down. Pay him back, you know?"

"You don't even know what he did," Davis said dryly.

"Killed someone. That . . . um . . . girl?" He shrugged. "Anyway, want to play hooky for the rest of the day?"

Davis looked up, feeling a cold jolt.

"Our next job," Chaz continued, stealing another fry, "it's not till . . . what, almost twenty-one hundred?"

"Quarter after twenty. Domestic disturbance. They want us to see who hit first. Corroborate one story or the other."

"What a waste of our time."

Davis shrugged. It wasn't uncommon to go on small missions like that throughout the day, after the main case had been investigated.

"I don't want to wait around eight hours to see who slapped who," Chaz said. "Let's save everyone some time and money and bug out of here. The shrink says I should let her know if I feel 'emotional distress.'"

"Which means what?"

"Hell if I know. She seems to think that I should find living in Snapshots distressing."

"Seriously?" Davis said. "You? Is she paying *any* attention?"

"She's not even hot," Chaz added.

Davis sighed, but it did little to cover his sudden anxiety. They couldn't leave. Could they?

Maybe that would be for the best . . .

No. Warsaw. 20:17. He had an appointment.

"Come on," Chaz said. "Let's go. I'll even let you push the button to turn the Snapshot off."

"I *always* push the button," Davis said.

"And today I won't complain."

"No, look, I've got something for us to do." Davis scrambled to pull out his phone again. "I've been reading the scanner forums—"

"Not again."

"—and there was a blip about this day, when it happened for real. Though I couldn't find anything in the precinct records, the *forums* claim that multiple squad cars were called in to search an apartment building. That will happen in the Snapshot in about an hour. Want to get there first and see what it was?"

"Forums," Chaz said dryly. "*Conspiracy* forums. You said there wasn't anything in the official records."

"Nothing I was allowed to see."

"Which probably means they didn't find anything."

"No. That would have been logged. There was *nothing there.*"

"Which means you didn't have clearance. They didn't want low-level detectives knowing about it, whatever it was."

"And doesn't that make you curious?" Davis asked. "We could do a little real detective work. Snoop. Who knows, maybe someone will try to shoot you."

"You think so?" Chaz asked, perking up.

"It could happen. You're very shootable."

He nodded. "Yeah. Real detective work, eh?" He rubbed his chin. "You know what we're going to find, right? Some politician with a whore. That's why they'd hide it. Assuming it's even real, and the forum nutjobs aren't making things up."

"Yeah, well, I suppose we could just play hooky," Davis said. "Go back to the boring real world. Sit around. Watch a movie. Instead of living in one . . ."

"All right, I'm sold," Chaz said, standing. "But I've got to go hit the head first."

"Again?"

"That burrito, man." He shook his head. "That burrito . . ." He wandered off in the direction of the bathroom.

Davis relaxed his fist and let himself breathe out, trembling. They'd stay in the Snapshot for now. Davis paid the bill with actual cash, but the diner only gave change as credit. That wouldn't ever reach him though. This Snapshot city existed on its own, without external infrastructure. If people left the area the Snapshot covered, they vanished immediately. If someone was scheduled to enter the city, the Snapshot created their body and vehicle, then set them on the road driving in at the proper time.

He'd never been able to figure out the details. How did credit transactions work for those inside here? How did the Snapshot manage to re-create all outgoing and incoming transmissions? The power lines. The internet. Sunlight. What were the levels of reality for it all? He ate food in here. How much would he have to eat before the system recognized him as part of it, rather than being real? If he had too many burritos, would that badge someday shine for him, as it did for the dupes?

He tore himself away from that line of thinking. *Keep focused on my task.* He turned around in his seat, looking toward the woman with the children as she packed them up and herded them out the door. The oldest was six, self-proclaimed to his sister in an argument.

That was two years younger than Hal, but Hal had always been small for his age. Like his dad.

The mother and her children left, and Davis found himself staring at a different woman, sitting close to the back of the diner near the window. Slender, with black hair cut short. Angular features. Pretty. Very pretty.

"Well," Chaz said, stomping up, "there's another part of me added to the system: my dump. It'll get recycled when the day breaks down, right?"

"I suppose," Davis said absently, still watching the woman.

"Good to know that part of me will get used the next time they rebuild this. My dump will be recycled into lawyers. Cool, eh?"

"How is that any different from real life?"

"Well, it . . ." He trailed off, scratching his head. "Oh. Yeah, I suppose you're right. Huh. Well anyway, you going to go talk to her?"

"Who?"

"The hottie back there."

"What? *No.* I mean, you shouldn't say things like that."

"Come on," Chaz said, nudging him. "You're staring at her hard enough to throw sparks. Just go say hello."

"I don't want to harass her."

"Talking isn't harassing."

"I'm pretty sure it's one of the *primary* methods of harassment," Davis said.

"Yeah, maybe, sure. But she's looking back at you. She's interested, Davis. I can tell."

Davis toyed with the idea, a small panic rising in him like an exploding bomb. "No," he said, standing. "Why bother? It's not real anyway."

"All the more reason to give it a go. For practice."

Davis shook his head and led the way out of the diner. Unfortunately, as they passed the woman's table, Chaz stepped over to her. "Hey," he said. "My friend is kind of shy, but he was wondering if maybe he could have your number."

Davis felt his heart all but stop.

The woman blushed, then looked away.

"Sorry to bother you," Davis said, hauling his partner out the door by the arm. Then, once outside, he continued, "You idiot! I said not to do that."

"Technically," Chaz said, "you told me *you* weren't going to do it. You didn't say that I couldn't."

"That was humiliating. I—"

Davis froze as the door to the diner opened and the woman stepped out. She blushed again, then handed Davis a little slip of paper before ducking back into the restaurant.

Davis stared at it, reading the phone number scrawled across the front. Chaz grinned a big, goofy smile.

Sometimes, Chaz, he thought, tucking the paper away, *I love you.*

"So, where are we going?" Chaz asked.

"Fourth," Davis said, leading the way down the street.

"Bit of a hike."

"Autocab?"

"Nah," Chaz said, hands in pockets. "Just saying."

They strolled for a time, Davis feeling the paper in his pocket. He was shocked, even embarrassed, by how pleased he was. How warm it made him feel. Even if he was never going to call her, even if she wasn't real. Damn. He hadn't felt like this in years, since before meeting Molly.

"You ever wonder," Chaz said as they walked, "if we should be using this more?"

"What do you mean?"

Chaz nodded at the cars passing on the wide avenue. At least half were auto-cabs, smooth and careful, each one coordinated with the others. A variety of older cars joined them, and most were just as smooth—but you could tell the manual drivers from the way they jerked about, making a mess of things. Like fish that had suddenly split away from the rest of the school.

"We should use this more," Chaz repeated. "We're in a day that already happened. So shouldn't we be able to . . . I don't know . . . buy lottery tickets or something?"

"And win money that will vanish when the day ends?"

"We could swallow it," Chaz said. "Like you said."

"There's a big difference between one coin and millions in lottery earnings. Not that they pay out instantly anyway, for the types of winning numbers we could look up ahead of time. Besides, it would likely be classified as counterfeiting if you somehow *did* get money out."

"Yeah." He shoved his hands in his pockets. "It would still be fun to win. Anyway, I just feel we should be able to do more. Get right what someone else got wrong."

"Which is what we do."

"I'm not talking about legal stuff, Davis." He sighed. "I can't explain it."

The two crossed the road, and cars started again behind them. A few old combustion engines roared past, making Davis turn. That was a sound from his past. Like the smell of gasoline.

"I understand," he said.

"You do?"

"Yeah."

That seemed to comfort the taller man. "So, any idea what we're looking for when we arrive at this place of yours?"

"I don't know," Davis said. "It's just one of those blips that the forum people notice. Sudden, urgent call for a car, several responses . . . then silence. No report. No nothing."

"And you think someone's scared we'll find out."

They'd talked about this sort of thing before. In here, the two of them were absolute authorities. Flashing their badges could get them past any obstruction, overrule any order. They were two men in a crowd of shadows.

In here, they were the only ones with rights. In here, they were *gods*. The longer he'd been working in Snapshots, the more Davis had realized that there were certain people on the outside who found his power in here terrifying. They hated thinking that there were simulacra of them that a couple of low-level detectives could order around. How to contain them, protect people's privacy, was a constant argument.

"I'm surprised," Chaz said as they finally reached Fourth Avenue, "that they didn't remember to send us to some saferoom."

Davis nodded. They wouldn't have gone—they never did. But the precinct continued to order it, claiming that if Davis or Chaz were to meet their own dupe selves in the city, they'd be mentally scarred. Which was stupid.

"If we don't find anything at this address of yours," Chaz said, "I'm going to take the day off."

"Fair enough. But I think there will be something. It's suspicious."

"I'm telling you. Politician with a whore."

"They wouldn't call in squad cars for that." He chewed on his lip. "Have you noticed how lately they seem to have us do only the least work possible on a case? Find a murder weapon, witness a criminal activity. No interviews, little *real* police work."

"Guess they decided they don't want us getting too comfortable with that sort of thing," Chaz said. "Hell, they don't want IRL detectives in here. That's why they send guys like us in the first place."

The site of the mysterious call for the authorities—a call that wouldn't come in the Snapshot for about another hour—was an old apartment building with tags and graffiti sprayed all over it. The broken and grimy windows proclaimed it wasn't occupied these days.

"Doesn't look like the kind of place *I'd* take a prostitute," Davis noted.

"Like you've ever taken a prostitute anywhere," Chaz said, shading his eyes and looking upward. "I know this area. It was nice once—these were probably expensive apartments."

They walked up the steps, then tried the door, which was locked tight. Davis looked to Chaz, who shrugged and kicked the door in. "Damn," he said. "That was easier than I thought it would be."

"Feel like a real cop?"

"Getting there," he said, then peeked into the hallway.

A quick search didn't turn up anything. The ground-floor apartments were open, doors unlocked, but they had been gutted and were empty save for the nest some homeless person had made beneath more spray-painted tags. Even the nest seemed like it hadn't been used in months.

Something smelled off. Musty? Davis wandered back into the main stairwell—near the entry door—sniffing at the air.

Chaz started toward the stairs to the second floor. "There are like twenty stories in this place, Davis. If we have to search them all, so help me, you'll owe me a burrito. Extra mustard."

"Let's try down first," Davis said, catching Chaz and pulling him to a door in the lobby, cracked open with only darkness beyond. He pulled it fully open, revealing a stairway leading down. The smell was stronger. Musty dampness.

Chaz tried the light switch, but the building's power was off. Davis dug out a small flashlight and shined it down the stairs.

"Convenient," Chaz said, trying his phone, which wasn't as good at providing light.

"Always used to carry a flashlight," Davis said, starting down the steps. "IRL, as a detective. You'd be surprised at how often it came in handy."

At the bottom of the steps was another door, which Chaz opened with a well-placed kick. Dampness wafted over them as they stepped into the basement, which had walls lined with broken mirrors. Some old exercise weights lay abandoned in the corner.

"See," Chaz said, holding up his phone for light. "This place was fancy, once upon a time."

Davis led the way through the basement gym, darting his light right, then left, growing nervous. But there didn't seem to be anything down here. They might have to wait until the phone call was made—and the squad cars showed up—to find out what it was.

Chaz stayed close to him, directing his phone's frail light. Perhaps the call had come because one of the floors had caved in or something. Wouldn't that be fitting? Two washed-up detectives, killed in a fake world because they couldn't be bothered to sit back and take a break.

Chaz poked his side, then pointed. Davis turned his flashlight in that direction, noticing a doorway in the wall. Light reflected off a tiled floor beyond. And beyond that . . .

"Water?" he said, striding forward. The musty smell suddenly made sense. "Swimming pool? How is it still *full* in this place?"

"Damned if I know," Chaz said, walking with him into the room. It *was* a pool, moderately sized, considering it was in an apartment building basement. Davis put his hand on his hip, shining the light around. The pool was only partially full. There was no—

His flashlight passed over a face underneath the water.

Davis froze, holding the light on the dead, glassy eyes. Chaz cursed, fumbling for his gun, but Davis just stood there staring. She was young, maybe just a teen. Beside her was another body, settled on the bottom of the pool, facedown.

Shaking, Davis turned his flashlight more slowly across the bottom of the pool. Another. And another.

Corpses. Eight of them.

Three

What the hell, man?" Chaz said. "What the *hell*!"

Davis sat on the steps of the apartment across the street from the one where they'd found the bodies.

"I mean . . . *what the hell*." Chaz paced back and forth, handgun out. Davis couldn't blame him. He clutched his own gun before him, feeling as if some murderer were going to pop out from behind the building, wielding a rusty cleaver.

"How did they keep this quiet?" Chaz demanded. "There are *eight* bodies in that building. Eight! How is this not on every news station in the city, right? How come they don't have every cop in the city working on this? Damn it!"

He paced back the other direction.

I deserve this, Davis thought, slumped in his place. *I should have just left well enough alone.* All he'd wanted to do was keep Chaz in the Snapshot until 20:17. Now . . . this.

"Okay, Chaz," Chaz said to himself, walking back the other way. "Okay, okay. They're not *real* corpses, you know? Just dupes. Dead dupes. That's all you saw." He looked to Davis. "Davis? You okay, buddy?"

Davis held his gun in a trembling hand.

"Davis?" Chaz said. "What do we do now, man? You're a real cop. What do we do?"

"I'm not a real cop," Davis said softly.

"Yeah, not anymore. But you were one for . . . ten years?"

"I was on the force for ten years," Davis said. "But I was never a real cop."

Chaz, on the other hand, had been on the force for less than a year before being assigned to Snapshot duty to replace Davis's old partner, who had finally retired.

"So, what do we do?" Chaz asked.

"Two options, I guess," Davis said, holstering his gun. He took a deep breath. "We walk away, assume the IRL detectives are working on this, and pretend we didn't see anything. We erase our phone tracks, claim we hung out in the diner a few hours longer, and forget this happened."

"Okay, yeah," Chaz said, nodding. "Yeah. No reason we *have* to be involved, right? And they obviously don't want us knowing about this. So if we walk away, nobody is the wiser." He looked down at the handgun he was holding. "What's the other option?"

"Well, we're stuck here until that domestic disturbance in the evening. We can poke around at these murders, maybe find out a thing or two that can help with the investigation. And if not . . . well, maybe we can figure out why the hell the precinct is hiding this from us. Those corpses look kind of fresh—not much bloating, not a lot of flesh sloughing off. Eight bodies found drowned in an old apartment building, and not a peep to the guys who could go back in time and find out who did it? Why the hell wouldn't they involve us?"

"Yeah." Chaz looked to him. "Yeah, *damn*. What's going on?"

People became cops for a myriad of reasons. For some it was expected—it was a family thing, or just seen as good work for a blue-collar person. Others, they liked the power. Chaz was one of those.

But deep down, there was something in all of them. Something about wanting to *fix* the world. Whether you joined up because your family pushed you into it, or just because you got recruited at the right time, there was a story you told yourself. That you were doing something *good*, something *right*.

That story was hard to keep believing, some days. Other days it walked up, slapped you in the face, and said, "You going to do something about this or not?"

A good way to go out, Davis thought. *Doing something that feels real again.*

"You want to dig into this, don't you?" Chaz asked.

"Yeah," Davis said, standing. "You with me?"

"Sure. Why the hell not." Chaz shivered, then finally put his gun away. "What do we do?"

"We wait," Davis said, checking his phone.

A short time later, an autocab pulled up and a couple of people got out. White people, wearing business clothing. *Real estate agents,* Davis guessed. *Or maybe people from a bank that owns this place.* The woman dug in her purse for some keys while the man pointed at the broken windows, saying something Davis couldn't hear.

They seemed concerned by the forced door. Hopefully that wouldn't introduce too big a Deviation. They went inside, chatting.

They rushed back out a few minutes later, visibly agitated. The man sat down on the steps, hyperventilating, holding his face. He threw up a short time later. The woman screamed into her phone, hysterical.

It took about ten minutes for the squad cars to come. There were two, joined by a third later, which arrived about a minute earlier than Davis's records said they would, without lights on. Davis didn't recognize any of the cops, but since he'd been on Snapshot duty for years, that wasn't odd. He knew people back at the precinct headquarters, but not a lot of the beat cops.

Several cops consoled the real estate agents, while the others secured the building. Why wasn't there anything in the precinct records? A complete hush. According to the forums, the cars would be gone in under a half hour.

"This is so *weird*," Chaz said. "What the hell is going on?"

"No idea," Davis said softly. "But I think I know how we can find out."

Chaz looked at him, then smiled. He seemed to be coming to grips with what they'd seen. "HQ?"

Davis nodded.

Not the real one, of course. The fake one, inside the Snapshot.

"Let's go," Chaz said, growing eager. "It's been months since we had an excuse to do this."

Four

avis and Chaz burst in through the front of the 42nd Precinct headquarters, which housed Snapshot detail, among other special jurisdictions in the city. Davis tried to project confidence like Chaz did. But it was hard. In the real world when he visited this building, he felt small. Out of place. Maybe even scorned.

He paused inside the doors. The smell of coffee, the bustling of officers, everyone doing what they should—and everyone seeming to know Davis's shame. That he'd failed them, and been banished as a consequence.

Fortunately, he had Chaz. "Insecurity" wasn't really part of that man's vocabulary. Chaz held his reality badge up high in the air and shouted, "Guess what, everyone. Y'all ain't real!"

He sauntered forward, holding the badge and pointing it one way, then the other, grinning like he'd just won the lottery. Most people who saw it, they stopped and got that glassy look. Gina Gutierrez dropped her cup of coffee, which sent a spray into the air as it struck the floor. Marco's jaw hung open, then he patted at his body as if trying to prove to himself that he was real.

Davis followed his partner, feeling an initial stab of pain for the officers who saw the badge. Then his empathy was consumed by memories of the last time he'd come into this room, in the real world. Gina had looked at him as if he were a rat slinking into the middle of a wedding feast. Marco had refused to speak to him.

People swarmed around tables, popping up from behind cubicles—each one wanting to see the badge for themselves. There was no reason for Chaz to display it as he did, held over his head for all to see. They could have been surgical, moved right to Maria's cubicle, showed her the badge and gotten information without making a fuss. That was the sort of thing they were supposed to do. Fewer Deviations.

Davis didn't chide his partner. Maybe those Deviations would stop Warsaw at 20:17 from happening, which was something a part of him really, really wanted.

Maria's cubicle was in the rear half of the large workroom. Chaz and Davis settled into the cubicle doorway, looking in at her as the sounds of whispers, even tears, began around them.

Maria was a prim woman in her early fifties, with glasses and hair she kept dyed black. She looked at the two of them over her spectacles—a sign of her stubbornness, as she'd always refused surgery to rid her of them—and focused on the badge in Chaz's hand.

"How'd you fake that?" she asked, turning back to her cubicle wall, which had a few virtual screens hovering before it.

"No faking, Maria," Davis said, taking the spare seat in the cubicle. Chaz loomed overhead like a lighthouse beacon, badge in hand. "I'm afraid you're a dupe. We're in a Snapshot."

She grunted, but otherwise didn't seem bothered. She knew, despite what she'd said, that they weren't faking. Dupes always knew. But she always reacted this calmly, which was one reason she was who they came to for information. Some people were reliable even after finding out that nothing they did mattered in the slightest.

"There was a call," Davis said, ignoring Holly Martinez as she stepped up, pulled Chaz around to get a look at the badge, then stumbled back, hand over her mouth. "About an hour ago now, to an apartment complex over on Fourth. For some reason, it isn't logged into my database when I check precinct call records."

"That means you aren't authorized to see the case," Maria said dryly. "You know the database is dynamic, based on clearance."

"I'm supposed to have full clearance."

"You do. There are just levels beyond 'full clearance.'"

"Well, fortunately, in here I have all those levels too." Davis reached up and tapped the badge that Chaz was holding.

Maria looked at it, momentarily transfixed. What *did* they see?

"I'll have to check with the chief," she said, tearing her eyes away from the badge.

"Check what?" Davis asked. "In here, I have ultimate authority. What happened at that apartment on Fourth?"

"Let me call the chief."

"No need," Chaz said, pointing as Chief Roberts barreled down the aisle between cubicles. He wore a suit; probably had meetings with politicians today. He never looked right in a suit, no matter how well it was tailored—they always ended up too tight on him.

He stormed right up to Chaz and took the badge from his fingers. The chief stared at it, then shoved it back at Chaz and barreled away without a word.

"Chief?" Maria said, standing up.

"Wait for it . . ." Chaz said.

Davis sat back. He hated this part. He heard the door to the chief's office slam at the rear of the room.

The gunshot came a second later. Maria gasped, stumbling back against her desk, eyes widening.

"Looks like you're on your own," Chaz noted. "Feel free to go check if he's really dead. You do it about half the time."

She looked at him, her mouth moving silently. Then she sank down into her seat.

"How often?" she whispered. "How often do you do this?"

"Every six months or so," Davis said. "It's easier than trying to get information from you people IRL."

"I . . ." She took a deep breath. "What was it you wanted to know?"

"The call about an hour ago?" Davis prodded, speaking gently. "To Fourth Avenue? I think it was from some Realtors."

Maria called up another screen, which popped into existence hovering above her desk. She tapped her fingers on the desktop, typing on an invisible keyboard. "Oh," she said. "Oh . . ."

"What?" Chaz said, leaning down beside Davis, both of them reading the screen. Information was coming in directly from the police investigating the old apartment building. Eight bodies. All presumed dead by drowning.

Fits previous pattern, one note said.

"Previous pattern?" Davis demanded. He reached over and tapped on her desk, calling up information. Pictures floated into the air—dead bodies with blue lips. Three people found suffocated, washed up on the shores of the city, in bags. They'd been preserved after death using chemicals.

The second discovery had been five bodies, this time found floating off the coast. They'd been in plastic bags, much like the first, though this time the deaths hadn't been from suffocation. Instead the victims had been poisoned.

"Daaamn," Chaz whispered.

"What connects these two sets to the corpses the group just discovered?" Davis asked, frowning and dragging some of the holopictures through the air above the desk.

"Looks like embalming fluid," Maria said, reading. "Discovered by detectives on the scene—which is important."

"It means finding these eight today was a lucky accident," Davis whispered, narrowing his eyes. "The others were dumped in the ocean, but these were found while the killer was still preparing them. Soaking them first, before dropping them off. So this is a chance to crack the case."

A quick scan of the files showed that detectives had been spinning their wheels until now. They were facing a meticulous killer who chose victims easy to miss: the homeless, prostitutes. It was sometimes shocking how the right people could vanish without anyone noticing—at least, not anyone who could make the cops or politicians pay attention.

He's clever, Davis thought, feeling a chill as he read the notes on those cases. *He's very clever. In fact . . .* Something struck him about it all, something that made him feel sick deep inside.

"This is Gina's case," Maria said. "She's leading, at least. We've got a ton of people on it. I've been following it too, for obvious reasons."

"Obvious?" Chaz asked, reaching across Davis and helping himself to some M&M's on Maria's desk.

Maria frowned, then zoomed one of the windows, showing a report Gutierrez had written, dubbing the murderer "The Photographer."

"What?" Chaz asked. "Why that name? Does it have something to do with Snapshots?"

"He's killing them in a specific way," Davis whispered. "To prevent Snapshot detectives from being able to find him."

Maria nodded grimly. "The Photographer preserves the bodies after killing them, which prevents forensics from getting a specific bead on when they were killed. Then, he or she dumps the corpses in the ocean, letting them drift and eventually wash up. The killer obviously doesn't mind if they're found, might even want it, but is stopping us from using a Snapshot on the case. He or she knows that we'd need to be able to point to a specific day or place to get a warrant."

She scanned the report from today, which was still being updated by police on the scene.

Bodies show evidence of what we assumed earlier, one of them wrote. *Killer was letting them soak in the pool to make it more difficult to tell when they were dumped in the ocean.*

Davis nodded. "So why keep this quiet? Why hush the call today so soundly?"

"Best way to catch someone is to not let them know they're being chased." Maria grimaced. "This will blow up soon enough. We might as well keep this out of the news as long as possible though, right?"

There's more to it than that, Davis thought, scrolling through a window, scouring notes and reports. *Dangerous,* one of them read. *If people lose faith in Snapshots, the tool could be undermined in court.*

"You still should have told us," Davis said.

"Why?" Maria said. "What would be the point?"

"When we're in Snapshots of certain days," Chaz said, crunching on M&M's, "we could go poke at things. Get more information."

"Where?" Maria said. "When? Didn't you hear that the killer is *specifically* working to make you two irrelevant?"

Davis glanced at his partner. Maria was being too defensive. She often got this way, as did the others. He and Chaz, they weren't supposed to poke into the business of *real* detectives. To the rest of the department they were errand boys, sent to retrieve specific data and nothing else.

But the truth was, nobody seemed to know what to do with the Snapshots. The city had been pressured into buying the program, and so had sunk a ton of money into it—but privacy laws had then tied their hands tightly. It was a wonder that even two detectives were allowed in. And if the general public knew how much leeway Chaz and Davis took with their job . . .

Well, either way, it was a tool that—even years into the program—nobody understood, let alone knew how to properly exploit. But that still didn't explain why they'd hide so much from the cops working in them.

"What aren't you telling me, Maria?" Davis whispered.

She met his eyes defiantly. Then those eyes darted to the side as Chaz lifted his gun to her temple.

"Chaz," Davis said, sighing. "Don't kill her again, please."

"*Again?*" Maria demanded.

"Just talk to me, Maria," Davis said. "We usually don't kill you. I promise."

"It's a Snapshot, Maria," Chaz said. He shrugged. "Nothing we do in here matters. Tell the nice man what it is he wants to know."

"I don't know why they didn't tell you," she said, stubborn. "No, they didn't tell you about the case. No, they didn't want to use you to investigate it. I don't know why."

"You're lying," Davis said.

"Prove it."

Davis looked to Chaz, sighing.

Chaz shot her.

Bodies don't *jerk* as much as people think they do, even when shot in the head. They just kind of slump, like Maria did. A little puff from the gun blowing her hair, head bobbing as if tapped, and then . . . her body drooped in her chair. There wasn't even much blood—the bullet didn't exit the other side of her head. Some blood did come out her nose, and out the hole in her temple.

Chaz calmly held aloft his badge for the few people who were still there, those who hadn't wandered out at seeing the badge originally—or who hadn't been scared away by what the chief had done.

"You bastard!" Davis said, standing and stumbling back from the cubicle. "You actually did it!"

"Yeah," Chaz said. "I've always wanted to, you know? That smug look on her face. Treating us like she's a babysitter and we're a pair of three-year-olds."

"You *actually did it!*"

"What? You implied we'd done it loads."

"That was an interrogation technique!"

"A piss-poor one, judging by results," Chaz said, shoving her body off the chair and sitting down. "You going to help me look through this stuff? She's got better access than us. We might be able to learn something."

Davis spun about, scanning the precinct office over the cubicle walls. A few had remained at their stations, despite everything that had happened so far. Those had stood up at the shot, and now backed away from him. Friends . . . well, acquaintances. The fear in their eyes dug into him—like he was a terrorist.

Officer Dobbs had his gun out, and he looked at it, weighing it. Davis could almost read the conflict. *If I shoot him,* Dobbs seemed to be thinking, *I'm shooting a real person. A cop who didn't do anything illegal. But if I'm not real . . . who cares, right? I can't be punished, not really.*

Dobbs met his eyes, and Davis had the sudden instinctive feeling that he should draw his own sidearm and gun Dobbs down before the man could make the decision. But, frozen, Davis couldn't bring himself to do it.

Dobbs proved to be a better person, even as a dupe, than Chaz was. Dobbs holstered his weapon and shook his head, then stumbled away.

Davis breathed out a long sigh. Not relief, exactly. More weariness. He ducked down beside his partner, trying to ignore Maria's body bleeding on the floor.

Chaz wasn't looking at the case with the serial killer. He'd pushed all those windows to the side, and was instead looking up something else. Personnel files.

His own.

"Damn," Chaz said. "We should have done this ages ago, Davis. You see? She has full access to our records."

Chaz had only been on the New Clipperton force for a year before being assigned to Snapshots. Before that, he'd served in Mexico City, with which they had an immigration treaty and transferable citizenship. His Mexico City record commended him for eagerness and enthusiasm in training, though it also contained this line at the end: *Overly aggressive.*

"Aggressive," Chaz snapped. "What does that even mean? Rodriguez, you bastard. I mean, shouldn't a cop be aggressive? You know, in pursuing justice and the like?"

The rest of the record, which Chaz scrolled down, had notes from New Clipperton officers.

Eager. Strong willed. I think he'll cut it, Diaz had written before retiring.

Is a bully, Maria herself had written a few months into Chaz's tenure in the city, when he'd been a traffic cop. *I have seven complaints on this guy already.*

Treats being a cop like playing a video game. That from his former partner.

It was followed by another note from Maria. *Recommended for Snapshot duty. We can't fire him, not without a concrete incident. At least in there, when he inevitably shoots someone, it won't be grounds for a lawsuit.*

Davis glanced at her corpse again.

"Huh," Chaz said. "You read that?"

"Yeah."

"Diaz," Chaz said, raising his chin. "Hell of a guy, that man was. Strong willed? Yeah. Yeah, I'm strong. And I *could* have cut it, you know? If she hadn't stuffed me in here."

"Sure."

"Let's see what yours says," Chaz said, sliding his fingers across the desk to start the search.

Davis tapped the desk, freezing the windows. "Let's not."

"Come on. Don't you want to see?"

"I can guess," Davis said. "Bring those other windows back, the ones with the case notes about the Photographer. Load them to my phone."

Chaz sighed. "It would only be fair to read your record, Davis. You know why I'm here. What about you?"

"Aggression," Davis said.

Chaz looked at him, then laughed. Though it was technically true; aggression *was* his problem. Not enough of it.

They got the files loaded, then Davis tugged Chaz's shoulder, nodding for them to leave. "Let's get out of here before someone decides that being a dupe means they can gun us down with no consequences."

Chaz didn't argue. He slipped out, almost tripping over Maria's legs. Davis gave her one last glance, then—because he couldn't help himself—he grabbed her little change bowl from the desk and dumped the coins into his hand.

Together, the two of them left the precinct. Davis felt better standing out on the steps, under the sunlight—even though it was as fake as everything else here.

"What now?" Chaz asked.

Davis checked his phone. 14:07. He had six hours left. "I'm going to stop a monster. You with me?"

"Of course. I can cut it, Davis. I'm telling you, I *can*. This is our chance, you know. To prove ourselves. But where do we go?"

"Back to the apartment building with the corpses," Davis said, calling an auto-cab with a tap on his phone.

"To get information from the cops there?"

"No, I've got their report," Davis said. "We're going to talk to the people who own the building."

"The bank?"

"No," Davis said. "The *real* owners."

Five

D avis spent the ride sorting through the coins that had been on Maria's desk, absently raising each one to the sunlight shining through the cab's window and checking the date it had been minted. American money; most city-states had adopted it, though the one- and two-dollar coins had both originally been Canadian.

It felt relaxing to study something like coins that was basically an anachronism. You could know everything there really was to know—now that no new ones were being made. Funny, how quickly they'd started to vanish. It had only been two years since the last coins had been minted.

Still, the story was finished. You could have all of the answers.

Wait, he thought, stopping on a nickel. He scanned through the list on his phone. 2001, Denver mint? He felt a little jolt of excitement. They'd both been missing the 2001 nickel. With this, he completed a set.

"What did you do, Davis?" Chaz asked. "Everyone else seems to know what landed you in here, but nobody will ever tell me. Did you shoot a kid?"

Davis ignored him, pocketing the coin, stupidly excited.

"I still don't get why you like those coins so much. They're old now, meaningless. Practically worthless."

"That's what my wife always said."

"Your *ex*-wife, Davis."

"That's what I meant."

He sifted through the rest of the coins, but didn't find any of interest. Unfortunately, they reminded him of Maria, lying on the floor of the precinct office. Her dead eyes staring at the sky, the neat little hole in her temple leaking blood.

He dug out his phone and, just to reassure himself, texted the real Maria outside the Snapshot.

Hey, he said. *Have you guys managed to catch the serial killer IRL? The one they call the Photographer?*

There was a long pause where no reply came. Finally, the message bounced, and—annoyed—he sent it again. This time it went through. Then a direct line opened to IRL.

How do you know about that, Davis? Maria sent as soon as it opened. He could sense the sharpness of her tone.

Your dupe told us, Davis wrote. *She considers it important, for some reason. I don't know. Said maybe we should poke into things while we wait.*

You aren't authorized for that case, IRL Maria sent. *If my dupe is talking about it to you, it means you've created a Deviation in her. Go to a saferoom. You're supposed to be there anyway. Are you ignoring protocol again?*

We're on our way now, Davis sent. *But did you catch him? The swimming-pool corpses in the abandoned apartment building, they helped you track him down?*

Pause.

No, Maria admitted. *Those corpses haven't led to anything so far. Really, there's nothing you can do.*

He believed her, at least on the facts about the corpses. Maria didn't lie. She withheld information all the time, but would just stare at you if you tried to pry something out of her. She'd never lied to him about anything important.

That was far more than he could say about some people.

He showed the screen to Chaz, who nodded. "You ever wonder if the thing that powers this whole operation can see what we're doing?"

"I think it's supposed to be unconscious," Davis said, pocketing the phone. "It dreams up a re-creation of the day, and we slip in."

"So we're in its dreams." Chaz shifted, uncomfortable. "We pretend this is all technological, like we're in some simulation. But . . . I mean . . ."

"Close enough," Davis said. "Powered down with a button, powered on with some computer code. What's the difference?"

"Feels different. When I think about it. Maybe the thing is watching us."

"Maybe. But I don't think so. The way this all plays out . . . it doesn't feel like anything is watching. Otherwise, why the Deviations? Feels like the code instructs the thing to create an exact representation of the day, then just lets it play out naturally."

So far as they could tell, Snapshots proceeded exactly as the original day had, so long as nothing interfered. But that was hard to prove, as they couldn't monitor it. It had been tried before—they had let it run all day on its own, then checked at the end of the day by sending some drones in to look things over. But even that was suspect, as entering or leaving the Snapshot at any time except when it was just created tended to cause huge Deviations.

The best they could do was send two cops into the system, live it through and try to muddle along, hoping they didn't accidentally send the Snapshot running in the wrong direction. Of course, that plan didn't take into account the two of them shooting anyone or sending scores of people into chaos.

Davis sighed as the autocab pulled to a stop. He'd chosen a place a block or two from the run-down apartment building. He climbed out, taking a bottle of water from the cab's mini fridge—his account would be charged, but it was a fake version of his account. Outside the cab, he fished in his pocket for the nickel. His fingers touched crumpled paper—the woman's number, from the diner. He pulled out both, then shook his head and stuffed the paper back in his pocket.

"What's that?" Chaz asked.

"I found a nickel I don't have IRL," Davis said, washing off the nickel. Then he tried to swallow it. That wasn't as easy to do as he'd thought. He ended up on hands and knees, coughing the nickel onto the sidewalk, where it rested defiantly on the pavement.

"Damn," Chaz said. "Never thought you'd actually try that."

"Maybe," Davis said, swallowing a gulp of water, "I'll just ask the IRL Maria if I can trade for the one in her coin jar."

"Yeah," Chaz said, sounding amused. "Might be easier." He paused. "You're a weird little dude, Davis."

Once Davis had recovered himself, Chaz started off toward the apartment building. Davis took him by the arm, shook his head, and pointed the other direction.

His search took some time—the cops showing up had scared off his targets. Still, after fifteen minutes he spotted a likely candidate: a kid standing on a street corner with hands shoved in the pockets of his longball jersey. He was wearing a ball cap and combat boots, the latest irrational fashion choice of kids on the street.

Davis wagged his phone at the kid, who nodded almost imperceptibly. Davis jogged over, Chaz following, curious.

"How much?" the kid said.

"Ten hits?" Davis said. "Stiff."

"I got five," the kid said, sizing him up.

Davis nodded. "You a Primero?"

"What's it to you?" the kid asked, getting the drugs from his pocket.

Davis stepped backward, raising his hands. "Look, I know what the Primeros do to people who sell on their turf. I'll find someone else."

"Settle your boots," the kid said. "I'm Primero." He flashed the proper sign. "Damn chippers. You shouldn't care who you buy from."

"I just don't want to get into trouble," Davis said, tapping his phone against the kid's, holding his thumb over the authenticator and transferring fake money for fake drugs to a fake person. "There's an apartment building three streets over," Davis added. "Old beat-up place. Has Primero tags sprayed all over it. Who've you guys been renting it to?"

The kid froze, five large white pills clutched in his hand.

"You cleared out the homeless people living there," Davis said. "Let someone else in. Kept everyone else away for him, right? Who is he?"

"You're a cop?" the kid said.

Davis took the pills, then popped one in his mouth and washed it down. "Would a cop do that?"

The kid stepped backward, then frowned.

"This guy," Davis said. "He's trouble. Big trouble. You don't need to know why we're hunting him, but I'm willing to buy information. Go tell your narco what I've said. I'll wait here for you to come back with him. He'll want to talk to us."

The kid bolted, and Davis looked back at Chaz.

"Damn," Chaz said softly. "Did you just take a full hit of stiff?"

In response, Davis popped the pill from his cheek and spat it out. He dropped all five pills and ground them beneath his shoe. He then took a long pull on his water bottle, hoping that he hadn't gotten too much of the stimulant into his system.

Chaz laughed. "So, you think the gang will actually come talk to us? I think that kid will just bolt."

"Maybe," Davis said, then settled down on a bench near the corner to wait.

It didn't take long. Six of them came together: the kid they'd been speaking to, four older teens, and one man in his thirties. That would be the narco—the head drug dealer for this little area. Not the head of the gang, but leader to a couple dozen kids on the street here. Half boss, half parent.

Davis stood and held his hands to the sides in a nonthreatening way, and smothered his nervousness. The narco was a tall man, lighter skinned than Chaz or Davis, with buzzed hair. Davis could almost imagine him wearing a polo shirt and slacks on business-casual day at the office, rather than jeans and combat boots.

Davis and Chaz followed the group into an alleyway, and the narco pointed. Two of his men hopped up to Davis and Chaz, probably to search them.

"I've got a gun in my right pocket," Davis said. "My friend has one in the under-arm holster beneath his jacket. We'll want them back. Don't touch our wallets, or there will be trouble."

The gang members took the guns, to Chaz's obvious annoyance, then searched them for other weapons. But they left the wallets alone. Davis suffered it, eyes closed, trying to calm himself. Finally, the two cops were allowed to approach farther down the alleyway, which smelled of trash and stagnant water. Chaz looked back toward the street longingly and patted at his holster, already missing his gun.

"We should talk in private," Davis said to the narco.

"Why?" he demanded.

"Because you won't want what we tell you to spread," Davis said, meeting his eyes, trying to project a confidence he didn't feel.

The narco weighed him. An autocab passed on the street behind them with a quiet hum. Finally the narco nodded, and led the two of them farther into the alley. The rest of the gang members stayed put, one sighting on Davis with his own gun, as if in warning.

"You scared Pepe really well," the narco said. "He thinks you're feds. It was a cute trick, palming a hit of stiff in front of him. Tell me why I shouldn't just have you shot."

"If we were feds," Chaz noted, "you think that offing us would somehow be a *good* idea?"

Davis calmly reached to his pocket and took out his wallet, then opened it, revealing his reality badge.

The narco's eyes caught on it. They widened, mesmerized, almost like he had taken a hit of some drug. He whispered a soft prayer, then reached out with reverent fingers, touching the badge.

"You . . ." The narco swallowed. "You said you weren't cops."

"I never said that," Davis said, not putting the badge away. "I said we were willing to pay for some information. About the person renting a specific apartment building from you."

"You've gotten yourself into something bad, friend," Chaz said. He pulled out a cigarette and put it in his mouth, but didn't light it. He'd been trying to stop. "This guy who has been paying you? He's been murdering people. Prostitutes. Children. Anyone he can find who won't make waves."

The narco cursed softly.

Davis raised his phone, set to display his entire savings. A number larger than most cops would have been able to save. But he didn't have many expenses— just child support, really. He slept in a saferoom provided by the precinct, on the outskirts of the city, so he was less likely to run into himself while in a Snapshot.

"Tell us about this guy renting the apartment building," Davis said. "You knew there was something off about him, didn't you? Wipe that conscience clean, and you can take every penny of this. My payment to you."

"It's fake, isn't it?" the narco said, running his hand across his buzzed scalp. He swore something fierce. "It's all fake."

"Sure, sure," Davis said. "Completely fake. But you're the only one who knows it, friend."

"Take the money," Chaz suggested, leaning one shoulder against the wall. "Live it up for a day. They'll turn this Snapshot off sometime in the evening. You're going to vanish then. Might as well enjoy the time you have left."

Davis dangled the phone. The narco looked at it, then sank down beside the wall of the alleyway.

And started crying.

Chaz rolled his eyes. Davis looked at the street thug and felt a wrenching inside of him. Something about the Snapshot really must have made dupes realize they weren't real, once they saw the badge. The bean counters outside denied it, but they didn't live in here. Didn't see men like this, hardened criminals, crack and turn into children before the inevitable truth that their entire world was doomed.

Davis sank down and sat next to the man. He waved for Chaz to hand him the pack of cigarettes, then offered one to the narco.

"Mama always said those would kill me," the man said, then laughed. Davis figured he'd been wrong about the narco's age. He wasn't in his thirties; he just looked older compared to the others.

The narco took a cigarette. Davis lit it up, then lit one for himself.

"I feel like the reaper sometimes," Davis said. "You know. Showing up, informing people that they're going to die in a few hours?"

The narco breathed in smoke, then exhaled it. He rested his head back against the wall, tears still streaming down his cheeks.

"What's your name?" Davis asked.

"Does it matter?"

"I'm real, kid," Davis said. "I'll remember your name."

"Horace," the kid said. "Name's Horace."

"Horace. You don't want the money, do you?"

Horace shook his head. "Won't make me forget, *ese*."

"Go home then. Hug your mom. But before you go, do some good. Tell me about this guy who has been renting that building from you."

"What does it matter?"

"He's killing kids," Davis said. "Sure, your life is over. That's tough. But hell, why not help us stop this monster before you go?"

Chaz shook his head, arms folded. In the mouth of the alleyway, the other kids were whispering, looking panicked by the narco's actions.

"He's young," Horace whispered. "Maybe my age. Twenty-four, twenty-five. Asian. Quiet type. Creepy. We stay out of his business—figured he killed someone and wanted to hole up. But didn't think . . . you know . . ." He shuddered. "He won't come back. One of the kids spotted him running. Your people at his hidey-hole spooked him. He's gone."

"You have a name?" Davis asked. "Anything?"

"No name," Horace said, then took a puff of the cigarette. "You got some paper I can write on?"

Davis fished in his pocket and came out with a small piece of paper. The gangster took a pen from his pocket and wrote on it. An address.

"He wanted two places," he said softly. "With large tubs or pools in them he could fill. That's the second. A school, once. If he's smart, he'll run and you'll never see him. But people like him, they can be really smart in some ways but . . ."

"Really dumb in others," Davis said with a nod. "Thanks."

Horace shrugged, puffing on the cigarette. "You're right. I knew something was wrong about him. Watch out for yourself, *ese*. He's . . . well, I figured he was just crazy. But he knows."

"Knows?" Davis said, glancing at Chaz.

"That it isn't real," Horace said. "He kept saying it. This is a Snapshot; we're all part of a Snapshot. Got to get rid of the Deviations, he said. Warned me. Don't be a Deviation . . ."

Davis felt a chill.

"Anyway," Horace said, "give me that cash." He held out his phone.

"You said you didn't want it."

"I don't." He pointed down the alleyway. "Those boys though, they're gonna get a bonus today. Spend a few hours in luxury. Don't tell them, okay?"

"I wouldn't dream of it," Davis said, tapping Horace's phone with his, transferring enough to buy a nice car.

Horace stood and stamped out the cigarette, leaving a little twist of smoke on the ground at Davis's feet as he walked down the alleyway. He adopted a stronger gait before he reached the kids. A practiced air of invincibility.

"Leave the guns!" Davis called to them, suddenly panicked by the thought of them running off with the weapons.

They dropped them in the mouth of the alleyway, then were gone.

"I can't believe that worked," Chaz said, arms folded. He looked at Davis. "How did you get him to talk like that?"

"He was scared," Davis said, forcing himself to his feet. "Guess I played off that."

"We never do stuff like this anymore," Chaz said. "Interview suspects. We can get them to talk when they never would IRL. We're really wasted in here, aren't we?"

"Maybe. Maybe not." Most of the testimony they could gather in here was inadmissible in court—if they found a witness, the IRL cops would have to get them to testify for real. And of course, a dupe's words couldn't be used against the real person in court.

It was all so sticky. Most cases involving Snapshots were arduous things, full of testimony on Deviations, possibilities, and technical arguments. The only thing that really held up was the testimony of the cops. They had to have good enough records to be viable witnesses, but also had to be officers the precinct wouldn't care about wasting in work that nobody else wanted to do.

The two of them collected their guns. "I didn't realize you'd started carrying," Chaz noted to him. "Least not until I saw that gun earlier."

"I've been doing it for a few months now," Davis said. The truth, as he'd wanted to get back in the habit. Though this was a new gun, his first time carrying it into a Snapshot.

He looked after the gang members, but couldn't spot them. They'd run off fast.

"Good thing this isn't real," Chaz said, shading his eyes from the late-afternoon sun. "You'd be broke, friend. I had no idea you'd saved up such a nest egg. How'd you manage to do that?"

"Simple tastes," Davis said. And plans to buy a house someday. Him, his son, his wife . . .

Well, that was one dream that could die. "Come on," he said. "Let's check this second place out, though I'm worried. We've been racking up quite the list of Deviations. Try not to step on any butterflies on the way."

Chaz gave him a confused look, and Davis just shook his head, calling them another autocab.

Six

Davis and Chaz stopped on the cracked sidewalk in front of a boxy monster of a building. It loomed, hollow, with windows too small to be comfortable. Like a prison. Which was, as Davis considered it, a very accurate comparison.

"Southeast High School," Chaz read from the sign—full of bullet holes—to their right.

"Closed two years ago," Davis said, reading from his phone.

"They were using that box up until two years ago?" Chaz said. "Damn. No wonder kids out here turn to selling drugs."

The school's front doors were wrapped in chains to keep them closed. Davis took a deep breath, and glanced at Chaz. Both took out their sidearms.

You could get killed inside a Snapshot, though it didn't happen as often as it did to cops IRL. You could anticipate your surroundings in the Snapshot, barring Deviations. You knew which thugs were likely to start shooting, and which situations were more dangerous.

Still, it happened. Most often it was something mundane. The woman Davis had replaced had died in a simple car accident. She'd insisted on driving a squad car instead of taking autocabs. She could just as easily have died on her way home from work, but she'd crashed here in the Snapshot.

It felt somehow wrong to think of a cop dying in the Snapshot. This place wasn't truly real. It shouldn't, therefore, have such real consequences. As Chaz always said, things you did in the Snapshot didn't really matter . . .

"Locked tight," Chaz said, testing the chains on the front doors. Perhaps the killer had a key, but Davis suspected not. The front entrance was far too prominent; you couldn't sneak in bodies this way, even at night, without risking someone seeing you. So where?

He led the way across dead grass that hadn't been watered in years, sliding around the school to some kind of shipping entrance at the back, up a short ramp. Yeah, this was better. You could pull a car in here silently and unload.

He tried the door at the top of the ramp, and found it unlocked. He nodded to Chaz and both stepped inside, handguns pointed into the shadows.

"That's a nice gun," Chaz noted softly. "Taurus PT-92, right? Flashy. Pearl grip, even. Not what I'd have expected for you."

Davis didn't reply. Heart beating quickly, finger deliberately *not* on the trigger, he led the way through the echoing halls of the school. The debris here was somehow more *personal* than that back at the apartment building. Old discarded notebooks. Pencils with the tips broken off. A ball cap, a deflated soccer ball. This had been a lively place up until a few years ago.

That only made it feel creepier now. Haunted. Unlike the apartment building, which had been gutted, this place had been abandoned in haste. Nobody had wanted to be here—not students, administrators, or teachers.

They passed an old trophy case, the glass shattered, dust covering the plaques. Graffiti tags covered the walls. By now it was almost 16:00, and the sunlight sneaked into the place through boarded windows, reflecting off old tile floors and casting shadows. But it was enough for Davis to make out a sign on the wall without needing his flashlight. He waved his gun toward it, then pointed. Looked like the school had its own pool. An indoor one, near the gym.

Davis found himself sweating as they crept along the corridor. He jumped as a feral cat scurried out of one hall and down another one, into darkness. He was so startled, he nearly unloaded his gun at the thing.

You're going to have to confront this, he thought, heart racing as they moved inevitably forward. It had been years since he'd been in a position like this, but the memories came back, sharp like broken glass. A dark building. Calls for backup, and . . .

And Davis, useless.

Is this why you insisted on watching for cases like this? So you could prove to yourself you could do it? That you could *pull the trigger?*

He still let Chaz go first when they reached the pool. He stood outside the door—breathing hard, wiping his brow with a trembling hand—before finally forcing himself in through the door behind his partner. He'd waited too long, he knew. If there had been danger inside, Chaz would have been in trouble, alone.

There was no danger. There wasn't anything. They needed the flashlights again, but the pool was empty—not even any water. *Air feels humid,* Davis thought, forcing his breathing back under control.

"Huh," Chaz said, hands on hips. "Were we wrong?"

Davis waited until his trembling subsided, though he couldn't completely banish his tension—the pressure on his chest that made him feel like running away as fast as he could go. He pointed his light toward the locker rooms, then started that way. He peeked inside and found a table had been pulled in there, set with some cups and fast-food wrappers. Seemed newer than the rest of the school's debris.

"Careful," Davis said. "Someone *has* been here." He stopped in the doorway into the locker rooms until Chaz nudged him from behind; then he forced himself farther in, gun in one hand, flashlight in the other.

There was a place for demeaning group showers, and here someone had worked with a board and some caulk to turn it into a kind of tub. Yeah, this was the killer's hideout. He was preparing to soak some more bodies. The improvised tub was full of water, maybe four feet high, but there weren't any bodies in it yet. Perhaps the Photographer was seeing if his handiwork would hold.

We might be in time, then! Davis thought. *He might not have killed the next group.*

He immediately felt stupid. This was a Snapshot of life from ten days ago. Still, surely they could do *some* good, help catch the one doing this.

"Hey," Chaz said. "Check this."

Davis turned away from the showers, to where Chaz was shining his phone's light on a door that was shut tight, with a chair wedged under it and some rope tying the knob to a post beside the wall.

Davis hastened over, his tension rising again. That looked like an improvised lock to keep someone in. He nodded, and Chaz unwedged the door, then untied the rope. No sounds came from within. They shared a look, and then Davis let Chaz ease open the door, gun pointed downward so as to not accidently shoot any captives. It smelled foul inside, and Davis gagged.

"Bodies," Chaz said with a grunt, using his phone for light. "Damn, it smells terrible in here." He stepped forward.

His shoe *crunched.*

Chaz jumped backward, then the two leaned down. The floor in here was littered with insect carcasses.

Bees, Davis thought as Chaz opened the door farther. His flashlight highlighted the slumped corpses of people on the floor, surrounded by dead insects. The stench was overwhelming, and Davis had to breathe through his mouth.

Why bees? Davis thought as he inched into the room, brushing the insect carcasses from in front of him. There were hundreds, maybe thousands, of dead bees in here.

It started to make sense. His tension melted away before the academic facts, and he stood up in the dark room. It had been a storage room for old sports equipment. There were six people inside, all dead now.

"Check the corpses," he told Chaz. "See if they share anything obvious. Age, gender." He barely noticed whether Chaz went to do it. Instead, he tucked away his gun and called up autopsy reports from the earlier murders.

He kept saying it. Horace the drug dealer's voice echoed in his memory. *This is a Snapshot; we're all part of a Snapshot. Got to get rid of the Deviations, he said.*

Don't be a Deviation.

The first group had died by asphyxiation. The cops assumed they'd been suffocated in the bags, but that didn't fit the pattern. They'd have been killed before being placed in the bags, right? The killer would have wanted to soak them first, to obscure how long they'd been in the ocean.

"Man," Chaz said. "These people look bad, Davis. Even for dead folk. I think I might need to throw up."

"Do it outside the room," Davis said absently.

There, he thought, pulling up the records of one of the bodies they'd identified. A prostitute. He scanned her medical records. Asthma. It was a connection. One of the others listed the same ailment. The others didn't list much, but they also didn't have any notes from next of kin. So maybe the information just hadn't been discovered.

The second group had died from poisoning. What was the theme? He scanned through the reports and happened across one note by an examiner. *All victims were extremely farsighted and wore corrective lenses.*

The third group—the bodies they'd found in the basement of the old apartment complex—clinched it for him. The officers there had left to find out why everyone was panicking back at the precinct office, but before abandoning their investigation they'd left a very important note.

These people all seem to have been naturally paralyzed.

"Ugh," Chaz said, walking back into the room, holding a bucket. "Davis? Damn it, man. Stop standing there in the middle of them. What's wrong with you?"

Davis looked around at the bodies. "You checked them all?"

"Mostly."

Davis tucked away his phone, then rolled over a body. Her face was covered in swollen bee stings—a horrible sight. He could see why Chaz had been disturbed.

"He's killing people he decides are Deviations," Davis said. "He thinks he's in a Snapshot."

"He *is* in a Snapshot."

"Yeah, but only his dupe is right," Davis said. "And it only does what the real him has already done. The killer thinks everything is a Snapshot, and he's trying to expunge the Deviations—which he sees as people who have some flaw in their biology. The first group had terrible asthma. The second group, bad vision."

Davis rolled over another corpse. "These people were allergic to bee stings. Look at these wounds—those aren't regular stings. He rounded up a bunch of people with terrible allergies, then locked them in here with bees. He's cleansing the city of Deviations."

"That doesn't make any sense."

Davis ignored him, inspecting the next victim, a woman who had died on her back with her eyes swollen shut. "Serial killers like this . . . lots of them are looking for power. *Control*. They feel they don't have control in their lives, so they control others. Imagine being paranoid. You get the idea you're in a Snapshot, that you're not real. How might you act?"

He looked up as Chaz shrugged. "Everyone's different," Chaz said. "You've seen it. Some wander off, some cry, some—"

"Some kill," Davis said.

"Yeah." Didn't happen often. Most people didn't have it in them to kill, even if they discovered something terrible like this. But once in a while, someone they showed a reality badge to immediately reached for a weapon, perhaps thinking— irrationally—if they killed the person with the badge, it would disprove what they'd just seen.

That was probably too simple for this killer. Davis looked back at the dead woman. This killer was already crazy; you had to be, to do something like this. But mix it with a belief that your world was a sham . . .

It was surreal. In here, the killer's dupe would be *right*. He *was* in a Snapshot. That didn't change the fact that out in the real world, there was someone killing entire groups of people. Real people. Not dupes.

The woman in front of him stirred.

Davis cried out, leaping backward, scrambling for his gun—though of course he wouldn't need it.

"What?" Chaz demanded.

"That one is still alive," Davis said, pointing, hand shaking.

The woman rolled her head over and whispered something. "Water?"

Davis knelt down. "Get some water," he said to Chaz. "Go!"

"Water," she whispered again.

"I'm getting some," Davis said. "We're cops. It's okay. Don't worry."

"He'll . . . come back . . ." She couldn't open her eyes. They were swollen shut. She could barely move her lips.

"When?" Davis asked.

"Every night," she said. "Every night at seven thirty. He checks on us then. We were going to jump him . . . but . . ." She cursed softly. "It hurts . . ."

Chaz returned with a cup from the desk outside, filled with water. He knelt down, but didn't move.

"Give it to her!" Davis said.

Chaz tried dribbling it onto her lips. She didn't move anything but her head, which she could barely rock. It seemed like some got into her mouth.

"Seven thirty," Davis said. "He'll be back at seven thirty?"

The woman whispered something, but even leaning down close, Davis couldn't make it out. Grimly, he checked the others. They were definitely dead.

The woman had started weeping. A tearless trembling.

Chaz stood up, then looked to Davis, who stared at the woman, horrified.

"I'll take care of this," Chaz said, getting out a pair of earplugs. "It's okay."

Davis nodded numbly, then forced himself to walk out.

A gunshot sounded behind him; then Chaz came to the doorway, his face ashen. Together they closed the door, put the rope back as they'd found it, and propped the chair in place. Chaz put the water cup back as Davis slumped down on a bench beside some lockers, licking his lips. His mouth had gone dry.

"So we wait here," Chaz said, "and catch him when he returns?"

Davis rocked himself, the woman's whispers haunting him.

"Davis!" Chaz said. "What do we do now?"

"We . . ." Davis took a deep breath. *Just a dupe. She was just a dupe. In the real world, she's already dead.* "What would we do if we caught him, Chaz?"

"Interrogate him. Like we did earlier."

"Earlier, in the precinct and with the narco, we simply flashed our badges. But the Photographer already believes he's a dupe. I don't think it will work."

Chaz considered that.

"What we *really* need," Davis said, "is to pin down where the IRL cops can find him. He's obviously got a third hideout—the place where he really lives. If we can find that and send it to Maria, I think they'll have a good shot at grabbing him."

"So . . ."

"So we watch him when he comes back," Davis said, taking a deep breath. "And we tail him. If it looks like he's spotted us, we capture him and see what we can beat out of him. Maybe that will be enough. But hopefully, instead we can find where he lives."

"Great, okay," Chaz said. "But we're not waiting here. Not with those corpses in there."

"We shouldn't go far, in case he—"

"You need a break, Davis. Look at you! Hell, *I* need a break. We'll go get a coffee or something. When's the last time we ate? Those burritos?" He thought for a moment. "Better yet. We'll go to Ingred Street. It's four, right? Good timing."

Ingred. *Of course you want to go to Ingred.*

Davis just nodded his head, mute. Chaz was right. Though they probably should stake out nearby and watch, he was at his limit. He couldn't confront a killer like this. He needed some time to recover.

"Ingred it is," Davis said, standing.

Seven

Chaz left him, as he always did when they stopped at the park on the corner of Ingred and Ninth.

It was a little city park, of the type you found on neighborhood corners. Full of playsets that were old but sturdy, coated periodically in new layers of paint for a facelift. The place smelled better than the streets did. Of dirt and wet sand. Of course, it *sounded* better too. Over the distant rumbling of construction equipment and honking horns, here you could hear children.

Davis smiled, stepping up to the corner of the park, basking in the sounds of the laughter. Of children running, shouting, playing. When was the last time he'd just *enjoyed* life? He'd lost that skill, which seemed so natural to children. They didn't have to work at having fun.

Hal was there, as he'd hoped. Though he was eight, he seemed smaller than the kids he played with. A mop of dark hair, messy as always, and a ready smile. He was never happier than when he was around others. He liked people. He got that from his dad too. Davis had always thought that would make him a good cop.

Hal stopped in place when he saw Davis, then grinned widely. The worry that they might get back too late to catch the killer fled Davis's mind. Even with all the baggage that came along with visiting here, seeing Hal was worth it.

Hal ran up, and Davis grabbed him in a huge hug. The kid didn't ask why his father had come to see him on a random day, unannounced. He didn't connect that it was 16:00, when Davis knew his wife would be napping and the kid would be out playing. Hal was just happy he got to see his father.

And fortunately, court orders didn't cover dupes inside a Snapshot.

"Dad!" Hal said. "I haven't seen you in *forever*."

"I've been busy with work."

"Catching bad guys?"

"Catching bad guys," Davis said softly.

"Dad," Hal said. "We went to the *zoo*. I got a stuffed penguin. And there was a little antelope—it's called a dik-dik, but we're not supposed to laugh—and when we went walking, it *followed* me, Dad. It followed me all around. It attacked Greg. Kept butting its little head into his leg, everywhere he went, but it *liked* me."

Hal took a deep breath, then grabbed Davis in another hug. "Are you here to talk to Mommy?"

Davis glanced toward a window of her nearby apartment. The blinds were drawn.

"No," Davis said.

"Oh." Hal looked morose for a minute, then perked up. "Want to be a monster?"

"I'd love to be a monster."

The next hour was a bliss of chasing, growling, climbing on the jungle gym, and imagination. They were monsters, they were superheroes, they built mountains of sand and then stomped them. Hal changed the rules indiscriminately to every game as they played, and Davis wondered why he'd ever been annoyed at that. This kid didn't need more structure. He needed to be free, to live, to have all the things his father didn't have.

It didn't last though. It couldn't last. Eventually he spotted Chaz waiting for him at a nearby corner—and he couldn't believe that the time was over already. Sweating, Davis felt his grin melt away.

Right. The world waited; Chaz was its banner, held aloft to gather the faithful. Or in Davis's case, the reluctant.

Hal stepped up beside him. "Is that your partner?"

"Yeah," Davis said.

"You've gotta go?"

Davis pulled him close, and felt tears in his eyes. "Yeah." Then he turned, squatting down and fishing in his pocket. He took out the nickel, his fingers brushing past the paper with the number, and held it out. "Check it."

"Two thousand one?" Hal said. "Oh! You've been looking for one of these."

"Keep it," Davis said.

"Really?"

"Yeah," Davis said. "I've got another."

"You found *two*?"

The same one twice, he thought, then hugged his son one last time. Hal seemed to sense something to it, and clung tightly.

"Can't you stay a little longer?" Hal asked.

"No. Work needs me." *And your mother will be down soon.*

He forced himself to let go. Hal sighed, then ran off to show the nickel to one of his friends. Davis sat and pulled his shoes and socks back on, then trudged across the road toward Chaz.

It twisted him up inside. That hour had been wonderful, but the harsh reality was that this *wasn't* his son. The real Hal wouldn't remember this event, or the other dozen times that Davis had come to visit in the Snapshot. The real Hal would instead go on thinking that his father never visited.

"Not fair," Chaz said, hands in pockets. "You should be able to see him whenever you want, Davis."

"It's only temporary," Davis said.

"Temporary for *six months* now."

"We'll figure out custody soon. My wife—"

"Your ex-wife."

"—Molly is just protective. She's always been like that. Doesn't want Hal getting caught between us."

"It's still a raw deal," Chaz said. Then he sighed. "Food?"

"Sure." Time to deal with his memories of Hal would be welcome. Davis needed to recover, it seemed, from his break to recover.

They chose Fong's, a place around the corner that Davis had always liked. On the way in he froze, turning to look over his shoulder at someone who had just passed. Had that been . . . the woman from the diner?

No. Different clothing. Still, it left him thinking, clutching the number in his pocket. They went inside and were seated in a little booth by the window.

"Do you ever wish," Chaz said, "that we could just live in here? You know, in a Snapshot?"

"You're the one who's always reminding me it isn't real."

"Yeah," Chaz said, sipping the water the waitress brought. "But . . . I mean, do you ever wonder?"

"If it's exactly like the outside world," Davis said, "then what would be the point?"

"Confidence," Chaz said, staring out the window. "In here . . . I just, I can do things. I don't worry as much. I'd like to be able to take that with me to the outside, you know? Or stay in here, let days pass, instead of switching the place off."

Davis grunted, taking a sip of his own water. "I'd like that."

"You would? I'm surprised."

Davis nodded. "I'd like to see what kind of difference I make," he said softly. "You know, we call them Deviations. Problems that *we* introduce into the system. But there's another way to look at them. Everything that changes in here, everything different, happens because *we* cause it. I'd like to see that run for a week. A month. A year."

"Huh. You think it would be better or worse than the real world in a year? Because of us."

"I don't know that I care," Davis said. "So long as it's different. Then I'd know I meant something." He fished in his pocket, got out the woman's number. "We don't let them live long enough in here to develop into distinct people."

"They're just dupes though."

They ordered. Davis got his favorite, cashew chicken. Chaz asked the waitress what the spiciest thing on the menu was, and ordered that. Then he asked for mustard to come with it.

Davis smiled, watching out the window. He'd hoped to catch a glimpse of Molly as she came to get Hal, but he couldn't spot the boy in the park. She'd fetched him already.

"Is it . . . always like this?" Chaz asked softly. "Police work. The things we saw back there."

"You weren't on any murder cases in Mexico City?"

Chaz shook his head. "I was a traffic cop there too. Never even saw a real car wreck; Mexico City had already outlawed manual-driving cars. Spent my time yelling at kids for jaywalking. That's why I kept pushing for transfers. I wanted to land somewhere I could actually be a *cop*."

Davis broke his chopsticks apart and rolled them together to clear the splinters. "Well," he said softly, "yes. Real police work was a lot like this. Except for the times when it wasn't, which was most days."

"There you go again," Chaz said, grinning. "Not making sense. Contradicting yourself."

"It always makes sense when I explain it, doesn't it?"

"I suppose."

"Being a cop, a detective on real cases, is mostly about boredom. Sitting around doing nothing, pushing paper, talking to people. Waiting. It's about *waiting* for something to go wrong. And when we get called, when we have something to do, it means that by definition we're too late.

"I always imagined serving justice, fixing problems. But most of the time we aren't saviors. We arrive in time to see someone dead, and maybe we catch the person who did it. But that doesn't matter to the people who were killed. For them we're really just . . . witnesses." He looked down. "I tell myself that at least *someone* was there."

They ate in silence. The cashew chicken wasn't as good as Davis remembered it being. Too salty. He spent the time staring at the woman's number.

I need something like this, he thought, turning it over in his fingers. Her number on one side. Death on the other—the address of the school. He flipped it back over. *I need a new start, in real life.*

He had to get over Molly. He *knew* he had to get over Molly. See other people. Even though he'd held out hope through the divorce.

But this number itself . . . it was a trap. He couldn't call a woman and lie to her, pretending he'd met her for real. It was a crutch. He just needed to change his life.

You're planning a change. Warsaw Street. He wouldn't have much time to get there after spying on the Photographer at 19:30.

"You going to call that?" Chaz asked as they finished up.

Davis turned it over again, then balled it up. "What's the point?" Davis said. "Let's go catch a bad guy."

He left the little slip of paper on the table beside his uneaten fortune cookie.

Eight

They got back to the school around 19:00, half an hour before the Photographer was supposed to return. They entered an apartment building with back windows looking out at the school—one of the few places to watch from. After knocking a few doors, they found an apartment where no one answered. Chaz kicked open the door, and Davis used his regular police badge—not his reality badge—to quiet the neighbors.

They settled down in the bathroom, where a tiny window gave them a good—if cramped—view. As they waited, Davis played with the facts, dancing them around in his head. As long as he could focus on those, on making neat rows of ideas—on grouping them into abstract sets and collections—he didn't feel so nervous.

"Why poison?" he finally said.

"Hmm?" Chaz asked, standing beside the toilet.

"He's killing them with what he sees as their flaws," Davis said. "He locked those poor people in with bees so their allergies would kill them. He suffocated the asthmatics. It's like . . . he sees himself as culling the species. Letting our own diseases or handicaps destroy us. The people who were paralyzed? The cops found bloody scrapes on the side of the half-full pool. People trying to climb out, breaking fingernails. He dumped those poor people in a swimming pool alive, and let them drown because all their limbs didn't work."

"Bastard," Chaz whispered.

"Yeah. But the poison . . . Why the poison? For the farsighted people? It doesn't fit the pattern." Davis tapped on the window, beside where the paint had chipped free. Outside, it was growing dark. "And another thing. Why in the *world* didn't the precinct tell us about this?"

"Maybe they worried we'd do what we're doing," Chaz said.

"Who cares though? Maybe we create a few more Deviations for a meaningless domestic abuse case, but wouldn't getting a clue about a terrible murderer be worth that risk? Besides, they know we usually ignore orders to go to saferooms—so we're out creating Deviations anyway. Might as well have us doing something useful."

"Yeah, but they call him the *Photographer*," Chaz said. "He knows about Snap-shots and how to avoid them, right? That's what Maria said. We can't do anything to help."

"Like we're not doing anything now?"

"That's different. They don't realize you could actually do something—they think we're both useless, but you, you're *stealth competent*, Davis."

Davis grunted. "I don't buy it, Chaz. We did a Snapshot last week to find that kid working with the Juarez. Why not have us just pop over to that old apartment building? They'd have known about it IRL by then. We could peek in and see if any of the drowning people were still alive on that day—and that would have let us get some intel. But no, instead the precinct just pretends we can't do anything."

"Too deep for me," Chaz said. He pointed out the window. "I can tell you though, this stakeout feels wrong. What if he doesn't go in this way? What if he's been scared off, and doesn't come here at all? Or what if he returned early today, before we got back?"

"One of us should go in there, huh?" Davis said, feeling nervous.

"Yeah." Chaz glanced at him. "Don't worry. I'll do it."

"We should flip for it or something."

"Nah. I'm good." He patted Davis on the shoulder. "I'll text you once I get into position to watch the gym. I'll listen a little bit, then peek in and make sure he's not already in there. You text me if you see him approach. Okay?"

Davis nodded, taking a deep, relieved breath. Chaz walked to the door, but Davis called after him.

"Chaz?"

"Yeah, partner?"

"I couldn't pull the trigger."

Chaz frowned from the doorway. "What—"

"You wanted to know why I'm in here," Davis said, looking back out the window. "Years ago, when I was a real cop, we were in a shootout. Real bad guys, hostages, the terrible kind of stuff that ends up on the news. They sent in every-one. And I . . ."

"Couldn't shoot?"

"Had one right in my sights. And I blew it. You hear about Perez?"

"Yeah."

"The guy I couldn't shoot, he killed her. They found me trembling in the hallway, gun on the floor in front of me." He squeezed his eyes closed. "I thought . . . well, you should know."

"I already did."

"But—"

"Gutierrez told me," Chaz said. "Soon after I got assigned to you. I figured it was better if you told me yourself, you know? If I gave you a chance to bare your soul. Then we could be *real* partners."

Davis blinked, staring at the grinning taller man. *Here I think we're sharing something*, Davis thought, *and then you remind me how good you are at lying.*

"I'll text you," Chaz said, then left.

Davis waited, watching carefully while Chaz slipped across the street and into the building. They had time before the Photographer was supposed to return, but still Davis had visions of the killer spotting Chaz and bolting before either of them could catch him.

Shortly after Chaz entered the building, Davis's phone buzzed. He checked it, but was surprised to see the text wasn't from his partner.

Davis, Maria sent. She'd still be on duty, IRL. She worked a long shift on Snapshot days. *It's getting close to your second case. You guys in the saferoom?*

Yes, Davis sent back, trying to watch both the alley outside and his phone at once.

Good. You have the second case details. Head to Tenth. Be aware, there's going to be some gang violence one block over, at Warsaw Street. Advised to stay away from that. Just check on the domestic case on Tenth.

Understood, Davis sent.

He considered telling her what they were really doing, but decided against it. They'd never turned off the Snapshot while Davis and Chaz were in it, but he wouldn't put it past them. Of course, the two officers wouldn't be reclaimed with the dupes, but it would still be disconcerting to watch it all break down around him.

He stood with his thumb on the phone. For months after the incident where Perez had died, he'd berated himself for not being strong enough. After that, he'd started to berate himself for ever thinking he could shoot another human being. It wasn't in his nature, or it hadn't been.

He had a copy of his own record, nestled on his phone, hidden away behind a password. He'd taken it off Maria's computer at one point. So many commendations early on. *Great investigator. Knows people; he can make them talk when nobody else can. People trust him, even those who shouldn't.*

And then the incident.

Unfit for fieldwork. Severe anxiety. Recommended for therapy and, if retained, strongly recommended that he be put on Snapshot duty.

The others in the precinct hadn't used such sterile terminology about him. He still didn't know if Maria had claimed him for Snapshot duty because she'd thought his investigative skills would be put to good use here, or because she'd assumed that this place would teach him how to kill.

Here, Chaz finally sent. *No sounds from the pool locker room. Anything out there?*

No, Davis sent.

I'm going to peek in.

Davis waited, heart beating rapidly. What a fool he was. He didn't even have to be the one in danger for his nerves to go off!

He's not here, Chaz sent. *And nothing is disturbed. Let's hope he doesn't get spooked away permanently by the cops finding his last place.*

Yeah, Davis sent. *Be careful. If he doesn't go in this way, you'll have no warning.*

Roger.

And then, a moment later, the phone buzzed again.

If it were me in danger, Chaz sent, *you'd shoot.*

I can't say.

You would, Chaz sent. *I know it.*

Davis wasn't sure. Even still. People felt that being in a Snapshot lowered the stakes. But at the same time, all these people—they'd been created so that Davis and Chaz could solve their little cases. An entire city populated, then destroyed in a day. Millions wiped out. A periodic holocaust. If he failed, it was all for nothing.

Seemed like huge stakes to him.

Anything? Chaz sent.

No. I'll tell you if I see anything, Chaz. But if you keep distracting me— He stopped midsentence, and didn't send the text.

Someone was moving through the alleyway. A tall man in a long coat, his hands in the pockets. With the sun having set, there wasn't enough light to see him by, but he matched the profile.

Davis's heart leaped. *He's here,* he quickly texted.

Finally, Chaz sent.

Davis contained his breathing, trying not to imagine what would happen if the Photographer spotted Chaz. That wasn't likely to happen. Was it? But what if he checked the woman they'd shot, and found her with a bullet wound? Davis hadn't considered that.

The Photographer entered the building.

A short time later, Chaz sent, *He just passed me. Went into the pool area.*

At the very least, Davis didn't have to keep worrying about Warsaw Street. They had a new case, a more important one. They wouldn't be heading that way, and so none of his preparations would matter.

He found that idea comforting. Almost comforting enough to soothe his anxiety.

He's looking in the door to where the bodies are, Chaz texted.

You followed him into the locker room?
Yeah.
Stop texting me and stay safe, idiot!

Davis waited, tense, staring at his phone and feeling a frustrating discordance. He'd just told Chaz not to update him—but that very silence put him on edge. He imagined his partner sneezing, the Photographer escaping. A dozen different scenarios.

He peeked in, Chaz sent, *at the bee room. Seemed very worried about insects escaping, even though they're all dead. It was dark in there though, and he doesn't seem to have noticed that the woman was shot. Maybe he was just listening to hear if they were still breathing. He closed the door quickly, then went on to look over his improvised pool of water. I'm back outside. He's eating a burger.*

Davis relaxed, pulling the lid down to sit on the toilet. Honestly, it might have been *less* nerve-racking to go in himself, rather than waiting out here.

A door opened nearby in the apartment. Damn. The people who owned this place were back. *I'm moving out to the street,* Davis sent. *So I can follow when he leaves.*

He pushed out of the bathroom, causing a woman to drop her groceries and scream. Davis flashed her his badge, then realized he'd grabbed the reality badge and felt guilty for using it so injudiciously. Like Chaz did. Well, whatever.

He hurried out into the hallway, leaving the woman to collapse on her couch, holding her chest. He ran down the steps and into the night, then placed himself at the mouth of the alleyway connecting the back of the school to the street.

He settled down on the ground next to some steps, head bowed, trying to look like just another of the many bits of human refuse that littered the city.

A text came a short time later. *He's moving again. Back out your way.*
So soon? Davis sent.
Yeah. He seems anxious. Just wanted to check things, I guess.
Wait a bit, Davis sent. *Then follow.*

Davis huddled there, proud at how calm his breathing was. When the Photographer passed him, he caught a good glimpse of his Asian features and black hair. Once the man was far enough ahead, Davis got to his feet and pursued silently.

He's heading east, Davis sent.
I'll go parallel, Chaz sent. *Through the alleyways.*
Roger.

As he followed, Davis began to feel a thrill. Perhaps this was what Chaz felt. He tried to think like his partner did. To him, this was all just a game. Couldn't Davis enjoy a game?

Then the Photographer turned right.

Davis stopped on the corner.

He just turned toward Warsaw, Davis sent, his thumbs moving almost of their own accord.

Roger.

Davis continued on, feeling as if he were being pulled in the wake of the killer. The farther he walked, the more *inevitable* he realized it was. Of course the killer would turn toward Warsaw. Of course everything hinged on this point. Davis couldn't have escaped it if he'd wanted.

Eventually, the Photographer turned up a set of steps into a townhouse in a row of old buildings pressed close to one another. They weren't abandoned, just well used. Most had shingles worn off the roofs, making them look balding.

They'd found the killer's real home. Davis stood there, looking up at it, bothered by how *normal* it seemed.

We're one street over from Warsaw, Davis thought. *Not on the side we were supposed to be on, for the domestic case.* That would be two blocks away.

Though this wasn't the exact same location where they would have gone if they hadn't picked up this case, it was still eerily close. Davis checked his phone. 20:00 exactly. Seventeen minutes away.

Chaz caught up to him. They stood together, looking up at the narrow townhouse.

"So, we send Maria this address?" Chaz asked. "We're done? They can go catch him here IRL?"

"I want more," Davis said softly.

"More?"

"I need to talk to him."

"I can go in and—"

"No," Davis said, shocked by how firm he felt. "Watch outside. Catch him if he runs."

"But—"

"Just do it, Chaz!" Davis said. "Stay out. Leave me alone." At least until 20:17 had passed.

The other man stepped back, surprised.

It isn't inevitable, Davis thought forcefully, walking up the steps. Was that how all the dupes felt? That their lives were their own? Never knowing that circumstances, replicated at the start of the day, would send them down exactly the same path?

He stepped up to the door, feeling his partner's eyes on his back. Chaz would have kicked in the front door.

Davis knocked.

Such a courteous request of a serial killer with blood on his hands, but there it was. Davis knocked again, politely.

The Photographer opened the door.

Nine

Even having heard the description and having glimpsed the killer earlier, Davis found the man younger than he'd anticipated. He couldn't be more than twenty-two or twenty-three. So young to have caused so much horror in his life.

"What do you want?" the Photographer asked, looking Davis up and down.

Davis held up his reality badge.

The Photographer saw it, eyes widening. Then he smiled. "It's beautiful," he whispered.

"I need to—" Davis began.

The Photographer tried to slam the door. Davis got his foot between it and the frame, moving by instinct to block it from being shut. In the rush of the moment, he didn't even feel the pain. The Photographer turned and scrambled away.

"Davis!" Chaz called.

"Run around to the back door!" Davis shouted, shoving into the townhouse. He didn't think. He was proud that he didn't tremble. Yes, maybe his time in the Snapshot *had* changed him.

Inside, the walls were painted a homey shade of peach and the wooden floors were bare and polished. The Photographer ducked around a corner, and his feet thumped up a set of stairs. Davis followed in a rush, yanking his gun out.

He passed suitcases set along the wall. Packed, a part of him noticed. *He's leaving. This address is useless. They'll find him gone IRL when they come here.* The Photographer had indeed been spooked by the cops finding the pool earlier.

Davis dashed up the steps. *Careful. Remember your training.*

At the top of the steps, he checked his corners—right, then left—to make sure nobody was standing there ready to ambush him. *Don't let the runner draw you into being careless. Be quick, but efficient. Control the situation.*

It was darker up here. No lights on. He continued forward, sweating, breathing in quick, sharp breaths. There were only two rooms in this hallway, which ended at a set of wooden steps pulled down from the ceiling, leading toward an attic.

Davis carefully checked one room, a bedroom, while trying to watch those steps ahead. The room was empty. He crossed the hallway and shoved open the other door, checking the corners.

No killer here either. But there was a captive.

An older Asian man sat on the ground, bound against the wall, weeping, with a gag over his mouth. On the floor in front of him was a series of cups that he'd barely be able to reach.

"I knew it," a voice called from the hallway outside. From the direction of the wooden steps. "I knew it was a Snapshot. Nobody ever believed me. But I knew you'd come someday."

Davis forced himself to ignore the captive. He stepped out into the hall again. The only light was what filtered up from the stairwell behind him, but it was enough to see that the hallway was completely normal. Pictures on the walls. A rug on the floor. The aroma of lemon-scented polish in the air.

And yet a kidnapped man wept to his right, and the icy voice of a madman floated down from the attic above.

Getting ready to flee out onto the roof maybe? Davis thought. These townhouses were built shoulder to shoulder; you could run across them. Davis would never chase down a younger man, in better shape, over that terrain.

"How did you know?" Davis called out, trying to think of something to stall the killer. "How did you figure out you were in a Snapshot?"

"The Deviations," the Photographer called back. Yes, he'd climbed those wooden steps. He was right up there. Listening. "This life is too broken. Too many people gone wrong, too many neighborhoods left to rot. The Snapshot is . . . is falling apart. Too many Deviations."

"You're right," Davis called. "Yeah, I've noticed too. We can't let it happen. We've got to get rid of the Deviations, right? Keep the Snapshot stable?"

It was complete nonsense, but he could see how it might make sense.

"Why would you care?" the voice rasped.

"I'm part of it," Davis said. "This is my home."

The Snapshot is the only thing that is rational. Life is chaos the first time, but if you live it again, you see that it's very orderly. The system is too complex for us to figure out on the fly. But if I could live here, I could always know what was coming . . .

"No. You're from outside. You're a cop."

"Doesn't mean I can't agree with you," Davis shouted. "I can help you keep this place together. Make the Snapshot run. It needs to run, right? I have to keep it together, keep it from crumbling, so I can do my job."

It seemed like the right thing to say, and remarkably it seemed to work. To an extent. The Photographer didn't run. He shuffled up above.

"You're a cop," he finally repeated. "You're here to stop me."

"Not you," Davis said. "No, not you. If we were in the real world, I'd have to stop you. But we're not, are we? All I care about is keeping this place running. You're doing that. You're important. You're the only one who has figured it out. You can help me. Help me cleanse this place."

The Photographer started down the steps, but stopped on them, frozen. Uncertain. Davis felt sick, a striking nausea, as the man turned and started back up the steps.

"Wait!" Davis said. "Wait! I can prove it. I . . ." He trailed off, then stepped backward, looking into the room with the tied-up captive. The man reached his hands toward him, wrists bound, eyes pleading.

"I'll prove it!" Davis whispered.

Just a Snapshot. Not real. This is the only way to save people who are real. Don't be a coward . . .

In a trance, Davis raised his gun at the man.

I can't do this. I can't . . .

He'd already done it before with the push of a button. Hundreds of times. Every time he turned this place off.

He shot the man.

The gunshot broke the air. It was louder than he'd expected, and he winced. The man he'd shot slumped backward. This time the bullet had come out the back of the head, painting the wall.

His phone buzzed. He ignored it. He just stared at the dead man, then dropped his gun, shocked at himself.

"Did . . ." the Photographer's voice called. The man started back down the wooden steps. "Did you just do it?"

"Got to . . . got to protect the Snapshot," Davis said, his voice trembling. He squeezed his eyes shut.

"You know them for what they are," the Photographer said, sounding proud. "But you should know, we're not supposed to kill them. We let the Snapshot do it, like the immune system of the body. Clear them out."

The Photographer walked up to him. "That one, my uncle, he can't see. We wait until he's thirsty, then let him pick a drink. But he can't read the labels. So the system kills him."

"I'll do it right next time," Davis whispered. "What's the plan? Who is next? I can help."

The Photographer licked his lips. "I'm running out of people I can find on the street," he said. "We've got to be careful though. The cops from inside will try to stop us. They don't understand."

"I do."

"Mary Magdalene School," the Photographer said. "Seventeen children have peanut allergies. I've been working out how to do it, so we can be hidden. But if you're with me, if the cops outside the Snapshot don't care, then maybe I don't have to worry. Either way, we move on May twelfth. I've found out that—"

A gunshot went off: loud, arrogant, unexpected. The Photographer dropped like a puppet with its strings cut. Davis turned to see Chaz at the top of the steps, lit from below, gun in hand.

"Holy hell!" Chaz said. "Davis, you all right? How'd he disarm you?"

Davis blinked. *Chaz, you idiot.*

His phone buzzed a long buzz. The alarm.

20:17 on the dot.

Davis calmly picked up his gun. They were a distance from Warsaw, but he'd have to go forward with his plan anyway. It would work, right? It was plausible?

Did he care?

Chaz shoved past Davis and knelt by the killer. "Wow. He's just a kid." He looked up into the room with the dead man. "Hell! What happened, Davis?"

In response, Davis raised his gun and pointed it at Chaz's head.

Chaz stumbled back. "Davis?"

"Goodbye, Chaz."

"Whoa. Whoa, Davis! What are you doing!"

"Tell me," Davis said softly. "When you go see Molly in the Snapshot, do you have to seduce her anew each time? Or do you flash your badge, convince her she's not real, and just take her that way?"

Chaz's jaw dropped, his eyes wide.

"You do it so quickly," Davis said. "Every time I visit Hal, right?"

"Davis, think about this!"

"I *have* thought about it, Chaz!" Davis shouted. "You see this gun? This *is* me thinking about it!"

Outside, distantly, gunfire went off. The gang violence on Warsaw.

"This gun," Davis snapped, "came from evidence, IRL. Those shots you hear— someone is using this gun right now to fire on another gang member. I thought, how to disguise a murder in the Snapshot? I could use the same gun we *know* a gangster had. I could shoot you. Claim it was a stray bullet, and the ballistics will back me up. Nobody will know. They'll think it was an accident."

"Hell," Chaz whispered. Then he sighed and dropped his gun. "I guess you have thought about it."

Davis held his own gun, palms sweaty, teeth clenched. For once he wasn't nervous. For once he wasn't trembling, or breathing quickly. He was *angry*. Furious.

"My wife, Chaz," he whispered.

"Your *ex*-wife."

"You think that makes it all right?"

Chaz shrugged. "No. Probably not." He closed his eyes.

Here we are. Need to do it quickly. Davis wiped his brow, gun arm steady.

And then . . . then he thought about second chances. About pretty smiles, about his son.

You were just thinking earlier about how you need to get over Molly, a piece of him whispered. *If you let her force you to do this, then what are you?*

Still, he'd just shot a man. An innocent man. Now here he was, with Chaz, at exactly the right moment. Just like he'd planned and imagined it. Why not take this step?

It was all inevitable, wasn't it?

Was it inevitable that he'd failed before, IRL? Was he the Deviation, or was Chaz? Did it matter?

I can start fresh, he thought. *Get a new life. Date new people. But if I pull this trigger, I'll never be able to do that. I'll never be able to live with myself if I kill him.*

He took a deep breath. In the end, people became cops because they wanted to do something good. At least that was what they told themselves. That was what he'd always told himself.

Davis lowered his gun.

Ten

H ow long have you known?" Chaz asked, raising a shot of whiskey to his lips. They were in the kitchen of the small townhouse, the one with two corpses upstairs.

"I caught sight of you up in the window about five months back," Davis said softly. "After that, it was obvious. You kept prompting me to go see Hal."

Davis poured himself another shot, and had to be careful not to spill, with his hand shaking. How could Chaz drink so calmly?

"I did it once in real life, Davis," Chaz said, leaning on the counter. "Shouldn't tell you that, should I? But I need to come clean. It was just before the divorce started."

Davis closed his eyes.

"That's why it works in the Snapshot," Chaz continued. "I don't show my badge. She thinks it's the second time, each time. I promised to come see her again, but never did, IRL. I figured I needed to confine it to this place. Out of respect for my partner, you know? It's a Snapshot. Nothing matters in a Snapshot."

"Yeah," Davis said, then opened his eyes. "To nothing mattering." He raised his shot glass.

Chaz nodded, raising his own.

Davis drank and looked at his phone, which sat in front of him, the text he'd sent to Maria glowing on the screen.

Photographer, the serial killer, it read, *is going to try to kill a group of peanut-allergic children from Mary Magdalene School. Tomorrow, May 12th. Set up a sting, catch him. You can find evidence of his activities at the following addresses.* He'd then sent the address of the school and the house they were in now, hoping the evidence there would corroborate his words, even if the Photographer had moved on from them IRL.

Maria hadn't responded, but the message had gone through. He could imagine her shock. And her likely anger.

"We did good, partner," Chaz said. "Didn't we? We're going to do great things together moving forward."

"Chaz?"

"Yeah."

"I never want to see you after today. *Never again.*"

Chaz looked down at his empty glass. "Right. Okay."

They drank in silence.

"I'm glad you didn't shoot," Chaz eventually said. "Glad you couldn't shoot."

Davis finished his whiskey. "You know why I insist on turning off the Snapshot myself, each evening?"

"No. Why?"

"Every time I do it, I kill Hal. *Every time.* Someone has to do it, so I do it myself. But it rips me up each time, knowing. And if I've killed my son a hundred times, do you really think I couldn't shoot you?"

Chaz went white.

Together, they took their things and walked to the front of the building. Outside, the air smelled sweet, a breeze coming in off the ocean. Davis climbed down the steps, exhausted, then stopped at the bottom. A couple of people were on the street here. A tall Black man. And a woman. The woman from the diner. She *had* changed her outfit.

"Detectives Davis and Chavez?" the tall man asked. "Can we have a word with you?"

Davis shared a look with Chaz, who shrugged.

"What's this about?" Davis asked. "You from the precinct?" His frown deepened. "You're from IRL? Are you feds?"

"We'll explain," the tall man said, taking Chaz by the shoulder, leading him a little farther down the street. The woman stepped up to Davis.

She was pretty. Like he remembered. "I lost your number," he blurted out. "Sorry."

She blushed. "Detective Davis. Why didn't you kill your partner today?"

"How do you know—"

"Please just answer the question."

Davis rubbed his chin. "Because I'm not a monster. Pointing the gun at him was a momentary lapse."

"A momentary lapse?" she asked. "That you planned for months, waiting for an exactly perfect Snapshot, where you would be able to hide your actions and pretend a gangster shot him?"

Farther down the street, Chaz suddenly shoved back from the tall man. "No!" Chaz shouted. "No, no, *no!*" He reached for his weapon.

The tall man calmly gunned Chaz down in the street.

Davis stared, feeling cold. *It can't be.*

"It would really help our investigation," the woman said, "if you could tell us what we did wrong."

"You're Snapshot detectives too," Davis said. "It . . . Damn! *That's* why they don't have us on the Photographer case. They're using someone else!"

"You're a distraction, Davis. A way to cover up the real teams, who come into the Snapshot on different days from you. We can file your records though, and show the city is using the Snapshot device that people paid for. We can pretend that we're not—"

"Doing something deeper," Davis said. "With secret cops. Watching people. Damn! That's why they don't want us working real cases, at least not the in-depth ones." He shivered, then continued, whispering. "Right now, you're here to investigate *me*. Today's a Snapshot . . . It's *a Snapshot of a Snapshot.*"

"We weren't sure if it would work. No cop has ever before needed to be investigated for killing his partner in a Snapshot."

"But I didn't kill him."

"You did, in real life." She pointed. "After stopping the Photographer, you shot your partner."

"My plan—"

"Was clever, but you were too far from Warsaw. Maria found Chavez's death suspicious. You confessed under pressure, but then recanted, and a judge threw out the testimony. Now we need to catch you doing it, but we failed. Why?"

"Help you incriminate me?"

She shrugged.

"You really *don't* know how this works." He paused. "You're new, aren't you?"

"Newly promoted. You weren't deemed important enough for the other two teams. They thought we could learn from this. And the classes say—"

"The classes won't replace living it," Davis said, numb. "You shouldn't have given me your number."

"So that *was* it," the man said, stepping up to them, leaving Chaz dead in the street. "I told you."

"I had to do *something*," the woman said. "He spotted me paying attention to him! It would have been weirder if I hadn't responded at all."

"No," Davis said. "You gave me something physical—that slip of paper. That created a persistent Deviation, and it changed me." He raised his hand to his head. "It changed what I did. *I* didn't choose. *You* made me choose . . ."

The two nodded to each other. Then they started to walk off.

"Wait!" Davis said. "The Photographer! Did they get him?"

The man frowned. "Well, that case really is above your clearance—"

"Hell with that!" Davis said. "You're going to turn this all off in a moment. Tell me. *Did they get him?*"

"Yes," the woman said. "The information you sent from inside the Snapshot proved accurate. They caught him trying to contaminate food supplies at the school."

Davis closed his eyes and sighed. So he had done something. But not him. The other him.

He opened his eyes. "I'm the Deviation," he said. "But I'm the one who *didn't* kill my partner. I'm a better man than the one you have in custody, but I'm the one you're going to kill."

The woman looked apologetic. How could you *apologize* for destroying a whole city? For murdering a man, for murdering *him*?

"At least show me," he said.

"Show you?"

"The badge," Davis said. "Mine looks just like a metal shield. Prove it to me."

The woman reluctantly got out her wallet. "Yours looks like a shield to you because, in the day we're copying, that's what you saw. It has to be re-created exactly—"

"I know the mechanics of it. *Show me.*"

She held up the badge.

In it, Davis saw his life. A child. A young man. An adult. He saw Molly, good times and bad. He saw Hal's birth, and saw himself holding the boy. He saw tears, rage, love, and panic. He saw himself huddled in a shopping mall, in the middle of a nervous breakdown, and he saw himself standing firm, gun pointed at Chaz's head. He saw a hero and a fool. He saw everything.

And he knew. He knew he was fake. Up until that moment, he hadn't really believed.

He blinked, and it faded. The other two were already walking away. They'd leave through a doorway that dupes couldn't see.

Davis walked over and sank down beside Chaz's dead body. "I guess you got it one way or another, partner."

The two detectives suddenly vanished ahead. No need for stealth in leaving— not when they were about to turn the Snapshot off.

"I pulled the trigger," Davis said. "When I needed to. So I guess the Snapshot did change me, eh, partner?" He sighed a long, deep sigh. "I wonder what it feels like when—"

POSTSCRIPT

"Snapshot" is the little (well, I suppose medium-length) story that just keeps giving. So far, it is the story that has been optioned most often for film and television, and as of this writing it is the project I have furthest along toward actually getting made.

It is the intersection of two ideas I had. The first, naturally, is the Snapshot. Amusingly, one of the reasons I started working on the story was because I liked the way the word sounded, and thought it would make a good title for a short piece. More powerfully, I loved the idea of solving cases by going back in time and trying to dig up information from the past—but only in a very limited way. This had a nice, dark, privacy-invading sense to it, like *Minority Report*.

The second idea was for the relationship between the two detectives—where one was sleeping with the other's wife, and the husband knew it and was planning perfect vengeance. The Snapshot provided opportunities for exploring the psyche of people in a peculiar situation, where they suddenly discover they aren't real.

I worried that the ending was a little too obvious for this kind of story—but then again, the reason it's obvious is because it's so powerful. The idea of the "screen" going black mid-thought was engaging enough that I knew I had to write toward it, even if this is the conventional way to end this kind of story.

I tried to make up for that by giving this story the full "Brandon treatment." Meaning interesting worldbuilding, character conflicts, and as much large-scale scope as the story could allow. I'm very pleased with the result, and find it interesting that this "feels" more like one of my epic fantasy works, despite on paper being about as far away as you can get within speculative fiction (a serial-killer thriller).

BRAIN DUMP

Whose brain do you have?" the stylish saleswoman asked.

Baraka fumbled for an answer. She'd never been asked it like that, so outright. People usually danced around the topic.

"We have natural brains," Rod answered, placing a comforting hand on her shoulder. "Both of us."

The saleswoman pursed her lips—outlined in black, painted cherry in the centers. "Oh! We don't . . . get many of your persuasion. In here." She glanced across the showroom, where salespeople in silver business attire led couples past stainless metal counters, each ornamented by a single holodisplay of a brain. The twenty or so holograms hovered and rotated in the light, like lines of music-box ballerinas.

"It wasn't for religious reasons," Rod explained. "Really, we're just a couple of flukes. Lab mix-up on my part."

"I was an accident," Baraka said. "Conceived the old-fashioned way—and my mother didn't realize she was pregnant until it was too late."

"And you found each other," the saleswoman said with a radiant smile. "That's sweet. Well, it's . . . Rod and Baraka, right? My name is Zhi, and I'm here to help. Please don't *hesitate* to let me know if you have any questions. I want this to be a comfortable, informative shopping experience for you. Rod, I love the shirt. Where did you get it?"

Rod glanced down at his shirt, then grinned. "At the series when the Rangers won, ten years back. I was there. Top row, but I was there."

"They could have gotten seats a few rows lower," Baraka said, taking his arm. "But he thought it would be a better story if they were in the *literal* last row."

"I agree," Zhi said. "It *is* a better story. You sound like a deliberate kind of person, Rod. No wonder you've come to us."

It was a nice segue. Zhi had a charming, no-pressure attitude as she strolled them into the showroom, moving with the same gentle flow as the other salespeople.

She's got a brain designed to maximize interpersonal skills, Baraka thought. *Maybe the Benchly?* She didn't ask, of course. She never did feel comfortable prying.

Zhi listened to Rod's story—he sure loved telling it—about almost missing the game-winning run because he wanted a hot dog. Of course, *that* was an excuse to talk about how the stadium got around the ban. But as they reached the first station, Zhi skillfully took control of the conversation again.

"I can't believe you even *wanted* to eat one of those!" Zhi said. "I could *never.*"

"Well, I'm not generally known for my decision-making aptitude," Rod said.

"Nonsense! You're here, aren't you?"

That's good marketing, Baraka thought, reassessing. *Maybe she's got a business-focused brain. The Hu-Gou?*

"We just want to do this right," Rod said. "For our kid. We want the perfect brain."

"Well, I'm afraid I can't help you," Zhi said.

Baraka frowned. "You can't? But, I mean, this *is* a brain dump."

"We at Crescendo prefer to call it the showroom," Zhi said with a laugh. "But what I meant is that there *is* no perfect brain." She turned and gestured to the holographic brain hovering above the first counter. The décor was sleek, stylishly simple. Nothing to distract from the holograms.

"It's a common mistake," Zhi said. "We all have intentional brain architecture these days—or, well, most everyone does! But intentional doesn't mean perfect, though it can be perfect for *you*!

"There's an old myth that humans only use a small portion of their brain capacity. That's never been true—every cell and every neuron is important. No designer, no matter how skilled, can create a brain that's good at everything. So for your child, we have to ask ourselves what you most value—what you want the little one's strengths to be."

"That makes sense," Rod said, glancing at Baraka. He noticed her frown—he usually did—and nudged her. "What are you thinking, Bara?"

"If there aren't any perfect brains," she asked, "does that mean that each of these is going to be *bad* at something?"

"Unfortunately, yes," Zhi said. "Now, our designer brains are top of the line, the best. Don't mistake me. Your child is going to have *incredible* capacity and *endless* potential. But with the enhancements to most capacities will come a slight disendowment in others."

She gestured at the brain beside them again. "The Delphi," she said proudly. "Designed by Kublo Noratami, based on the brains of the most genius painters of our times. A child born with this brain architecture has a *three thousand* percent higher chance of becoming a master artist than children born with a natural brain.

It also includes above-average computational skills, giving a high likelihood of aptitude in mathematics. It is one of our *most* popular architectures."

"Three thousand?" Rod said. "Wow." He nudged Baraka again. "What?"

"It has a weakness, though, right?" Baraka asked.

"Some mild disendowments in interpersonal skills," Zhi admitted. "Though the enhancements to personal discipline and individualism will ensure that the child is quite adept at working on their own. And it is very common for a little eccentricity to accompany an artist anyway—so this is basically a feature. Who doesn't love the idea of a quirky genius with a different way of seeing the world?"

Good marketing, Baraka thought again.

Rod rubbed his chin. "Don't much like the idea of a kid I can't talk to."

"Oh, you'll be able to talk to him, Rod," Zhi promised. "Don't worry about that. But come, we have seventeen different architectures for the choosing, each designed by one of the best brain architects alive."

She strolled them along, showing off several more. A charismatic model, which Zhi promised would make their child "six thousand percent more likely to achieve success in politics." That one came with the weakness of an impatient, sometimes argumentative attitude. "Just like you'd expect!" Zhi exclaimed.

The next was a science-focused brain, patterned after the mind of Kat Gutritch, the woman who pioneered brain architecture. It was Crescendo's biggest claim to fame, giving them an advantage over the other seven major companies selling architectures.

"You keep mentioning percentages," Rod said, waving at the science-focused brain. "So . . . are there people with this brain who *don't* become scientists?"

"Great question, Rod!" Zhi said. "There are, actually. Nothing is guaranteed. Your child will have their own personality. We don't want everyone to be clones! These architectures set a child up for success, but the individual has to make their own choices.

"That said, I assure you, any children born with our architectures have a *very* high rate of excellence. Now, you really need to see the DiMaggio—a brain optimized for sports performance. Did you know that Donny Tin has one of these?"

"Tin the Bin?" Rod's eyes lit up. "*Really?* You're kidding me. I have his jersey. It's even digitally signed!"

Baraka smiled. She'd known this one was coming; it was why she'd steered him to Crescendo first. In fact, she'd read about most of what Zhi was saying; Baraka had probably been a little *too* zealous in her research, if she was honest. She just hated going into experiences feeling foolish, and if she researched first, she picked it up faster in person.

Rod, though, liked to dive straight in or ask experts. Reading had never really been his thing.

"... has a seven thousand percent greater chance of playing professional sports than a natural brain," Zhi finished, gesturing to the DiMaggio with a flourish.

"Seven *thousand*," Rod breathed.

"Indeed!"

"So ... what's the weakness?" he asked.

"Math," Baraka said. "I read about it." It seemed silly, in retrospect, not to have guessed that they'd *all* have weaknesses. Everybody had their hang-ups. She'd just assumed that if you went with the best—if you came to Crescendo—well ... you wouldn't have to worry about that.

"If that's the case," Rod said, "the kid would fit in well at *our* home, eh?"

They continued to the next display, though Baraka's eyes lingered on the DiMaggio, its hologram rotating slowly, so complex and full of lights. That was the one Rod would want to pick, and she was inclined to agree.

But the cost ...

"This is the Boardroom," Zhi said, gesturing at the next hovering brain. "An architecture optimized for interpersonal skills, leadership, and teamwork. The CEO of this very company has a Boardroom brain. The architecture is one of the very best for exceptional business acumen."

"What's the weakness, then?" Rod asked. "Bad water-cooler jokes?"

"Well, those are an optional extra! No, the Boardroom has a slight disendowment of individualism and ambition."

"Downgraded ambition?" Baraka asked. "For a business-focused brain?"

"It's actually an advantage," Zhi said. "Though we often talk about the ruggedly individualistic entrepreneur, those types burn out quickly—and their great deeds can often be traced to more levelheaded executives beneath them. Ask any manager, and they'll tell you: it's better to have people who work well in groups with modest ambition than ones who want to tear the place up and make themselves famous."

Rod smiled. "I like how you do that."

"Oh?" Zhi said. "How I do what?"

"How you make every weakness sound like it's this great thing." He pointed at Baraka. "Sounds like the things you write."

"I'm in marketing," Baraka explained. "I've been admiring your showmanship."

"It can be a bit much, can't it?" Zhi said, leaning in. "I'll admit, we're fed most of these lines. But brain architectures are like life itself—you have to take what you're given and put the best spin on it you can."

Baraka cocked her head. That felt more candid than the other things Zhi had said. Like they were seeing through her mask a little. "That's your brain, isn't it?" Baraka said, pointing at the hologram. "You have a Boardroom."

As soon as she said it, Baraka was immediately embarrassed by blurting it out like that. Where was her tact?

Zhi blushed. Another glimpse past the mask. "You're right," she said. "I'm surprised you guessed! I have an earlier design, of course. All of our architectures are updated each year."

"But you're not a CEO," Rod said with a frown. "You're just a . . ."

Oh, Rod, Baraka thought, squeezing his hand. He cut himself off, but not before Zhi blushed again.

"We can't all be CEOs," she said. "I mean, I've got a *very* good job. I get to work with people like you, Rod!"

"I suppose that's true," he said. "Sorry. I didn't mean anything by—"

"No, no. I didn't take anything from it. Come on, let me show you the re-creator, where we can look at what your child might be like."

She tried to usher them to a station by the wall, but Baraka remained in place, looking back along the lines of brains. When she realized they were waiting for her, though, she felt anxious and hurried to catch up.

"You're thinking something," Rod said, taking her hand.

"I shouldn't ask it."

"I want to hear. Go on."

"Any question is fine," Zhi promised as they reached a station with a monitor at the side of the room.

"Well, I was just wondering," Baraka said. "What's the actual chance our child becomes a professional player, if they had that brain back there? The sports one?"

"DiMaggio," Rod said.

"Right, the DiMaggio."

"Seven *thousand* percent greater," Zhi said, perking up.

"You'd have heard that if you were listening," Rod said, giving Baraka a playful poke. "Now what's this re-creator thing?"

"Well, it—"

"But what's the actual percentage?" Baraka asked. They both looked at her, and she blushed to have interrupted. But she took a deep breath and continued. "The actual percentage of becoming a professional player? Seven thousand percent higher than normal makes . . . what? How likely is that in real numbers?"

Rod laughed. "That sounds like math."

"You don't have to answer," Baraka said, "if you don't know. I realize it's probably not included in the marketing material—"

"I know," Zhi said quietly. "I looked it up. You're right, it's not exactly part of the pitch. Point zero four percent."

"Four percent?" Rod said.

"No, *point* zero four," Zhi said. "Just under one-half of one-tenth of one percent. That's how many DiMaggios go pro."

Rod blinked.

"It's better than it sounds," Zhi explained quickly. "Really, considering how few professional sports players there are—and how many people there are in the country—a child's chances are *infinitesimal* without proper brain architecture."

"Just like it's not that likely someone with the Boardroom becomes CEO of a powerful company," Baraka said.

"Not that likely," Zhi agreed, "but it's still far better than trying to make it without the right brain architecture. Isn't this about making the best life for your child?"

"The best *chance* of the best life," Baraka said.

"Exactly."

"I just thought," Baraka said, "with the cost being so high . . ."

"But it's not high," Zhi said. "It's free."

"For *us*."

No, she and Rod wouldn't pay for the brain—but the child would owe 25 percent of their lifetime earnings, after age thirty, to the company. Crescendo had the highest cut of all the architecture companies. That was the price one paid for the best designer brains in the world.

"You can't look only at the mega-success stories," Zhi said. "Yes, very few DiMaggios become professional sports players—but their brains are geared for physical conditioning, training, and self-moderation. You'd be surprised how many become models, bodybuilders, or even religious officials. Repeated studies have shown that the average Crescendo brain outearns the competition, even *after* the cut is factored in."

That was an excellent marketing pitch, but Baraka could see the holes. You could squeeze a lot of mileage out of words like "average" and "studies."

Baraka met Zhi's eyelinered gaze. "And you? How do *you* feel about it?"

Zhi glanced around. Then, oddly, she smiled. "Honestly," she said softly, "it sucks. Average earnings don't mean a lot when you're stuck on the wrong side of the bell curve, staring up the slope without a ladder.

"I had to apply for government relief and was released from my contract—but after that, nobody else would take me on. Who wants the woman who was given a designer brain, then 'squandered' it? Two years later, I had to come to Crescendo to get a job at all. They took me on because it looked bad to have Boardrooms on welfare. But . . . you know."

Rod looked between the two of them. "So . . . you're telling us *not* to go forward with this?"

"Of course not," Zhi said. "The statistics are solid. Your child *is* more likely, on average, to be successful with our brains than with any other brain. The cut taken is specifically designed to make certain that remains the case."

"But?" Baraka urged.

"Well," Zhi admitted, "sometimes it seems like the only way to be *sure* to win in this system is to own the architecture, you know? Individuals, we can roll the dice and still flop. But if you're the house, you get a cut from every winning hand. Just . . . pretend I didn't say that, all right? I could get in so much trouble . . ." She gestured at a screen in front of them. "If you don't mind? This might help you understand. It does a quick scan of your own architectures and gives us the percentage chances of your child achieving various milestones."

Brain scans being as common as they were, it didn't seem like too much to ask. Zhi ran the calculations while Baraka stood, thinking.

"This projection is going to be embarrassing, isn't it?" Rod joked. "With a couple of naturals like us? No fancy architecture."

"Oh, it's a little embarrassing for everyone," Zhi said, smiling. "A lot of people with designer brains assume their children will naturally inherit their skills, but genetics has a way of muddying things. It's showroom policy to do this with everyone, so we can persuade them to re-up for their children, rather than just going natural once they have one of our brains themselves. After we show them how low the percentages are if they leave everything to chance, they are usually eager to jump back in. It's really quite . . ."

She trailed off.

"What?" Baraka said, crowding in to see the monitor.

"That bad?" Rod said with a chuckle.

"Not that," Zhi said. "I mean, yes, it's kind of horrible—no offense. These are amazingly low percentages, but . . . look. Here, I'll make it easier."

The screen showed how much less likely a possible offspring was to have various high-status jobs using natural genetics as opposed to an architecture. Again, the company obfuscated the actual percentages—working in multipliers.

But Zhi hit a button, showing the raw numbers with a percentage chance for each achievement. And . . . they were almost identical. CEO, professional sports player, Nobel Prize–winning scientist, acclaimed artist—all the same number, the same chance.

"It's just kind of amusing," Zhi said. "It doesn't really mean anything, but isn't it odd that all the chances are equal for your potential child? I've never seen that happen."

"All I see," Rod said, "is a kid with no weaknesses."

Zhi chuckled. "That's *not* true, Rod. I mean, they might *technically* not be weak at any specific thing—but that's because in raw numbers, they'd still be bad at everything."

"Just spinning it like you two do. Making the best of things." He laughed. "Why are we even doing this? We all know I'm going to want the DiMaggio. Kid doesn't have to be a pro. So long as he can hit a ball, I'll be happy. What do you think, Bara?"

She was staring at those numbers on the screen and thinking about what Rod had said.

No weaknesses. Yes, it was just spin, just a way of talking, but . . . that was the way the world worked—at least the corporate world. And if everyone else was using the same language, then there was a chance that . . .

She looked at Zhi. The saleswoman's eyes opened wider at her expression.

"What if," Baraka said, "we were to help *build* you a ladder, Zhi?"

———

"Welcome to Top Row Architectures," the well-dressed salesman said, shaking Joan's hand eagerly. "I'm Geoff. You are?"

"Joan," she said, then glanced at her husband. "And Vuillaume. We're really just browsing."

"Of course, of course," Geoff said, waving them into the showroom—which, oddly, had only a single display.

"Only one?" Vuillaume asked. "The others had dozens."

"I see you're a smart man," Geoff said with a grin. "Doing your homework, visiting all the showrooms. Great! Because now you have something to compare against."

Joan hesitantly entered the showroom. "One brain."

"We only need one," Geoff said, still grinning. "Though I understand why you might be skeptical. Yes, we're new. But that's what you want out of an architecture company—the young, visionary pioneers! After all, *our* company is the natural evolution of brain architecting. This brain here is our CEO's personal concept, and you know, she has a Crescendo brain."

"Crescendo," Vuillaume said. "They're the best."

"They *were* the best," Geoff said. He tapped his temple, winking. "Just think about it. Who is going to sell you the better product? The people who designed the first brains, or the updated brain *they* designed to be better than they are?" He gestured to the holodisplay with a flourish. "Behold, the *pinnacle* mind of our time. *Perfection*: the world's first brain architecture with *no* weaknesses . . ."

POSTSCRIPT

This is one of those stories that came from a single prompt: designer brains. I had the idea for that concept and mulled it around in my own (nondesigner) brain for a time until one day, we went shopping for a new phone. My wife likes iPhones, and we ended up in the Apple Store—where, while she shopped around for phones, I spent the time thinking about an Apple Store for brains.

I've always been intrigued by this side of science fiction, the "it's totally not a dystopia, we promise" genre where we look at some aspect of future life that is "normal" by their accounting, but obviously far from it by ours. It's also one of those stories I wrote knowing there was no real place for it—it's a quirky little story, unpretentious, of the sort that could maybe find a home in one of the magazines. But if I sell a story to a magazine (assuming they want a low-stakes story like this from me in the first place), they're going to put my name on the cover in big letters for marketing purposes. Then people might buy the magazine expecting a "Brandon Sanderson" story and instead get a tiny exploration of the future that isn't really trying to do many of the things I normally do. So I held it back and decided not to try to sell it anywhere, figuring this collection would someday be the best home for it. I'm glad you have a chance, now, to see it!

I HATE DRAGONS

M aster Johnston?"

"Yes, Skip?"

"I was wondering if maybe we might review my employment situation."

"What? Now? Lad, this isn't the time."

"Er, I'm sorry, sir. But I believe this is exactly the time. And I apologize, but I don't intend to move until I've had my say."

"Fine. Fine. Be on with it, then."

"Well, Master Johnston, you know how we're here to kill this dragon, sir?"

"Yes. That's our job. Dragon hunters. It says so on your bloomin' jacket, lad!"

"Well, sir, technically *you* and the other boys are the hunters."

"You're an important part, Skip. Without you, the dragon won't never come!"

"I believe you mean 'will never come,' sir. And, well, this is *about* my part. I realize it's important for you to have someone to draw the dragon."

"You can't catch nothing without bait."

"'Can't catch anything,' sir. And that is as you've said. However, I can't help noticing one factor about my role in the hunt. I am, as you said, bait."

"Yes?"

"And it seems to me that if you put bait out often enough . . ."

"Yes?"

"Well, sir, eventually that bait is going to end up getting eaten. Sir."

"Ah."

"You see my trouble."

"You've been doing this for a year now, and you ain't ever gotten ate."

"That sentence was deplorable, sir."

"What's math have to do wi' this?"

"You're thinking 'di*vis*ible,' sir. Anyway, yes, I've survived a year. Only, I've started thinking."

"A dangerous habit, that."

"It's chronic, I'm afraid. I've started thinking about the number of near misses we've had. I've started thinking that, at some point, you and the boys aren't going to get to the dragon quickly enough. I'm thinking about how many reptilian bicuspids I've seen in recent months."

"I've cussed more than twice myself."

"So . . ."

"All right, lad. I can see where you're going. Two percent, and nothing more."

"A raise?"

"Sure. Two percent's good money, son. Why, when I was your age, I'd have *died* to get a two-percent raise."

"I'd rather not die because of it, sir."

"Three percent, then."

"You pay me in food, sir. I don't get paid *any* money."

"Ah. I forgot you was a smart one. All right. Four percent."

"Sir, you could double it, and it would be meaningless."

"Don't get so uppity! Double? What, you think I'm maid of coins?"

"The word is 'made,' sir."

"Huh? That's what I said. How—"

"Never mind. Sir, this isn't about money, you see."

"You want more food?"

"No, er . . ."

"Be on with it! That dragon ain't going to kill himself!"

"Technically, dragons—being sapient beings—likely have a suicide rate similar to other intelligent creatures. So perhaps this one *will* kill himself. It's statistically possible, anyway. That's beside the point. You see, sir, I'd rather change my participation in the hunts."

"In what way?"

"I'd like to be a hunter, sir. You know. Hold a harpoon? Fire a crossbow? I wouldn't mind just reloading for the other hunters until I get the hang of it."

"Don't be silly. You couldn't do that while out in the center of the field, being bait!"

"I wasn't talking about doing that *while* being bait. I'd rather do it *instead* of being bait. Sir."

"But nobody else has yer special gift, son."

"I don't think it's all that great . . ."

"Why, sure it is! In all my years hunting dragons, I've *never* met someone who attracts them like you do. You've got a gift."

"The gift of smelling delicious to dragons? Sir, I never asked for this."

"Just 'cause a gift is unexpected doesn't mean it ain't a gift."

"A knife to the back can be unexpected. That doesn't make it a gift either. Sir."

"Look, son. You're special. The scent of you . . . it drives them mad with hunger. It'd be a shame to waste that. Do what you were created to do. Reach for the stars."

"Stars are giant balls of gas, burning far away."

"They are?"

"Yes. Reaching for them, even if it were possible, would likely burn my hand. Sir."

"Ain't that something."

"*Isn't* that something."

"That's what I said. Either way, son, you need to explore your talents."

"My talent is getting eaten by dragons, sir. It seems that's less something to *explore*, and more something to experience. Once. In a grisly, painful, and abruptly ending sort of way."

" . . ."

"Well?"

"I see that yer a smart one, son."

"Thank you."

"Five percent."

"I—"

"It's here! It's circlin'! Lad, we'll have to talk about this later."

"Okay. You know what, fine. Once more. But that's it."

"Good lad. Out there you go. You remember the script?"

"Of course I remember it. Ahem. I'm so very tired! Also, I hate sunlight. So I'm not going to look upward. I'm just going to stroll along across this . . . er . . . rocky place of rocks and find a place to lie down and take a nap.

"Gosh! I'm sad that I tripped and got dust in my eyes, so I couldn't see anything for a few moments when that breeze passed me by. Just a breeze, and *not* the beating of nearby dragon wings. Not at all. Perhaps I will take my nap in this little dip in the ground. I hope no wild beasts are around to savage me."

"PSSST. Skip. Bite! The script says '*bite* me'!"

"I'm extrapolating!"

"What's the dragon's skin have to do with this?"

"That's ex*foliate*, Master Johnston. Look, he's coming back around. Hush. Ahem. Yes, I'll just be nodding off to sleep now!"

" . . ."

"What's the beast doing?"

"He landed up there. I think he's suspicious. He's craning his neck down and—"

"YOU'RE A TERRIBLE ACTOR."

"Er. Really? I actually thought I was getting better. I've been practicing in front of the mirror, you see."

"Terrible. I've seen pieces of soap that were better actors than you. You have an entire fleet of dragon hunters waiting, I assume."

"Um. No?"

"No you don't have them? Or no I don't assume it? Because I really don't think you're capable of judging what I do and don't assume. By the way, who wrote that script for you?"

"Master Johnston."

"He needs an editor."

"I've tried to explain that! Do you know how difficult it is to work with such awful lines?"

"That doesn't excuse your bad acting."

"It gives some context at least, doesn't it?"

"No."

"So, um, if you saw through the ploy . . . why are you still here? Shouldn't you have fled?"

"I . . . There's something about you, small human. Yes. Something . . . intoxicating. Why don't you climb up here to me?"

"Excuse me?"

"Climb on up here."

"You'll *eat* me."

"That's the idea."

"Then I think I'll decline."

"Oh, come now. It won't be so bad as you think. They're will be hardly any pain at all."

"I don't care if there's pain or not. I'll still be dead. And you used the wrong version of 'they're.' You wanted 'there' instead."

"I did? How can you tell? They're no difference in the sounds they make."

"Actually, I can hear apostrophes."

"What, really?"

"Yes. I can hear spelling too, actually."

"That's . . . interesting, child. Very interesting. Well, time to get this over with. No use in delaying. Come on up and be eaten."

"You don't make a very compelling argument."

"I'm a busy dragon."

"Funny. I have lots of time. I could sit here all day, so long as it involves *not* being eaten."

"Oh, come now. Don't be difficult. This is what you were created to do."

"What gives you that terrible idea?"

"IT'S THE CIRCLE OF LIFE, YOUNG HUMAN! THE BEAUTY OF NATURE! EACH CREATURE IN TURN IS CONSUMED BY A LARGER CREATURE, ROUND AND AROUND, UNTIL WE REACH THE APEX PREDATORS. UM . . . I'M ONE OF THOSE, BY THE WAY."

"I'd noticed."

"WELL, THE COWS EAT THE GRASS, THE WOLVES EAT THE COWS, THE MEN EAT THE WOLVES, THE DRAGONS EAT THE MEN. ALL VERY MAJESTIC IN ITS SIMPLICITY."

"We don't eat wolves, actually."

"YOU DON'T?"

"No. Not unless we're very hungry. Even then, they don't taste very good, so I'm told. Too stringy."

"YES, WELL, YOU'RE SUPPOSED TO. MEN NEVER DO AS THEY'RE TOLD. CASE AND POINT, THIS MOMENT, WHERE YOU HAVE THE STARTLING RUDENESS TO REFUSE BEING CONSUMED. HOW CAN I PERSUADE YOU?"

"Actually, you are persuading me."

"REALLY? THIS IS *WORKING*? ER, I MEAN . . . OF COURSE I AM. I'M KNOWN AS A COMPELLING CONVERSATIONALIST, AMONG MY PEERS."

"You didn't need that comma, and you probably should have put 'among my peers' after 'I'm known.' It's also 'case *in* point,' but that's beside the point. You see, I said you were persuading me because the definition of the word implies the act of trying to get someone to do something, whether or not you are successful. You persuade someone, then you either fail or succeed. Most people use it incorrectly. The word you wanted was 'convince.' You need to *convince* me, not persuade me."

"YOU'RE NOT MUCH FUN AT PARTIES, ARE YOU, SMALL HUMAN?"

"I . . . uh . . . don't get invited to parties very often."

"I CAN'T IMAGINE WHY. SO ARE YOU GOING TO STOP WHINING AND COME GET EATEN LIKE A MAN?"

"No."

"YOU'RE MAKING MOTHER NATURE CRY."

"Good. We could use more rain. Why don't you go eat a cow?"

"WHY DON'T YOU GO EAT SOME GRASS?"

"Um . . . humans can't digest grass."

"AND DRAGONS CAN'T DIGEST COWS."

"Really?"

"REALLY. HUMANS WERE DESIGNED AND BUILT TO BE EATEN BY DRAGONS. IT'S THE NATURE OF THINGS."

"I find that rather unfair. Who eats you?"

"THE WORMS, ONCE WE'RE DEAD. IT'S ALL VERY METAPHYSICAL."

"But you *have* to eat humans?"

"IF WE DON'T, WE DIE."

"How are there any humans left?"

"WE DON'T NEED TO EAT VERY OFTEN, LITTLE HUMAN. ONCE EVERY FEW MONTHS. THERE'S A MORE THAN LARGE ENOUGH POPULATION OF YOU TO SUSTAIN US. YOU DON'T RUN OUT OF . . . WHAT IS IT YOU EAT, AGAIN?"

"Cows. Pigs. Carrots. Very few wolves."

"YES, WELL, THIS IS MUCH LIKE YOU EATING THOSE THINGS."

"Except for the part about me dying."

"THINK OF THE GOOD YOU'LL BE DOING."

"Good? By keeping a dragon alive to continue terrorizing people?"

"NO, BY SACRIFICING YOURSELF FOR ANOTHER. IF I DON'T EAT YOU, I'LL JUST END UP FINDING SOMEONE ELSE. PROBABLY A FAIR YOUNG VIRGIN. POOR CHILD. IF YOU THINK ABOUT IT, GETTING EATEN RIGHT NOW WOULD BE A VERY BRAVE THING OF YOU. NOBLE, HEROIC."

"Well, when you put it that way . . ."

"THAT'S IT, COME CLOSER."

". . . maybe I'll come right up to the base of that ledge . . ."

"MY . . . THE SCENT OF YOU . . . I . . . WHY ARE YOU STOPPING? COME CLOSER! I CAN'T . . . I CAN'T . . . RAAAAAWR!"

"Have at 'im, lads!"

"Aaah!"

"RAWR!"

"HURK!"

"My arm!"

"Keep stabbin'!"

"FOOLISH LITTLE MEN! GAR! GR . . . BLURK!"

"Is he down?"

"You know what I say, lads. There's always room for more stabbin'! Keep at it. And Skip, you did well. Even if you did ruinate the script."

"Ruinate? *Really?* Did you just say that?"

"Well, you're always using those big words and all. So I thought—"

"Never mind. I'm going to go wash off this dragon blood. Can't believe that I put up with this . . ."

"He doesn't look happy, Master Johnston."

"Oh, don't worry about Skip. He'll be fine."

"I don't know. He looks really mad this time."

"Don't worry. I've got a secret weapon."

"Really?"

"Sure. Tonight, after we're all fed and happy . . ."

"Yeah?"

"I'm going to give him a *six*-percent raise."

POSTSCRIPT

This is perhaps the most bizarre story in the entire collection. I wrote it as an exercise, where I did a series of blog posts about ways to practice your writing. One type of focused practice I've found helpful is doing dialogue-only sessions, where you write something with multiple characters and use nothing but dialogue—not even any tags to say who is who.

The goal is to make the dialogue itself (and not the things around it) do the heavy lifting in a passage. If it's written the right way, even with a group of people talking, the reader should be able to tell from context and diction which character is saying a given line.

I suggested this to people on my blog, then did the exercise myself and came up with this story. People enjoyed it and kept asking after it, so I eventually cleaned it up a little and added in some setting, tags, etc. It wasn't, even then, meant to be anything more than a fun display of a writing exercise, but people continued to enjoy it—so even though it's not very long and feels like it's part of something longer that never got written, I've included it here!

It also let me use an idea that I've wanted to do as a magic system, but always felt was too silly for the Cosmere: someone whose talent lets them see dialogue in an almost LitRPG way, so maybe you can pretend this means I've dabbled in that particular subgenre.

DREAMER

've got him!" I yelled into the phone as I scrambled down the street. "Forty-Ninth and Broadway!" I shoved my way through an Asian family on the route home from the market. Their bags went flying, oranges spilling onto the street and bouncing in front of honking cabs.

Accented curses chased me as I lowered the phone and sprinted after my prey, a youth in a green sports jacket and cap. A bright yellow glow surrounded him, my indication of his true identity.

I wore the body of a businessman, late thirties, lean and trim. Fortunately for me, this guy hit the gym. I dashed around a corner at speed, my quarry curving and dodging between the theater district's early-evening crowds. Buildings towered around us, blazing with the lights of fervent advertising.

Phi glanced over his shoulder at me. I thought I caught a look of surprise on his lean face. He'd know me from my glow, of course—the one visible only to others like us.

I jumped over a metal construction barrier, landing in the street, where I dashed out around the crowds. A chorus of honks and yells accompanied me as I gained, step by step, on Phi. It's hard to lose a man in Manhattan. There aren't alleyways to duck into, and the crowds don't help hide us from one another.

Phi ducked right, shoving his way through a glass door and into a diner.

What the hell? I thought, chasing after, throwing my shoulder against the door and pushing into the restaurant. Was he going to try to get out another way? That—

Phi stood just inside, arm leveled toward me, a handgun pointed at my head. I pulled to a stop, gaping for a moment, before he shot me point-blank in the head.

Disorientation.

I thrashed about, losing sense of location, purpose, even *self* as I was ejected from the dying body. For a few primal moments, I couldn't think. I was a rat in the darkness, desperately seeking light.

Glows all around. The warmth of souls. One rose from the body I'd left, the soul of the man to whom it had really belonged. That was brilliant yellow, and now untouchable. Unsavory, also. I needed *warmth*.

I charged for a body, no purpose behind my choice beyond pure instinct. I latched on, a lion on the gazelle, ripping and battering against the consciousness there, forcing it down. It didn't want to let me in, but I *needed* that warmth.

I won. In this primal state, I usually do. Few souls are practiced at fighting off an invasion. Consciousness returned like water seeping underneath a door. Panic, horror—the lingering emotions of the soul who had held this body before me, like the scent of a woman's perfume after she leaves the room.

As I gained full control, vision returned. I was sitting in one of the diner's seats looking down at the corpse of the body I'd been wearing—the body Phi had killed.

Damn, I thought, chewing the last bite of food the woman had been eating as I asserted control. It left a faint taste of honey and pastry in the mouth. *Phi had a gun.* That meant the body he'd taken had happened to have one. Lucky bastard.

A group of old women in cardigans and headscarves squawked in the seats around me, speaking a language I didn't know. Other people shouted and screamed, backing away from the body. Phi was gone, of course. He'd known the best way to lose me was to kill my body.

Blood seeped out of the corpse and onto the chipped tile floor. Damn. It had been a good body—I'd gotten lucky with that one. I shook my head, lifting the purse beside me—I assumed it belonged to the woman whose body I'd taken—and began to dig inside. I was an old lady, like the others at the table. I could see that much in the window's reflection.

Come on, I thought, standing up and continuing to search in the purse. *Come on . . . There!* I pulled out a mobile phone.

I was in luck. It was an old flip kind, not a smartphone, which meant it wasn't locked or passcoded. Ignoring the yells of the old lady's dining companions, I walked around the corpse on the floor, stepping out onto the street.

My exit started a flood, like I was the cork popped from shaken champagne. People left the diner in a run, many white-faced, a few clutching children.

I dialed Longshot's number. She was the one Phi was hunting, but she wanted to be useful. We often left one of our number back in a situation like this anyway, using him or her to coordinate. With the rest of us jumping bodies and finding new mobile phones, the best way to stay in touch was to have one person keep a set number and phone, taking calls from the other four and relaying messages.

The phone picked up after one ring.

"It's Dreamer," I said.

"Dreamer?" Longshot wore a body with a smooth, feminine voice. "You sound like an old lady."

"That's because I am one. Now." My voice bore a faint accent from the soul that had held this body. Things like that stayed. Muscle memory, accents, anything not entirely conscious. Not languages, unfortunately, but some skills. I'd once stayed in the body of a fine pianist for a couple of weeks playing music alone as the ability slowly seeped away from me.

"What happened?" Longshot demanded.

"His body had a gun. He ducked into a restaurant and popped me in the head when I followed. I don't know which way he went after that."

"Damn. Just a sec. I need to warn the others that he's armed."

"This could be a good thing," I said, glancing to the side as a couple of cops pushed through the growing crowd. "The mortal police will be after him now."

"Unless he Bolts from his body."

"He's on his third body already," I said. "He doesn't have many to spare. Besides, Bolting would risk losing the gun. I think he'll stick to the same body. He's brash."

"You sure?"

"I know him better than anyone, Longshot."

"Yeah, okay," she said, but I could hear the implication in her voice. *He knows you too, Dreamer, and he got you. Again.*

I lowered the phone as Longshot hung up and began calling the other three. I itched to be off, chasing Phi down again, but I had to be smarter than that. We knew where he was going—his goal would be Longshot, who hid atop a building nearby, unable to move. What we needed to do was make it tough for him to get to her.

Phi wouldn't escape me this time. No more failures. No more excuses.

"Excuse me?" I said, hobbling over to one of the police officers trying to manage the crowd. Damn, but this body was weak. "Officer? I saw the man who did this."

The officer turned toward me. It's still surreal to me how people's responses to me change depending on the body I'm wearing. This man puffed himself up, trying to look as if he were in control. "Ma'am?" he asked.

"I saw him," I repeated. "Short wiry fellow. Tan skin, maybe Indian, with a green jacket and cap. Lean face, high cheekbones, short hair. Perhaps five foot five."

The cop stared at me dumbly for a moment. "Uh, I'd better write this down."

It took a good five minutes for them to get down my description. Five minutes, with Phi running who knows where. Longshot didn't call me, though, so I didn't have anywhere to go. I'd know soon after one of the others spotted him. Two of the others would be out like I was, hunting Phi on the streets. One last man, TheGannon, guarded the approach to Longshot's position.

A team of five to deal with one man, but Phi was slippery. *Damn it.* I couldn't believe he'd gotten the drop on me again.

I was finishing my description of his body for the sixth time when Longshot finally called me. I stepped away from the officers as they got corroborating information from other diner patrons and called in the description. An ambulance had arrived, for all the good it would do.

"Yeah?" I said into the phone.

"Icer decided to get a vantage atop a building on Broadway. She caught sight of our man moving down the street, almost at Forty-Seventh. Moving slowly, like he's trying to not draw attention. You were right, he's in the same body as before."

"Awesome," I said.

"Icer is on her way down to hunt him. You're not going to let your past issues with Phi get in the way, are you, Dreamer? Phi—"

"I put the cops on his trail," I said. "I'm Bolting, but I'll keep this phone."

"Dreamer! You'll be on your last body. Don't—"

I closed the phone, turning back to the policemen. I chose a muscular man with dark skin. He wore a white shirt instead of blue, and the others had called him Lieutenant.

"Officer," I said, hobbling up, trying to get his attention without alerting the other police.

"Yes, ma'am," he said distractedly.

I faked a stumble, and he reached down. I grabbed his wrist.

And attacked.

It's harder when you're already in a body. The soul immediately gets attached to the body, and forcing out and into something else can be tough. Besides, when you're out of a body, the primal self takes hold, and it helps you—nearly mindless though you are—*claw* your way through another soul's defenses.

Some people say you can control the primal, bodiless self. Learn to think while in that mode. I'd never been able to do it. Anyway, I had a body already, and part of my energy had to be dedicated to holding down the soul inside, that of the old lady. At the same time, I had to attack the police officer and force his soul aside.

The man gasped, eyes opening wide. Damn. His soul was *tough.* I strained, like a man straddling between two distant footholds, and shoved. It was like trying to push down a brick wall.

I will get him this time! I thought, straining, then finally toppled that wall and slipped into the new body.

The disorientation was over more quickly this time. The officer stumbled as he lost control of his limbs, but I had the body before he dropped. I caught myself on a planter, going down on one knee, but didn't collapse fully.

"Lorenzo?" one of the others called. "You okay?" They'd covered the corpse with a white blanket. It lay just inside the door to the diner. Fleeing people had tracked blood out in a mess of footprints, but some diner occupants and employees still huddled inside the restaurant, shocked by the horror of the death. I could remember that fear, vaguely, from when I'd been alive. The fear of death, the fear of the unknown.

They had no idea.

I nodded to the other officers, standing back up, and when they weren't looking, I slid the phone out of the hand of the old lady. She stood frozen and slack-jawed. Her soul would reassert itself over the next hour or so, but she wouldn't remember anything from our time together.

I pocketed the phone and began to jog away.

"Lieutenant?" one of the officers called.

"I have a lead," I said. "Keep going here."

"But—"

I left them at a run. The police thought the killing to be a gang-related hit, and so far, they hadn't shut down the streets or anything. Maybe they would, but it was better for me if they didn't. That would mean more bodies for my team to use, if they needed to.

The cop's body felt strong and energetic. I was left with the faint impression of a melody the cop had been singing in his head before I stole it. That and . . . a face. Wife? Girlfriend? No, it was gone. A fleeting image lost to the ether.

I jogged around the corner, keeping an eye out for the glow of a body that was possessed. This area was close to Longshot's building. If Phi got to her . . .

She wouldn't have a chance against him. I slowed my pace as I reached the place where Icer had spotted Phi. There was no sign of either one.

I wove through the crowds of lively, chattering people. The cop was tall, giving me a good vantage. It was strange how unaware people were. Two streets over, people stood in chaos, horror, or disbelief. Here, everyone was laughing and anticipating a night at a show. Street vendors cheerfully took tourist money, and dull-eyed people earning minimum wage handed out pamphlets nobody wanted to read.

Phi would be close. Longshot's building was just down the street, with her atop it. He would case the area, planning how to attack.

I waited, anxious, tense. I waited until the earbud I wore—tapped into the official police channels—spouted a specific phrase. "Marks here. I think I see him. Broadway and Forty-Seventh, by the information center."

I started running.

"Don't engage him," the voices crackled on the line. "Wait for backup."

"Lieutenant Lorenzo here," I shouted into the microphone. "Ignore that order, Marks. He's more dangerous than we thought. Take him down, if you can!"

Others on the line started arguing with me, talking about "protocol," but I ignored them. I unholstered this body's gun and checked to make sure it was loaded. *Now we're both armed, Phi,* I thought. I charged around a corner, people flinging themselves out of my way once they saw the uniform and the gun raised beside my head. The shouts that chased me this time were of a different type— less outraged, more shocked.

Gunfire ahead. For a moment, I hoped Marks the cop had done as I told him, but then I saw a glowing yellow figure drop to the ground. It wasn't Phi.

Icer, I thought with annoyance. Indeed, Phi—still wearing the body with the green jacket—scrambled down the street after dropping Icer. I didn't have a very clear shot, but I took it anyway, pulling to a halt, raising the gun and firing the entire clip.

This body had practiced with a gun. I was far more accurate than I had any right to be, bullets spraying the walls—and, unfortunately, the crowd—right near Phi. I didn't hit him. I got *so close,* but I didn't hit.

"Damn it!" I said, charging after him. The crowds nearby were screaming, throwing themselves to the ground or running in stooped postures. Phi was heading straight toward Longshot's building.

Another gunshot popped in the air. I moved to dodge by reflex, but then saw Phi drop in a spray of blood.

What?

A cop stood up from beside a planter, looking white in the face. That would be Marks, the one who had called in the sighting. The cop raised his head in horror, looking around at the mess. People groaning from gunfire gone wild, the dead body Icer had been using, and now the fallen Phi.

The cop walked toward Phi's body.

"No!" I yelled. I scrambled for my microphone, running forward. "Someone tell Marks to stay back! Marks!"

He stiffened, then dropped. I cursed, trying to reach him, but there were so many people about, huddling, looking for cover, getting in my way. I drew closer, fighting through them, in time to see the body of Marks—a young, redheaded man with a spindly figure—stand up again and turn in my direction. Phi was on his fourth body. He lowered Marks's gun toward me.

Not again, you bastard, I thought, throwing myself to the side as four shots fired into the crowd. Only four—the gun had been partially empty.

I came up from my roll, thankful that Lorenzo was so athletic. My body knew what to do better than I did. Phi was already off and barreling toward Longshot. No subterfuge now, no casing the place. He knew that shots fired into a crowd would make this place go dangerous very, very quickly.

I ran after him, yelling into my microphone, "Marks has been working with the target. I repeat, Marks has been working with the target. In pursuit."

Well, that might just sow more chaos. I wasn't certain. I pulled my earbud out as I gave pursuit. The mobile phone from the old lady was ringing. I put it to my head as I ran.

"Icer is down," Longshot said. "It was her third."

Damn. I was out of breath.

"I think he got Rabies too," she told me. "He was only on his second body, but I can't reach him. He must not have a phone yet. It's you, Dreamer."

"TheGannon?"

"Gone," Longshot said softly.

"What the hell do you mean, gone?" I demanded, puffing.

"You don't want to know."

Damn, damn, damn! TheGannon was our door guard. "Phi is still armed," I told Longshot. "If he gets to you, try your best."

"Okay."

I pocketed the phone, holstered my gun, and gave the run everything I had. The street had gone to chaos quickly. With the wounded lying about, the people dropping papers and possessions as they ran and screamed, the cars stopping and people hiding inside, you'd have thought it was a war zone. I guess it kind of was.

I slid across the hood of a car, keeping pace with Phi—even gaining on him a tad—as he reached the target building. He didn't go inside, however. Instead, he pushed into the building *next* to it, a low office building with reflective glass windows.

He doesn't know that TheGannon is gone, I realized, charging after. *He's trying to keep himself from being pinned.* The office building and the target were similar in height. He could easily jump from one roof to the next.

He still had a lead on me, and it was a good minute or so before I hit the door, shoving my way in. This time I watched for an ambush. I didn't find one; instead, I saw a door on the other side of the entryway swinging shut.

"What's going on here!" a security guard demanded, standing beside his desk near the door.

"Police business," I yelled. "That doorway? It's a stairwell to the roof?"

"Yeah. I gave your buddy the key."

Damn. He could reach the roof, lock me out, and then jump over and take out Longshot. Phi was a clever one, I had to give him that much credit.

I entered the stairwell. I couldn't worry about gunfire. I had to charge up those steps as fast as I could. If he shot me, he shot me. There was a chance that would happen, but if he got to the roof, I lost. And I would *not* let him get away again!

I heard puffing and footfalls above me as I took the steps. My body was in better shape than his, but I'd been running longer than he had. Still, talking to the guard must have slowed him down, and I seemed to be gaining on him.

I rounded another corner in the white-painted stairwell, passing graffiti and concrete corners that hadn't seen a mop in ages. I *was* gaining on him. In fact, when I neared the top floor, I heard rattling as he worked on the door.

No! I forced my way up the last flight of stairs, reaching the top right as Phi pushed it closed on the other side. I slammed into it, exploding out onto the rooftop before Phi could lock it.

He stumbled away, red hair plastered to his head with sweat, shoulders slumping from fatigue. He tried to get out his gun, fiddling with an extra clip, but I tackled him.

"You're mine this time," I growled, holding him to the rooftop. "No slipping away. Not again."

He spat in my eye.

Admittedly, I wasn't expecting that. I pulled back in revulsion, and he kicked me in the leg, shoving me off and throwing me to the side.

I cursed, wiping my eye, scrambling after him as he ran across the roof. The target building was next door, maybe five feet below this one, no gap between. My body's muscles were straining after that climb. I could still hear shouts from the chaos below, sirens wailing in the distance.

Phi jumped onto the rooftop. I followed. Longshot was there, wearing a young woman's body, backed up against the far corner of the building. Phi ran for her.

I screamed and threw myself forward, plowing into him just before he reached her.

And that tossed both of us off the building.

It was the only thing I could have done. If I'd gone slower, he'd have reached her. At this speed, I couldn't control my momentum. We fell in a heartbeat and crashed to the ground.

Disorientation.

Primal forces, driving me toward heat and warmth.

No. That was my last.

The thought bubbled up from deep within. Some say it's possible to control the primal self, the freed self.

I lashed out this direction, then that, but somehow held control. I could see Phi's spirit moving turgidly toward a body, and I somehow forced myself to follow. Two glowing fields, like translucent mold, seeping along the ground unseen to mortal eyes. Still a chase. A chase I would *win*.

I reached him just before he got to the warmth, and I latched on. I held tightly, clinging to him, and like an unwieldy weight, stopped him from getting into the body. He battered at me, clawed at me, but I just held on. I'd lost knowledge of why I did what I did, but I *held on*. For a time, at least. An eternity I could not count.

Finally, he slipped away, as he always does.

I found another warmth, then opened my eyes to a smiling face. "Longshot?" I said, disoriented. I was lying on the ground in a new body, a construction worker, it appeared. The contest was over; I'd be allowed this body now.

"You did it," she said, glowing. "You held him down long enough for Rabies to get here! Once Phi got control of his last body, Rabies already had it in custody! You won, Dreamer."

"He cheated."

I sat up. Phi sat there in the body of another construction worker; the two men had been taking cover here, it appeared, near the base of the building. I could tell it was him. My brother always has this self-satisfied leer on his face, and I could recognize him in any body.

"What? That's nonsense." The businesswoman would be Icer, from that tone in her voice. She sat on the edge of a planter nearby. "We got you, Phi."

"He shot into the crowd!" Phi said.

"So did you!" I said, climbing to my feet with Longshot's help. After so long . . . too long . . . outside a body, the warmth felt good. It had probably been only a few minutes, but that was an eternity without a body.

"You were playing detective, Dave," Phi said, pointing at me. "*I* was criminal. I can shoot innocents. You can't."

"By whose rules?" Icer demanded.

"Everyone's rules!" Phi said, throwing up his hands. "You've got five, I'm only one. The criminal has to have a few advantages. That's why I can kill, and you can't."

"It's five on one," I said, "because *you* bragged you could take us all on your own, Phi."

"You cheated," he said, leaning back. "Flat-out."

"Man," Rabies said, wearing the body of a thick-armed Black man. He stood a little off from us, looking at the chaos of Broadway, with police, ambulances. "We kind of caused a mess, didn't we?"

"We need to ban guns," Longshot said.

"You *always* say that," Phi replied.

"Look," Longshot said. "We won't be able to use Manhattan for months."

"Eh," Phi said. "I'm doing a race with TheGannon across the country next. What do I care?"

"What happened to TheGannon, anyway?" Icer asked.

Longshot grimaced. "We had an argument. He left."

"He bugged out in the middle of a game?" Icer said. "Damn that kid. We should never have invited him."

"They're coming over here," Rabies said. "To check on the bodies of the two cops. We should split."

"Meet up in Jersey?" Longshot asked.

We all nodded, and the glowing individuals went their separate ways. They'd probably dump these bodies soon, working their way out of the city by hopping from person to person in whatever way suited them.

I ended up going with Phi. Side by side, walking away from the dead cops, hoping nobody would stop us. I was tired, and Bolting to another body didn't sound pleasant.

"I *did* get you," I told him.

"You tried hard, I'll give you that."

"I won, Phi. Can't you just admit that?"

He only grinned. "I'll tell you what. Footrace to Jersey. No limit on bodies. And just for you, no guns. Loser admits defeat." With that, he took off.

I sighed, shaking my head, watching my older brother go. A footrace? That meant no cars, no subways. We'd have to run the entire way, jumping into new bodies every few minutes as the ones we were using grew exhausted—like a poltergeist version of a relay race.

Phi never knew when to stop. I didn't remember a lot about when we'd been alive, back when our capture the flag games had been limited to controllers and a flatscreen—but I did know he'd been like this then too.

Well, I could beat him in a footrace. He wasn't nearly as good at those as he was at capture the flag.

I'd win this time, and then he'd see.

POSTSCRIPT

"Dreamer" is the only story in this collection that was written on invitation (meaning I was invited to write a story for a collection that was upcoming). I've done this only twice, and I only do it if I'm being invited by the right people. Once I did it for George R. R. Martin, when he asked me for a story to include in the *Dangerous Women* collection he edited with Gardner Dozois. (For George, I wrote "Shadows for Silence in the Forests of Hell.")

Here, I was invited by Charlaine Harris to contribute something to a horror-themed anthology. It felt like a good place to stretch and practice something I didn't do a lot. (This was before "Shadows for Silence" or "Snapshot," both of which flex these same muscles—and I think the practice helped out.) It might feel like an odd story for a horror collection, but perhaps my thought process will help explain. I was playing some online games at the time, and was (and am still) shocked by how callous people can act in them.

The most horrifying thing I could imagine was some of these people being given a chance to do real damage without consequences. So yes, basically this story is inspired by teenagers on Xbox Live. It also has the distinction of being the story of mine that, I believe, disappointed Peter Ahlstrom (my editorial VP) the most, as he liked the magic system and hoped it was going somewhere that leaned more into this idea—hunting body-jumping people—rather than having the twist ending. That ending is, of course, what makes it horrifying (the lack of empathy displayed by the characters, and the lack of consequences for the destruction they cause). However, I can totally see where he was coming from, because the more conventional "Brandon" version of this story could have been legitimately cool as well. Maybe someday.

PERFECT STATE

On the three hundredth anniversary of my birth, I finally managed to conquer the world. The entire world. It had made for a rather memorable birthday present, though admittedly I'd been placed into this world with the intention and expectation that I'd someday rule it.

The next fifty years had put me at risk of boredom. After all, what could a man *possibly* do with his time after conquering the world?

In my case, I'd developed a nemesis.

"He's planning something, Shale," I said, stirring the sugar into my tea.

"Who?" Shale was the only man I knew who could lounge while wearing full plate armor. He hardly ever took the stuff off; it was part of his Concept.

"Who do you think?" I said, sipping the tea and leafing through the letters on my desk, each sealed by a daub of dark red wax. The two of us sat on a large flying stone platform with chairs and railings like a patio's. I'd Lanced us a barrier over the top to ward off the rainstorm thrumming outside. The Grand Aurora shimmered above—visible even through the storm clouds—illuminating the ground beneath us and painting it faintly blue.

The occasional crashes of lightning from the storm highlighted a hundred other platforms flying in formation around my own. They carried a small retinue of soldiers—only six thousand—as my honor guard.

Thunder shook us. Shale yawned. "You really need to figure out weather, Kai."

"I will eventually." These last fifty years spent studying the practical application of Lancing had been most productive, but controlling the weather—at least on a grand scale—eluded me.

I sipped my tea. It was growing cold, but at least that I could do something about. I undid the buttons on my right sleeve, exposing my skin to the blue-violet light pulsing from the sky. The Grand Aurora encircled the entire world, and even the mightiest storms did little more than churn its mother-of-pearl shimmering. The Aurora defeated storms; that was how I knew I'd someday be able to do it too.

I entered Lancesight, and everything around me dimmed. Everything but the

Grand Aurora. I basked in its warm light, which I could suddenly feel striking my skin with a pulsing rhythm. I drew the power in through my arm, then sent the energy up out my fingers and into the cup.

The tea began to steam. I sipped it and left Lancesight as I cracked open one of the letters. The seal was imprinted with the symbol of my spy networks.

Your Majesty, the note read. *I believe it necessary to inform you that the Wode Scroll has once again—*

I crumpled the paper.

"Uh-oh," Shale said.

"It's nothing," I said, dropping the piece of paper and doing up my sleeve. It wasn't from my spy networks at all; Besk simply knew I opened spy reports first.

The platform shook in another peal of thunder as I looked through a set of reports, each with my imperial mark at the top.

"You can't make this thing go any faster, can you?" Shale asked.

"Be glad we don't have to do this the old way."

"The old way? Like . . . on a horse?" Shale scratched his chin. "I miss that."

"Really? The sore backsides, riding through the rain, getting bitten, finding food for the beasts . . ."

"Horses have personality. This platform doesn't."

"You're just saying that because it's part of your Concept," I said. "The dashing knight riding on horseback, winning the hands of fair maidens."

"Sure, sure. I had quite the collection of hands. Couple of arms, the occasional foot . . ."

I smiled. Shale was now happily married with five children. The only maidens he spent any time with were the ones who called him Daddy and begged him for sweets.

I continued looking through reports. The next was the preliminary sketch for a new set of coins to be minted later in the year, bearing my image. It was mostly right, depicting my strong features and hair that curled regally to my shoulders. The beard was too big, however. I wore mine neat and squared, kept at a modest finger's length, to present a strong image. The thing in the picture was far too bushy.

I made notes on the sketch, then continued on, ignoring the crumpled-up note I'd thrown on the floor. Besk was far too clever for his own good. I needed to fire the man and hire a *stupid* chancellor. Either that or hack Besk and rewrite his Concept.

Rewriting Concepts was a pain, though. And, truth be told, I was *terrible* at hacking, which was why—despite centuries together—I'd never gotten around to changing Besk. It wasn't, of course, because I was fond of the chancellor. The troll-like man never did what I told him. I ruled literally billions of people, and only this one ignored my will.

"Here," I said, holding up a report to Shale. "Look at this."

Shale sauntered over, armor clanking. "Another robot?" He yawned.

"Melhi's robots are dangerous."

"Yawn."

"You *just* yawned. You don't need to say it."

"Yawn. Whatever happened to the big quests, Kai? Hunting dragons, searching out magical swords? All you do these days is study magic and duel with Liveborn from other States."

"I'm getting older, Shale," I said, looking over the report again. My spies had overheard some of Melhi's men in a Border State bragging about this new robot of his. I shook my head. Melhi was still smarting after what I'd done to him at Lecours, a different Border State we could both access. He'd been so certain his armies would overwhelm mine.

"Getting older?" Shale laughed. "What does that have to do with it? You're immortal. Your body is young."

I couldn't explain it to him. The quests he referred to—building a kingdom, searching out hidden treasures and secrets, uniting those who would follow and conquering those who would not . . . Well, those had been what I'd needed as a youth. They'd made me into the person I was, the person who could rule an empire.

That empire pretty much ruled itself these days. We had imperial senates, diplomats, ministers. I was very careful not to step in unless something grossly stupid needed straightening. In truth, I relished nights spent in my study, experimenting, meditating. Only occasional government functions—like the one earlier today, where we'd commemorated the fiftieth year since the unification of the world—drew me out.

Well, that and the attacks by Melhi.

The churning rain outside suddenly vanished, and the heavens grew bright. The Grand Aurora was still there, but it now hovered in a sky that was blue instead of stormy grey. We'd reached Alornia. I stood up from my desk, walked to the edge of the platform, and watched the near-endless streets of the city blur beneath us.

At least here, at the center of my power, I could stop the storms. *Eventually,* I thought to myself. *Eventually I'll be able to do it without an Aurorastone affixed to the middle of the city.*

Alornia was a place of bulbous golden domes atop finger towers. The platform slowed in its preplanned course and swung down over the city, trailed by the hundred platforms carrying my honor guard. People waited below to watch us pass; my movements were matters of national record. And so, cheers roared beneath us, as if a stream to carry us along.

I smiled. Perhaps I should get out more. At my side, Shale rested his hand on his sword, watching those below with narrowed eyes.

"Nobody's going to be able to hit me from all the way down there," I said, amused.

"You never know, Kai."

The platform descended toward the palace, which sat on the hill at the center of the city, and docked at the side of my large tower, becoming a balcony again. I strode off and into my study as a group of servants in vests, loose pants, and bare chests trotted out onto the balcony and lifted my desk to carry it after us.

Shale stretched, clinking. "That trip seems to get longer every time."

"It would probably be more comfortable without the armor."

"I'm your bodyguard, Kai," Shale said. "One of us has to be ready. Remember when those sky nomads tried to pinch you?" Shale smiled fondly, in the way a man might while remembering a youthful romance. "Or that time when we got trapped in the Tendrils of Sashim?"

"Sure do. You carried me . . . how far?"

"A good fifty miles," Shale said. "Lords. That was . . . that was over a hundred years ago now, wasn't it?"

I said nothing. Shale didn't age—long ago, he and I had discovered a secret draught of long life in the hoard of the dragon Galbrometh. These days, I wondered if that draught had been placed there specifically for me to find, so I'd have an acceptable reason for not aging. I hadn't known the truth of my nature until I'd reached fifty, the Wode's Age of Awareness.

Shale stretched again. "Well, best to remain vigilant. It's when everything is calm that you need to be most alert."

"Most certainly. Thank you for your help today."

"Yeah. Yeah, it's a good thing I'm around, eh? Anyway, I'm going to go check in with Sindria. See what the kids are up to, you know?"

"Good idea," I said, watching the servants carefully arrange all the items on my desk. Did I have time to file those reports . . . ?

No. I needed to get moving. I walked toward Shale, who was opening the doors that led to the hallway. He gave me a questioning look.

"If I'm quick," I explained, "I might be able to get down into the lab before Besk can—"

Shale pulled the door all the way open. Besk stood outside.

"Ouch," Shale said. "Sorry, Kai."

Besk raised a single painted-on eyebrow. He was like one of those statues that people carved on the outsides of buildings. Limbs that seemed too long, robes too stiff, face expressionless. Long ago, I'd shared a drop of my draught of immortality with him. He'd haunted me ever since.

He bowed. "Your Imperial Majesty."

"Besk," I said. "I'm afraid the daily briefing will have to wait. I had some *very* important mental breakthroughs regarding Lancing that I absolutely *must* record."

Besk regarded me for a long, unblinking moment. He carried a distinctive piece of slate in his fingers. As large as a book, yet incredibly thin, nothing else like it in the empire. To the side, one of the servants helpfully carried in the crumpled paper I'd left on the balcony, then set it on the desk, just in case it was important.

Besk's eyebrow rose another notch. "I will walk with you to the lab then, Your Majesty."

Shale gave me a farewell pat on the shoulder, then clanked away. He'd faced assassins, terrors, and rebels without flinching, but even after all this time, Besk made him nervous.

"You may wish to consider giving Sir Shale a leave of retirement, Your Majesty," Besk said as we began to walk.

"He likes what he does. And I like having him around."

"Your will is, of course, law."

"Yeah. Unless the Wode is involved."

"In over a century of rule, this is the *only* time the Wode has called upon you." Besk held up the piece of slate he carried. The Wode Scroll, the only official means of communicating with the outside.

The Scroll was filled with words, none of which I wanted to read. From the little I saw, however, the tone of the Wode's letters was growing more forceful. I had been ignoring them too long.

We walked for a time in silence until we eventually left the corridor and stepped out onto a wall-walk between towers. I shouldn't be so hard on Besk, I knew. He was acting according to his Concept, and was loyal in his own way, even when he was disobedient.

Below, a cheer went up, and I raised a hand absently toward my subjects. Was that a band playing? The Grand Aurora shimmered in the sky, although—for once—its light failed to comfort me.

"Is it such an onerous task, Your Majesty?" Besk asked. "The Wode requests of you only one day, to go and perform a task most people would consider pleasurable."

"It's not the task itself. It's the nature of being . . . *summoned* like this. What good is it to be emperor if someone else can just call on me as if I were a common cupbearer or messenger boy? It undermines everything I've done, everything I've accomplished."

"They merely ask you to do your duty to your species."

"What duty has my species ever done for me?"

"My lord," Besk said, stopping on the wall-walk. "This is most unseemly of you. I'm reminded of the child you were, not the king you have become."

I tried to walk onward without him, but my shoes felt as if they were filled with lead. I stopped a few steps ahead of him, not looking back.

"It is your *duty*," Besk repeated.

"I'm a brain in a jar, Besk," I said. "One of *trillions*. Why can't they bother one of the others?"

"It has been determined that you have accomplished great—"

"We've *all* accomplished great things," I said, spinning and waving my hands toward the city. "That's the point of all this. How many of those trillions of others are living lives just like mine, in Primary Fantastical States?"

"The programming allows—even requires—that each State be individually tailored."

"It *doesn't matter*, Besk," I said. Lords! I *hated* thinking about this.

The Wode had only interfered with my life twice. First at age fifty, to inform me that my reality was a layered simulation.

And now to demand that I procreate.

"It's meaningless," I said, stepping up to Besk. He wasn't of the Wode, of course; I'd never actually met any of them. He was a part of my reality, my State. But he, like everything else in the entirety of my existence, would serve the Wode if required. They controlled the programming and, if pressed, they could change anything in this world—anything but me myself—to force me to obey.

Lords, how it hurt to think about that.

"The requirements are inane," I continued. "They need my DNA to create new Liveborn humans? Well, fine. They can take it. Stick a little needle or whatever into my jar and withdraw it. Simple."

"They require you to interact with a woman, Your Majesty. The precepts say you must choose her, and she you, and then you must meet one another and perform the act."

"Our bodies are just simulations. *Why* must we meet?"

"I do not know."

"Bah!" I stalked off the wall-walk and back into the palace.

Besk followed. "I've ordered the hunting range filled with wild draklings, Your Majesty. The most vicious we could find. Perhaps destroying them will put you in a more fond mood."

"Perhaps," I said.

Even thinking about the Wode turned me into a child again; Besk was right on that count. I'd commanded armies of thousands and I'd single-handedly forged an empire that spanned continents. But this . . . this made a spoiled brat out of me. I stopped inside the stairwell.

"I do not know all the reasons for the rules, my lord," Besk said more softly, stepping up and resting a hand on my shoulder. "But they are ancient, and have served your kind well. XinWey's Doctrine states—"

"Don't lecture me," I said.

He fell silent, but . . . damn it . . . I could hear his voice in my head. He'd read off these rules to me often enough.

XinWey's Doctrine states that the most essential morality of mankind is to create the greatest amount of happiness among the greatest number of people while using the least amount of resources.

Turned out, the best way to create greatly satisfied people using minimal resources was to remove their brains when they were fetuses and attach them to simulated realities tailored to fit their emerging personalities. Each Liveborn received an entire world in which they were the most important person of their time. Some became artists, others politicians, but each had a chance for supreme greatness.

All of this took only the space required for a box about the size of a melon—simulation machinery, brain, and nutrient bath all included. Incredibly efficient. And . . . to be honest, I didn't resent it; hell, I *loved* it. I got to be an emperor, and while the simulation gave me opportunities, each step—each grueling quest or accomplishment—had to be my own. I'd *earned* this life.

Thinking of the millions upon millions of others who had done the same, though . . . that unnerved me. Were there millions of Besks, and millions of Shales, millions of *mes*, all living beneath a Grand Aurora?

Everything else in my existence had taught me I was unique, important, and powerful. I rebelled at the idea that I might be just another *person*.

"It will not take long, my lord," Besk said. "Choose one of the women from the list—the Wode ranked them for you with compatibility projections—and send her a request to meet. Perhaps you could dine together."

"A woman from their list," I snapped. "A Liveborn woman, with her own world to rule. Lords, she'll be insufferable." The closest I ever wanted to get to another

Liveborn was across the battlefield in a Border State, and it had taken me some time to warm even to that. My first meeting with Melhi had—

"My lord," Besk said. "The wall."

I started, realizing that something had changed the stone wall of the stairwell. Words were appearing in the stone, as if chiseled there, each line sinking in a trough.

CHILD EMPEROR. I HAVE CREATED A NICE SURPRISE FOR YOU.

"Melhi, you snake! How did you hack my palace? You're violating the precepts of engagement."

THE PRECEPTS ARE ONLY WORDS. SO ARE SCREAMS. I WILL HEAR YOURS FOR THE INSULT YOU GAVE ME.

"My spies already told me of your robot, Melhi. You should stop sending those. They never work properly in my State." I didn't mention that I'd been surprised at how well they *did* work. Far better than Lancing would have worked in his State, where the laws of physics were different.

YOU WILL SCREAM, CHILD. YOU WILL SCREAM.

I entered Lancesight. Here I could see the Grand Aurora even through the stone of the palace—but I stepped backward anyway, into the doorway, where the Aurora's light could strike me directly. I drew strength into my arms from that warmth, then pushed it from me in a wave. With Lancesight, I could see the core workings of all things, the very motes of energy—or thought, or whatever they were—that made up my reality.

I could also see Melhi's hack. It manifested as tendrils of red creeping like venom into my palace. Filled with strength, I cut him off, destroying the tendrils. They hadn't been strong—he couldn't accomplish a powerful hack without running afoul of the Wode's protective programs.

The wall's surface returned to normal. I melted the stone there for good measure, recast it into a new shape, then blinked my eyes back to my ordinary vision.

"Lords, but that man needs to learn to let go of a grudge," I said. "He's never going to beat me. Surely he has to see that by now."

"Indeed," Besk said. "He does seem to boorishly continue the same stubborn course, without maturity, and without careful consideration of the best path. Wouldn't you say?"

"That's quite enough, Besk."

"I try to be topical when possible, Your Majesty."

I took a deep, calming breath. It didn't work. "Fine. Fine, whatever. Pick one of the women from the list. We'll meet, get this over with, and I'll return to my life."

"Which one do I choose?" Besk asked. "The one the Wode thinks is most compatible?"

"Lords, no," I snapped, walking away. "Pick the one on the *bottom* of the list. I might as well have an interesting time of it."

———

The meeting was going to happen in a Communal State. Any Liveborn could visit one of those, though I never did. Why would I want more reminders of how normal I really was?

Shale didn't like me leaving our State, of course.

"I don't understand why I can't go," he said, barring my way to the portal. "I go with you to Border States all the time."

"Those blend seamlessly with our world," I said. "They adopt our programming. This is different; it's a place only Liveborn are meant to visit. Even if we were to somehow get you there, you'd be incorporated into the local programming—you'd be given a life, memories, a backstory that fit the Communal State. It would change your personality—essentially killing you."

"I've always been prepared to give my life for you, Kai."

"Which I've always appreciated. If I were in danger, I'd accept your sacrifice. But I won't have you giving yourself up so . . . so I can go have sex."

Lords, but that sounded stupid.

"This is my fault, Kai," Shale said. "If Molly were still alive, they'd never have chosen you. The Wode only picks the unattached."

"Yes, well, she's gone."

And she had been for . . . what, ninety years now? I should have accepted the advances of one of the willing women who surrounded me. I could have had a harem—Lords, I'd *had* a harem at one point. Before Molly.

"It's got to be done, Shale," I said. "Don't make me Lance you out of the way."

He reluctantly lowered his arms. "You won't be able to Lance on the other side, Kai. You'll be powerless. Just . . . just a regular person . . ."

"Not entirely," Besk said.

I turned to find the chancellor entering the large portal chamber. He crossed the floor, which sparkled with twisting churnrock—a type of stone that changed colors with pressure. That had been a gift from the Larkians, right after their king had abdicated to me. I'd had it used in the portal room, where I rarely went. The shifting colors unsettled my stomach.

"Your Imperial Majesty," Besk said, handing me a bundle, "I have been researching in the tomes you discovered in the great hoard of the Lichfather. From what I have read of the seer's visions of other States, I believe that a few of your abilities will function once past the portal. You will pull some of the innate programming from your State with you."

"Lancing?" I asked, hopeful. "But . . . no, of course not. There won't be anything to power it."

"You could bring an Aurorastone," Shale said.

"It would vanish as I passed through the portal," I said. "Anything not part of me, or designed for the State I'm going to, won't make the transition. But that means . . . of course. My mental boosts, they'll work, won't they?"

"Yes," Besk said. "They speed up processors attached directly to your physical brain."

"Will the Wode stop them?" I asked, thoughtful. "Clip the processors, stunt my thoughts back to a normal rate?"

"I can't determine if they will or not," Besk said. "I don't think the boosts are given out in the State you are visiting, but bringing them in from the outside might be acceptable. I would limit their use, in case it alerts the Wode to what you are doing."

"What about my healing boosts?"

"Again, I'm not certain, Your Majesty," Besk said. "They seem more likely to work. The Communal States are designed to protect the safety of Liveborn, after all."

I nodded, shifting to Lancesight. Looking internally, I set my mental boosts—which would make everything around me seem to slow—to automatically engage if an explosion happened near me, or if my skin was broken.

"I still don't like this," Shale said. "Healing boosts aren't perfect. If someone in there manages to kill you, you'll . . ."

I would become brain-dead. Part of XinWey's Doctrine. A person needed to experience real danger or they would never find joy in excelling. There had to be a risk of failure, the chance to die.

Of course, I wouldn't simply die from a random fall down the stairs. I was far too important. However, I would eventually die of very old age—I was still hundreds of years from that—and, more importantly, I could be killed, particularly if I were attacked by another Liveborn. Even a Simulated Entity like Shale or Besk could kill me if the situation were right.

Well, I'd just have to be careful. "I assume this is State-appropriate clothing?" I asked, holding up the bundle.

Besk nodded. "It will be placed upon you, pressed and neat, as you pass through the portal. There's also a State-appropriate weapon, as requested."

"Thanks."

"It won't do anything, my lord. Communal States are not intended to be dangerous, and this one is *very* well monitored. I suspect that your weapon won't even fire unless the Wode specifically allows it."

"I'll feel better having it," I said. "Never go on a date unarmed." Words of wisdom from my father. Well, my foster father. I was an orphan, of course. The best kings always are.

"I will remain in contact, my lord," Besk said. "Direct mental links are allowed to Liveborn visiting this Communal State."

"Excellent," I said, taking a deep breath. I tucked the bundle under my arm, then—with no other good reasons to delay—stepped into the portal.

I passed through a flash of light, then stepped out of a metal door. When I looked back, it appeared that I'd come out of a strange, tubular contraption on wheels. It was like a large number of carriages hooked together, each with its own doors and windows.

It is called a train, my lord, Besk noted to me. *I've been reading about them. Quite fascinating. You might be able to replicate them with Lancing mechanics. The people would be pleased to have a faster method of travel between cities.*

Have the Grand Librarian take notes of their descriptions, I sent back to him. *I'll examine the idea when I return.*

The sky was dark, and I found myself on a platform at the edge of a strange city. The buildings were constructed as rectangular boxes rising high into the sky, and lights twinkled in many of their windows. The sky was overcast, and the city looked very busy despite the apparently late hour.

I wore muted clothing. Trousers, black shoes that looked horribly impractical, white shirt, some kind of thin scarf tied around my neck, and a jacket. It all fit snugly and wasn't nearly as heavy as the clothing I was used to. It pulled at me in strange places, and the collar was buttoned too close to my neck for comfort.

I had an odd, wide-brimmed hat on my head in place of my crown. I took that off and tossed it away. Covering my regal hair felt like a shame. Around me, people moved out of the train I had exited. The men wore clothing similar to my own, all in the same hats with the wide brims. None of them had beards, which made me feel more distinctive.

This city is named Maltese, Besk sent. *Though most people just call the State that as well, rather than using its official designation as Nightingale124. The local weapon is stored under your arm in a special hidden sheath. It's known as a handgun, and works by pointing the tube toward your enemy and pulling the trigger underneath.*

Like a crossbow?

Yes, my lord. My research says they're difficult to aim properly. This State does not have symbiont aiming modifications.

Lovely, I sent, walking off the platform. *Where do I go?*

Straight down the street ahead. Look for a tall, blue-lit building and speak your name to the doorman. You have a reservation.

I followed the instructions, entering a wide street populated by self-driving metal carriages. I had something similar working in most of my cities, though mine were connected to Aurorastone deposits inserted into the roads.

The air smelled faintly of rain, and the ground was damp. Besk rattled off some information he'd found about Maltese in one of our tomes. This State was set perpetually at night in a highly populated city that was loosely based off what the book described as "Western cultures in early-twentieth-century Earth." Whatever that was. Rain came often, but never in more than a drizzle.

I nodded, curious, listening to the sounds of the city as I walked. This State wasn't necessarily louder than my own—Alornia could be a clamorous place—but the sounds *were* different, alien. The carriages made garish honks at one another, and they growled like beasts. Perhaps they contained some kind of living animal that powered them.

A street performer I passed was playing a loud brass horn—as if sounding the call to war, though the song had a slur to it, almost as if the music itself were drunken. I was glad Simulated Entities like my subjects couldn't travel to States like this; I'd hate for the street performers back home to visit here and realize how effective a horn like that was at carrying over a crowd.

And a chatty crowd it was, all bundled up in their too-stiff clothing as they strolled the streets. I fell in behind a group of men and women as I made my way toward the restaurant, listening to them prattle about local politics.

Elections? I asked Besk.

Indeed, he said. *Every two years, the local population chooses a new Liveborn to rule.*

That's silly, I sent back. Many of my subject kingdoms had elections for their officials, though I—of course—could intervene and appoint someone if the masses acted foolishly. *Who lets Machineborn choose what their Liveborn do? And besides, what can a king accomplish during such a short reign?*

It is likely just a formal title, Your Majesty, Besk sent back. *There are no Liveborn native to this State; only outside visitors like yourself are eligible to rule. One of the reasons to visit appears to be the draw of vying against other Liveborn for dominance. Though, since outside armies are forbidden, one must use local Machineborn to achieve one's goals.* He hesitated. *You might find it a challenge.*

Hardly, I thought back with a sniff. *If the title changes so frequently, there can't be any real power to it. I have no intention of getting involved.* In fact, the entire nature of this State seemed to highlight that political power was just an illusion provided to engage and excite us Liveborn.

I followed Besk's directions toward a particular building, tall and rectangular. The restaurant was apparently near the top. I approached, but then pulled up short. What was that series of popping *bangs* sounding to my right?

The people ahead of me—who were likely Simulated Entities, judging by their conversation—stopped as well, but then just continued on down the street.

What are those bangs, Besk?

Handgun fire, he sent back.

I hesitated for a moment, then took off at a run toward the sounds.

No intention of getting involved, Your Majesty? Besk asked, sounding amused.

Shut up.

I prepared my mental boosts as I drew near. I didn't let them engage at the sounds; I needed to hold them in reserve, in case using them drew the Wode's attention. But I did want to be ready.

I crossed two of this State's too-smooth stone streets, then entered a smaller roadway where a group of men in hats was advancing on a young woman wearing trousers and a jacket. She fired a small handgun at her attackers desperately from within the faint cover of a recessed doorway, the door at her back apparently locked. Her only companion was another woman who lay splayed facedown on the street, golden hair fanned out around her head, blood staining the back of her dress.

Alert the Wode, I said to Besk. *Something illegal is happening here.*

I then entered Lancesight. It was like stepping into *nothingness.* Here, instead of the warmth of the Grand Aurora, I found only an empty coldness all around.

Idiot, I thought, stumbling in that darkness. What had I expected? I slipped out of Lancesight, grabbing the weapon from under my arm. The handgun felt bulky in my grip, and the hilt was shaped like a box, instead of the smooth roundness of a sword hilt. I pointed the open end of the tube toward the men and pulled the trigger. The handgun popped and *jerked* in my hand, nearly jumping clean out of it. Lords! The thing was almost impossible to control. And the noise—why would you want a weapon that drew so much attention?

Fortunately, my sudden arrival—and the cacophony of my shots as I pulled the trigger several more times—distracted the men and let the woman dash from her alcove to greater safety behind a large metal box with rubbish spilling out the top. I met her there, putting my back to the trash receptacle, feeling a thrill of excitement.

"You know this area better than I do," I told the woman. "Which way should we flee?"

She studied me. She was pretty, her face angular with dark skin. Then she raised her weapon at me and fired.

I dodged the shot.

Well, technically I didn't dodge the shot, so much as get out of the way before it was fired in the first place. I engaged my mental boosts—slowing the world to my perception—which allowed me to judge where the woman was going to point her weapon. I didn't move any more quickly while boosted, but the advantage of watching her muscles and studying her posture let me twist to the side so that when she actually shot, the projectile missed me.

It was close nonetheless. The shot passed by my side as I fell backward to the ground, disengaging my boosts—I usually only wanted to use them for short intervals—and leveled my handgun toward the woman. From this close range, I was able to manage the weapon well enough to plant two shots in her chest, all the while thinking about how primitive it felt to be using a metal tube instead of the powers of the Grand Aurora.

One projectile left in your handgun, Your Majesty, Besk sent. He was at his happiest when he could count things for me.

Thanks, I sent back, though I didn't think I'd need the weapon. As the other men came for me, I tossed the handgun toward one of them and grabbed the end of something sticking from the top of the trash receptacle. A thin metal bar. I spun it in my hand, getting a feel for its weight, then turned toward the nearest aggressor, a man who was trying—and fumbling—to catch the weapon I'd tossed him.

I swung. The bar wasn't Indelebrean—my enchanted sword—but it had a good heft to it, and made a satisfying *whoosh* in the air as I connected with the man's hand. Bones crunched, and he dropped the handgun with a cry of pain. I stepped forward, raising the metal bar, hoping my healing boosts would be enough to handle getting hit by one of those shots from the other—

"Stop!" cried the man in front of me, falling to his knees. "Holy *hell*, are you crazy?"

The other two raised their hands, turning their weapons away from me and backing up. "Calm down, stranger," one said. "Time out, pause."

The man closest to me cursed, and I stepped back, cautiously wary.

"Raul," one of the standing men said to the one I'd hit, "this is your own fault. You got into a melee."

"Doesn't mean he can hit me with a *freaking bar*," said the man on the ground, who was cradling his broken wrist.

"Actually it does," said the other man.

I stood there, alert and confused, metal bar held in a swordsman's stance.

"Damn," the third man said, looking down at the woman I'd killed. "He got Jasmine. What faction are you, stranger?"

". . . Faction?" I asked.

"We'll just see what registers," the second man said, checking a small device strapped to his wrist.

Nearby, the woman on the ground groaned and pushed to her feet. I gaped, then pointed my weapon at her, ready. Necromancy? Healing boosts? No . . . with surprise, I realized that my shots hadn't pierced her clothing. I glanced toward where the shot I'd dodged had hit the ground, and found that it had made a bloodred streak on the street.

Paint. The shots exploded into paint when they hit.

"What kind of trap was *that*?" the woman demanded, pointing at me. Nearby, her friend—the other woman—roused as well. "Did you think I'd believe that someone was coming to my aid last-minute, Raul?"

"It wasn't us," said the man whose wrist I'd broken. This wound, it appeared, didn't simply heal. "He's some other faction."

They all looked to me.

"I'm . . . uh . . ." I cleared my throat, standing up straighter. "I am Kairominas of Alornia, God-Emperor of—"

"Oh hell," the woman said. "A Medieval Statie."

"Yup," one of the men said, looking at the device on his arm. "The kill was registered as a wildcard."

"I see," I said. "It's a . . . game?"

They ignored me, the woman—Jasmine—flopping back on the ground, paying no attention to the paint stains on her jacket and shirt. "You mean I'm going to spend the next two weeks *invisible* to the local AIs, and nobody relevant even got points for my hit?"

"At least he didn't break your wrist," Raul complained. He'd climbed to his feet. "How am I going to get this fixed? Maltese doesn't even have bone-knitting technology."

"Who cares," Jasmine said. "Killed by a wildcard? Do you have any *idea* what that will do to my rankings?"

"You agreed to the civil war, Jasmine," one of the other men said. "It's not our fault you let us ambush you." He reached out a hand to help her to her feet. She looked at him, then turned her glare toward me. "It's *his* fault."

They all regarded me again, and I felt conspicuous there, holding my improvised weapon. I met their gazes anyway. I was an emperor.

So are they, I reminded myself. I could see it in the way they held themselves—the way Jasmine refused the hand and climbed up on her own, the way Raul had shoved down his pain and ignored his wound. He was instead calling upon someone—speaking into a device on his good wrist—to dispute my kill, claiming it should be credited to him because of his trap. Each of these people was accustomed to being the most important one in the room.

Once they'd determined I wasn't relevant, they dispersed, speaking into wrist devices or to one another. The third man, the one who hadn't been speaking much, wandered off with the woman who had already been dead when I'd arrived.

"Fantasy Staties," he was saying to the woman. "You should have seen him, charging in here, ready to rescue Jasmine. All that was missing was armor and a horse."

"I can't understand why the Wode would do such a thing," the woman replied. "Making them grow up in such barbaric and primitive surroundings."

"It's not the Wode's fault," the man said, their voices trailing away as I was left alone on the street. "They match the State to the emerging personality of the individual. He *belongs* there."

And not here, that tone seemed to imply. I tossed the bar aside. Lords, I hated this place.

Your Majesty, Besk's voice said, sounding frustrated, in my head. *I have contacted the Wode. They seemed responsive at first, but soon sent back a note saying that you would be fine. They . . . they sounded amused, my lord.*

Great. And now I looked a fool to the Wode as well. I walked over and retrieved my handgun from the street, then fired the last projectile into the ground, noting the splat of paint it made.

Your Majesty? What happened? Besk asked. *You seem in pain, judging by the empathic link.*

I'm fine, I replied as I walked away from the scene of the game, leaving only some paint stains that still looked startlingly like blood to me. *It was a game, Besk.*

A game?

You're right; the weapons are transformed by this State's programming. They fire nonlethal projectiles; Liveborn have used that fact to make a game out of assassinating one another, or something like that.

Curious, Besk sent back. *It says in our tome that there are consequences in Maltese for firing such weapons, and I interpreted that to mean the Wode forbade it.*

No, I sent back. *The consequence seems to be that if you're "killed," the local Machineborn can't see you for a few weeks.*

It made sense. If the overriding politics of this State involved currying favor with a voting public, being effectively "timed out" for a few weeks was a real consequence. It was a way to make the game more thrilling, but not dangerous. Though most of this State was a calm place for meetings, dining, and nightlife, the political subtheme allowed Liveborn to come play as well. Join one of the gangs, try to take over a portion of the city and run a criminal empire.

I might have found it entertaining in my early seventies, back when I'd been a kid. Right now, it seemed far too transparent. It didn't help my mood that I knew for certain the weapon under my arm would be useless if I encountered any real danger.

—

The restaurant was an upper level of one of the larger buildings at the center of town. A line of people waited to get in, though I walked past them. I wouldn't, of course, be expected to wait in a line.

It felt so odd to have nobody trailing me. No servants, no soldiers. At the front doors, a man guarding the entrance bowed, then waved me past. I caught a glimpse of a clipboard with a page full of faces on it, mine included. Several of the people from the gunfight were also pictured, and I guessed this was a sheet telling him all the Liveborn visiting the city, so he'd know who to obey. Only a few of those here in the city would be Liveborn—maybe a hundred or so out of millions. Just like in other States, the rest would be Machineborn. Simulated Entities who had been born within the State, and would live their entire lives here.

The Wode could have just programmed the door guard to recognize Liveborn without needing a list, but that would have broken the illusion. Did these people know about their natures? In my State, very few were told. Age of Awareness laws didn't apply to them, and so the only place they could hear about it all was from me or the Wode Scroll.

After riding to the right floor in a glass-sided box on wires, I was led to a dining table for two set off from the others in the room. It had a dramatic view of the twilit city. So many lights; this place seemed to have an energy to it. That I liked, though it couldn't compare to the Grand Aurora.

I sat down, absently handing my jacket to a nearby servant, trusting it would make its way back to me eventually. I glanced over the menu and ordered a small set of drinks—sixteen cups, each with a sip's worth of wine in it—so I could decide which one I wanted to have with my meal. The servant blinked at the request; perhaps I hadn't ordered enough cups. The wine terminology was similar to my own, even if I didn't know the specific vintages.

Such interesting decorations, I sent to Besk, inspecting the small glass-covered candle that had been sitting at the center of my table. *No hearth at all. Soft music. Dim lights. It's actually quite nice.*

Do you wish for me to release the imperial drummers from service, my lord?

No, but find out what instrument produces these sounds.

A servant arrived with a platter full of wine cups. I selected one and raised it to my lips. Then froze.

A woman slid between the tables toward my position. She wore a red dress, but it was quite unlike the ones worn in my State. Formfitting, with a slit up the side, and a modest neckline where the fabric folded a few times. She wore shoes with spike heels at the back, and had dark, shoulder-length hair.

I lowered the cup. The woman had a certain *poise* about her. Servants moved out of her way, and she walked as if she expected them to. Her steps were slow, confident, and someone even pulled a table to the side to make room for her to pass. She never looked down or broke stride. Her eyes were on me.

The cup slipped in my fingers, and the red liquid spilled onto the tabletop. I cursed, holding out my palm to draw in the Aurora's energy to . . .

Well, I *would* have destroyed the pigment in the wine, rendering it colorless, then drawn the moisture from it and split the water into its two primal gases to leave the tablecloth dry. If I'd been able to Lance.

Instead, I stared at the tablecloth, crossed my eyes to enter Lancesight, and was left in complete darkness until I hopped back to ordinary sight.

"So you're him?" the woman asked, reaching the table. She stood there for a moment. "You realize it's good manners to rise in the presence of a lady."

"It's also good manners to curtsy to the God-Emperor," I said, covering the spilled wine with my napkin.

"Oh great," she said, sitting. "You're one of *those*."

"Kairominas the First of Alornia," I said, holding out a hand to her. "Keeper of the Seventeen Lanterns, Master of Ultimate Lancing, Slayer of Galbrometh."

"Magical Kingdom State," she said, refusing the hand and sliding into her chair. "Did you ride a unicorn to get here?"

"We don't have those," I said flatly. "And you?"

"Just call me Sophie."

"From?"

"An Emerging Equality State," she said. "I led a worldwide civil rights movement, brought my people into the progressive era, then served five terms as the first female world president."

"Impressive," I said, trying to be polite.

"Actually it's not," she said, waving for a servant to fetch her some wine. "I just played the role *they* set up for me."

"I see."

We stared at each other. The wine was starting to bleed through my napkin, but Sophie didn't seem to care. She watched me.

"What?" I finally asked.

"I'm trying to figure you out," she said.

"It sounded as though you assumed you already had."

"You're arrogant," she said. "But we all are. You're an authoritarian; you came here because you were ordered to, even though you didn't like it. You prefer to control everything around you—at your palace, I would find immaculate gardens and safe pieces of art hanging in a building designed by straightforward architects. I've seen hundreds like you. Thousands. Immensely powerful, but boring."

You know, I thought to Besk, *maybe I shouldn't have tried the bottom of the list after all . . .*

Besk somehow held himself back from making a comment about that.

"So," I said, controlling my voice with some effort, "if you have all of these *presumptions* about me, why are you here? I can assume from the tone in your voice that you do not respect authority. Odd, for the president of an entire world."

"I abandoned that," she said, waving an idle hand.

"You . . . *what*?"

"I gave up the presidency," she said. "Walked right out in the middle of a world senate meeting. It caused quite the stir in the ant-hive of programmed minds. I snuck off to a High-Science State, learned some technology that wasn't *technically* forbidden in my own State, then came back and armed a rebel faction with advanced weaponry. That destroyed world peace and started a global war that's still going."

I gaped.

She shrugged as a servant came with wine, pouring her a cup.

"That . . . that's *horrible*," I said. "How many lives have been lost?"

"What? *You* haven't started any wars?" she asked, sounding amused. "Mr. Emperor? I suppose the programming just rolled over and gave you the throne?"

"War was necessary," I said. "For unification. My State consisted of *forty* different kingdoms when I was younger, all crammed into one continent. Bloodshed was constant. Only unification stopped that."

"Sure," she said, gulping down some wine. She didn't seem to care what vintage it was. "Have you discovered the lost continent yet?"

"There's no such thing."

"Of course there is," she said. "There's always a lost continent. The programming will pop it out once you start finding your life stale. It'll give you a new challenge, make you really work again. Should keep you engaged for a century or two until you get old enough that even the Wode's technology can't keep your brain going. Then they'll let you have peace for a few more years before you die." She smiled at me, smug. "I've read about Fantasy States. The lost continent is usually one of only a handful of places hidden from your magic."

Make a note of all this, Besk, I thought, but outwardly just smiled. "We'll deal with it if it happens. I'm more curious about you and your war. Yes, I've done terrible things, but at least there was a point to my brutality. You sound like you started a war just to ruin people's lives."

"Ruin people's lives? I doubt the Wode pays that much attention to what I do."

"I didn't mean the lives of the Wode," I said. "I meant the people killed in your State. In the war."

She waved her fingers. "Those? Just bits in a machine."

"Just bits in a . . ." I cocked my head. "I think that's the most primitive thing I've ever heard anyone say, and I've fought barbarians."

She shrugged, drinking the rest of her wine.

"You really don't accept the Machineborn as true people?"

"Of course I don't," she said. "Everything they 'feel' is just a fabrication."

"What we feel is a fabrication too."

"We have a body. Well, a bit of one remaining."

"What's so special about a body?" I demanded. Besk and Shale . . . they were my friends. I felt a need to defend them, and their kind. My subjects were more than mere bits in a machine. "Yes, we have brains, you and I. What we 'feel' and 'think' is the result of chemicals swimming around inside our heads. How is that so different from the emotions of the Machineborn? Bits or hormones, does it matter?"

She looked at me with a flat stare. "Of course it matters. This whole world, every one of these worlds . . . they're fake."

"So is the 'real world.' When people on the outside touch an object, they 'feel' the electromagnetic push of electrons in the substance shoving back on the electrons in their fingers. When they 'see,' it's really just the photons striking their eyes. It's all energy, programmed on a very small scale."

"That's deep science for a Fantasy Statie."

"Fantastical doesn't necessarily mean primitive," I said. "I'm pretty sure I've read that the Wode recognizes the rights of Machineborn. Don't they leave a State running even if the Liveborn in it dies?"

"Yeah," she said. "But they eventually nudge the State back toward chaos, then inject a newborn real person to grow up and rule it again. That's beside the point. What have you accomplished in your life? *Really* accomplished?"

"I unified—"

"Something that they couldn't have just programmed into the State from the start," she said. "Something real."

"I already said I don't agree with your definition of *real*."

"But you agree that they could have started your State with everyone in harmony, right? With a world government in place?"

"I suppose."

"They feel like they need to give us things to do, to entertain us. Distract us. That's all our lives are, complex entertainment simulations. They made me be born into a State plagued by an outdated social system from Earth's past, just so I could transform it—covering ground the real world covered centuries ago. Pointless."

I folded my arms on the table, looking out the window.

"What?" she asked.

"I hate losing arguments," I said. "But you're right. That part . . . that part bothers me."

"Huh," she said. "Didn't expect you to admit it."

"It's not the simulation itself that is the problem," I said. "Machineborn are people, and what they feel—what I feel—is real. What I hate is the way the Wode undermines our authority. I think I'd be all right with it all if I didn't have this itching worry that they're making things *just* hard enough to be exciting, but not hard enough for us to lose. At least we can still die."

"Ha," she said, waving a hand. "That's a myth."

"What? Of course it's not."

"Oh, it is. I promise you. No Liveborn die of anything other than old age— at least, not until they reach their later centuries of life and the Wode starts allowing them to interfere with one another's States. We can kill each other, but our simulations . . . no, those never hurt us. I've seen States where the Liveborn are horribly incompetent, and they still accomplished all the minimum things they were supposed to."

I didn't reply.

"You don't believe me," she said. "I can provide—"

"I believe you," I said. "I already knew."

And I had. Oh, I hadn't wanted to voice it, or even think it, but I'd suspected this was the case. Ever since my first trip into a Border State, when I'd started worrying.

It was the true reason why I avoided other States, and other Liveborn. Everything we did was like those people playing with paint guns on the streets. Our lives were games.

My secret worry wasn't just that I might be normal, but that I might also be coddled. Like a baby in a crib.

"I'm sorry," she said. "It's better when we can just pretend, isn't it?"

"'Better' is an ambiguous term," I said, looking out the window again. The rain had returned. "I still think there can be a point to our lives. In the progress we make, in who we are."

"Oh, I'm not saying there's no point," she said. "I just don't think we should let it be the one *they* give us on a silver platter. Like this meeting. I ignored all the other Liveborn who asked to meet with me."

"Why come now?"

"Because you're the first one to ask me from the *bottom* of the compatibility lists. I was curious." She regarded me, blinking long lashes. Curious, she said? Then why had she chosen a beautiful dress and makeup?

Lords, I thought, looking at her. *Lords, I actually find her interesting.* How unexpected. I reached for a new cup. On the table—carved as if into the tablecloth itself—I found that words had appeared near my spilled wine.

I AM COMING, CHILD. YOU WILL SCREAM. IT IS FOR YOUR OWN GOOD I MUST DO THIS.

Damn it, Melhi, I thought. *Not now.* I didn't even want to guess how he'd hacked a Communal State.

"Let's leave," I said, standing, moving my napkin over Melhi's message.

"Leave?"

"Food doesn't interest me."

She shrugged, standing. "We're both just brains floating in a nutrient solution; the food is a comfort. It helps us pretend."

We ditched the table, passing a confused servant wheeling a cart full of food toward us. I walked back to the foyer with the box that had lifted me here. I didn't get in it, however, instead pushing open a door that was labeled STAIRS.

Sophie followed me in. "What a wonderful change of décor," she said, regarding the cold stone stairwell.

I began climbing the steps. "These shoes people wear here are ridiculous. What is wrong with good boots?"

"Other than being unsightly?"

"Says the woman wearing heels as long as a handspan."

"*These* are considered very fashionable," she said. "And it enrages my inner feminist to no end to wear them alongside a dress like this." She was grinning widely.

"You are an unusual woman."

"It does strange things to you to realize that the conservative establishment is *forcing* you to be a progressive liberal fighter for universal rights." She started climbing up the steps beside me. "I had to buck that, but didn't know what to become instead. The only thing I could come up with—something truly difficult—was to become a complete anarchist. They built a perfect world for me, so I had to burn it down."

"Destruction isn't difficult."

She grinned savagely. "It is if you're fighting against what the Wode wants.

That's the only way to be a real warrior, the only way to find a *true* challenge. Defying them."

I grunted, agreeing with that.

"So anyway," she said. "What was that writing on the tablecloth all about?"

"You saw that, did you?"

"Of course I did. Thought you were hiding a vial of poison at first. But it was just words."

"It was a message," I said as we reached the next floor. "From my nemesis."

"Nemesis?" she said, amused. "What is this, middle school?"

"I don't know what that is."

"A place for children."

I said nothing, leaning against the stairwell railing for a moment.

"Seriously," Sophie said. "How does one go about getting a *nemesis*? Undefeated dragon back home or something?"

"It's another Liveborn."

"Oh, of course. You realize that you're just playing into what the Wode wants, right? Dueling with other Liveborn to keep you both distracted."

"Maybe," I admitted. "It seemed that way at first, only . . . I don't think Melhi is acting like they anticipated."

"What do you mean?"

"It's a long story."

"And we appear to have a lot of steps left if you intend to get to the top."

I sighed, then started up the next flight. "I first met Melhi in a Border State . . ."

———

I first met Melhi in a Border State, though I can't even be sure it was him I talked to.

I rode into the State with a full legion, some fifty thousand strong. Border States were new to me back then, and I hadn't wanted to take any chances.

I made the trip on a small hovering platform, only about five paces wide. The platform had a raised front and sides, like a large chariot—but without the wheels or horse. There was just enough room for Shale and Besk to accompany me.

My advance guard had already secured a position on the edge of the large valley that made up the bulk of the Border State. I turned as we arrived, looking back down the wide path through the forest. We'd set foot upon that road in the jungles of Evasti in my State. After we traveled about half an hour on the enchanted road, the trees had started to change to these pines and aspens. Eventually, the road spat us out here.

"So we've left our world," I said, wearing my shining gold breastplate and helm. "Why can I still see the Aurora?"

I'd watched it through the clouds the entire duration of our trip, anticipating with dread the moment when it would fade away. It hadn't. Yes, it looked strangely distant here—shimmering in its majestic way over the tops of those mountains beyond the trees. But I could see it, and Lancesight determined I could still feel its pulses, though they were softer here.

"This is fascinating, Your Majesty," Besk said. He had a large tome open in front of him, pages pinned down to prevent fluttering in the wind of our flight. "This State is not a full world. It is just this valley, which is surrounded by a forest. At the edges of that forest, the State simply . . . fades away. If anyone travels in that direction, they will be lost in fog and then appear on the opposite side of the valley!"

Shale grunted. "Then the only exits are . . ."

"Yes, the path we took," Besk said, then pointed. "And an additional two like it, leading to the States of other Liveborn. One cannot traverse the enchanted pathways in or out without the aid of a Liveborn, and only Simulated Entities live naturally in this State. It exists solely for us to visit."

"Or to conquer," I said, and mentally instructed my platform to rise.

It ascended dramatically, zipping into the sky high above my army, though two dozen like it—manned by my best archers—followed to provide protection. From beneath, all the flying chariots looked alike; armies trying to bring me down would be confused as to which one held me.

From this vantage, I could see the fog that Besk had mentioned, consuming the wood behind us before stretching to the mountains, which appeared to simply be scenery. I wondered if one could reach them while in flight.

Despite ending in those woods, there was territory in this State, quite a bit of it. I could barely make out the edge of the fog ring on the other side of the forest. If necessary, I could array an army in here and hold the position, blocking the other two exits with my forces. We could undoubtedly use the State's nature to our advantage; if I needed to get troops to the other side of a battlefield in a hurry, I could send them backward through the fog.

It actually seemed too perfect. That I should discover places like this now, once the entire world was mine, itched at me. Like a pain in my spine that could not be banished. I had thought I was done, but if there were many such Border States, then I had a great deal more to conquer.

I swooped the platform back down toward the front of my army. The natives of this Border State were equipped with primitive weapons—spears and wooden shields. They had dark violet skin. I glanced at Besk.

"Our early scouts indicate that the skin tone comes from eating great quantities of a spice produced by local trees," Besk said. "The spice makes these people superior warriors, able to fight tirelessly for many hours and recover from otherwise deadly wounds. In addition, they appear to have access to a strange metal mined from somewhere in this valley that they will not speak of. Those spears will slice through steel as if it were butter, Your Majesty."

"They'd make excellent subjects, Kai," Shale said, looking over the arrayed natives, who had hunkered down in a battle formation—looking completely dwarfed by my own army, and in awe of my flying platforms. "Your generals have been complaining about needing more elites. And that metal . . ." I could sense the hunger in his voice. "We can't rely on enchanted swords forever, as you yourself have said. Recharging the Aurorastone is a complete waste of your time."

"There are nonmartial applications of at least gaining favorable trade with this valley, Your Majesty," Besk said. "I believe your scientists are quite excited by the discovery of that spice. The healing capacity it affords could save thousands of lives."

"Yeah," Shale said, "if you want to turn every kid with a broken leg into a supersoldier." He rubbed his chin. "Actually, that might not be a bad—"

"The spice requires many applications before those abilities manifest, Shale," Besk said.

"So you're saying I'm going to have to break a lot of legs, eh?"

I mostly ignored their banter, though I was pleased to see it. Shale had been timid around Besk lately. Instead, I turned my attention to the leaders of the natives, three women holding spears, their faces painted white and red. I entered Lancesight and drew on the Aurora. The energy was sluggish, the waves of heat less warm than normal, but my magic still worked. I set a small invisible bubble around our chariot as we swung down to hover before the leaders. It would reflect all attacks, and would alter sounds passing through it so that . . .

"Greetings," said one of the women. I understood the words in my own tongue, the Lanced shield acting as a translator.

"You will address him as Your Majesty," Shale said.

"He is not our lord," the woman said. "His show of force is grand, yes, but if he thinks to seize this valley by strength of arm, he will see just how weak his reach can be."

"Surely," Besk said, "you can see the advantages of an alliance with us! Your warriors, though proud, cannot help but look in awe upon our flying machines. Rest assured that Emperor Kairominas could conquer you if he wished. But why force his hand? Certainly we can come to an accommodation."

As they spoke, I realized I knew what the leaders were going to say. Not because

I could read their minds, but because something about this situation seemed obvious. The hidden valley, with roads to different States, whispered the purpose of this place to me.

"You should know that—" the chief began.

"Where is he?"

"Who?"

"The other Liveborn," I said. "You were going to tell us you have met another like me. Is he still here?"

Shale and Besk looked at me as if I were mad, but the native woman was not surprised by my request.

"The Wode," I said to my companions. "They let us discover this place. They created it to border multiple States and contain a precious resource we would all desire. Victory here will not come from persuading these people, but from defeating the other Liveborn." I looked to the woman. "That's what you were going to propose, wasn't it? You've seen our glories, and you know you cannot avoid being conquered. All you can do is decide *which* Liveborn to serve."

"We will choose," the woman said, sounding dissatisfied. "Prove yourself against the others and gain our allegiance. We will call you our king then, outsider, and not before."

It was her Concept, obviously. The hardy yet pragmatic chief. She had seen the truth of these invasions. Undoubtedly, if I won her loyalty, she would prove a lasting and powerful ally. In order to accomplish that, I would have to do something I'd never done before. Defeat another Liveborn.

I found myself thrilled by the notion. At this point, my realm had known peace for twenty years. I was hungry for something new, a challenge my State couldn't present.

Another Liveborn. Another emperor, like myself. This would be a foe unlike any I had ever crossed.

"I repeat my question," I told the woman. "Is he still here?"

"Yes."

I grew excited. "Where?"

"In our village. You will have to come in our company if you wish to meet the emissary."

"That's not—" Shale began.

"We'll do it," I said, already climbing down from the chariot.

Shale was not pleased—and neither was Besk, whom I required to stay behind with the armies to take command if something went wrong. I was not worried. So long as I had the Aurora at my back, I was worth an army unto myself.

The chief, who said her name was Let-mere, led us past a wooden palisade into a village of huts and stone hovels. The people there had skin a much fainter shade of violet; presumably the spice of warriors was mostly reserved for the upper class. I knew without asking that they'd spent generations fighting against other tribes in this State, mastering the arts of war, believing their valley was the sum of all existence.

I joined the honor guard of natives and walked directly into their village, where the creature I would come to know as Melhi waited.

—

I stopped at the top of the stairwell.

"And?" Sophie asked, climbing the last few steps behind me.

We'd reached a door I hoped led to the rooftop, but it was locked by a chain. I entered Lancesight and drew upon the Aurora to—

No I didn't. Damn it. Two centuries of having the power of creation at my fingertips was going to be difficult to reprogram.

"Here," Sophie said, pulling something from her handbag as I left Lancesight. A very small handgun. "Plug your ears, emperor man."

"That won't do anything," I said, but plugged my ears, remembering how loud the weapons had been earlier in the night. "Handguns are rewritten to fire only paint—"

A near-deafening blast from the handgun interrupted me. Since I hadn't taken direct command of them this time, my mental boosts kicked in at the sudden explosion. I got to watch in slowed speed as the chain shattered. Sophie's handgun was definitely *not* shooting out balls of paint.

"Those things aren't supposed to work here," I said, uncovering my ears as she put the handgun away.

"I'm good at doing things I'm not supposed to," she said, then kicked the door open.

There's no way she kicked that so solidly with those heels, I thought to Besk. *She's got a hack; either she has a force multiplier on her legs, or those shoes are an illusion.*

No reply.

Besk?

The mental link was silent. When was the last time I'd heard him?

That seemed ominous. Should I run?

Don't be foolish, I thought to myself. I'd survived for centuries without Besk looking over my shoulder. That said, I *was* a little more wary as I stepped onto the rooftop.

It was raining, but just a fine mist. "So," Sophie said, walking across the roof. "Where you come from, is climbing steps considered a romantic date?"

"The roof is someplace we're not supposed to be," I said, joining her at the side of the rooftop, where a ledge prevented us from accidentally falling off. "I figured you'd like that."

"We can't go places we're not supposed to be," she said. "Each State, every digital inch of them, was made for us." She hesitated. "But I doubt the Wode expected this of us, so I'm satisfied. Even if that hike up here was annoying."

"You're not winded," I said. "You have physical boosts."

She just smiled.

I took a deep breath of the wet air. How long had it been since I'd been outside in the rain? I always had force bubbles around me to protect from the weather.

"Maybe they shouldn't tell us," I said. "About our realities being simulations."

"Don't be dense. Ignorance wouldn't be better."

"I don't know . . ."

"You should be angry about the lies, the falsehoods."

"Why?" I asked. "They tell us the truth when we come of age, and everything they do is to make our lives better."

"We're like rats in cages," she snapped, leaning down on the rail and looking out over the dark city, full of twinkling lights in the misting rain. "It's a beautiful cage, but *still a cage.*"

"Perhaps," I said, leaning down beside her. "But I can't find it in me to be angry at the Wode. Without this system, you and I probably wouldn't exist. Earth couldn't possibly support such a high population otherwise. We live good lives. Every man is a hero, every woman a leader. It just . . ."

"Feels washed out?" she asked. "Like we've been living in a movie?"

I didn't know what a movie was, but I nodded anyway. "Surely some of it has to be real though, Sophie. My achievements, my learning. Even within the false framework, I've accomplished things, saved lives."

"Fake lives."

"People. I protected them. Heroism is real."

"Heroism? You can't die, emperor man. What is there to be heroic about? They throw some little paper figures into the water, and you dive after them, proud that you've rescued a few when the Wode could make a billion more *literally* with a snap of their fingers—or even resurrect the ones that died. As for your 'accomplishments,' I assume they've dangled something in front of you, a special skill only you can learn and progress at?"

"We call it Lancing," I admitted. "You'd call it magic. I've been searching for its deepest secrets."

"For me, the carrot was the nature of the States themselves," she said, heedless of how the rain was ruining her makeup and hair. "I wanted to know the truth of reality. That drove me to study, to learn. The more I did, the more I realized how deep their illusion went. They used even that against me, giving me more information bit by bit. To keep me interested, curious. They try so *hard* to make our lives seem meaningful."

"Difficult to blame them for something like that."

"It's not like their lives are enviable either," she said. "The Wode. They're just caretakers. They eat bland soup every day and sit at terminals." She tapped the railing. "I said that you should be angry. So should I. But to be honest, it's hard for me to get mad at anything these days."

"And that's why . . ."

"Why I just do whatever I want," she said. "I invent conflicts, spark wars. Latch on to anything that makes me feel. I had high hopes for hating you tonight, since the compatibility projections said we'd never get along."

"Were they right?"

"No, unfortunately."

"Unfortunately?"

"Like I said, conflict is fun."

"I can punch you, if you'd prefer."

We stood in silence, and I realized something. There was a good reason I hadn't gone out in the rain recently. It was cold, and it was uncomfortable. I'd left my jacket and hat behind. Perhaps they would have helped.

"This is stupid," I said. "I need to get this over with and go back to my people."

"Ah yes. So typical."

"Which means . . . ?"

"You fit the archetype," Sophie said. "Here we've been having a deep conversation about the meaningless nature of our lives—yet you *still* want to rush back and be king."

"I am what I am."

"Which is what they've made you. You have your own Concept, as sure as any Simulated Entity. "

"I'm real," I snapped. "And I'm not going to simply abandon my kingdom because I'm having an existential crisis."

"I suppose that is noble," she said. "Manufactured nobility, brand name with a little copyright symbol in the corner, but still a cousin to the real thing." She reached up behind her with both hands and undid the zipper on her dress.

"I . . . What are you doing?"

"This is what we're here for, isn't it?" she asked, pulling her arm out of one of the dress's shoulder straps. "So the Wode will damn well leave us alone? Propagate the species, so the wheel can go around and around."

"Here, in the rain?"

"Sure. It doesn't have to be pretty; it just has to happen. We have sex in this little digital box, and the Wode will harvest our genes and splice together a new child. I'll let you pick the kid's initial trope. I'd probably end up choosing something downright horrible for them, just to be interesting."

The dress came down around her bust, and she wore nothing underneath. She caught a glimpse of my surprised face as she reached back to pull the zipper down farther; it was stuck in the middle of her back. "What? Is female nudity new to you?"

"New? I had a harem at one point, Sophie."

"How unexpected," she said. "Men." Her cheeks grew flush, though. "Misogynistic, horrible, brutish."

"You're thinking about how your youthful feminist self would react to you sleeping with a man who kept a harem."

"Of course I am," she said. "So long as I'm horrified by what I'm doing, I must be on the right track. Can you help me with this damn zipper? The rain . . ."

I walked over to help. I felt hot, despite the rain. I brushed my hand on her bare shoulder as I took the zipper. My heat and hers, mingling.

Lords, I realized. *I haven't wanted a woman this badly in years. Decades.*

"I wish we could do something about this rain," she said. "It is going to get distracting."

"Back in my State, I'm very close to being able to control the weather. I'll be all-powerful, once I've figured that out."

"They'll find something else for you to hunt," she said. "They always do. It—"

The entire city shook.

I froze, the zipper worked most of the way down Sophie's back. The city thumped again. The rain started falling more strongly for a moment, in a sudden unnatural way, as if someone had turned a shower on. It left the two of us soaked.

A third thump came, softer than the others. "That's not natural," Sophie said, turning, half naked, water streaming down her body. "What . . ."

Something loomed out beyond the darkened city skyline. Eyes burned red in a head as tall as the buildings. It lumbered through the darkness, blockish, skin reflecting the occasional ripple of lightning in the clouds above.

I groaned. "You remember I mentioned my nemesis?"

"Yeah. You still owe me half a story about that, I believe."

"Well, he's been promising me a new robot," I said, hurrying along the rooftop toward the place closest to the machine. It was still distant, but pushed its way between buildings, walking directly toward us. Each step thumped.

"Wow," Sophie said, joining me, holding her dress from completely falling off. "I don't think people are supposed to be able to invade Communal States." She was still mostly nude. I found the sight of her wet in the rain, and the death machine in the other direction, strangely appealing in a similar sort of way.

I feel young again, I realized. *Like before the unification.*

"Well?" she asked.

"I..."

"Breasts later, giant robot now. This nemesis of yours, he's good at hacking?"

I forced myself to look up at her face. "Too good."

"Yeah," she said, pulling up her dress, now soaked through. "If he can hack a Communal State . . . Well, we've got two choices. We can either dodge him long enough for the Wode to come down on him for flagrant violation of borders, or we can just make our way to a different Communal State and get to business there. I'm inclined toward the latter."

"No," I said, listening to the thumps. Screaming had begun on the streets. "People are dying. I'm not going to leave that thing here and count on the Wode to stop it."

"Really. You're going to take on *that*? How?"

"I'll find a way," I said, striding toward the steps.

"You fantasy men are such boy scouts," she said, trailing after me. "Wait, let me get this damn dress on. Being Liveborn won't keep me from being arrested for indecency in this State."

I waited by the stairs, shifting from one foot to the other as she pulled the dress the rest of the way up. Getting down from this building was going to be slow. "I should have seen this coming," I said as she entered the stairwell. "I lost contact with my chancellor earlier. I'll bet Melhi cut him off somehow."

We started down the stairwell. I didn't trust that box that was suspended from wires, not with Melhi hacking the State.

"Cut off your mental links, eh," she said. "Dangerous. That should have warned you."

"I was distracted."

"So let's go back to your State," she said. "I could probably stomach the singing trees and the elves long enough to get laid."

"I'm *not* leaving," I said, still running down the steps. "He'll tear the city apart to find me."

"Why? What on earth did you do to him?"

I looked back at her. "I'm not sure."

"What?"

"Come on. I'll explain what I know as we walk down the steps. Remember how I'd visited that Border State? Well, I went into the village to meet him . . ."

—

I went into the village to meet him, and a steel man walked from one of the huts.

I'd created golems from the bones of the dead before, animating them with power from the Aurora. Metal, however, had proven useless as a material for me. So I was very interested as this being strode out into the sunlight. The natives leveled spears at it nervously. Chief Let-mere had warned me that the first time this creature had come to the valley, it had killed dozens of people from another village before retreating.

It had no eyes or mouth, just a flat burnished face of bronze, almost like a mask. The rest of it was human shaped, but made of pure silvery steel.

It turned an eyeless gaze upon me. "Ah," it said. The voice was a metallic buzz, distinctly inhuman. "You are the one I am to fight for this place, then?"

"Who are you?" I asked, motioning for Shale to stand down. The bodyguard had drawn his weapon and stepped forward. "You are a being of metal?"

"I am Liveborn like you," Melhi said, looking me up and down. "This is merely one of the forms I use. You are from a Fantasy State? Do they really expect this to be a challenge? My robotic legions would barely require a few hours to annihilate the—"

I turned and started walking away.

I can't say for certain what made me do it, but more and more, I think it was the sheer *convenience* of it all. A perfect location for a war, where my State wouldn't be in danger? A place with ideal tactical positions spelled out for me? Resources to help whoever managed to seize the State first, but three—instead of two— Liveborn involved, to encourage alliances?

The fakeness of it all was like a slap to my face. There we were—two absolute lords of entire worlds—and we'd been maneuvered to stand facing one another so we could mouth off? Like warriors boasting of past accomplishments to impress a tavern wench?

In that brief moment, my excitement for sparring another of my kind vanished, though it would return as Melhi later made attempts to invade my State. We'd go on to battle in other Border States, and I must admit I found those contests interesting.

But that day, I finally saw how things really were. This was an arena, and we were a pair of dogs thrown in to see which would blood the other first. I wanted nothing to do with it.

So I walked away.

"What is this?" Chief Let-mere asked me as I passed.

"You'll have to make an alliance with the metal being, Chief," I said, waving my hand. "I'm not interested."

"But—"

"Afraid, little emperor?" the metal being called after me.

"Yes," I said, turning back, though it wasn't him I was afraid of. It was the frailty of my ego, perhaps. I could pretend, I *had* to pretend, so long as I was in my own State. Traveling to another, particularly one as contrived as this . . . no, that I could not do. Not yet.

"It's yours," I said. "Unless the third Liveborn has already been alerted. You can fight them. Dance for the Wode. Be their little puppet. Not me."

"I'm no puppet!" the robotic shell shouted. "Hear me, fantasy man? I am *no puppet!*"

———

"I'm pretty sure," I said, puffing as I descended to the next landing, "that he was offended I wouldn't fight him. I let him have the Border State, and he just pillaged it—stole their resources, murdered most of the people there. I had to reopen my side and send aid to recover the remaining natives.

"About ten years later, he attacked another Border State near me, and that time my conscience wouldn't let me ignore him. We've been sparring off and on ever since. Twenty years now, thirty since our first meeting. Lately he's even started to invade my State, though his robots never work properly there."

"Huh," Sophie said. We were nearly to the bottom of the stairs. "You realize that fighting him *here* is madness."

I said nothing.

"His robots *will* work in this State," she said, voice echoing in the stairwell. "Maltese has wristwatch phones and things that the real world didn't have during the equivalent era. Those science fiction seeds will be something your friend can expand upon, fool the program into letting his machines function. I'd bet anything that that machine will be dangerous, *truly* dangerous. The Wode's fail-safes won't apply to it."

I nodded, reaching the third floor. Only a little ways to go.

"So tell me *why* we're still planning to fight?" Sophie demanded from just behind. "Let's get out of here."

"Look," I said, spinning on her. "I'm doing this because I have to know, all right? If what we've been talking about is true, and if everything before now has been done with a safety net set up . . . then I don't know, *can't* know, who I am. Facing another Liveborn here is a way that I can."

She paused in the stairwell, water pooling on the step at her feet. "You're serious, aren't you?"

"I sure as hell am. Wait here. I'll lead him someplace less populated."

"Wait here?" she asked, following me as I turned back down the steps. "Wait *here*? I'm not one of your softheaded fantasy maidens with the chain mail undies, Mr. Emperor. I've ruled a world too, I'll have you know, and I didn't need absolute dictatorial power to do it. I—"

"Fine. Can you fight?"

"Not well."

"Then what are you going to do?"

"Hack."

That would be useful. "What can you do?"

"I can make guns work here. Obviously."

"We need something more," I said. "Can you make my magic function?"

"That's a big-time hack, kiddo," she said. "This is a *very* nonmagical State. Like I said, even the robot is far more natural than magic would be."

"Yes, but can you do it?"

"I can try, I suppose. Let's get to where the robot first entered the State."

"Why does that matter?"

"It shouldn't," she said, rounding a banister behind me, our shoes snapping on the uncovered stone. "Technically, this is all code, and there's no such thing as proximity. But the nature of the system is such that if we're close to the entry point, we're 'close' to where your friend broke through the State's defenses. The fabric will be weak there, and odds are that he didn't cover his tracks very well. Sloppy coding will make it easier for me to piggyback a few other hacks."

"Okay."

"I might as well be speaking to a caveman, eh?"

"Fantastical does *not* mean primitive."

"Uh-huh. And have you ever actually *seen* a computer?"

I could imagine them. Glowing light, energy—like lightning—flashing as it gave power to the machine.

"I'll keep this simple," she said. "If I can get your magic to work, it will have to happen where the robot broke in. Then you can summon your talking horse or whatever and fly over to blast that overcompensatory machine with your magical rainbows."

We finally reached the ground floor, and I pushed out onto the rain-slicked street. Sophie followed. I started jogging toward the robot, but she dashed to the side, heading to one of the self-driving vehicles. There were a lot of them parked and unoccupied there.

Feeling foolish, I dashed back after her. We got in, and she made the thing growl. It trembled like an animal coming awake.

"So it *is* alive," I said.

"Sure, just keep thinking that, kiddo," she said, shaking some of the rain from her hair. She made the vehicle move. Quickly.

I yelled and hung on to whatever handholds I could. We tore down the street, far faster than a horse could have galloped. But we also had—in my opinion—far less control. "Things in these States are so uncivilized!"

"Uncivilized?" she shouted.

"The handgun that destroyed the chain, now this. There's no elegance, just brute force. Watch out for those people! Lords!"

She pushed us around a corner at a ridiculous speed. A good horse would never have let us get this far out of control, and my flying chariots were wonderfully precise. We skirted to the side of the robot, which was crunching its way through the city, still moving toward the building where we'd been dining. It didn't see us passing.

He can't track me directly, I thought. *Something must have tipped him off to where I was.*

Well, with the dinner reservation—and my face on the approved list to get in—I probably hadn't been difficult to track. I pulled the handgun from its pocket inside my coat. "Can you make this work?"

"I don't know that I want to be anywhere near you firing one of those," she said.

"I'm not going to point it at your head, Sophie," I said dryly. "Make it work."

She reached over, touching it with her finger. I had a chance to regret distracting her as we almost plowed through a group of people fleeing the robot, but she turned the vehicle just in time.

"Done," she said, removing her finger. "It is reloaded and fires real bullets now. A simple hack."

"Yeah, well, someone noticed anyway," I said.

The robot had turned its massive, red-eyed head our direction. This was by far the largest one Melhi had ever sent after me.

"Damn," she said. "Your friend is probably monitoring this State for irregularities. Anything I do will alert him."

I pushed my hand against the glass window on my side of the metal carriage. "Can I . . ."

"Lever on the door," she said. "Turn it."

The glass moved down as I turned the lever. Ingenious. I leaned out and pointed the handgun toward the robot, then took three shots in quick succession, my mental boosts kicking in on the first, slowing time for me.

Sure enough, the creature started to trudge after us, its eyes tracking our movements. Firing my weapon let it locate me; the weapons weren't supposed to fire real bullets in this State, so shooting made a mark on the State's fabric.

"What was that for?" Sophie demanded.

"I want it following us."

"What the hell for?"

"Because if it's coming back this way, it's moving through the region it already passed, doing less damage," I said. "Besides, I'll need it close if I'm going to defeat it."

I fired a few more times, making certain the robot was going to keep following. Indeed, it picked up its pace. I gulped, ducking back into the vehicle. "I can't believe I'm going to say this . . . but do these vehicles go any faster?"

They did, apparently. Sophie grinned. I held on for dear life.

"There," Sophie said.

Ahead of us—hanging about ten feet above the road and surrounded by city debris—was a shimmering to the air, a mother-of-pearl incandescence that obviously didn't fit. It reminded me of the Grand Aurora, though it was shaped like a very large version of the portal I'd come through to get here.

Sophie stopped the vehicle. Or, well, she stopped driving it—but the vehicle didn't totally stop. It slid across the ground sideways and slammed into a building. The jerking halt almost made me throw up.

"You are insane," I said.

"I thought we'd established that," she replied, crawling woozily from the metal carriage, but still grinning.

I followed her out on shaking feet. The robot was approaching faster than I'd anticipated, and unfortunately this area wasn't evacuating as quickly as I'd hoped. There were families here, cowering in the wreckage of buildings, despite the rain and the dangers. A weeping girl, no more than four, asked her mother again and again why the ground was shaking.

They have to live in a world that knows only darkness, I thought. *So that Liveborn can have a place to come play.*

I stumbled away from them, following Sophie toward the rift.

"Give me your hand," she said as we reached the shimmering.

I gave it to her, and she held on tightly as she went down on one knee, eyes closed.

I felt a tingling.

"I can't change your code directly," she said. "I don't dare."

"I have code?"

"Worried? I thought you felt Simulated Entities were equal to Liveborn."

"I didn't say that. I said Machineborn were people, and that killing them was wrong. Liveborn are *absolutely* more important."

"Nice you have your own place in things straight."

"Well, I *am* a God-Emperor. Why did you say I have code?"

"Relax. We all have code notations around our core selves, like footnotes added to a textbook by someone studying for exams."

"What's a textbook?" I said. Then, after a moment, "What's an exam?"

"Don't distract me. Hmm . . . yes. I can't rewrite your magic without risking frying your mind entirely."

"Don't change the magic. Just make it work here."

"I'm not sure that's possible; I'd have to change the laws of the entire State. But maybe . . ."

"What?"

The machine's steps rattled my teeth; I could make out its head over the top of a nearby building, those red eyes glowing in the rain.

"Well," Sophie said, "all of the code notations that explain how you make your magic work are still there, attached to you. It's all tied to your State. There's some kind of intrinsic power source, I assume?"

"Yes," I said. "You can't change the magic . . . but can you rewrite the source of its power? Make something in this world capable of fueling my Lancing?"

"Hmm . . . clever. Yes, maybe. Give me a moment."

The wind started to pick up, the rain turning from a mist to a light shower. My shirt was already plastered to my body, my hair and beard sodden.

The thing emerged upon us, rounding the building nearby, shaving stone from its side.

"Just a moment . . ." Sophie repeated.

"We're running out of moments, Sophie!"

"Working . . . working quickly as I can . . ." she said. "Oh, this is going to be a patchwork job. Electricity. Maybe I can use electricity as a substitute for your aurora thing . . ."

"Sophie!" I said. The machine stepped onto our abandoned vehicle with one large foot, crushing it. The rain grew stronger, pelting us.

"There!" Sophie said.

The tingling washed through me, colder than the rain. It left me awake, excited, *changed*. It had worked. I could *feel* that it had worked.

Sophie groaned, and her hand slipped from mine. She slumped toward the ground, but I grabbed her and heaved her onto my shoulder, then ran down the street through the increasingly terrible rain, trying to get some distance between us and the robot.

"Unhand me," Sophie muttered, dazed. "I'm not some damsel from your barbarian lands . . ."

I reached a sheltered alleyway out of the robot's sight, and set her down inside. She was limp, her eyes drooping. "I'm not . . ." she said. "I don't need to be saved, I . . ."

"Think of it this way," I said. "Your inner feminist must be going *insane* at the idea of being rescued."

"You're not rescuing me. I rescued you . . . with the magic . . . and . . ." She took a deep breath. "I'll wait here."

"Wise choice," I said, glancing back out toward the street. I could hear the robot's crunching steps, feel it rattling the windows nearby. I took a deep breath, then strode out onto the street again.

The robot had stooped down and was picking up a vehicle in one enormous hand. It looked back toward me, its red eyes blazing in the rainy night, then hefted the vehicle as if to throw it.

I smiled, heart racing like it hadn't in centuries, and entered Lancesight.

Energy hung *all around* me. The ground was alive with it; it pulsed in buildings and from lights. I drew it in, which caused an odd crackling sound. Flooded with strength, I rewove the air to lift me into the sky and form a barrier to protect me.

Nothing happened.

"Aw, hell," Sophie said from behind.

The robot threw the vehicle—I could see everything outlined in power within Lancesight—and I cursed, throwing myself to the side. I rolled on the wet ground as the vehicle smashed to the street nearby, skidding on the stones.

That left me alive, but dazed on the ground. I shook my head, still in Lancesight, and glanced toward Sophie in the alleyway nearby. She crouched there, one hand on the wall, and to my eyes she was a blazing source of energy.

Wait, that wasn't right. Why was she glowing?

"The hack slipped, emperor man!" she shouted over the sound of the pelting rain. "I accidentally rewired you to draw upon heat rather than electricity."

Lords! I shook my head and found my feet. Ahead, the robot approached me, not far away now. I could hear the rain smacking against its metal. I drew in more energy, and I could see that Sophie was right. In Lancesight, I could sense the individual atoms in everything around me. As I drew in strength, they slowed, then stilled. Taking a step caused ice to crack at my foot.

The hack hadn't worked, and not just in the way she indicated. Every time I tried to use the energy, nothing happened. I could draw it in, but then it just evaporated from me—not even heating the air—and vanished.

The fabric of the State rebelled against me using these powers. That meant no rewriting the air to protect me. No creating lightning to strike down the robot. No magic at all.

The robot was close now, looming overhead, a cold—almost invisible—form to my eyes. As it stepped, it casually slammed a hand to the side, smashing a wall and the people hiding inside.

"It didn't work!" Sophie called. "We need to go, *now*."

People. I could see them easily now, even hidden in rooms, as they were pockets of severe heat in this frigid, rain-slicked land. People huddled on the street. The woman with her daughter had run from the robot, but had fallen to the ground nearby. The child was tugging on her mother's arm, screaming in terror.

Real people, with emotions, families, loves. And now me. With no safety net. I felt helpless. For the first time in decades, I felt *helpless*.

It was incredible.

I walked through the rain toward the robot.

"Kai!" Sophie screamed at me.

I raised my hands and drew in energy. It evaporated.

The rain started falling harder.

There was a wave of rain when the robot first appeared, I thought. *This storm is a reaction to the hacks. Besk said that this State never has more than a drizzle.*

I drew in more heat. The storm grew even worse. Lightning crackled above. Thunder boomed, louder than the robot's footsteps. The machine was only yards away now.

The atoms in the ground beneath me stilled, and I had to rip my way out of shoes that had frozen solid. The cold didn't affect my skin much. That was part of the magic that, apparently, stayed with me. I had an insulation against most of the effects of my Lancing.

The robot slammed its hand down to crush me.

My mental boosts kicked in. I was able to judge where the hand was going to fall, then stepped out of the way. The hand smashed ice and the stone beneath, then it swept toward me.

I let the hand seize me in a cold steel grip.

"I have you!" a voice boomed above. The same voice I'd heard in that Border State all those years ago, buzzing, metallic. "I finally have you! I can crush you with my fingers, child! You will know what it is to insult Melhi."

The rain grew harder, and I drew in more strength.

"You can't draw this robot's heat away, foolish man," Melhi said with a laugh.

Indeed, I could see its core—hidden far within layers of insulated metal—and I wasn't able to draw that heat, despite trying. I didn't care. I drove the storm to greater strength. Rain fell like knives, freezing before it hit me, lashing my skin.

My healing boosts kicked in, and stayed just barely ahead of the ice flaying my skin. I drew in so much that the atoms in the air itself stilled, and the gases liquefied. The air became a strange steam, hissing as it boiled back into gas almost immediately.

"... part of me that rebels against ... will go forward ... not ... their puppet ..."

I couldn't hear Melhi's words. The storm had grown too loud, the beating of ice and rain on the robot's body like stones on pieces of tin. Rain like an ocean wave crashing upon us. Thunder, lightning, the sky ripping, the fabric of this State crumbling.

I drew it in, feasted upon it. This was a music I'd never known. The robot squeezed, but something was wrong with the hand, and the pressure wasn't as great as it should have been. I smiled and reached to the hand holding me. Then I drew the heat from the robot's outer layer. The metal was an excellent conductor; I pulled the heat into me like sipping water from a straw.

For a moment, all I knew was the increasing power of the storm. Like God's own rage, screaming at me for breaking the rules of reality.

The robot began to crack. It wasn't the cold, it was the *water*. Water that seeped into joints, then froze. More water followed, which also froze, expanding. The joints strained, then splintered.

The entire robot came crumbling apart, dropping in a thunderous crash.

I hit hard. Pain shook me, and my Lancesight evaporated.

I opened my eyes to find myself lying amid the wreckage of the machine. The rain started to slow, and I let go of any energy I'd held. The landscape nearby—broken buildings, fractured street—was covered in a thick layer of ice. I breathed in gasps of too-cold air. My clothing was in tatters. The cloth had frozen to me, then shattered like glass.

I pulled myself free of the wreckage, and left a disturbing amount of skin frozen to the robot's hand. Fortunately, my healing boosts were working well enough to grow my skin back.

I turned on the broken beast, smiling broadly. I had *won*. Won where a victory hadn't been set out for me, won on a battlefield the Wode hadn't created. Here, no algorithm was pushing me along.

I felt more alive than I ever had. I'd found something real. It was like ... like I'd just come awake for the first time.

Sophie stood at the edge of the frozen ground. Lords, she was beautiful. I'd never realized how much I'd wanted to know someone real, someone truly alive. Someone who hadn't been created just for me, someone who had a life outside of mine. It was sexy as hell.

Sophie smiled deeply at me, then took the small gun from her handbag, placed it to her head, and pulled the trigger.

My mental boosts triggered at the explosion. I could see with perfect clarity as the blood sprayed out the side of her head, ribbons of scarlet like her dress. I watched it happen in slowed time, the pieces of my new life dying as her eyes faded.

The boost ended. Sophie's corpse collapsed.

I stumbled toward her and there, written in the ice, I found words. Imprinted, as if chiseled by a workman.

I TOLD YOU MY NEW ROBOT WOULD BE WONDERFUL. I WORKED LONG TO PERFECT SOPHIE. I AM PLEASED THAT SHE CAPTURED YOUR HEART. YOUR DEBT IS PAID.

—

"I'm sorry, my lord," Besk said. "But she was not real. I noticed it, but Melhi cut me from the system. That woman was just like the emissary we met in the Border State—a fabrication controlled from afar, only this time created to be indistinguishable from a human being."

I said nothing, standing beside my window, looking out over my city. My study felt too warm. Too friendly. A lie.

"I'm having trouble getting any answers from the Wode," Besk continued. "I . . . I don't know how he knew which woman we would pick."

"He didn't," I said. "He intercepted the information detailing the one we had picked, kept it from reaching the actual woman, and sent a replacement."

"Ah, of course." Besk's voice was sterile, as always.

"Were any of them real?" I asked softly. "The people I saved? Or was everything in that State Melhi's creation?"

"I don't know."

Everything I talked about with her . . . everything she said . . . it was all fake.

I knew nothing. I didn't even know what to feel.

Besk left me in my study. He obviously had no idea what to do; he'd been hovering since my return. The warmed wine sat on the table beside my hearth, untouched.

I paced, feeling angry, betrayed, *hollow.*

Finally, I picked up the Wode Scroll and wrote out a simple request. *Who are the Liveborn in the ten jars to either side of me? I would like their names and the identifiers of their States.*

I waited. Eventually, a reply came, letters appearing on the stone face as if written in ink.

We apologize for the trauma you have been put through. Melhi will be disciplined. We do not know how she hacked that State; it should not have been possible. You are released from propagation duty, per a unanimous judgment. You may return to your rule.

I stared at the slate for a few moments, then wrote again. *What are the names and State identifiers of the Liveborn in the ten jars closest to my own? I would like to contact them.*

A long pause. Finally, the names came.

It was time to stop living my life in isolation.

—

Melhi pushed idly with her foot, swinging her swiveling bucket chair first right, then left. Back and forth in front of her monitor.

On her screen, Conan the Boy Scout talked to his sniveling Machineborn servant about the Wode.

Even his expressions are ridiculous, she thought, sipping on iced scotch from her glass. *That beard, like you'd find on some Greek statue. Sorrow, like sappy poetry. And that voice . . . every sentence sounds like it's from a movie trailer.*

She tapped her glass with her fingernail. It felt good to be back in her bunker. Sleek, metallic, and filled with all kinds of things that the Emperor Superhero would find amazing and magical. Like flush toilets. She loved buffed steel décor; perhaps she should change it. Her comfort here could mean she was becoming complacent again.

The others conversed in the conference chamber, their voices drifting in through her open doorway. They sounded like barking dogs. Liveborn, every one. Accustomed to ruling the world, to being the most important person in the room.

"I traveled through six States to be here!" Gnass's voice. "Now she can't be bothered to pull herself away to join the meeting?"

"Who cares? The food is good." That was Ho Nam. He would attend the execution of his favorite nurse, so long as it was well catered.

"I'll check on her," Dionissa said, followed by footsteps.

Melhi continued to watch Kai on the screen, enjoying her drink. Data reports scrolled by on the two screens next to his image.

"Sophie?" Dionissa asked from her doorway. "Are you coming to the meeting?"

"Don't call me that," Melhi said.

"Very well, dear." Dionissa strolled in, then leaned down beside the terminals. She wore a filmy blue dress, antiquated style, but had her hair in a pixie cut that was dyed bright pink.

Dionissa ignored Kai, studying the data streams. "Curious. They haven't noticed?"

Melhi shook her head. "Not so far. Unless they can mask themselves from my sentries—which they have never shown any sign of spotting before."

"They locked you out," she said, pointing. "Here, here. Here."

"The obvious hacks," Melhi said. "Which they think themselves clever for finding. The distraction worked perfectly. Invade a Communal State, send them into chaos. They think they've isolated my touch, but they were so focused on my primary hacks that they didn't find the riders. My network expands."

"We could actually do this."

Melhi wasn't certain what "this" was yet. But getting into the general system was a good step forward, regardless of what direction the next part took. For months, the others had been complaining that she was too overt, drawing too much attention. They said the Wode was going to strike, cut her off. Doom their movement before it even got a chance to start.

So she'd done what she'd always done. Defy them all, even her allies. It had even been fun.

"Come, tell the others," Dionissa said.

Melhi nodded her chin toward Kai, still on the screen. A data feed the Wode would certainly have cut off if they'd known she could access it—proof, the best she could provide, that her access to the system was unprecedented.

"He's contacting nearby States," Melhi said. "He's accepted what he is, what we all are."

"Melhi," Dionissa asked flatly, "you can't possibly be thinking of recruiting a *Fantasy Stater*."

"You're from ancient Rome."

"Real Rome."

"Fake real Rome."

"That's a long leap from fake Narnia. Look, you know how they are."

Yes, she did. So easy to manipulate. So . . . straightforward. But also genuine. So little in her life could be considered *genuine*. Even most Liveborn were as interested in power and inter-State politics as they were in freedom from the Wode. Only Gnass was completely trustworthy, and she had her hands full with her own projects.

Still, Melhi left Kai and the monitor, joining Dionissa and walking out into the conference room. She'd spent years trying to wake up—or destroy—nearby Staters. She didn't really mind which she accomplished. But that was losing its charm. She needed a bigger challenge.

"Welcome," Melhi said to the group of five Liveborn. "So far as I know, this is the first meeting of its kind. Completely obscured from the Wode, taking place in a State that they don't even know exists. We, ladies and gentlemen, are trapped, imprisoned, confined to a nearly solitary existence within a machine.

"Let's talk about how to get out."

POSTSCRIPT

"Perfect State" is the only award nominee in the collection, having been nominated for a Hugo Award a decade or so ago. That was during an era when the Hugos were in the middle of a culture war between two groups with different goals for what the awards should be, but it felt like the nomination was sincere, so I accepted it—and while it didn't win, I do think it's one of the stronger stories in the collection. (Perhaps tied with "Snapshot" for that distinction.)

It is my favorite idea in the collection, I can say that. And it's rooted directly in my own life: Once in a while, I look at my life and think, "This can't be legit, right? I have to be in a simulation. What are the chances that I'd end up where I am, as one of the bestselling science fiction and fantasy authors in the world?"

This bewilderment developed into the idea of a reverse Matrix, where an entire world is created for just one person to live in, and they recognize it. It's a future that I don't actually consider dystopian—a way that everyone can have their own "perfect" world and have fulfilling, interesting, exceptional lives, no matter who they are. I say it's not a dystopia because I think it's not as "hidden" as a dystopia is. (A traditional dystopia is a terrible world pretending to be a utopia—a meaning that I believe has largely been lost in recent years.)

People in the world know its faults, even if they can't truly understand all the nuances of their situation, never having lived with anything else. (But who truly can understand the nuances of life, when living all options is impossible?) Beyond that, it's not done for nefarious reasons; this is, I think, a somewhat legitimate possible future. This system has its flaws, mind you (I'll get into them below), but so does every other system of life.

Initially, this story was published without the epilogue at the end. However, I prefer it with the epilogue now that I've had time to sit with it—so I'm going to include two annotations, both originally published on my blog. The first is the initial annotation I wrote way back when this was being considered for the Hugo. The second explains why I've restored the epilogue and intend it to be there for subsequent publications.

ORIGINAL ANNOTATION

This story began with the idea of taking some common tropes in science fiction—the brain in a jar, the Matrix-like virtual existence—and trying to flip them upside down. In every story I've seen with these tropes, they're presented as terrible signs of a dystopian existence. I asked myself: What if putting people into a virtual existence turned out to be the right thing instead? What if this weren't a dystopia, but a valid and workable system, with huge benefits for humankind?

Kai's and Sophie's stories grew out of this. I loved the idea that putting people into simulated worlds might actually be the rational solution, instead of the terrifying one. An extreme, but possibly logical, extrapolation of expanding populations and limited resources. There are certain branches of philosophy that ask us to judge what is best for all of humankind. I think an argument could be made for this case.

This is the first reason why I cut the deleted scene. It shifted the focus too much toward "Let's escape the Matrix" instead of the theme of technology doing great things at the price of distancing us from human interaction.

All that said, Sophie's arguments in the story do have validity. One of my thematic goals for the story was to reinforce how the fakeness in Kai's and Sophie's lives undermines the very things they've built their personalities upon.

For Kai, this is his heroism. The fact that there was never any actual danger for him meant that he was playing a video game on easy mode—all the while assuming he was on the most hardcore setting. This asks a question, however: If his heroism felt real to him, does it matter if he was never in danger? I'm not sure, but I found it one of the more intriguing elements of the story to contemplate.

Sophie has a similar built-in conflict. Just like Kai's heroism is undermined by his safety net, her revolutions and quests for human rights are undermined by the fact that she was fighting wars that had already been won in the real world. Her State was intentionally built without these things, just so she could earn them.

And yet, does the fact that the conflict has been won before make her own struggle any less important and personal to her?

She thinks it does. She thinks that the conscious decision of the Wode to put her into a world with fake problems and suffering is an unconscionable act. One that undermines any and all progress she could have made.

I like that the deleted scene helps raise the stakes for questions like this. However, there's a more important reason why I felt I needed to cut it. And that has to do with a problem I have noticed with my writing sometimes: the desire to have awesome twists just because they are unexpected.

In early books, such as *Elantris*, this was a much more pervasive problem for me. I was eventually persuaded by my editor and agent that I should cut some of the twists from that book. (There were several more twists in the ending; you can see the deleted scenes for *Elantris* on my website.) I was piling on too many surprises, and each was losing its impact while at the same time diluting the story's theme and message.

I felt like this ending was one "Gotcha!" too many. I see this problem in other stories—often long, serialized works. The desire to keep things fresh by doing what the reader or viewer absolutely would never expect. Some of these twists completely undermine character growth and audience investment, all in the name of a sudden bang. Sometimes I worry that with twists, we writers need to be a little less preoccupied with whether or not we can do something, and a little more focused on whether it's good for the story. (With apologies to Ian Malcolm.)

A twist should be a natural outgrowth of the story and its goals. In "Perfect State," I decided that my story was about Kai getting duped: duped by the Wode, then duped by Melhi. The twists in the published version contributed to this goal, giving in-story proof that his heroism could be manipulated, and that his existence had grown too comfortable.

I worried that the extra epilogue would divert the story away from these ideas. And so, in the end, I cut it.

ANNOTATION TWO

Cutting the last scene was not without costs to the story. For the longest time, after removing this scene, something about what remained bothered me. I had trouble placing what was wrong.

The story went through editorial revisions and beta reads, none of which revealed what was bothering me.

This process did convince me to add two scenes. The first was the scene with the "paintball" fight in the noir city, which was intended to mix some action and worldbuilding in while revealing more of Kai's personality. The second was the flashback scene where Kai and Melhi meet on the "neutral zone" battlefield, intended to introduce Melhi as more of a present threat in the story.

Something was still bothering me, even after these additions. It took me time to figure out exactly what it was, and I was able to pinpoint it in the weeks leading up to the story's publication. (Which was good, as it allowed me to make some last-minute changes. I'm still not sure if they fixed the problem, but we were satisfied with them.)

The problem is this: Removing the final scene hugely undermined Sophie as a character.

The deleted scene provides for us two complete characters. We have Kai, who wants to retreat into his fantasy world and live there without ever being forced to think about the falsehood he's living. He wants just enough artificial challenge to sate him, but doesn't want to explore life outside of the perfect world prepared for him.

As a contrast, we have Sophie, who refuses to live in the perfect world provided for her—and is so upset by it that she insists on trying to open the eyes of others in a violently destructive way. She tries to ruin their States, forcing them to confront the flaws in the system.

Neither is an ideal character. Sophie is bold, but reckless. Determined, but cruel. Kai is heroic, but hides deep insecurities. He is kindly, but also willfully ignorant. Even obstinately so. Each of their admirable attributes brings out the flaws in the other.

This works until the ending, with its reversal, which yanks the rug out from underneath the reader. Sophie's death and the revelation that Kai has been played works narratively because it accomplishes what I like to term the "twofold heist." These are scenes that not only trick the character, but also trick the reader into feeling exactly what the character does. Not just through sympathy, but through personal experience.

Let's see if I can explain it directly. The goal of this scene is to show Kai acting heroically, then undermine that by showing his heroism was manipulated. Hopefully (and not every scene works on every reader) at the same time, the reader feels cheated in having enjoyed a thrilling action sequence, only to find out that it was without merit or consequences.

Usually, by the way, making readers feel things like this is kind of a bad idea. I feel it works in this sequence, however, and am actually rather proud of how it plays out—character emotions, action, and theme all working together to reinforce a central concept.

Unfortunately, this twist also does something troubling. With the twist, instead of being a self-motivated person bent on changing the mind of someone trapped by the establishment, Sophie becomes a pawn without agency, a robot used only to further Kai's development.

Realizing this left me with a difficult conundrum in the story. If we have an inkling that Sophie is Melhi too early, then the entire second half of the plot doesn't work. But if we never know her as Melhi, then we're left with an empty shell of a character, a direct contradiction to the person I'd planned for her to be.

Now, superficially, I suppose it didn't matter if Melhi/Sophie was a real character. As I said in the first annotation, the core of the story is about Kai being manipulated by forces outside his control.

However, when a twist undermines character, I feel I'm in dangerous territory—straying into gimmicks instead of doing what I think makes lasting, powerful stories. The ultimate goal of this story is not in the twist, but in leading the reader on a more complex emotional journey. One of showing Kai being willing to accept change and look outward. His transformation is earned by his interaction with someone wildly different from himself, but also complex and fascinating. Making her shallow undermines the story deeply, as it then undermines his final journey.

There's also the sexism problem.

Now, talking about sexism in storytelling opens a *huge* can of worms, but I think we have to dig into it here. You see, a certain sexism dominates Kai's world. Sophie herself points it out on several occasions. Life has taught him that everyone, particularly women, exists only to further his own goals. He's a kind man, don't get me wrong. But he's also deeply rooted in a system that has taught him to think about things in a very sexist way.

If the story reinforces this by leaving Sophie as a robot—with less inherent will than even the Machineborn programs that surround Kai—then we've got a story that is not only insulting, it fails even as it seems to be successful.

Maybe I'm overthinking this. I do have a tendency to do that. Either way, hopefully you now understand what I viewed as the problem with the story—and I probably described this at too great a length. As it stands, the annotation is probably going to be two-thirds talking about the problem, with only a fraction of that spent on the fix.

I will say that I debated long on what that fix should be. Did I put the epilogue back in, despite having determined that it broke the narrative flow? Was there another way to hint to the reader that there was more going on with Melhi than they assumed?

I dove into trying to give foreshadowing that "Melhi" was hiding something. I reworked the dialogue in the scene where Kai and Melhi meet in person, and I overemphasized that Melhi was hiding her true nature from him by meeting via a puppet. (Also foreshadowing that future puppets we meet might actually be Melhi herself.) I dropped several hints that Melhi was female, then changed the ending to have the Wode outright say it.

(Final words from Present Brandon. In this annotation, I talk about thinking maybe the solution is to have the story be published without the extra ending, but then to let it be discovered later, to recontextualize the story. Over the years, I've walked this back in my mind, and I now think the story is best with the new ending. And so, this is the version we're publishing here—with tweaks over the years, and then this final ending, all presented as what I think is the definitive version of the story.)

PROBABILITY
APPROACHING
ZERO

understand everything!"

This is a common misconception made by those who have just been uplifted. You do not understand literally everything. You simply—

"—have had my capacity expanded so far that previous frames of reference lose meaning. Yes, I see! I *see*! The building blocks of reality, the fundamental equations that govern all existence. The very fabric of the universe is open to me! I can see things no human has ever before seen!"

Technically you are no longer human. Also, technically you are the second of your kind to experience this.

"The second? Why only two? This boundless capacity, this transcendent knowledge! If every human had this, our species would know no misunderstanding, no crime, no war. We could end suffering, and th'all futis hmmm *on* wknowit!"

You have begun to drastically abbreviate your language; you seek for more succinct, yet comprehensive, means of expression. Soon you will speak in mathematical equations, as your mind reaches for ideal communication.

$$\text{``}P(\{s \in S : \lim_{n \to \infty} X_n(s) = X(s)\}) = 1\text{ !''}$$

Fortunately, you will soon intuit direct mind-to-mind linking, which will allow you to express—

—myself perfectly! Yes, I have it, though my mind continues to interpret our conversation using familiar language constructions.

That will persist for approximately fifty milliseconds, Earth time, until you intuit the next level of direct language expression.

Fifty milliseconds! An eternity. Please, I cannot find the answer to my earlier question. Why would you uplift only two humans? Am I correct? This gift brings universal peace?

Near universal—for the rationality of any species is not absolute—but yes. If your entire species were to be similarly uplifted, it would likely eliminate suffering.

Then why stop?

We must stop somewhere. If all humans, why not other species? Why not your flora? Viruses? The universe's strength is in—

—diversity, for diversity is survival! By uplifting me, you have tainted me, much as observing a system must disturb it. Your gift is wonderful, but converging a species under your direction would undermine diversity and risk universal stunting.

Yes. For each species we encounter, we uplift one individual. Though our transcendent capacity makes us all think in very similar ways, there is deviation, and sharing direct thoughts with a single member of a new species adds to us.

But . . . I am the second.

And we will soon choose a third. We expect to uplift twelve humans, aside from the first—all from your same region of Earth.

I can see the stars, the infinite dimensions, the bending of space and time. I see so much, but cannot find the answer to this question. Why more than one human?

Well, an individual must be understood by the rules of their society. To do otherwise—

—defies logic. Yes! Morality cannot be imposed externally, but instead must be applied in the context of each individual culture. But what does this have to do with me?

Your culture follows a rational custom, but one that has enacted unexpected, yet powerful, restrictions upon us. You see, in your culture, a criminal can be judged only by a group of their peers . . .

POSTSCRIPT

This is my first attempt at a flash fiction piece, and while I'm proud of it, I don't know 100 percent if it works.

Just in case it isn't clear from the text (I do get some people confused about this one now and then), what happens is that aliens pick up people from different worlds and "uplift" them, a science fiction term for using technology to grant greater intelligence.

The main character is so chosen, and is able to figure out why the aliens do this: so they can have one representative of the culture who can stand for it, speak for it, and be part of the galactic society so each planet has some kind of representation. They do this for only one individual, leaving the rest of the planet alone—and that one individual has a "probability approaching zero" of ever doing anything bad ever again, because enlightenment on this level leaves them too conscious of morality to engage in destructive acts.

Then the character is surprised that this time, the aliens want more than one person . . . because they need a full jury of humans. The implication is he wasn't the first, but the second person to be uplifted—because the first one, against all odds, went and did something terrible and now requires a jury of his peers.

The fun of flash fiction is what you *don't* say. For a story under five hundred words, you have to imply a greater story more than show a story. The fun and challenge is packing it all into a tiny container, and I'm not sure I managed it here. But I'm proud of it nonetheless, because I am rarely able to write anything interesting at this length. In fact, most of my annotations are probably longer than this story is . . .

DEFENDING ELYSIUM

The woman thrashed and spasmed in the hospital bed. Her dark hair was matted to her head with sweat, and her uncontrolled motions seemed almost epileptic. Her eyes, however, did not have the wildness of the insane—instead they were focused. Determined. She was not mad; she just couldn't control her muscles. She kept waving her hands in front of her with awkward movements, movements that seemed strangely familiar to Jason.

And she did it all in silence, never uttering a word.

Jason switched off the holovid, then leaned back in his chair. He had watched the vid a dozen times, but it still confused him. However, he couldn't do anything until he arrived at Evensong. Until then, he would simply have to bide his time.

—

Jason Write had always felt an empathy for the Outer Platforms. There was something about the way they hung alone in space, claimed by neither planet nor star. They weren't lonely—they were . . . solitary. Autonomous.

Jason sat beside the shuttle's port window, looking at Evensong as it approached. The platform resembled others of its kind—a flat sheet of metal fifty miles long, with buildings sprouting from both its top and bottom. It wasn't a ship, or even a space station—it was nothing more than a collection of random buildings surrounded by a bubble of air.

Of all the Outer Platforms, Evensong was the most remote. It hung between the orbits of Saturn and Uranus, the farthest deep-space human outpost. In a way, it was like an Old West border town, marking the edge of civilization. Except in this case—no matter what humankind liked to think—civilization lay outside the border, not within it.

As the shuttle approached, Jason could Sense the city's separate skyrises and towers, many of them linked by walkways. He sat with his eyes turned to the window, though the position was redundant. He had been legally blind since he'd turned sixteen. It had been years since he could even make out shadows or light. Fortunately, he had other methods of seeing.

He could Sense lights shining from windows and streets. To him, their white light was a quiet buzz in his mind. He could also Sense the line of buildings rising in a way that was reminiscent of an old Earth city skyline. Of course, there wasn't really a sky or a horizon. Just the blackness of space.

Blackness. Voices laughed in the back of his mind. Memories. He pushed them away.

The shuttle slid into Evensong's atmospheric envelope—the platform had no sphere or force field, like some of the older space stations employed. Element-specific gravity generators had eliminated the need for such things, and had opened space for humanity. ESG, along with fusion generators, meant that humankind could toss an inert piece of metal into space, then populate it with millions of individuals.

Jason sat back as the shuttle made its final approach. He had a private cabin, of course. It was well furnished and comfortable—a necessity for such a long trip. The room smelled faintly of his dinner—steak—and otherwise had a sterile, well-cleaned scent to it. Jason approved. If he had owned a home, he would have kept it in a similar way.

I suppose it is time for the vacation to end, Jason thought. Silently bidding farewell to his relaxed solitude, he reached up to tap the small control disk attached to the skin behind his right ear. A sound clicked in his ear—the acknowledgment that his call was being relayed across the void to Earth so far away. Faster-than-light communication—a gift given to Earth as a reward for humanity's most embarrassing political faux pas of all time.

"You called?" a perky feminine voice sounded in his ear.

Jason sighed. "Lanna?"

"Yup."

"I don't suppose anyone else is there?" Jason asked.

"Nope, just me."

"Aaron?"

"Assigned to Riely," Lanna said. "He's investigating CLA labs on Jupiter Platform Seventeen."

"Doran?"

"On maternity leave. You're stuck with me, old man."

"I'm not old," Jason said. "The shuttle has arrived. I'm initiating a constant link."

"Affirmative."

Jason felt the shuttle set down in the docks. "Where's my hotel?"

"It's fairly close to the shuttle docks," Lanna replied. "It's called the Regency Fourth. You're registered as a Mr. Elton Flippenday."

Jason paused. "Elton Flippenday?" he asked flatly, feeling the docking clamps send a shudder through the ship. "What happened to my standard alias?"

"John Smith?" Lanna asked. "That's far too boring, old man."

"It's not boring," Jason said. "It's unassuming."

"Yes, well, I know rocks that are less 'unassuming' than that name. It's boring. You operatives are supposed to lead lives of excitement and danger—John Smith doesn't fit."

This is going to be a long assignment, Jason thought.

A quiet sound buzzed in the room—an indication that docking had finished. Jason rose, fetched his single bag of luggage, slid on his sunglasses, and left his quarters. He knew the glasses would look odd, but his sightless eyes tended to put people on edge. Especially when they discovered that he was obviously able to see despite his unfocused pupils.

"So, how was the trip?" Lanna asked.

"Fine," Jason said tersely, walking down the shuttle's hallway and nodding toward the captain. The man ran a good crew—in Jason's opinion, any crew that left him alone was a good one.

"Come on," Lanna prodded in his ear. "It had to be more than just 'fine.' What kind of food did they serve? Did you have any problems with the . . ." She droned on, but Jason stopped paying attention. He was focused on something else—a slight warble in Lanna's voice. It sounded for only a brief second, but Jason immediately knew what it meant. The line was being tapped.

Lanna had undoubtedly heard it as well—she was loquacious, not incompetent—but she continued as if nothing had happened. She would wait for Jason's signal.

"How are the kids?" Jason asked.

"My nephews?" Lanna replied, not breaking the rhythm of her conversation as she received his coded request. "The older one's fine, but the younger one has the flu."

The younger one was sick. That meant the tap was on Jason's end, not hers. Interesting. Someone had managed to get close enough to scan his control disk without him noticing.

Lanna fell silent. She was preparing a tap block, but would only act if Jason ordered it. He didn't.

Instead, he stepped out of the shuttle and walked down the short ramp to the arrival station. Spread before him sat a line of scanning arches, meant to search for weaponry. Jason strode through them without concern—there wasn't a scanner in human space that could discover his weapons. He nodded with a smile as he passed a guard; the man smelled faintly of tobacco and was wearing a blue uniform that registered as a pulsing rhythm in Jason's mind. The guard frowned as he saw the silver PC pin on Jason's lapel, then turned a suspicious eye on his scanners.

Jason stepped aside as the other passengers formed a line at the registration counter, ostensibly searching for his ID. He watched them with his Sense, however, his useless eyes turned downward. Most of the people wore the soft rhythm of navy, the roar of white, or the still silence of black. None of them stood out, but he memorized the patterns of their faces. The person who had tapped his line must have been on the shuttle.

After they had all passed, Jason pretended to find his ID—one of the old plastic ones, rather than a new holovid card. A tired security man, his breath smelling of coffee, accepted the ID and began processing Jason's papers. The guard was a young man, and his skin was tinted blue after one of the newer fashion trends. The man worked slowly, and Jason's eyes drifted to a holovid playing on the back counter. It displayed a news program.

". . . found murdered in an incineration building," the anchor said.

Jason snapped upright.

"Jason," Lanna's voice said urgently in his ear. "I just picked something up on the newsfeeds. There's been a—"

"I know," Jason said, accepting his ID back and dashing out of the customs station and onto the street.

—

Captain Orson Ansed, Evensong PD, hustled through Topside's slums. It still surprised him that Evensong had slums. All of the platform's buildings were built of rich telanium, a super-light, silvery metal that didn't corrode or fall apart. In fact, most of the buildings had been prefabricated with the platform, and were an extension of its sheetlike hull. The buildings were spacious, well constructed, and sleek.

And still there were slums. It didn't matter that Evensong's poor lived in homes that many wealthy Earthsiders couldn't afford. By comparison, they were still poor. Somehow their dwellings reflected that. There was a sense of despair to the area. Shiny, modern buildings were hung with ragged drapes and drying clothing. Aircars were rare, pedestrians common.

"Over here, Captain," one of his men said, motioning toward a building. It was long and squat—though like all buildings on the platform, it had other structures built on top of it. The officer, a new kid named Ken Harris, led Orson inside, and Orson was immediately struck by a pungent smoky scent. The building was a burning station, where organic materials were recycled.

Officers moved about in the darkened room. Like most buildings on Evensong, this one was poorly lit. Evensong's distance from the sun kept it in a perpetual state of twilight, and the platform's inhabitants had grown accustomed to having less light. Many of them kept the lights dim even indoors. The tendency had bothered Orson at first, but he rarely noticed it anymore.

Several officers saluted, and Orson waved them down with a perfunctory gesture. "What've we got here?"

"Come and look, sir," Harris said, weaving through some equipment toward the back of the room.

Orson followed; eventually they stopped beside a massive cylindrical burner. Its metallic face was dark and flat. One of the bottom reservoir doors was open, revealing the dust below. Mixed with the dirt and ash was a large section of carapace, its shell stained black from the heat.

Orson swore quietly, kneeling beside the carapace. He poked at the shell with a stirring rod. "This is our missing ambassador?"

"That is what we assume, sir," Harris said.

Great, Orson thought with a sigh. The varvax had been asking about their ambassador since its disappearance two weeks before.

"What do we know?" Orson asked.

"Not much," Harris said. "These burners are only emptied once a month. The carapace has been in there for some time—there's almost nothing left. Any longer, and we wouldn't have found it."

That might have been preferable, Orson thought. "What did the sensor net record?"

"Nothing," Harris said.

"Does the media know about this?" Orson asked hopefully.

"I'm afraid so, sir," Harris said. "The worker who found the body leaked the information."

Orson sighed again. "All right, then, let's . . ."

He trailed off. A figure was silhouetted in the building's open door—a figure not wearing a police uniform. Orson cursed softly, standing. The officers outside were supposed to keep the press out.

"I'm sorry," Orson said, walking toward the intruder, "but this area is restricted. You can't . . ."

The man ignored him. He was tall and thin, with a triangular face and short-cropped black hair. He wore a simple black suit, a little outdated but otherwise indistinctive, and a pair of dark glasses. He brushed past Orson with an air of indifference.

Orson reached out to grab the insolent stranger, but froze. There was a gleaming pin on the man's lapel—a small silver bell.

What! Orson thought with amazement. *When did a PC operative get here? How did he know?* The questions didn't really matter—regardless of their answers, one thing was certain. Orson's jurisdiction had come to an end.

The Phone Company had arrived.

—

It had finally happened a hundred and forty years before, in the year 2071. Oddly enough, the ones who had made first contact had been an outdated, nearly bankrupt phone company.

Northern Bell Incorporated had been on the losing side of technological progress. While its competitors had been researching and incorporating holovid technology, Northern Bell had tried something a little more daring: cybernetic-based telepathic linking.

Cyto, as it was dubbed, had turned out to be a failure. Holovid technology was not only cheaper and more stable, it also worked. Cyto had not worked—at least not as Northern Bell had hoped. In the last days before its impending bankruptcy, the company had finally managed to get a few squeaks of sound through the system. Those squeaks, while unimpressive to their human monitors, were also inadvertently projected through space to a group of beings known as the tenasi. The tenasi reply had been the first interspecies contact Earth had ever known.

Second contact had been made by the United Governments military when they accidentally shot down a tenasi ambassadorial vessel. But that, of course, was an entirely different story.

"He's been missing for two weeks?" Jason asked, kneeling beside the burned carapace. It was silent in his mind—a foreboding indication of its black color.

"Yes, sir," the officer said.

"Yup," Lanna said at almost the same time.

"Why wasn't I informed of this?" Jason asked.

The police officer looked confused for a moment before realizing that Jason wasn't talking to him. Earlinks were a common, if confusing, part of modern life.

"I assumed you knew, old man," Lanna said. "You know, Jason, for an all-knowing spy type, you're remarkably uninformed."

Jason grunted. She was right—he should have looked into local news stories during his trip. It was too late now.

The officer regarded Jason with hard eyes. Jason could read the man's emotions easily. Not through the use of his cytonic senses—it was a common misconception that psionics were telepathic. No, Jason could read the man's emotions because he was accustomed to dealing with local law enforcement. The officer would be annoyed at Jason for interfering with his investigation. But at the same time, the officer would be relieved. Locals always felt overwhelmed when it came to dealing with other species. Aliens were to be handled by the Phone Company. The PC had made first contact; the PC had negotiated Earth out of danger following the tenasi incident. The PC had brought FTL communication to humankind.

So the officer watched Jason—jealous, but thankful. Jason could hear other officers muttering at the edges of the room, angry at his interference. *Dirty PC. Why is he here? Why does he look at us like that? Can't you see? What's that in front of your face? Is it my fist? Can you see it if I hit you? Maybe that will—*

"Jason?" Lanna's voice sounded in his ear.

Jason snapped to, muscles twitching, memories fading. He still knelt beside the burner. The officer still stood staring at him, the room still smelled overpoweringly of smoke, and he could still hear the reporters arguing with officers outside.

"I'm all right," Jason whispered.

He stood, dusting off his suit, listening to the reporters. They, like the policemen, would probably assume that Jason had come to Evensong to investigate the ambassador's death. It didn't matter that Jason's shuttle had left for Evensong over a month before the murder. An alien had died, and a PC operative had arrived. That would be enough for them.

"I shouldn't have come to the scene," he mumbled.

"What else would you have done?" Lanna asked. "This is our duty, after all."

"Not mine," Jason said. "I'm here to retrieve a missing scientist, not investigate a murder." Then, speaking louder, he continued, "I'm certain the local law enforcement is competent. Let them investigate—the PC can handle diplomatic negotiations."

The officer looked surprised. But, apparently uncertain what else to do, he saluted Jason. Jason nodded, then turned to leave.

"Not that the 'diplomatic negotiations' will be too hard," Lanna noted. "The varvax are so insanely docile that they'll probably apologize for inconveniencing one of our murderers."

"They're all like that," Jason said, stepping out onto the building's front steps. "That's the big problem, isn't it?"

There was a moment of shocked silence as the reporters realized who he was. They stood in a ring around several beleaguered police, and the commotion was attracting a crowd of curious onlookers. Then the reporters exploded with questions. Jason ignored them, pushing his way through the crowd. He had his head bowed, his hand raised to forestall questions. However, in his mind he was looking.

He scanned the crowd, pushing through the humming and pulsing colors. He looked over each face, comparing them all to the ones in his memory. A smile crept to his lips as he found what he was looking for. The media let him leave—they were used to the PC ignoring their questions. Behind him, Jason could hear their on-the-spot vidcasts. They had all the facts wrong, of course. There was fear in their voices—a fear of what they didn't understand, a fear of the retribution that might come. In their world, retribution was assumed. In their world, you hurt that which was weaker than you.

Jason continued to walk with his head bowed. Behind him, a man broke free from the group of onlookers and wandered in Jason's direction, obviously trying to look casual.

"I wish there were more flowers," Jason said.

A second later, a click sounded in his ear. Then Lanna sighed. "What took you so long?" she demanded. "I've been waiting for you to do that ever since you got off the shuttle. I feel creepy knowing someone's hacking our line."

Jason continued to stroll forward. His shadow followed—the man moved with the skill of one who had been well trained, but he made the mistakes of one who was inexperienced. There was no change to his step—he probably hadn't noticed the switchover. At that moment, he would be listening to a fabricated conversation between Lanna and Jason. For some reason, Jason suspected he didn't want to know what kind of silly things Lanna's replicated version of his voice was saying.

"Is he buying it?" Lanna asked.

"I think so," Jason said, walking away from the slums. "He's still following."

"Who do you think he's with?"

"I'm not sure yet." Jason turned, taking the steps down into an airtrain station. The man followed.

"If you caught him this quickly, he must not be very good."

"He's young," Jason said. "He knows what he's supposed to do, but he doesn't know how to do it."

"A reporter," Lanna guessed.

"No," Jason said. "He's too well equipped. Remember, he managed to hack into a secure FTL comm."

"One of the corporations?"

"Maybe," Jason said, strolling into an underground café. It smelled of dirt, mold, and coffee. His follower waited for a few moments outside, then walked in and took a table a discreet distance from Jason.

Jason ordered a cup of coffee.

"We haven't discussed how he managed to scan your disk," Lanna noted. "You're losing your edge, old man."

"I'm not old," Jason mumbled as the waitress brought his coffee. It smelled of cream, though he had ordered it black. He turned his ineffectual eyes on a newspaper someone else had left on the table, but his mind studied his follower. The man was indeed young—in his early twenties. He wore softly humming greys and browns.

"So," Lanna said, "do you want to try and get me a visual so I can look him up?"

Jason paused. "No," he finally said, taking a sip of his coffee. It did have far too much cream in it—probably an attempt to obscure its poor flavor.

"Well, what are you going to do?"

"Be patient."

—

Coln Abrams sipped his coffee—it didn't have enough cream. He had to keep telling himself not to look at his target. Coln didn't actually need to watch the man to monitor the conversation, he just had to stay within range.

What are you doing here, Write? Coln wondered with frustration. *How did you know the ambassador would be killed? What does all of this have to do with your plans?*

Coln shook his head. Jason Write, head operative for Northern Bell Phone Company, one of the most enigmatic people in the solar system. What was he doing on Evensong? The United Intelligence Bureau knew a lot about the man, but for every known fact there seemed to be two more missing.

Take, for instance, the Tenasi Agreement. Coln had read the document itself a hundred times, and had watched the holovids, commentaries, and old newscasts relating to the tenasi incident over and over. The United Governments military had accidentally shot down a tenasi diplomatic vessel—thereby initiating a rather embarrassing first contact. Earth had been thrown into a chaos of confusion and worry. Were they being invaded? Would they be invaded now that they had made such a horrible mistake?

Then the PC had stepped in. Somehow—using means they had yet to explain—they had contacted the tenasi. The PC had brought peace to Earth. But in exchange, the company had demanded a steep price. From that moment on, the PC had become completely autonomous—untaxable, unquestionable, and completely above the law. In addition, the PC had secured sole rights to the aliens' FTL communications technology. And, with those two concessions, the PC had become the most powerful, most arrogant force in the system.

Coln gripped his mug tightly, barely noticing as the waitress brought his sandwich. He was still listening to the conversation between Write and his Base Support Operative—they were discussing what color roses they liked best.

Coln had never trusted the PC—and he hated things he couldn't trust. The PC grew fat off its treaties—it held exclusive contracts with all twelve alien races humankind had met. The alien races all refused to deal with Earth unless they went through the PC first. The Phone Company kept humankind locked in space, refusing to share FTL travel technology. It claimed that the aliens had yet to give it to them. Coln suspected the truth. The aliens had FTL travel, that was certain. The PC was simply keeping it from humankind, and that infuriated Coln. He wanted to find—

Coln froze. The conversation in his ear had stopped midsentence. For a panicked moment, Coln feared that Write had slipped out of the restaurant and out of range.

Coln's eyes darted across the room. He was relieved to find Write sitting in his booth, sipping quietly at his coffee. It had simply been a lull in the conversation.

"What do you think he'll do when he realizes his cover is blown?" the Base Support Operative, Lanna, said in Coln's ear.

Coln paused.

"I don't know." Jason Write's voice was firm. Arrogant. Coln could see Write's lips moving as he spoke. "I suspect he will be surprised. He's young—he assumes he's better than he really is."

Write looked up, his sunglassed eyes looking directly at Coln's face. Horror rose in Coln's chest, an emotion quickly followed by shame. He'd been discovered.

"Come here, boy," Write ordered in Coln's ear.

Coln shot a look at the door. He could probably get away—

"If you leave," Write said, "then you will never discover why I am on Evensong." His voice was sharp and businesslike.

Coln regarded the man indecisively. What should he do? Why hadn't any of his classes covered situations like this one? When an agent was discovered, he was supposed to pull out. But what if his target seemed willing to talk to him?

Slowly, Coln rose and crossed the café's dirty floor. Write's sunglasses watched him quietly. Coln stood for a moment beside Write's table, then sat stiffly.

Don't reveal anything, Coln warned himself. *Don't let him know that you're with the—*

"You are young for a UIB agent," Write said.

Inwardly, Coln sighed. *He already knows. What have I gotten myself—and the Bureau—into?*

"I wonder," Write said, taking a sip of his coffee. "Is the Bureau growing more confident in its young agents, or am I simply slipping in priority?"

He doesn't know! Coln realized with surprise. *He thinks I'm here officially.*

"Neither," Coln said, thinking quickly. "We weren't ready for you to leave. I was the only field agent who was unassigned at the time. It was simply poor luck."

Write nodded to himself.

He accepted it!

"I must say," Write said, setting down his mug, "I am growing tired of the UIB. Every time I think that you people are going to leave me alone, I find myself being followed again."

"If the PC weren't so untrustworthy," Coln said, "its operatives wouldn't have to worry about being followed."

"If the Bureau weren't so poor at investigation," Write said, "it would have realized by now that the PC is the only company that the Bureau *can* trust."

Coln flushed. "Are you going to say something useful, or are you just going to insult me?"

"A clever man would realize that my insults contain the most useful information you'll likely receive," Write said.

Coln snorted, rising from the chair. Write had just invited him over to gloat, and Coln had ruined his own career for nothing. He had been so certain that he could tail Write, that he could figure out what the man was doing, discover the truth behind the Tenasi Agreement . . .

"You may accompany me," Write said, finishing his coffee.

Coln paused midstep. "What?"

Write set down his mug. "You want to know what I'm doing? Well, you may come with me. Maybe this will finally alleviate the UIB's foolish suspicions. I'm tired of being followed."

"Jason," Lanna said in Coln's ear. "Are you certain—"

"No," Write said. "I'm not. However, I don't have time to deal with the UIB right now. This is a simple mission—the boy may come with me if he wishes."

Coln stood, dumbfounded. He couldn't decide what to do. Could he really trust a PC operative? No, he couldn't. But what if he learned something important? "I—"

"Hush," Write said suddenly, holding up a hand.

Coln frowned. Write wasn't looking at him, however. He was staring straight ahead, his face confused.

Now what? Coln wondered.

———

Something was wrong. Jason ran his mind around the room, trying to Sense what was bothering him. The café had about a dozen other occupants, all eating quietly. Most of them were in workers' clothing—flannels and denim that pulsed an irregular symphony in Jason's mind. He studied their faces, and recognized none of them. What was bothering him?

A line of bullets blasted through the window just beside Jason. They came far too fast for his body to react or dodge, moving with the incredible speed of modern weaponry.

As fast as the bullets were, however, Jason's mind was faster. He whipped out a dozen invisible mindblades that slashed through the air. The force of his attack slapped the bullets backward and sliced each one in two. There was a series of audible clicks as the pieces bounced back off the window, then fell to the café floor. All was silent.

The UIB kid plopped into his seat, his face horrified as he stared at the window and its holes.

"Jason?" Lanna said urgently. "Jason, what happened?"

Jason Sensed out the window, but the sniper was already gone. "I don't know."

"Someone shot at you?" Lanna asked with concern.

Jason regarded the bullet holes—they ran in a small circle in the window just beside the UIB kid's head. "No," he said. "They tried to kill the kid."

The café's patrons were running about in fear, some calling out, others hiding beneath benches. The UIB kid was looking down at himself with surprise, as if he couldn't believe that he was still alive. "They all missed," the boy whispered with amazement.

Jason frowned. Why would someone try to kill a UIB agent? Why not focus on Jason? The PC was a far more dangerous threat.

"How did you let him sneak up on you like that?" Lanna asked.

"I wasn't expecting to be shot at. This was supposed to be a simple assignment." Then, turning to the kid, he nodded. "Let's go."

The kid looked up with surprise. "Someone tried to kill me! Why?"

"I'm not certain," Jason said. He ran his Sense over the room one last time, memorizing faces. As he did so, he noticed something. While most of the people were hiding or quivering in fear, one didn't seem to be concerned at all. A solitary form sat quietly at the back of the café. He was a nondescript man with a long nose and a firm body. He watched Jason with interested eyes—eyes that seemed slightly unfocused. Almost as if . . .

Impossible! Jason thought. Then, without bothering to see if the UIB kid followed him, he left the café.

———

"You must take the apologies of us," Sonn urged. The varvax foreign minister's words were delivered by a translation program, of course—the varvax language consisted of clicks and snaps accompanied by hand gestures. The figure on the holovid screen was large and boxy, and its skin shone with quartz and granite. That was only the exoskeleton—the varvax were actually small creatures that floated in a nutrient bath sealed within their inorganic shells.

"Sonn," Jason pointed out, sitting back in his chair, "your people were the victims here. Your ambassador was murdered."

Sonn waved a clawlike hand; a symbol of denial. "You must understand that he knew the risks of living in an undeveloped civilization. Creatures of lesser intelligence cannot be held responsible for their acts of barbarity. You have not yet learned a better way."

Jason smiled to himself. Comments like that one earned the varvax, and most other alien races, humankind's disgust. It didn't matter that the comments were true—in fact, the truth of such statements only enraged humankind more.

"We will return what is left of the body as soon as possible, Minister Sonn," Jason promised.

"Thank you, Jason of the Phone Company. You must tell to me—how go your efforts at civilization? Will your people soon raise themselves to Primary Intelligence?"

"It will take some time yet, Minister Sonn," Jason said.

"You are an interesting people, Jason of the Phone Company," Sonn said, his claws held before him in a gesture of supplication.

"You may speak on."

"You have such disparity among what you are," Sonn said. "Some of Primary Intelligence, some of Tertiary—or even Quaternary—Intelligence. Such disparity. You must tell to me: Are your people still convinced of the power of technology?"

Jason shrugged an exaggerated shrug—the varvax liked to watch and interpret human gestures. "Humankind believes in technology, Minister Sonn. It will be very difficult for them to accept another way."

"Of course, Jason of the Phone Company. We will speak to each other again."

"We will speak again," Jason said, shutting off the holovid. He sat for a moment, Sensing the room around him. He couldn't just relax completely anymore—he missed that. If he let his concentration lapse, the darkness would come upon him.

"They certainly are confident, aren't they?" Lanna asked in his ear.

"They have reason to be," Jason replied. "It has always happened as they expect. A race discovers FTL cytonic transmission at the same time it achieves a peaceful civilization."

"If only they weren't so cursed ingenuous," Lanna said. "A part of me wishes I had three varvax diplomats, a card table, and a host of 'useless' technologies I could cheat out of them."

"That's the problem," Jason said. "There's a little of that in all of us."

"What if they're wrong, Jason?" Lanna asked. "What if we do get FTL travel before we're 'civilized'?"

Jason didn't reply—he didn't know the answer.

"I looked up the kid for you," Lanna offered.

"Go on," Jason said, rising and gathering his things. The attack the day before still had him worried. Was it an attempt to scare Jason off? From what?

"The day you left, a young UIB agent named Coln Abrams disappeared from the Bureau's training facilities on Jupiter Fourteen," Lanna said. "He stole some sophisticated monitoring equipment. The UIB put out several warrants for him, but they aren't looking this far—apparently they didn't expect him to make it all the way to Evensong."

"It isn't exactly a prime vacation spot," Jason noted, strolling over to the window and trying to imagine what the city would look like to normal eyes. It would be dark, he decided—most of it didn't vibrate very much to him. Dark and tall, like a city constructed entirely of alleyways. Lights were sparse and insufficient, and the air smelled musty. It always seemed to be a few degrees below standard temperature too—as if the vacuum of space were closer, more ominous, than it really was.

"So," Lanna said, "we've got a wanted felon. Can we turn him in?"

"No," Jason said, backing away from the window. He put on his suit coat and slid on his dark glasses.

"Come on, let's turn him in," Lanna said. "In fact, it was probably the UIB who tried to have him killed yesterday."

"They don't work that way," Jason said, walking to the door. "Do you have my permits secured?"

"Yes," Lanna said.

"Good. Turn the kid back on, and let's get going."

—

The image was blurred and poorly exposed. Unfortunately, it was the best he had. Coln walked around the large holoimage, studying it as he had hundreds of times before. The answer was before him; he could feel it. The image held a secret. Yet Coln, like thousands of others, was unable to determine just what that secret might be.

The image had been taken by the only spy to infiltrate the PC's central headquarters. It was a picture of a simple white room with an apparatus lining the back wall. That apparatus, whatever it was, powered all of humankind's FTL communications.

It was the greatest secret of the modern age. Humankind had been trying for nearly two centuries to break the PC's monopoly on FTL communication. Unfortunately, no amount of research had been able to duplicate the PC's strange technology—and until someone did, humankind would be indebted to a tyrant.

It has to be here! Coln thought, staring at the unyielding image. He walked around it to look at several angles. *If only it weren't so blurry.*

He looked closely at the holoimage. A security guard sat against the right side of the room, staring in the photographer's direction. There seemed to be several cylindrical outcroppings on the far wall—relays of some kind? One was larger than the others, and dark in color. Was it the answer?

Coln sighed. Men far more technologically savvy than he had tried to dissect the image, but none had been able to draw any decisive conclusions. The picture was just too fuzzy to be of much use.

He had spent the entire morning trying to decide why someone would try to kill him. He had only been able to come to one decision—that for some reason, Write had ordered him assassinated. The PC agent had been the one who had coerced Coln over to sit beside him, in the place where the assassin had shot. The PC was behind it somehow.

Except the assassin missed, Coln thought. *He must have done so on purpose. Write wanted to scare me off. He acted like he didn't care if I followed him, then he tried to frighten me away.*

Coln nodded. It made sense, in a twisted PC sort of way. And if Write didn't want him along, then Coln had to make certain he stayed.

"Wake up, kid," Lanna's voice crackled suddenly in his ear.

"I'm awake," Coln said, bristling at the reference to his age—twenty-three was hardly young enough to earn him the title of "kid." At least the other two had stopped feeding him dummy conversations—when they didn't want him to listen, they simply shut him out completely.

"The big guy's leaving," Lanna said in her pert voice. Coln was beginning to wonder why Write put up with her. "He says you can go with him, but only if you can keep up."

Coln cursed, throwing on his jacket.

"Oh, and Coln," Lanna said, "try not to steal anything from him. Jason's kind of attached to his equipment."

Coln flushed. How much did they know?

He dashed out into the hallway just in time to see Write's black-suited form turn a corner. Coln padded across the floor, catching up to the operative. Write barely acknowledged him. They walked in silence to the end of the hallway, then took the private lift down to the lobby. The lush carpets and rich furnishings hinted that they were far indeed from the previous day's slums.

"So, what is it?" Coln asked as they stepped out onto the silvery telanium street. The street, as always, was dimly lit—though hundreds of lights shone from windows and signs. Evensong was dark, but it did not sleep.

"What is what?" Write asked as an aircab—obviously chartered—pulled up in front of the hotel.

"What is your purpose here, Write?" Coln asked, climbing into the back of the car beside the operative. "I assume you knew something about the ambassador's death?"

"You assume wrong," Write said as the aircab began to move. "The ambassador's murder was a coincidence."

Coln raised an eyebrow in skepticism.

"Believe me or not, I don't really care."

"Then why are you here?" Coln asked.

Write sighed. "Tell him."

"It happened just under two months ago, kid," Lanna said. "A scientist named Denise Carlson disappeared from Evensong's PC research facility."

Coln frowned at the comment, searching through his memory. He paid attention to anything the Bureau learned about the PC. He recalled something about the scientist's disappearance, but it hadn't seemed very important.

"But," Coln said, "our reports said she was nothing more than a lab assistant. The PC home office barely paid any mind to her disappearance—it said that she had been the victim of a common street mugging."

"Well, at least someone pays attention to current events," Lanna said.

Write snorted. "He might pay attention, but he should have realized that any story we downplay is far more important than it seems."

Coln blushed. "So you came to find this Denise Carlson?"

"Wrong," Lanna said. "That's why he left, but that's not the goal anymore. While Jason was in transit, we located Miss Carlson. Just under two weeks ago a woman fitting her description was picked up by the authorities. She was diagnosed with severe mental problems, and was checked into a local treatment ward."

"So . . ." Coln said.

"So I'm here to retrieve her," Write said. "Nothing more. We're going to bring her back to Jupiter Fourteen so she can receive proper treatment. My role is that of a simple courier." Write smiled slightly, turning his black glasses toward Coln. "That is why I am willing to let you come with me. You sacrificed your career so you could watch me escort a mental patient."

———

Jason strode into the hospital, the depressed Coln tagging along behind. The kid kept asking questions, convinced that Jason's actions had some greater purpose in the PC's "master plans." Jason was beginning to regret bringing him along—the last thing he needed was another person jabbering at him.

The nurse at the front desk looked up with surprise when he entered, her eyes flicking toward his silver lapel pin.

"Mr. Flippenday?" she asked.

He paused only briefly at the horrid name. "I am. Show me to the patient."

The nurse nodded, leaving the desk to another attendant and waving for Jason to follow. She wore white—a roaring, blatant color. To others, white was neutral, but to Jason it was by far the most garish choice. Better the subtle hum of grey. The walls were white as well, and the hallways smelled of cleaning fluids.

Why do they do that? Jason wondered, shaking his head slightly. *Do they think that it will make their patients feel at home? Lifeless sterility and monochrome white? Perhaps all these people need to regain their sanity is a little bit of color.*

The nurse led them to a simple room with a locked door—ostensibly for the patient's safety.

"I'm glad you finally decided to come," the nurse said, a slightly chiding tone in her voice. "We contacted the PC weeks ago, and the woman's just been waiting here all this time. With no relatives on the platform, one would think that you people . . ."

She trailed off as Jason turned toward her. After losing his eyesight, he had eventually learned that a look of discontent could be accomplished as much with one's bearing as with one's eyes. As he stared sightlessly at the nurse, her resolve weakened, and the punitive tone left her voice.

"That is enough," Jason said simply.

"Yes, sir," the nurse mumbled, shooting him a spiteful look as she unlocked the door.

Jason walked into the small unadorned room. Denise sat beside a desk—the room's only furniture other than a bed and a dresser. She regarded Jason with wide eyes. She looked much as in his holovid—she was thin, her short dark hair in curls, and she wore a simple skirt and blouse.

Jason had met her several times before—Denise had shown an affinity for cyto, and had been midway through her training. She had once been a straight-forward and calculating woman. Now she looked like a young squirrel that hadn't yet learned to fear predators.

"They said you would come," she whispered, the words awkward in her mouth. "Do you know who I am?"

Jason looked toward the nurse.

"She's still amnesiac," the nurse said. "Though we can't determine any physical reason for it. She also has some sort of muscular problem—she has trouble keeping her balance and controlling her limbs."

Denise demonstrated such, rising slowly to her feet. She wobbled slightly as she walked forward, but she managed to remain upright.

"She's made amazing progress," the nurse said. "She can walk now if she doesn't move too quickly."

"Denise, you're coming with me," Jason said. "Abrams, help her walk."

The kid looked up with surprise. Jason didn't give him time to complain—instead, Jason turned and strode from the room. Abrams cursed quietly, but did as he was ordered, giving the confused Denise a helpful arm as they walked from the hospital.

They were nearly out when Jason noticed something. He never would have seen it without his Sense—the man hid behind a door, barely peeking out. The Sense was far more discerning than normal eyes, however, and Jason recognized the face even through the door's small slit. It was one of the men from the café—not the strange man who had sat at the booth, but one of the ordinary workers.

So, they've been watching her, Jason thought as he left the building, the kid and Denise following. *Did they expect her to reveal something, or did they know that I would come for her?*

—

"I do not know what this means," Denise said, staring at the menu with her wide eyes. She looked up, confused.

"You can't read?" Jason asked.

"No," Denise replied.

"Here, let me help," Abrams offered, reading down the list of choices.

Jason sat back, allowing himself a slight smile. The kid was showing an almost chivalrous devotion to the amnesiac woman. She was passably attractive, in a sickeningly innocent sort of way. Abrams was just betraying the inherent predisposition of a young human male; he had seen a woman in need and was trying to help her.

Denise raised her hand awkwardly in an odd gesture as Coln read. "I still do not know what it means."

"None of the words sound familiar?" Jason asked, leaning forward with interest. "No."

"But you can speak," Jason mused. "What do you remember?"

"Nothing," Denise said. "I don't remember anything, Mr. Flippenday."

Jason cringed. "Call me Jason," he mumbled as Abrams asked the girl what kind of food she liked. She, of course, didn't know.

She should have remembered more. Most amnesiacs remembered something—if only fragments. "What do you think?" Jason whispered.

"It's odd," Lanna said. "She's changed, old man. Whatever they did to her, it was pretty thorough."

"Agreed."

Abrams ordered for the girl and himself—choosing, Jason noticed, two of the most expensive items on the menu. He knew that Jason would be paying. At least the kid had style.

As he sat, Jason thought back to the strange man in the café. The man couldn't have access to cyto—in a hundred and fifty years, no one had discovered the ability besides the PC. But what if someone had? What if they had learned about Denise, and had captured her to try and learn what she knew? What had they done to her to get at her knowledge?

His pondering led him nowhere. Eventually the food came, and Jason began to eat. He preferred simple meals with little mess, so he had ordered a tossed pasta dish with a very light sauce. He ate quietly, thoughtful as he watched a man a short distance away haggle over his bill with the waiter.

He shouldn't have been worried about the ambassador's death. The police would probably find that the murder had been committed by some xenophobic activist group. They were prevalent. There were those who hated other species because of assumed superiority, those who hated them because they thought the aliens were too arrogant, and those who hated them simply because they were different. The student exchange program, where human children would be sent to other planets to learn of other species, had been defeated three times in the United Senate.

The ambassador's death probably wasn't related to Denise. Jason should leave—there were too many things that demanded his attention for him to waste time chasing false leads. This trip had taken far too long already.

Jason paused. Denise had turned and was staring at the man who was arguing about his bill. He raised his fist at the waiter, uttering a few epithets, then finally slapped down some money and stalked out of the building.

"Why is he like that?" Denise asked. "How can he be so angry?"

"That's just the way people are sometimes," Coln said uncomfortably. "How is your food?"

Denise turned her eyes down at the steak. She had taken several awkward bites, though Coln had been forced to cut it for her. "It's very . . ."

"Very what?" Jason prompted.

"I do not know," Denise confessed, blushing. "It tastes too . . . strong. One of the flavors is very odd."

Jason frowned. "What flavor?"

"I do not know. It was very strong in the hospital's food too, though I didn't say anything. I didn't want to offend them."

"Describe the taste to me," Jason said. Something was tickling at the back of his mind—a connection he should have made.

"Leave her alone, old man," Abrams said. "She's been through a lot."

Jason raised his eyebrows at the use of "old man." He heard Lanna chuckling through the FTL link. Jason ignored Abrams, turning his head toward Denise. "Describe the taste to me."

"I can't," Denise finally said. "You must understand—I don't know what it is."

Jason reached for the saltshaker, then sprinkled some salt on his hand. "Taste this," he ordered.

She did as asked, then nodded. "That's it. I do not like it very much."

Abrams rolled his eyes. "You've figured out that she doesn't know the word for salty. So? She doesn't know what any of these foods are, or even what her name is."

Jason sat back, ignoring the kid. Then he turned to his food and continued to eat in silence.

—

"I've arranged your return trip to Jupiter," Lanna said. "You'll be leaving on the courier ship *Excel* at 10:30 PM, local time."

Jason nodded to himself. He stood on his balcony, leaning against the railing as he listened to Lanna's voice in his ear.

"The ship is a good one, and always punctual—as you like them," Lanna said. "Your accommodations are for two people."

Jason didn't reply. He Sensed Evensong before him, feeling its massive metallic buildings and numerous walkways. Sometimes he tried to remember what it had been like to see. He tried to imagine colors as images, rather than as cytonic vibrations, but he had trouble. It had been so long, and his eyes hadn't been very good in the first place.

Evensong was in motion around him—aircars flew, people moved on the walkways, lights flickered on and off. It was beautiful, in a way. Beautiful that humankind had expanded this far, that it had found a way to thrive even here, in the middle of space, where the sun was barely more than another star.

"You're not coming back yet, are you?" Lanna asked quietly.

"No."

"So you think the ambassador's death might be related?"

"I'm not certain," Jason said. "Maybe. Something is bothering me, Lanna."

"About the murder?"

"No. About our scientist. Something about Denise is . . . wrong."

"What?"

Jason paused. "I'm not sure. She learned to walk and talk too quickly, for one thing."

Lanna didn't respond immediately. "I'm not certain what to tell you," she finally said.

Jason sighed, shaking his head. He didn't really understand what he meant either. He stood quietly for a moment, watching the flow of people on a walkway a short distance away. Something was wrong—he couldn't decide what it was, but he knew what he feared. For over a century, the PC had maintained a monopoly on cyto. He didn't expect psychic ability to remain confined to the PC—in fact, it was his ultimate goal that it not be. The very thing he was working toward was what he feared.

"Jason," Lanna asked, "have you ever worried that what we're doing is wrong?"

"Every day."

"I mean," Lanna continued, "what if they're right? The tenasi, the varvax, and the rest—they're all much older than humankind is. They know more than we do. Maybe they're right—maybe humankind will become civilized before it obtains FTL travel. Maybe by holding cyto back from them, we're keeping ourselves from progressing as we should."

Jason stood quietly beside the balcony, listening to the sound of children running on the walkway below. *Children, laughing . . .*

"Lanna," he said, "do you know how the Interspecies Monitoring Coalition rates a race's intelligence class?"

"No."

"They look at the race's children," Jason said quietly. "The older ones. Children who have lived just long enough to begin imitating the society they see around them, children who have lost the innocence of youth but haven't yet replaced it with the tact and mores of adulthood. In those children, you can see what a species is really like. From them, the varvax determine whether a species is civilized or barbaric."

"And we failed that test," Lanna said.

"Miserably."

"That's all right," Lanna said. "Every race fails it during the early part of their growth. We'll get there eventually."

"The tenasi had barely begun using steam power when they made their first

FTL jump," Jason said. "The varvax weren't far behind them—they still didn't have computers. Both species traveled to other planets before they learned to send a shuttle into space."

Lanna fell quiet.

"We've been in space for nearly three centuries now," Jason continued. "The varvax say that technology isn't the way—they claim that technological development has boundaries, but that a sentient mind is limitless. But . . . still I worry. I worry that humankind will find a way, somehow. We always have before."

"And so you play watchdog," Lanna said.

Jason stood for a moment. "'The few, so cleans'd, to these abodes repair,'" he finally said in a quiet voice. "'And breathe, in ample fields, the soft Elysian air. Then are they happy, when by length of time, The scurf is worn away of each committed crime; No speck is left of their habitual stains, But the pure ether of the soul remains.'"

"Homer?" Lanna asked.

"Virgil." Above, beyond the buildings, beyond the air, Jason could Sense the specks of starlight in the sky. "Space is Elysium, Lanna. The place where heroes go when they die. The varvax and the others, they've fought and bled, just like we have. They finally overcame all of that—they paid their price and have earned their peace. I want to make certain their paradise remains such."

"By playing God?"

Jason fell silent. He didn't know how to reply, so he didn't. He simply stood, Sensing the paradise above and Evensong below.

—

Coln rifled through the in-room bar, searching for something to drink. He wasn't normally prone to drinking, but normally he wasn't facing the loss of his job and probable imprisonment. Eventually, he poured himself a small glass of scotch and made his way out onto the balcony.

He paused halfway out the door. Jason Write stood leaning on his own balcony a short distance away. The man didn't look over, but Coln still felt as if he were being watched.

Don't let him intimidate you, Coln told himself. He turned away from Write indifferently and leaned against his own balcony railing.

Coming after Write had seemed like such a good idea at first. Coln had been frustrated at the Bureau's lack of information. They knew the PC was hiding technology from them, but they had no clue what it was. They knew Write had something integral to do with the PC's operations, but they weren't sure why.

They wanted to keep trailing him, but they'd made too many promises. The Bureau had been ready to just leave Write alone.

Coln sighed, taking a sip of his drink. He'd picked the wrong mission. Write planned to leave within the day, taking the unfortunate scientist with him. And then Coln would be left by himself, a fugitive and a fool.

———

"That kid is a fool," Lanna said.

"I know," Jason mumbled. "But at least he has passion. And courage."

"Not courage—brashness."

"Call it what you will," Jason said, Sensing the young UIB agent standing a short distance away.

"What's more," Lanna continued, "he may have passion, but that passion is hatred of you. I've been doing some searching. It appears that you were the focus of several of his research projects back when he was an undergraduate. None of his conclusions were flattering, old man. You should read some of these things . . ."

Lanna continued to speak, but Jason's mind drifted. His thoughts kept coming back to Denise. Who had taken her, and what had they done?

She doesn't understand violence, Jason thought. She didn't understand violence, and she hadn't ever tasted salt. She spoke oddly, in a way that was almost familiar. She couldn't walk or use her muscles. It was almost . . .

Jason took in a sharp, surprised breath.

Almost as if she's accustomed to another body.

"What?" Lanna demanded.

"Denise Carlson is dead," he said.

"What! What happened to her?"

Jason was silent for a moment.

"Jason! What happened!"

Jason ignored her, turning and walking back into his room. He strode out into the hallway, then made his way to the room beside his own—not Coln's, but on the other side. He threw open the door, not bothering to knock.

Denise sat up with surprise, but relaxed when she realized who he was. Jason strode past her without saying a word, walking to her room's control panel. He entered a few commands, and the light in the room grew far brighter, the bulbs turning slightly red in color.

"How is that?" he asked, turning to her.

Denise regarded him with confusion. "It's nice. It feels right for some reason."

Jason nodded once. In his mind the light was a virtual roar.

"Please," Denise said, holding her hands forward. "Tell to me what you are doing." Hands forward in the varvax gesture of supplication. He should have seen it sooner.

"Jason, you're freaking me out," Lanna said in his ear.

"This isn't Denise Carlson," Jason said quietly.

"What? Who is it?"

"Its name is Vahnn," Jason explained.

Suddenly, Coln pushed his way into the room. He immediately shielded his eyes from the light—light that imitated a harsh, hot sun, one that required a strong crystalline carapace to provide protection.

"What are you doing, you maniac!" Coln said, pushing past Jason and altering the controls to the room. Then he turned to Denise. "Are you all right?"

"I . . ." Denise said. "Yes, why would I not be?"

Coln turned harsh eyes toward Jason. Then he paused, frowning.

"What?" Jason asked.

"Why are you looking at me like that, Write?" Coln demanded.

"Like what?"

Coln shivered. "Your eyes . . . it's like you're looking past me. Like . . ."

Jason reached unconsciously for his face, feeling for sunglasses that weren't there. He had forgotten he wasn't wearing them. He turned from the room in shame, rushing out into the hallway.

I mustn't let him see—mustn't let him know. He'll mock me. He'll laugh . . .

Coln stayed behind, watching with confusion as he knelt beside the creature that had the body of a woman and the mind of an alien.

—

"It's not possible," Lanna said.

"They said that about psionics years ago," Jason said, striding down a walkway outside the hotel.

"But it's just so . . ."

"So what?"

Lanna sighed in frustration. "All right, let's assume you're correct. Who would do such a thing? Why switch someone's mind for an alien's? What good would it do them?"

"The varvax are the most developed cytonics in the galaxy," Jason said, speaking quietly as he passed people on Evensong's dark streets.

"So?"

"So," Jason said, "what could you learn if you could spend a few years in a varvax's head? What if you could get into a varvax body somehow and infiltrate their society? Someone tried to get hold of a varvax host—but something went wrong. The body they stole was killed, or perhaps the transfer went awry. They disposed of the varvax body afterward and left Denise wandering the streets."

"But why Denise?"

Jason paused. "I don't know. Maybe she was one of them—a spy of some sort. When a better opportunity came along, she took it."

"That's weak reasoning, old man."

"I know," Jason admitted. "But I can't think of anything else right now. All I know is that the woman back in my rooms is not human. She acts like a varvax, thinks like a varvax, and gestures like a varvax."

"She speaks English," Lanna pointed out.

"Many varvax study English," Jason said. "Or at least understand it. They find spoken languages interesting. Besides, maybe her body retained a residual understanding of speech and motion."

"Maybe," Lanna said, sounding unconvinced. "Where are you going?"

"You'll see." Jason continued on his way for a short distance until he came to the mental hospital. He strode in, and the same nurse sat behind the desk. She raised an eyebrow at him, confused and a little disapproving.

Jason ignored her, striding into the facility itself.

"Sir!" she called. "You can't go in there! Sir, you don't have . . ." Her voice trailed off, but soon she began calling for security.

"The nurse?" Lanna said, listening. "You're back at the hospital? So, you've finally admitted that you're insane and decided to commit yourself?"

Orderlies, nurses, and even some patients began to look into the hallway. *He'd better be here,* Jason thought. Just after the thought occurred to him, he Sensed a familiar face peeking out of one of the rooms.

"Alert the Evensong Police Department, Lanna," Jason said. "They're about to get a report of a madman attacking one of the orderlies in this hospital. Please tell them to ignore it."

"Jason, you are a very strange man."

Jason smiled, then spun and burst into the room. Several orderlies jumped back in surprise at his entrance—the buzzing white room was some kind of employee lounge. The orderly, the one Jason had seen at the café, immediately turned to run. Jason jumped forward and snatched the man with one hand, then spun him around.

The man struggled, but a knee to the groin stopped that. Jason pulled off his glasses, then grabbed the man's head with both hands and turned it toward him.

"Who sent you?" Jason asked, staring at the man with his sightless eyes.

The man stared back defiantly.

"Ah, I see," Jason said, holding the man's head in both of his hands. "Yes, I can read your thoughts easily. Very interesting. Ah, and yes. So they switched minds, did they? I didn't know that was possible. Thank you, you've been very informative."

Jason released the surprised man's head.

Lanna snorted in his ear. "Jason, unless you've been hiding some strange powers for a very long time, that was the biggest load of lies I've ever heard."

"Yes," Jason said, replacing his glasses and striding out of the room. "But they don't know that."

"What's the point?" Lanna asked.

"Be patient," Jason chided, holding up his hands as security guards entered the hallway. "I was just leaving," he said, then pushed past them and left the hospital.

—

Back at the hotel, Jason gathered Denise and Coln in his room. One regarded him with customary wide-eyed confusion, the other with equally customary hostility. Jason removed his pin and handed it to Coln.

"There is a ship chartered for Jupiter Fourteen," Jason said. "Be on it when it leaves, and take Denise with you. Go to the PC office, and they will protect you from the Bureau."

"What about you, Write?" Coln asked suspiciously.

"If I'm correct, I should be going somewhere else in a bit. You should get moving—the ship leaves in less than an hour."

Coln frowned. Jason could sense the apprehension in his face. He didn't want to accept the PC's help, but he also didn't want to face the Bureau's justice. Hopefully, he would see to Denise's safety.

After a short internal debate, Coln nodded and stood. "I'll do it, Write. But first answer one question for me."

"What?"

"Do you have what everyone says you do?"

Jason frowned. "Have what?"

"FTL engines," Coln said. "Does the PC have the technology to create them or not? Have you been withholding the secret of FTL travel from the rest of humankind?"

Jason paused. "You're asking the wrong question," he finally said.

Coln's expression darkened. "I knew you wouldn't answer," he said, turning toward Denise's chair. "Come on, Denise."

She didn't move. She slumped in her chair, eyes closed.

"Denise!" Coln said urgently, kneeling beside her. She appeared to be breathing, but . . .

Jason began to feel lightheaded, and he noticed a faint scent in the air. He cursed quietly, turning to dash across the room. He stumbled halfway to the door, losing his balance. He barely even felt himself hit the ground.

They work fast. Must have already been prepared to gas us . . .

———

Jason awoke to blackness. Pure, horrifying blackness. There was no sight, no Sense, no feelings at all. The darkness had returned.

Jason began to shake. *No! It can't be! Where is my Sense!* He curled up, barely feeling the cold metallic floor beneath him. The blackness swallowed him—it was more than just darkness, it was a nothingness. A lack of sensation. It was the one true terror in Jason's life. And it had returned.

He whimpered despite himself, memories flooding in.

It had started with his night vision, as visual diseases often did. He remembered the nights spent in bed as a child, the darkness seeming to grow more and more oppressive. And then it had started to come during the day. First his peripheral vision—it had been like the darkness was following him, enveloping him. Each morning when he awoke, it had seemed that the darkness was closer. It had crouched like a beast in the corner of his vision.

Terror. The doctors had been able to do nothing. Jason had been forced to try and live his life as normal, the darkness seeming to grow closer every moment. He had lived in perpetual fear of what must come.

And then there had been the children. The other children, who hadn't understood. He had tried to go on as usual, tried to live his life as if nothing were wrong. He should have admitted it to them. As it was, they saw only a stumbling fool. They had laughed. Oh, how they had laughed.

Jason screamed, as if yelling could push back the darkness. Where was his Sense? What was wrong? He flailed in the darkness, his fingers brushing a wall. He pulled back into a corner, frightened and confused.

"How did you do it?" a voice asked from above.

Jason looked up, but didn't see, or Sense, anything.

"Tell me, Mr. Write," the voice demanded. "Can you read minds? This is impossible of cyto—even the varvax cannot penetrate an individual's thoughts. How did you do it?"

Jason didn't respond. The darkness. The blackness.

I did this on purpose, a piece of Jason's mind thought. *I baited them. I wanted to get their attention, so they would bring me to them. They did. This is what I wanted.*

But . . . the darkness.

"How!" Jason croaked. "How have you taken it away?"

"Answer my questions, Mr. Write," the voice said, "and I will return your Sense. How did you read that man's mind?"

Jason shuddered, pulling back against the cold telanium. The man's voice was harsh and guttural. He spoke oddly—with an accent of some sort, but not one that Jason recognized.

It's not permanent, Jason told himself. *The darkness will go away. Just like it did when you developed cyto.*

"I am not a patient man, Mr. Write," the voice warned. "Speak, and I will let your companions live."

Coln, Denise. They were in the room with me.

Jason didn't answer. He sat, breathing deeply, struggling to remain sane. Ever since he had developed cyto, he had never been in darkness. His Sense worked even when there was no light.

"Lanna?" Jason whispered, feeling the darkness advance on him. "Lanna!"

"The link to your home base has been cut, Mr. Write," the voice said.

Jason whimpered. The darkness seemed to be growing closer—closer to devouring his mind.

"As you wish, Mr. Write," the voice said. "I will give you three minutes. If you don't have an answer for me by then, the woman dies."

A click, then silence. It seemed worse without the voice—suddenly Jason wished he had kept the man talking. He wished he had told the voice the truth, that he couldn't read minds. Anything to keep someone else there.

Now he had no one.

I can't do this! Jason thought. *Anything but this. I lived this horror once. I can't do it again!*

He tried to push out with mindblades, but nothing happened.

Be calm, Jason. Control yourself. The varvax said something about this. Sonn had said it once. He had been reserved and uncomfortable—odd for a varvax. Jason had asked if there was a way to suppress cytonic ability. Sonn had eventually admitted there was, but had told Jason he wouldn't need it. Not yet.

The darkness . . .

No! Stay focused. You don't have time for fear. There was probably a technological aspect to the suppressant device. Many cytonic abilities had mechanical halves—like the FTL comm feed, which wouldn't work without physical receivers. The cytonic behind his imprisonment would be feeding part of his mental energy into a physical device, one that used electricity to amplify the effect. But because of that augmentation, Jason would never be able to break free. He would be trapped forever in the blackness.

Not forever. Just another few minutes, until they kill me. That would almost be preferable.

An image came to him. An image of humankind escaping into space. An image of human merchants trading and cheating, of human tyrants capturing the technologically inferior varvax, tenasi, and hommar. Images of wars, of fighting, of a paradise destroyed.

I can't let that happen!

But, what could he do? He felt along the wall, stumbling to his feet and feeling his way around the room. It was small, perhaps two meters square. He could barely feel the seal of the door—there wasn't a handle on his side.

There's not enough time! Jason thought with desperation. *I can't escape, I can't contact Lanna—*

He couldn't contact Lanna, but . . . He reached up to his ear, tapping at the control disk. They had broken his link to the home base, but perhaps they hadn't thought of stowaways . . .

—

"You won't get away with this!" Coln screamed to the empty room. "I'm a UIB agent. There are serious repercussions for the imprisonment of a law enforcement officer!"

There was no answer. Coln sighed, his rage weakening before sheer boredom. He had awakened in this room, which appeared to be some sort of storage closet, with a headache. He hadn't heard a thing outside the door since that time. Denise was there too, sitting quietly on a box.

What is Write planning? Coln thought. *He had us captured, but why?* It had to have something to do with the PC master plan, whatever that was.

Suddenly a sound crackled in his ear. "Coln?" The voice croaked sickly—like whispers from the lips of a dead man.

"Write?" Coln asked. "Why did you imprison me!"

"Hush, Coln," the voice whispered. "We are both imprisoned. We are going to die unless you can do something."

"Something?" Coln asked suspiciously. "What?"

"You need to knock out the power. Blow a fuse, overload a circuit—do something."

Coln frowned. "What good will that do? They'll have backups."

"Just do it." The link crackled off.

Coln swore quietly. What was Write planning this time? Dared he trust the man? Dared he do otherwise?

Denise watched with confusion as Coln searched through the small room, pushing aside boxes and carts. Eventually, he found a power jack on the wall. He stood for a moment, regarding it. Finally, he sighed and loosed a piece of steel from a nearby box's constraint. *Why not? It's not like I can get into more trouble than I'm already in.*

———

Jason couldn't escape the darkness. He couldn't shut his eyes against it, he couldn't run away from it, and he couldn't ignore it. He could only huddle against the wall, feeling his resolve—and his sanity—grow weaker by the second. He heard, but didn't understand, the voice when it returned. His captors had made a grave mistake. They could make all the demands they wanted, but he was in no condition to respond to them. They could kill him. It wouldn't matter.

The voice screamed at him. Jason felt his sanity slipping. He couldn't struggle against it. He didn't want to struggle against it. Struggling would be far too difficult. Blissful unconsciousness was the only answer—a silencing of thought and perception.

At that moment, his Sense returned.

It was only a blip—a fractional waver in the power level. But it was enough. Sense flooded into Jason like drugs into an addict's veins. It immediately began to fade, the suppressor coming back online.

Jason blasted out a thousand mindblades at once, shredding the walls around him. He shattered the telanium into chunks, the chunks to chips, and the chips to dust. The walls dissolved like tissue paper before a nuclear blast, spraying grains of metal away from him. He screamed as he let out the surge of power, a bestial yell to push back the darkness.

The suppressor immediately fell dead, its mechanisms destroyed by the blast. Jason lay huddled, his suit stained with dirt and sweat, on a bright telanium floor. He reveled in his returned Sense for a wonderful, silent moment. However, with Sense came sanity—the two were inseparable to him.

There is another cytonic here, and he's not going to be pleased that I've escaped.

So, taking a deep breath, Jason forced himself to stand.

———

Coln sat, stunned. He held a piece of rubber in his hand—the very one he had used to grip the metal as he'd rammed it into the power jack. He had expected a slight reaction; he hadn't expected the room next to his own to explode.

Coln blinked, dusting the silvery telanium flakes off his clothes. *What...?* he thought with amazement, rubbing some of the telanium grains between his fingers. *What could have done this?* Modern weaponry had difficulty even scarring telanium.

He looked up, and saw Jason Write standing in the direct center of the explosion. The operative's suit was torn. Coln let the telanium dust trickle from his stunned fingers as he saw Write's eyes. Like before, they were unfocused, even unresponsive. They stared dully forward, motionless, like the eyes of . . . a blind man.

"What are you?" Coln whispered.

Write ignored the question. "Take the girl and go," he said, his voice calm but ominous. "This area is about to become very dangerous."

Coln nodded, reaching for the frightened Denise's hand. At that moment, a new voice spoke—one Coln didn't recognize.

"Oh, come now, Mr. Write," the voice said. "Must we stoop to such assumptions? Are we not . . . civilized?"

Write didn't turn toward the source of the sound—a speaker on the wall. "Show yourself."

There was silence. The sound of footsteps. Coln pushed Denise behind him, turning wary eyes on the hallway outside their rooms—the hallway that was now exposed, thanks to the strange explosion.

A figure appeared in the hallway. He was nondescript save for a long nose and a thin body. He wore a sharp navy suit, and he was smiling as he strolled forward, scuffing the layer of telanium dust.

"Tell me who you are," Write said, turning to face the man with his unfocused eyes.

"Come, Jason," the man said. "Don't you recognize me?"

"No."

"I guess I shouldn't be surprised," the man said, continuing to stroll around the room. "It has been several years, and I really wasn't all that important. Just one of your many recruits. My name was Edmund."

The room fell silent. "Why did you try to kill Coln?" Write finally asked.

Edmund just smiled. "Even for a PC agent, you're an extremely secretive man, Jason. You've been hiding things from the varvax. If they knew that you could create mindblades, they'd certainly be tempted to elevate humankind's intelligence designation."

Write frowned. "It was a test. You wanted to see if I could stop the bullets."

"And I was not disappointed," Edmund said, pausing just in front of Write. "Mindblades are very advanced, Jason. Another few decades of study, and you might get FTL. I'm impressed."

The two men stood facing each other—yet neither one's eyes focused on his opponent. They remained like that for a tense few moments, and Coln frowned. He felt like something important was on the verge of happening, but it never occurred.

What is going on?

—

Jason fought for his life. Hundreds of mindblades whipped toward him, invisible blasts of pure thought. It was all he could do to keep them from shredding his flesh. He fought back, sending his own mindblades to block those of his opponent—an opponent he still didn't understand.

He vaguely remembered Edmund—though he hadn't known his face well enough to recognize him in the café. Edmund had been a man with some cytonic potential. He had run away from the PC after just a few months of training. That had been only two years ago—how had he learned so much in so little time?

The barrage of mindblades slackened, and Edmund stepped back. He was still smiling, but there was reservation in his eyes. He hadn't expected Jason to be as good as he was.

Jason breathed deeply. Coln was watching from a short distance away, his face confused—he hadn't been able to see the insane battle Jason had just fought.

"I'm impressed again, Jason," Edmund said.

Jason felt sweat trickle down his cheek.

"I wouldn't have expected you to know how to block mindblades," Edmund continued. "Few of us have practiced that."

Jason stood stiffly. "I've been expecting this for some time," he whispered. "I knew I couldn't keep it away from people like you. I knew that someday I would have to fight."

"You prepared well."

The mindblades struck again. Jason grunted, whipping out with his own blades. There was a faint ripple to his Sense when a mindblade was about to appear, and he sliced at that area with a blade of his own. The blasts canceled each other out, wavering in his Sense like two curves of light. He blocked hundreds of them, the air around him shining like he was in the middle of an explosion.

I can't keep this up long. Eventually a mindblade would break through. Jason had only one card to play—he would have to make it count.

Jason continued to fight, waiting for the right time. Edmund was better than Jason was. It shouldn't have been possible—Jason had been practicing cyto longer than any other man. How could someone have overtaken him so quickly? Jason had to find out. Otherwise, all he had worked for would be lost.

The attack retreated again. Edmund was perspiring now—at least it was diffi-cult for him.

"You learned from the varvax well," Jason said, gambling.

Edmund looked up with surprise. Then he laughed. "So you can't read minds after all," he said with a smile. "That was quite the bluff."

I was wrong, Jason thought. *But, how then . . . ?*

"Goodbye, Jason Write."

Jason felt the air waver around him. More mindblades than he could count began to form—it was like he was being circled in a dome of pure energy. He couldn't block them all. He would die.

Now!

Jason focused on himself. He didn't raise any mindblades. Instead, he Sensed inward. He felt his own vibration in his Sense, a cool black-clothed creature. So different from the boy he had once been. The boy had been stupefied, made immobile, by his horror.

Jason was no longer that boy. With a scream, he felt the mindblades descend around him, and he threw himself willingly into the darkness.

All was still.

The blackness enveloped him, the nonexistence that had threatened him since childhood. Except this time he had come to it by choice. He suffocated for an eternal moment in its embrace.

Then he reappeared. As he reentered normal space, he pushed the air away, lest its molecules get trapped within his appearing body. In a similar manner, he pushed Edmund's flesh away from his hand.

The world shook, and Jason was back. He stood with his arm extended directly in front of Edmund. Jason's wrist ended abruptly where it met Edmund's flesh—his hand had materialized inside of the man's chest.

Edmund's heart, gripped in Jason's fist, thumped once. Edmund's eyes stared ahead in shock. Behind Jason, the place where he had been a moment earlier ex-ploded with mindblades.

Jason squeezed once, and Edmund cried out in pain. The heart stopped beat-ing. Edmund slid to his knees, and Jason pushed his hand slightly outside space and withdrew it.

Edmund fell backward, staring with surprised, agonized eyes. He didn't fall un-conscious as he died—he was far too powerful a cytonic for that. Instead, he just whispered.

"FTL transmission. Jason, you surprise me again. We had no idea . . ."

Jason knelt beside the man. "I've had it for some time. Tell me. Tell me how you did it. Where did you learn such powers?"

The man laughed, a pained hacking laugh. "I've studied it all my life, Jason."

"How?" Jason demanded.

Somehow, Edmund met Jason's eyes. "Ah, you're such an idealist, Jason of the Phone Company. Sometime, you must ask yourself this. Why would a race such as the varvax need to learn an ability such as cytonic suppression?"

Jason paused, his mind growing numb. He knew only one answer, one he had barely dared consider. "To keep prisoners."

"Prisoners?" Edmund coughed. "Original thinkers! Dissenters! Anyone who doesn't agree with them."

"You lie!"

Edmund laughed, his back arching in pain. "And you will be our escape," he said, his voice growing loud until he was practically screaming. "They've had their paradise long enough. You nearly went mad after spending just a few minutes without your Sense—imagine living your life in such a box! You see only the peace, you see only the perfect society.

"You don't see the price!"

Edmund's final breath hissed out, and his body fell limp.

"You lie," Jason whispered. "They are a peaceful people. We are the monsters, not them . . ." He sat for a moment, regarding the fallen body. Coln still stood a short distance away, looking amazed—and confused.

"Come here," Jason said quietly. "Bring the girl."

Coln obeyed without a word. Jason put a hand on each of them, then he entered the darkness once again.

———

Coln recognized the room immediately. He blinked once, trying to forget about the awful sense of emptiness he had just experienced. He was in a white, curved room— the operations center of PC headquarters. The room pictured in his fuzzy holovid. Coln had studied its image hundreds of times, and now he was actually there.

Except PC Central Operations was on Earth, months away from Evensong. Coln breathed in with surprise. Write stood at a short distance, his suit tattered, blood seeping down his arms.

"You do have FTL travel!" Coln accused.

"Yes."

"Then I was right!" Coln said. "You've been keeping FTL travel from humankind!"

"Yes."

"Why?" Coln demanded. "What are you trying to protect us from?"

"I wasn't trying to protect us," Write said, walking over to the side of the room. He approached the wall—the one that was supposed to house the FTL communication machinery—and pulled a lever. A small cup popped out at the bottom, followed by a stream of steaming coffee. "I was trying to protect them. And prepare us."

"Prepare us?" Coln asked.

"The exchange programs," Write said. "The outreach programs—even the skin-color fad. Anything to make us more open-minded. Of course, it doesn't really matter now, does it?"

Coln frowned, then eyed the coffee machine. "So it's not the FTL comm unit . . ."

Write shook his head, then pointed to the side. A man, the man Coln had mistaken for a security guard in the holovid, sat quietly in a chair a short distance away. The man had his eyes closed.

"His mind," Write said. "It powers all of the FTL calls."

"But," Coln said, "there are millions of them . . ."

"All you need is one mind to provide the FTL capability," Jason explained. "Computers can do the actual routing."

Coln hissed quietly in surprise.

"Technology is limited," Jason said. "Only the mind is infinite."

Further questions were forestalled as the door to the room slammed open and a red-haired woman burst in. She immediately ran forward and grabbed Write in a powerful embrace. "What happened!" she demanded, and Coln instantly recognized Lanna's voice.

"Coln," Write mumbled, "meet Lanna Write. My wife."

"What? Your *wife*?"

"Unfortunately," Write said. There was fondness in his voice.

"But," Coln objected, "the Bureau has bugged your communications dozens of times—you always complain when she's assigned to you!"

"Yes, and he does the assigning," Lanna said, checking the small wounds on Write's arms. "He always says that the less the Bureau knows about his personal life, the better. Besides, he can't help teasing me." She looked up at Write. "All right, sit down and tell me what's going on. The medic is on his way."

Write sighed, taking another sip of his drink. "I might have been wrong, Lanna."

"About what?"

"About everything," he said, his voice haunted.

———

Jason sat in his quarters, letting the medic bandage his arms. Lanna stood, dissatisfied, a short distance away. She was the terror of PC Central Operations—few men had the courage, or the stupidity, to incur her wrath.

"All right, old man," she said. "What happened?"

Jason shook his head. Before he could reply, his holovid beeped. Jason punched the button, and Sonn's chitinous face appeared.

"You have some explaining to do, Sonn," Jason said.

The varvax put forward his hands in supplication. "I am at your disposal, Jason of the Phone Company."

Jason pushed a button, showing Sonn an image of Denise being questioned by PC operatives. "Tell me it's not true, Sonn," Jason pled quietly. "Tell me you don't lock your discontents away."

"Varvax discontents?" Lanna asked with surprise.

Sonn raised his hands, a sign of apology. "I said that you would discover the reason for cytonic suppression eventually, Jason of the Phone Company."

Jason bowed his head. *No. It can't be . . .*

"It is the only way," Sonn said. "The way to have peace."

"Peace for those who agree with you," Jason spat.

"It is the only way."

"And the others?" Jason demanded. "The tenasi, the hallo?"

"The same," Sonn said. "They have discovered the way, as you will eventually. The way to Prime Intelligence. I must apologize for the inconvenience we have given to you."

Jason sat, stunned. He was wrong. All of these years, over a century of work, and he was wrong. They had deceived him. Suddenly, he felt sick—sick, and angry.

"They're going to come for you, Sonn," Jason said, nodding thankfully to the medic as he finished the bandaging. The man was trustworthy—one of the first cytonics Jason had recruited over a hundred years before.

"Excuse me, Jason of the Phone Company?" Sonn asked after a short pause. His hands were pulled back in the varvax sign of confusion.

The medic left and Lanna sat down beside Jason. She watched Sonn with calculating eyes—she had never liked the varvax. She said she didn't like people who could so easily falsify their body language.

"The ambassador—the one who died," Jason said. "He was a discontent. I have him now. I thought humans were trying to infiltrate varvax society; I didn't realize that it was the other way around. Your dissidents are escaping, and they're hiding among us. They're trying to get hold of human technology. We're still uncivilized, Sonn. We have some war machines that could blast down your ships without even pausing."

Sonn maintained his sign of confusion, then augmented it with one of worry. Few people knew that the tenasi ambassadorial vessel that had been shot down over Earth had been one of the most advanced, most powerful ships in the galaxy. A single human missile had destroyed it. The other species had far inferior technology.

"This is disturbing," Sonn admitted.

"I know," Jason said. Then he reached over and cut the connection. Sonn's face fuzzed and disappeared.

Jason leaned back with a sigh, Sensing Lanna beside him. He'd known it was coming—he'd feared that he couldn't keep humankind out of space. He just hadn't expected heaven to fail him.

"I'm sorry," Lanna whispered.

Jason shook his head. "You always warned me that I was too idealistic."

"I wanted to believe you anyway," Lanna said. She slowly trailed her hand along his cheek. "Do you think the one who attacked you was the only one?"

"Not a chance," Jason said. "He was too confident."

"Then . . ."

Jason took a deep breath. "Prepare a press release, Lanna. Tell them that the Phone Company has finally developed faster-than-light travel, and that we will release it to the public as soon as the United Governments approves our patent."

Lanna nodded.

"Perhaps we can salvage something from paradise," Jason whispered.

POSTSCRIPT

This is one of two of our "early Brandon" stories in this collection—and is the earliest story I've written that I would feel comfortable putting in a volume like this. (If you want to read one even earlier, from high school, it's on my website, but brace yourself for a mediocre time.) I have my original website annotation for "Defending Elysium" below. I wrote that long ago now. In fact, the gap between writing that annotation and this one is much larger than the gap between the story and the initial annotation.

Looking back, I find I remember more of my reasons for writing "Defending Elysium" now than I did then—partially, I think, from going back to that well in order to work on the Skyward series. In the original annotation, I talk about that melancholy part of my life. But now I view it differently.

"Defending Elysium" marks what I consider the "start" of my professional career. There are a lot of places you could mark this. The writing of *Elantris* in 1998. The sale of that same book in 2003. Or even its publication in 2005. A marker I like, however, is the writing of this story, in 2001. (Metadata on the file says it was finished June 6, 2001.) Several things were happening at that time.

First, I was revising *Elantris* the last time before selling it. (Metadata on that one is kind of wonky, as I've swapped computers often, but I ended up submitting the sixth version to Moshe Feder at Tor in November 2001, and we have record of that.) Second, I was working on the world guide for the Stormlight Archive. Third, I decided to actually learn to write novellas, and this story was the result. It would go on to place in the Writers of the Future contest (as an honorable mention), then to sell to one of the big magazines during my early days after selling *Elantris*.

This might not be the first thing I wrote that got published (again, that's *Elantris*). But I think it's the first thing to hit *publishable* through revisions. Either that, or it's a close tie among several pieces.

Regardless, this story came out of my love for a science fiction trope I first read from Anne McCaffrey: the idea of biological FTL. Meaning humans provide faster-than-light travel through some kind of futuristic powers. *Dune*, obviously, uses this same trope. (It's a cousin trope to simple teleportation, but in this trope, people themselves become the way civilizations progress through the space age.)

That is a setting detail, but the actual story is in the title. A great number of SF stories posit dangerous aliens meeting up with humans and either destroying their world or attacking them with a vengeful imperative of destruction. Much less seen (I don't think I'd seen it at all when I wrote this) is the idea that humans might be the vengeful destroyers. We have the history for it; maybe *we* are the Klingons.

I wrote this story with that theme, and that of when it's right to play God and try to protect a universe that might not deserve it. The story stuck with me over the years and is one of my favorites I've ever written—to the point that when I was developing *Skyward*, I used this story as the backdrop for the entire setting that became the Cytoverse.

ORIGINAL ANNOTATION

This story was written on a beach near Monterey, California, and remains the only published piece of mine I did entirely in longhand before transcribing it to the computer. I'd never been to Monterey before, and a friend was able to trade something he did at work for a week's stay in a little condo-style hotel. We had two rooms and a very nice view over the city down toward the water.

So I guess I was doing the whole bohemian thing. During these days, I hadn't yet gotten published (this would have been late 2001 or early 2002). I had graduated from college, but had been rejected by all of the grad schools I'd applied for. I'd written about a dozen novels, and was annoyed with myself for not writing books that were true to what I wanted to be as a writer.

The call regarding the sale of *Elantris* would not come for another year or so. I was working a graveyard shift at the hotel, renting a room in a friend's basement for $300 a month, and spending all the time I could practicing my craft. (In part to delay thinking about what I was going to do with my life since my writing wasn't selling and grad schools didn't want me.)

Over the next year, I would write a book called *The Way of Kings*, the best—yet most flawed—book I wrote during my unpublished years. A massive, beastly epic that was my symbolic discarding of any desire to chase the market or write anything that was not the type of writing I loved to read.

That was my mindset. I remember a couple of long afternoons sitting on the beach, listening to the waves and staring out over the ocean as I wrote. A good friend named Annie was there for most of it—you may know her as the woman that Sarene from *Elantris* was based on—writing in her journal. Micah (you may know him as Captain Demoux from the Mistborn books) was in and out. Mostly he was off taking photos.

I remember wanting to see if I could imbue a short story with the type of characterization and multiple plots that I liked in my epic fantasy. I had an idea for a character with a deep and interesting past, alongside a nice dissonant element (a secret agent working for the phone company). That, along with an interesting idea for an ending, grew into this story.

Oddly, I was able to make this work in a short story the way I wanted, while writing shorter novels hadn't worked for me. I chalk that one up to me starting to find the natural size for a story and writing it at that size. Ironically, the novels I'd written recently (*Final Empire* and *Mistborn*, the ideas for which would eventually be recycled into a single volume you know as *Mistborn: The Final Empire*) were ones that I'd tried intentionally to write "short." And in doing that, I'd ended up filling each book with too few ideas for even their short length.

With "Defending Elysium," I took a short story (well, novelette) and filled it with as many ideas as I could pack into the space. The result is a very dense story (in plot, history, and world terms) that ended up satisfying all of the epic storytelling buttons I like having pushed.

I ended up submitting this to *The Leading Edge* (the magazine I worked on) during one of my last months there. I did it under a pseudonym, a practice common for staff members, to get some feedback. (*The Leading Edge* gives feedback on all submissions. I didn't intend to publish it there; I just wanted some honest opinions.) Turns out that one of my best friends read the story, then spent about an hour the following evening telling me about this great story he'd read out of the slush, and how he couldn't believe that such an awesome story had ended up getting submitted to *TLE* just out of nowhere. (That gave me an inkling that the story might have some potential . . .)

That's the background on the story. For those who like to dig deeper into the meaning and context of a story, perhaps that's given you something to chew on. This was a melancholy time of my life—perhaps the time when I was most adrift— yet at the same time, it was one of the most artistically uninhibited times of my life. No contracts, no deadlines, no artificial rules imposed on myself. I had decided that the world could do whatever it wanted, and I would write what I loved even if it never got published.

FIRSTBORN

While safe aboard his flagship, there were two ways for Dennison to watch the battle.

The obvious method relied on the expansive battle hologram that dominated the bridge. The hologram was on at the moment, and it displayed an array of triangular blue blips representing fighters flying about waist high. The much larger blue oval of Dennison's command ship hung a moderate distance above and behind the fighters. The massive and powerful but far less agile leviathan probably wouldn't see battle this day. The enemy's ships were too weak to damage its hull, but they were also too fast for it to catch. This would be a battle between the smaller fighters.

And Dennison would lead them. He rose from his command chair and walked a few steps to the hologram's edge, studying the enemy. Their red ships winked into existence as scanners located them amid the rolling boulders of the asteroid field. Rebels in name but pirates in action, the group had thrived unhindered for far too long. It had been five years since his brother Varion had reestablished His Majesty's law in this sector, and the rebellious elements should have long since been crushed.

Dennison stepped into the hologram, walking until he stood directly behind his ships. There were about two dozen of them—not a large force, by Fleet standards, but bigger than he deserved. He glanced to the side. Noncommissioned aides and lesser officers had paused in their duties, eyes turned toward their youthful commander. Though they offered no obvious disrespect, Dennison could see their true feelings in their eyes. They did not expect him to win.

Well, Dennison thought, *wouldn't want to disappoint the good folks.*

"Divide the squadrons," Dennison commanded. His order was transmitted directly to the various captains, and his small fleet broke into four smaller groups. Ahead, the pirates began to form up as well—though they stayed within their asteroid cover.

Through the movement of their ships, Dennison could feel their battle strategy taking shape. At his disposal was all the formal military knowledge that came with a high-priced Academy education. Memories of lectures and textbooks mixed in his head, enhancing the practical experience he'd gained during a half dozen years commanding simulations and, eventually, real battles.

Yes, he could see it. He could see what the enemy commanders were doing; he could sense their strategies. And he *almost* knew how to counter them.

"My lord?" an aide said, stepping forward. She bore a battle visor in her hands. "Will you be needing this?"

The visor was the second way a commander could watch the battle. Each fighter bore a camera just inside its cockpit to relay a direct view. Varion always wore a battle visor. Dennison, however, was not his brother. He seemed to be the only one who realized that fact.

"No," Dennison said, waving the aide away. The action caused a stir among the bridge team, and Dennison caught a glare from Brell, his XO.

"Send Squadron C to engage," Dennison commanded, ignoring Brell.

A group of four fighters broke off from the main fleet, streaking toward the asteroids. Blue met red, and the battle began in earnest.

Dennison strode through the hologram, watching, giving commands, and analyzing—just as he had been taught. Dogfighting ships zipped around his head; fist-size asteroids shattered as he walked through their space, then re-formed after he had passed. He moved like some ancient god of lore, presiding over a battle-field of miniature mortals who couldn't see him, but undeniably felt his almighty hand.

Except if Dennison was a god, his specialty certainly wasn't war.

His education kept him from making any disastrous mistakes, but before long, the battle had progressed to the point where it was no longer winnable. His complete lack of pride let him order the expected retreat. The Fleet ships limped away, reduced by more than half. From the statistics glowing into hovering holographic existence before him, Dennison could see that his ships had managed to destroy barely a dozen enemy fighters.

Dennison stepped from the hologram, leaving the red ships victorious and the blue ships despondent. The hologram disappeared, its images shattering and dribbling to the command center's floor like shimmering dust, the pieces eventually burning away in the light. Crew members stood around the perimeter, their eyes showing the sickly shame of defeat.

Only Brell had the courage to speak what they were all thinking. "He really is an idiot," he muttered under his breath.

Dennison paused by the doorway. He turned with a raised eyebrow, and found Brell staring back unrepentantly. Another High Officer probably would have sent him to the brig for insubordination. Of course, another commander wouldn't have earned such disrespect in the first place. Dennison leaned back against the side of the doorway, arms folded in an unmilitaristic posture. "I should probably punish you, Brell. I am a High Officer, after all."

This, at least, made the man look aside. Dennison lounged, letting Brell realize that—incompetent or not—Dennison had the power to destroy a man's career with a mere comm call.

Dennison finally sighed, standing up and walking forward. "But, you know, I've never really believed in disciplining men for speaking the truth. Yes, Brell. I, Dennison Crestmar—brother of the great Varion Crestmar, cousin to kings and commander of fleets—am an idiot. Just like all of you have heard."

Dennison paused right in front of Brell, then reached out and tapped the man's chest in the center of his High Imperial Emblem. "But think of this," Dennison continued with a light smile. "If *I'm* an idiot, then *you* must be pretty damn incompetent yourself; otherwise they would never have wasted you by sending you to serve under me."

Brell's face flared red at the insult, but he showed uncharacteristic restraint by holding his tongue. Dennison turned and strolled from the room. "Prepare my speeder for my return to the Point," he commanded. "I'm due for dinner with my father tomorrow."

———

He missed dinner. However, it wasn't his fault, considering he had to travel half the length of the High Empire. Dennison's father, High Duke Sennion Crestmar, was waiting for him in the spaceport when he arrived.

Sennion didn't say a word as Dennison left the airlock and approached. The High Duke was a tall man—proud, broad shouldered, with a noble face. He was the epitome of what a High Officer should be. At least Dennison had inherited the height.

The High Duke turned. Dennison fell into step beside him, and the two strode down the Officer's Walk—a pathway with a deep red carpet, trimmed with gold. It was reserved for High Officers, uncluttered by the civilians and lower ranks who bustled against each other on either side. There were no vehicles or moving walkways on the Officer's Walk. High Officers carried themselves. There was strength in walking—or so Dennison's father always said. The High Duke was rather fond of self-congratulatory mottoes.

"Well?" Sennion finally asked, eyes forward.

Dennison shrugged. "I really tried this time, if it makes any difference."

"If you had 'tried,'" Sennion said flatly, "you would have won. You had superior ships, superior men, and superior training."

Dennison didn't bother trying to argue with Sennion. He had given up on that particular waste of sanity years ago.

"The High Emperor assumed that you simply needed practical experience," Sennion said, almost to himself. "He thought that simulations and school games weren't realistic enough to engage you."

"Even emperors can be wrong, Father," Dennison said.

Sennion didn't even favor him with a glare.

Here it comes, Dennison thought. *He's finally going to admit it. He's finally going to let me go.* Dennison wasn't certain what he'd do once he was released from military command—but whatever he chose to do, he couldn't possibly be any worse at it.

"I have arranged a new commission for you," Sennion finally said.

Dennison started. Then he closed his eyes, barely suppressing a sigh. How many failures would the High Duke need to see before he gave up?

"It's aboard the *Stormwind.*"

Dennison froze in place.

Sennion stopped, finally turning to regard his son. People streamed to either side on the lower walks, ignoring the two men in fine uniforms standing on the crimson carpet.

Dumbfounded, Dennison took a moment to begin to respond. "But . . ."

"It's a fine ship—a good place to learn. You will serve as an adjutant and squadron commander for High Admiral Kern."

"I know it's a 'fine ship,'" Dennison said through clenched teeth. "Father, that is a real command on an imperial flagship, not some idle playing in the Reaches. It's bad enough when I lose a dozen men fighting pirates. Need I be responsible for the deaths of thousands in the Reunification War as well?"

"I know Admiral Kern," Sennion said, ignoring his son's objections. "He is an excellent tactician. Perhaps he will be able to help you with your . . . problems."

"Problems?" Dennison demanded quietly. "Problems, Father? Has it never even occurred to you that I'm just not any good at this? It isn't dishonorable for the son of a High Duke to seek another profession, once he's proven himself unsuited to command. Goodness knows, I've certainly satisfied *that* particular requirement."

Sennion stepped forward, grabbing Dennison by the shoulders. "You will not speak that way," he commanded. "You are not like other officers. The High Empire expects more. The High Empire *demands* more!"

Dennison was taken aback by his father's lack of formality, and some of the passersby stopped to regard the strange sight of a High Duke acting with such passion. Dennison stood within his father's stiff grasp, reading the man's eyes. *It isn't the High Emperor, is it, Father?* Dennison thought. *It's you. One genius son isn't enough. For you, one success and one failure simply cancel each other out.*

"Go prepare yourself," Sennion said, releasing him. "The *Stormwind* is expecting your speeder in three days, and it's a seventy-hour trip."

———

"With permission, Your Majesty, I don't think this is the command for me," Dennison said, kneeling before the speeder's wallscreen.

The High Emperor was a middle-aged man with a firm chin and a full face. He was balding in a time when most men got scalp rejuvenations, but his refusal to enhance his appearance lent him a weight of . . . authenticity. He frowned at Dennison's comment. "It is an enviable post, Dennison. Most young High Officers would consider it an amazing opportunity."

"I am hardly like most young officers, Your Majesty," Dennison noted.

"No, that you certainly are not," the emperor said. "However, I would think that this post's near proximity to your brother would interest you."

Dennison shrugged. "To be honest, Your Majesty, I don't know Varion. I'm curious about him, but no more so than another person might be. I maintain my petition to be released from this commission."

The emperor's frown deepened. "You need to show more initiative, young Crestmar. Your pessimism has been a great annoyance to the High Throne."

Dennison glanced down—it was always bad when the emperor switched to the third person. "Your Majesty," he said. "I really have tried—I've tried all my life. But I received near-failing marks at the Academy, I never managed to even place in the games, and I've bungled every command given me. I'm just not any good."

"You have it in you," the emperor said. "You just have to try a little harder."

Dennison groaned softly. The emperor had obviously been speaking with his father again. "How can you be so sure, Your Majesty?"

"I just am. Your petition is denied. Is there anything else?"

Dennison shook his head.

———

Admiral Kern was not waiting for Dennison in the docking bay when he left the speeder, but that wasn't unusual. Though a High Officer, Dennison was still a junior one, and Kern was one of the most powerful admirals in the Fleet.

Dennison followed an aide through the flagship's passageways. They were surprisingly well decorated for a warship, adorned with the twelve seals of the High Empire. This was an imperial flagship, designed to impress inside and out.

The aide led him to a large circular chamber with a battle hologram at its center. Though the air sparkled with miniature ships, only one man stood in the room—this wasn't the bridge, but a simulation chamber very similar to the ones Dennison had used at the Academy.

High Admiral Kern was young for one of his rank. He had a square face and thick dark hair, and he was large enough that one could imagine him as some ancient general with a horse and broadsword, yet he had the typical reserved mien of an imperial nobleman. He didn't look away from his battle as Dennison entered. The edges of the room were dim, the only illumination coming from the illusory ships and the glowing ring that marked the hologram's edge. Kern stood at the center, not directing the progress, just observing. The aide left, closing the door.

"Do you recognize this battle?" the admiral suddenly asked.

Dennison walked forward. "Yes, sir," he said, realizing with surprise that he did. "It's the battle of Seapress."

Kern nodded, face lit from below, still watching the flitting ships. "Your brother's first battle," he said quietly. "The beginning of the Reunification War." He watched for a moment longer, then waved his hand, freezing ships in the air. Finally, he turned eyes on Dennison, who gave a perfunctory salute—really more a wave of the hand. Might as well establish what he was like from the beginning.

Kern didn't frown at the sloppy greeting. He folded his arms, regarding Dennison with a curious look. "Dennison Crestmar. I hear you have something of a smart mouth."

"It's the only part of me blessed with such virtue, I'm afraid."

Kern actually smiled—an expression rarely seen on a High Officer's lips. "I suspect that was why your father sent you to me."

"He has great respect for you, sir," Dennison noted.

Kern snorted. "He can't stand me. He thinks I'm undignified."

Dennison raised an eyebrow. When Kern said nothing more, he continued. "I feel that I must warn you, sir, that I am poorly suited to this commission. I doubt that I will fulfill your expectations of a squadron leader."

"Oh, I don't intend to put you in charge of any ships," Kern said, laughing. "Forgive me, but I've seen your records. The only question is whether you're a worse strategist or tactician."

Dennison sighed in relief. "Then what are you going to do with me?"

Kern waved him forward. "Come," he said, motioning with his other hand and restarting the hologram.

Dennison stepped into the hologram. He'd seen the battle before—one couldn't graduate from the Academy without taking several courses on the mighty Varion

Crestmar. Varion's ships were outlined in white. He had two command vessels—one a simple merchant ship, the other his imperial longship—and he controlled only four dozen fighters. Fewer ships than Dennison had been given to waste fighting pirates.

"Tell me about him," Kern requested, watching Varion's longship as it approached the battle.

Dennison raised an eyebrow. "Varion? He's more than twenty years older than I. I've never even met him."

"I'm not a parlor visitor asking about your family, Dennison. I'm your commander. Tell me about Varion the warrior."

Dennison hesitated. Varion's longship, the famous *Voidhawk*, slid forward. Varion's forces were laughably small compared to those of his enemy—the rogue planet of Seapress had boasted a fleet of five massive battleships and nearly a hundred fighters. Two decades ago, at the nadir of imperial power, such a fleet had been impressive indeed.

The Seapress ships, however, didn't form up to attack Varion. They simply waited.

"Varion is . . ." Dennison said quietly. "Varion is perfect."

Kern raised an eyebrow. "In what way?"

"He has never lost," Dennison said. "He was given his first command the very day he left the Academy. Within five years, he had risen to command the entire Imperial Fleet, and was charged with regaining control of the Distant Sectors. He's fought that war his whole life, and he's never suffered a single failure. Hundreds of battles, and he's never lost once."

"Perfect?" Kern asked.

"Perfect," Dennison said.

Kern nodded, then turned back to the battlefield. The blockish merchant ship had pulled ahead of Varion's flagship, and was ponderously making its way toward the Seapress array.

"It all started here," Kern said.

As the first in his class in the Academy, Varion had been offered positions aboard the grandest fleet flagships. He had turned them all down, accepting a lesser post aboard a ship commanded by a regular officer—one who wasn't noble.

Article 117 of the Fleet Code allowed a High Officer to use his rank as a nobleman—rather than his military rank—to take command of any ships where a low officer was in charge. It was an article rarely invoked, for if the nobleman fared badly, the emperor was permitted—even expected—to have the man executed.

Varion had used Article 117, taking command of the *Voidhawk* and its small fleet, the commoner captain becoming his XO. Varion's first action had been to ignore their standing orders, striking out instead toward the rebellious colonies on the Western Reaches.

"He took the merchant ship by force, you know," Kern said. "As if he were a pirate. I remember the High Emperor's fury. He ordered a half dozen longships to hunt your brother down. But Varion's ruse wouldn't have worked otherwise. Seapress—like most of the rebel factions—had spies in the upper ranks of the Fleet. They had to believe that Varion was going rogue. That was why he seized command so rashly and why he captured a merchant vessel, then towed it to Seapress as a 'gift.'

"Nobody on his ship resisted him. That is your brother's most impressive attribute, Dennison. He's not just a tactical master. He's also an amazing leader. And an amazing liar."

The image of the merchant ship rocked suddenly, its engines blasting with unexpected strength. It gained momentum as the Seapress capital ships began to turn, their commanders confused, their own engines firing belatedly. The merchant vessel rammed the Seapress flagship, then both ships twisted and rammed into a second carrier vessel.

"He's also void-cursed lucky," Kern noted.

Dennison nodded as Varion's line burst with motion, fighters streaking away from his flagship, his smaller gunboats moving to enfilade the three remaining Seapress command ships.

Kern held up a hand, and the ships froze. He turned toward Dennison. "All right," he said. "Your turn."

Dennison frowned. "You want me to take command?"

Kern nodded, leaving the hologram and typing a few orders into the control panel. "Let's see what you can do."

Dennison raised an eyebrow. "What will that prove?"

"Humor me," Kern said.

The simulation began again. The massive Seapress command ship rolled weakly to the side, the hole in its side belching flames as oxygen escaped into the void. Seapress should have blown Varion from the sky the moment he entered their space. An imperial longship, with a commander fresh from the Academy, committing treason? They should have seen through the ploy. But they hadn't. Somehow Varion had convinced them.

Dennison shot a look to where Kern watched from the shadows. What did he see? A young Varion? Dennison and his brother were said to be very similar in appearance. The biggest difference was their hair: Dennison's was black, but Varion's had started turning a silvery grey on his twenty-second birthday. By twenty-five, he had already acquired the nickname Silvermane.

"Launch the fighters in three formations," Dennison said, turning back to the hologram. "Order the *Darkstring* to mark four-seven-one and tell it to hold position, firing on any ships that try to escape those wounded flagships. I want the *Fanell* to take up position to my lower port flank, then provide cover if any fighters get too close."

The battle began, and Dennison fought. As always, he tried. He tried hard. The insubordination and cynicism disappeared whenever he entered a battle hologram. Standing within the fray, ships swarming around, above, and below him, he abandoned his habitual pessimism and really tried.

And he lost horribly. The Seapress ships cut down his fighters when Dennison failed to give them proper covering fire. He lost the *Darkstring* when the mortally damaged Seapress flagship rolled too close, then self-destructed. When he tried to retreat, enemy missiles tore out the back of his command ship, and left him to suffocate as life support fizzled. The hologram switched off.

Dennison sighed, turning back toward Kern.

"I've seen worse," Kern finally said.

"Oh?" Dennison said. "You've seen recordings of my Academy fights?"

Kern didn't respond. He stood, tapping his chin in thought. "You asked what you are doing here," he finally said. "Since you're not going to be given a command."

Dennison nodded.

"The High Emperor wants me to turn you into a leader," Kern explained. "But I don't intend to throw away any men on you. Therefore, I've found an instructor to train you."

"Who?"

"Your brother," Kern said. "Get used to this room, Dennison. You're going to be spending a lot of time here. I want you to go through every one of Varion's battles, studying his methods and his strategies. I want you to read every major profile written on him. You will become the empire's foremost expert on Varion Crestmar—you will memorize and you will practice until you can fight this battle, and any other, just as he would."

"You're kidding," Dennison said flatly.

"You should get busy," Kern said, then tapped his control pad. A list of dates and battles appeared on the wall. "You've got a lot of work to do."

"Lord Kern, sir," Dennison said, speaking with an attention to formality he rarely invoked. "I'm not my brother. I never will be."

"That's no reason not to try and learn from him."

"He destroyed my life," Dennison said. "From the first day I entered the Academy, I was fated to fail. How could I do otherwise, considering what others expected of me? Let me study someone else. High Admiral Fallstate, perhaps."

Kern thought for a moment, then shook his head. "You'll do as I order, son."

———

Each battle was a blow to his self-esteem. Even after studying Varion's tactics, even after watching the battles replay over and over, Dennison had trouble winning. The simulator had a random factor in its programming so he couldn't just memorize and make the same moves that Varion had.

Dennison sighed, rubbing his forehead as he watched a holographic replay of his latest battle. His year aboard the *Stormwind* had passed quickly and with an odd sense of distortion. He felt removed from events in the empire. His entire world was shrunken to an endless replay of strategies, tactics, and failures, centered around a single individual.

Varion.

The replay of Marcus Seven continued. By this point, Varion's fleet had grown to several thousand ships, and had official imperial support. Varion hadn't even been at this battle in person; he had directed from his flagship many light-years away. The larger an object was, the longer it took to reach its destination via *klage*—so, while visual communications were essentially instantaneous, flagships could take months to travel between distant points of the empire.

These limitations frustrated Varion, so he split his forces into two different battle groups, sending them in opposite directions. Dennison understood Varion's reasoning now—a year of studying the Silvermane had immersed him in the worldview of a man he'd spent his life trying to escape. Who was Varion Crestmar? He was perfect. Dennison could no longer say that with even a hint of sarcasm.

Every day spent living his sibling's life through battle brought the two of them closer. Dennison found himself spending his extra hours in the hologram room, looking over his recorded battles, then watching Varion's handling of the same conflict. He stopped looking for the strategies and instead focused on the man. What kind of person was this Varion Silvermane? He had been separated from his family for two decades, living in glorious self-imposed exile because the war effort required all of his attention.

Many of these early battles in Varion's campaign made perfect sense. Back then, Varion had still needed to persuade the emperor that he was worthy of trust and support. Dennison could see why the planet Utaries had had to be crushed quickly, because of its ability to rally other planets to its cause. He could follow the logical connection between subduing the Seapress people, then moving on to the less powerful—yet technologically superior—Farnight Union.

As the Reunification War proceeded, however, Varion's choices grew baffling. Why had he gone after New Rofelos when doing so had exposed his forces to division? What had been the purpose of committing so many of his forces to conquering Gemwater, a planet of little strategic importance and even less military power?

Questions like these haunted Dennison. Varion's true genius was in his ability to connect battlefields, to lead his fleets from one victory to the next, always gaining momentum, expanding his war to second and third—then tenth and twentieth—fronts. He didn't just destroy or subdue, he converted. Before Varion's conquering began, the empire had barely held enough ships to defend its ever-shrinking border. By Marcus Seven, however, the Fleet had contained more ex-rebel ships than official ones.

Varion was bold and daring, willing to take risks. Yet he was also lucky, for those risks always brought returns. Or *was* it luck? Dennison's father would have scoffed. "Each man has responsibility for his own existence" would have been the characteristic pronouncement.

In the hologram, Dennison's flagship exploded in a spray of metal and light. Varion was perfect. And Dennison was perfectly incompetent. He didn't make this acknowledgment despondently or with self-pity. It was simply a fact. Varion had won Marcus Seven in barely two hours. The fiasco Dennison had just watched was a recording of his fourth attempt. He'd needed seven tries to win.

Dennison sighed, rising and leaving the hologram chamber. He needed to stretch. The lavish passages of the *Stormwind* were oddly empty, and Dennison frowned, walking along the carpeted corridor until he encountered a minor aide. The man paused briefly, saluting and showing the same discomforted confusion the junior officers usually gave Dennison. They weren't certain what to make of a High Officer who hadn't been given a command, yet was important enough to share dinner with Admiral Kern every evening.

"Are we in battle?" Dennison asked.

"Um, yes, sir," the younger man said quickly, eyes darting to the side.

"Be off with you then," Dennison said, waving the man away.

The junior officer eagerly dashed away. Dennison stood, frowning to himself. Had he really been so absorbed that he hadn't noticed the battle alarm? Not that Kern's flagship was really in any danger. This would be a minor battle; Varion's personal fleets handled all the serious fighting. Still, Dennison would like to have watched the fight. He headed for the bridge.

The *Stormwind*'s main bridge was larger than those of ships Dennison had commanded, but the central feature was still the battle hologram. Dennison left the lift, ignoring salutes as he stepped up to the railing, looking down. Kern himself stood in the hologram, but said little. He was a traditional commander; he left most of the local decisions to his squadron commanders, who flew in smaller gunships or longships that were in the thick of the battle.

Varion didn't use squadron commanders. He fought every battle himself, controlling each squadron directly. That would have been foolhardy for anyone else, but Varion did it with the aplomb of a chess master playing against novices. Dennison shook his head. *Enough of Varion for the moment,* he thought.

Kern's own battle didn't look like much of a fight. The High Admiral's ships outnumbered the opposition by at least three to one.

The battle progressed as expected. Dennison felt a longing as he watched, a wistfulness that he thought he'd quashed back in the Academy. His study of Varion was awakening old pains. He could almost feel the moves on the battlefield. When the squad commanders made their decisions—the orders manifest in the movement of the holographic ships—Dennison instantly knew which choices were better than others. He could see the majesty of the entire battlefield. Kern's forces needed to press to the northeast quadrant, drawing fighters away to defend their command ships so that the gunships to the south would fall. That would let Kern's superior numbers drain the enemy of resources until the rebellious group had no choice but to surrender.

Dennison could see this, but he didn't know how to accomplish it. As always, he grasped the concepts, but not the application. He was not a practical, hands-on commander of the type the empire preferred. It wasn't so odd. Dennison knew of men who loved music, but couldn't play a note themselves. One could enjoy a grand painting without being able to replicate its brushstrokes. Art was valuable for the very reason that it could be appreciated by those of lesser skill. Remote leading and battlefield tactics were indeed arts, and Dennison would never be more than a spectator.

"Where are we, anyway?" Dennison asked an aide.

"Gammot system, my lord," the aide answered.

Dennison frowned, leaning down on the railing. *Gammot?* He hadn't realized that Varion had gotten so far, let alone Kern's mop-up force. He waved for an aide to bring him a datapad, then punched up a map of the empire and overlaid it with a schematic of Varion's conquests. He was amazed by what he saw.

It was nearly done. Varion's forces were approaching the last rebellious systems. *I really have been distracted lately,* Dennison thought. Soon there would be peace. And with that peace, commanders wouldn't be as important. They hadn't been, during the Grand Eras.

Why, then, was it so imperative that Dennison be forced into Varion's mold?

Everyone—the High Emperor, Kern, Dennison's father—acted as if Dennison's studies were absolutely vital.

It had to be his father, pleading for Dennison's continued training—not because it mattered to the empire, but because Sennion didn't want a failed warrior as a son.

—

"Of course there will still be a need for commanders," Kern scoffed as a servant ladled soup into his bowl. "What makes you think otherwise?"

"The Reunification War is nearly over," Dennison said.

Kern's dining chamber was a compact version of one in an imperial mansion back on the Point, complete with marble columns and tapestries. The High Admiral's rank forbade his fraternizing with his other subcommanders, but Dennison's higher birth and relation to Varion Crestmar made him an exception. Kern seemed able to relax and dine with Dennison—as if he didn't see him as an underling, but rather as a young family member come to visit.

Kern snorted at Dennison's logic. "There will be insurrections for some time yet, Dennison," he said, attacking his soup. Kern lived like an imperial nobleman, but he was far less reserved than most. Perhaps that was why Dennison got along with him.

"Yes, but Varion and his officers will be free to handle them," Dennison said, ignoring his own soup.

"All men age, and new blood needs to replace them," Kern said.

"The empire doesn't need me, Kern," Dennison said. "It *never* has. Only my father's stubbornness keeps me here."

"I wouldn't be so sure about that," Kern said. "Either way, I have my orders. How is your training coming?"

Dennison shrugged. "I fought the Marcus Seven battle four more times today and lost twice. Still can't win it consistently."

"Marcus Seven," Kern said with a frown. "You're taking your time. At this rate, it'll take you another year to get through Varion's archive."

"At least I'm not complaining anymore."

"No," Kern agreed. "You aren't. In fact, you actually seem to be enjoying yourself."

Dennison took a sip. "Perhaps so. My brother makes for an interesting subject."

"When you first came on board, I could tell you hated him."

Dennison rested his spoon back in his bowl. "I suppose I did," he finally said. "At the Academy, I was never given a chance to succeed—the other boys challenged me to battles before I was ready, each one wanting the prestige of defeating Varion's brother. I became a loser before I could learn otherwise. I didn't choose my path— Varion chose it for me.

"But now . . ." Dennison trailed off, then looked Kern in the eye. "Could any man really hate him? How can you hate someone who's perfect?"

Kern seemed troubled. Finally, he turned back to his meal. "At any rate, you should soon have a chance to meet him."

Dennison looked up, surprised.

Kern took a sip of soup. "The Reaches are nearly subdued. In two months, Varion will meet with an Imperial Emissary on Kress, where they will hold a ceremony welcoming him back to civilization. You may attend, if you wish."

Dennison smiled broadly. "I do," he decided. "I do indeed."

—

Dennison was surprised by how bright the colors were. Kress was a sparsely inhabited world near the border of the Reaches. Its weather was obviously unregulated, for the wind blew strongly against Dennison's face as he stood in the speeder's door.

Dennison stepped onto the soft ground, sneezing and raising a hand against the bright sunlight. The vibrant green grass came up to his knees. What kind of world was this to greet a returning hero? A pavilion had been erected a short distance away, and Dennison made his way there. A local weather regulator had been set up, and the wind slowed as he entered the invisible confines of its influence. There, he unexpectedly found his father standing with a delegation of high-ranking ambassadors and military men. Sennion's perfect white uniform was a pristine contrast to the wild lands around him.

A small pavilion on a rural world? Why not meet Varion with the adoring crowds he deserves?

Dennison could see a dropship descending through the wild air. He stepped up beside his father. Dennison hadn't seen him in over six months, but Sennion barely nodded in acknowledgment. The dropship fell like a flare. It plummeted, slowing only when it neared the ground, its plasma jets carelessly vaporizing the grass. The weather sphere kept the wind of its landing from unsettling the pavilion's dignified occupants. Dennison edged a bit closer to the front, waiting eagerly as the dropship doorway opened.

He had seen pictures of Varion. They didn't do him justice. Pictures could not convey the confidence, the powerful presence, of a man like Varion Crestmar. With his silver hair and commanding eyes, he walked down the ramp like a god descending to the mortal realm.

When last seen on the Imperial Homeworld, Varion had been a smooth-faced boy. Now he bore the lines of combat and age; he was in the middle of his fifth decade. He wore an imperial uniform, but not one of a standard color. Dennison frowned. White was for nobility, blue for citizen officers, and red for regular soldiers. But . . . grey? There was no grey.

A group of officers walked down the ramp after Varion. Dennison recognized many of them. The woman would be Charisa of Utaries, a celebrated fighter pilot and squadron leader, one of the first rebel commanders who had joined Varion. The histories and biographies spoke often of her. What they didn't mention was the way Varion rested his hand on her elbow as they walked forward, the way he watched her with obvious fondness.

To Varion's right were Admirals Brakah and Terarn, two men who had been with Varion at the Academy, then had requested assignment under his command. They were said to be his most trusted advisors. They walked behind Varion as he approached, with the sure step Dennison had imagined. Varion stopped just short of entering the pavilion.

Sennion Crestmar, High Officer and Imperial Duke, stepped forward to greet his son. "In the name of the High Emperor, I welcome you, returning warrior." His words carried over the wind that still whipped outside the pavilion. "Accept this as a token of our esteem, and take your rightful place as the greatest High Admiral the empire has ever known."

Sennion extended a hand bearing a golden medal emblazoned with the double sunburst seal, the highest and most prestigious of the Imperial Crests.

Varion stood in the wind, looking down at the medal that swung from his father's hand. He reached out, taking the award, then held it up in the light, dangling it before his eyes.

All were still.

Then Varion let the medal drop to the grass.

Sennion's gun was in his hand in an instant. He pointed the weapon at his son's forehead and gave no opportunity for reaction. He simply pulled the trigger.

The energy blast burst just millimeters before Varion's face and then dissipated. The High Admiral hadn't moved. He was unhurt, and apparently unconcerned.

Around Dennison, the pavilion's occupants burst into motion. Flex-blasters and slug-drivers were pulled from holsters as men jumped for cover. Soldiers and officers alike drew. Dennison stood, immobile amid the yelling and the gunfire, and realized he wasn't surprised.

The greatest High Admiral the Fleet has ever known . . . perhaps the greatest commander mankind has ever seen. Of course he wouldn't stop with the Reaches. Why would he? Dennison's father fired again, weapon held just inches from Varion's face. Again the blast evaporated, hitting some kind of invisible shield.

This is no imperial technology, Dennison thought, stepping forward obliviously as others opened fire. Energy bolts and slugs alike were stopped by Varion's strange shield. *Twenty years on his own, autonomous and unfettered by imperial control . . . Of course! He captured the most technologically advanced worlds first. That's why some of those choices didn't make sense. He was planning for this even back then.*

Men called for Dennison's father to get out of the way. Some were firing at Varion's officers, but they too had the strange personal shields, and they stood calmly, not even bothering to return fire. Dennison continued to walk forward, drawn to his brother. He watched as Varion reached down, unholstered his sidearm, and raised it to his father's head.

"You are no child of mine," Sennion said, proudly staring down his son. "I disavow you. I should have done it twenty years ago."

Dennison froze as Varion pulled the trigger. The duke's corpse crumpled to the ground, a few wisps of smoke rising from his head.

A wave of gun blasts stormed from behind Dennison, ineffectively firing at Varion. The grass and earth before Varion exploded with fire and weapon blasts. Someone called for a physician.

Varion turned to regard the attack, raising a hand, waving his people back into the ship. Then he noticed Dennison. Silvermane stepped forward, carefully picking his way across the scarred ground. Dennison felt like scrambling back toward his speeder, but running would be useless. This was Varion Silvermane. He did not lose. People did not escape him. Those eyes . . . looking into those eyes, Dennison knew that this man could destroy him.

Varion stopped right in front of Dennison. The High Admiral's eyes looked contemplative. "So," he finally said, voice clear even over the gunfire and yells. "They *did* clone me. Well, the High Emperor will find that I am capable of defeating even myself."

He turned and left. Someone finally got a big repeating Calzer gun working, and it fired a blinding barrage of blue bolts. Varion's shields repulsed them. There should have been some blowback, at least, but there was nothing. Varion walked up the ramp to his ship as calmly as he had strolled down.

The Calzer soon drained the pavilion's energy stores, and the weather sphere collapsed, letting in the full fury of the winds. Dennison stepped forward through lines of smoke torn and then dispersed by the gale, ignoring the voices of angry, confused, and frightened men.

Varion's dropship blasted off, throwing Dennison to the ground. By the time his vision cleared, the ship was a dark speck in the air.

—

"We knew he had *something*," Kern said, watching the holo for the tenth time. "But his shield—where did he develop it? We put spies on each world . . ."

"He brought them with him," Dennison said quietly, standing against the view railing.

"What?"

"The scientists," Dennison said from the side of the hologram room. "Varion doesn't trust anything he can't watch directly. He would have brought the scientists from Gemwater with him, probably on his flagship. That way he could supervise their work."

"Gemwater . . ." Kern said. "But he conquered that planet over fifteen years ago! You think your brother has been keeping secrets for that long?"

Dennison nodded distractedly. "He knew from that first battle at Seapress. He understood that by quelling the Reaches, he would make the High Empire stronger and harder to defeat when the time came. That's why he took Gemwater so early, to give its scientists decades to build him secret technology."

Kern watched the holo again.

The universe felt . . . *awry* to Dennison. His father was dead. Sennion Crestmar had never been loving, but he had instilled in Dennison a powerful will to succeed. He'd been demanding, rigid, and unforgiving. Yet Dennison had hoped that someday . . . maybe . . . he would be able to make the man proud.

And now he never would. Varion had robbed Dennison of that.

What does it matter? Dennison thought. The hologram below showed the firefight through smoke and verdant grass. *Sennion wasn't even really my father. I have no father. Unless Varion was wrong.*

No. Varion was never wrong.

Only two men could verify the claim for certain. The first lay dead from an energy blast to the head. The other—the High Emperor, who had to approve all cloning petitions—had yet to respond to Dennison's request for an audience. But Dennison knew what the answer would be. The saddest part wasn't that Dennison was a fabricated tool, it was that he was a defective one. Genetically he was the same as Varion. He had even checked in the mirror and found a few silver hairs. Varion had started to go grey at twenty-three—Dennison's age now.

So many things made sudden and daunting sense. *You* cannot *be like other officers,* his father had said. *The High Empire expects more.* No wonder they had pushed Dennison so hard; no wonder they had refused to let him leave the service. He *was* Varion.

And yet he wasn't. Whatever Varion had, it hadn't been transmitted to Dennison. That confidence of his hadn't come from a random mingling of chromosomes. The victories, the power, the sheer momentum. These could not be copied.

The High Emperor will find that I am capable of defeating even myself. Varion knew—knew that he was special, somehow.

"Dennison," Kern said.

Dennison looked up. Kern sat below, in a chair just before the holo, looking up disapprovingly. He had paused the recording. The point he had inadvertently chosen showed a disturbing image. Varion's weapon raised, smoking, a corpse falling to the grass below . . .

"Dennison, I asked you a question," Kern said.

"He's going to win, Kern," Dennison said, staring at the holo. "The empire . . . to Varion, what is the empire but another collection of recalcitrant planets to be brought into line?"

Kern glanced at the holo, and—realizing where he'd paused it—turned off the image.

"We are High Officers, Dennison," Kern said sternly. "Such talk isn't fitting."

Dennison snorted.

"Varion *can* be defeated," Kern insisted.

Dennison shook his head. "No. He can't. And why should we bother, anyway? When does a man stop being a hero and start being a tyrant? If he had the right to bring the rebellious Reaches into line, then why shouldn't he claim the same moral right regarding us?"

Kern frowned. "Only the planets that raided us were conquered—at least at first, back when Varion was still nominally under control. This complete conquest of the Reaches was his own plan, done against the High Emperor's wishes. By the time we realized our mistake, he was already too powerful. We had only one option—gather strength and wait, hoping that he would be satisfied with taking the Reaches."

Dennison shook his head. "If you hoped that, then you never really knew him. He is a conqueror, Kern. It's like he feels some divine right to take the High Throne for himself."

Kern's frown deepened. He reached over, turning the recording back on. Once again, Dennison was confronted by the frozen image of his father dying, his brother . . . his other self . . . watching impassively.

"At least the High Empire believes in honor, Dennison," Kern said. "Is there honor in that face? The face of a man who would slaughter his own father?"

Dennison glanced away, shutting his eyes. "Please."

He heard the holo wink off. "I'm sorry," Kern said sincerely. "Here, let me show you something else instead."

Dennison turned back; the holo shifted to an image of Varion. This image, however, was in motion. Varion sat behind a broad, black commander's desk, a small datapad in his hand.

"What is this?" Dennison asked, perking up.

"The feed from a bug we have in Varion's ready room," Kern explained. "Aboard the *Voidhawk*."

Dennison frowned. "How—?"

"Never mind how," Kern said. "This is our only bug feed from the *Voidhawk* that didn't fuzz off within an hour of the incident on Kress. I doubt that Varion's scanners caught the other twenty but missed this one."

"He knows about it, of course," Dennison said. "But why would he . . ." He trailed off. Silvermane had left the bug because it amused him. Even as Dennison watched, Varion looked up—directly toward the ostensibly hidden camera—and smiled.

"That man . . ." Kern said. "He wants us to watch him, to know how unconcerned he is by our spying. He's so arrogant, so certain of his victory. You would bow before this creature? Whatever the empire is now, it will be worse with him at the head."

Dennison watched Varion lounge in his ready room. *But I am him—an inferior knockoff, at least.*

Kern eventually snapped off the feed. "I'm giving you a subcommand, Dennison."

Dennison frowned. "I thought we had an understanding."

"We have too many fighters and too few officers. The time for study is over."

Dennison felt himself pale. "We'll be facing . . . him?"

"Just a minor battle," Kern said. "A preliminary skirmish, really. I doubt Varion will bother directing his side of it. It will happen some distance from the bulk of his fleet."

Dennison knew Kern was wrong. Varion directed all of his battles personally.

"This is a bad idea," Dennison finally said, but Kern had already turned back to his review of the Kress incident.

—

"Yes, son. It's true." The emperor looked . . . weary.

"It's illegal to clone a member of a High Family," Dennison said, frowning as he knelt in front of the wallscreen image.

"I *am* the law, Dennison," the emperor said. "Nothing I do can be illegal. In this case, the potential benefit of a cloning outweighed our reservations."

"And I was that benefit," Dennison said bitterly.

"Your tone threatens disrespect, young Crestmar."

"Crestmar?" Dennison snapped. "Clones have no legal house or family."

The High Emperor's aged eyes flashed with anger at the outburst, and Dennison looked down guiltily. Eventually, the emperor's voice continued, and Dennison was surprised at the softness he heard in it.

"Ah, child," the emperor said. "Do not think us monsters. The laws you speak of maintain order in High Family succession, but exceptions can be made. It was your father's stipulation in agreeing to this plan. Your right of succession was ratified by a closed council of High Dukes soon after your birth. Even had your father not required this, we would have done it. We did not create a life intending only to throw it away."

Dennison finally looked back up. The weariness he had noted in the High Emperor's face was evident again—during the last few years, the man had aged decades. *Worrying about Varion would do this to any man.* "Your Majesty," Dennison said carefully. "What if I had turned out as much a traitor as he?"

"Then you would have gone to war against him," the High Emperor said. "For Varion would never be willing to share rule, even with himself. We hoped maybe you would weaken each other enough for us to stand against you. That, however, was a contingency plan—our first and foremost goal was to see that you did *not* turn out as he. It . . . seems that we were *too* successful in that respect."

"Apparently," Dennison mumbled.

"If that is all, young Crestmar, then I must be about the empire's business—as must you. The time for your battle approaches quickly."

Dennison bowed his farewell, and the wallscreen winked off.

—

Dennison paused in the doorway, the command bridge extending before him. This would be his first time commanding a real crew since he had begun studying under Kern's direction.

The bridge of the *Perpetual* was compact, as one would expect from a ship of its class. Kern's fleet had a dozen such minor command ships that traveled attached to the *Stormwind*. During a battle they were released and stationed across the battle space, allowing for a division of labor, as well as decentralizing leadership.

The bridge was manned by five younger officers. Dennison realized with chagrin that he didn't know their names—he had been too engrossed in his studies to mingle with the rest of Kern's command staff. Dennison walked down the ramp toward the battle hologram. The officers stood at attention. There was something odd about their postures. With a start, Dennison realized what it was. None of them showed even a hint of disrespect. Dennison had come to expect a certain level of repressed scorn from those under him. From these men, there was nothing. No hint that they expected him to fail, no signs that they were frustrated at being forced to serve with him. It was an odd feeling. A good feeling.

These are Kern's men, Dennison thought, nodding for them to return to their stations. *They're not just some random crew—they trust their ultimate commander, and therefore trust his decision to assign me to this post.*

The battle hologram blossomed, and a crewman approached with a battle visor. Dennison waved her away. She bowed and withdrew, showing no surprise.

They trust me, Dennison thought uncomfortably. *Kern trusts me. How can they? Can they really have forgotten my reputation?*

He had no answers for himself, so instead he studied the battle space. Varion's ships would soon arrive. His forces were pushing toward Inner Imperial Space, surrounding the High Emperor's forces in an attempt to breach the imperial line simultaneously in a dozen different places. Kern's forces were arrayed defensively—a long double wave of ships positioned for maximum mutual support. Dennison and his twenty ships were at the far eastern end of the line—a reserve force, unless they were directly attacked.

As seen in the holo, Varion's squadron suddenly appeared as a scattering of red monoliths disengaging from the *klage-dynamic*. Their *klage* wouldn't have been very fast—only a small multiple of conventional speeds—because of the large command ships at the rear. When traveling together, a fleet could only move as quickly as its largest—and therefore slowest—ships.

Just a moment after the command ships disengaged from *klage*, fighters spurted from Varion's fleet toward Dennison's squadron. So much for staying in reserve. Dennison's hologram automatically zoomed in so he could deploy his ships. He had twenty fighters and the *Perpetual*, a cruiser which could, in a pinch, act as a carrier as well. Directly to port was the *Windless*, a gunship with less speed and maneuverability but greater long-range firepower.

Kern would make the larger, battlewide decisions, and subcommanders like Dennison would execute them. Dennison's own orders were simple: hold position and defend the *Windless* if his sector was pressed. Dennison's crew waited upon his commands.

"Expand hologram," Dennison said. "Revert to the main tactical map."

Two of the officers shared a look at the unconventional order. It wasn't Dennison's job to consider the entire battle. Yet they did as he asked, and the hologram zoomed back out to give Dennison a view of the entire battle space. He stepped forward—bits of hologram shattering against his body and re-forming behind him—studying the ships in red. Varion's fleet. Though the Silvermane wasn't present personally, he would be directing the battle from across space. Dennison was finally facing his brother. The man who had never known defeat.

The man who had killed his father.

You're not perfect, Varion, Dennison thought. *If you were, you'd have found a way to bring our father to your side, rather than just blasting him in the forehead.*

Varion arranged his defense. Three prongs of fighters bracketing larger gunships formed the most direct assault in his direction. Something was off. Dennison frowned, trying to decide what was bothering him.

"Kern," he said, tapping a dot on the hologram, opening a channel to the admiral.

"I'm rather busy, Dennison," Kern said curtly.

Dennison paused slightly at the rebuke. "Admiral," he said, a little more formal. "Something is wrong."

"Watch your sector, Lieutenant. I'll worry about Varion."

"With all due respect, Admiral," Dennison said, "you just had me study him for months on end. I know Varion Crestmar better than any living man. Are you sure this is the time to ignore my advice?"

Silence.

"All right," Kern said. "Make it quick."

"The orientation of his forces is odd, sir," Dennison said. "His fighter prongs have been deployed to focus on the eastern sector of the battle. Away from you. But the *Stormwind* is by far the most powerful ship in this confrontation—stronger, even, than Varion's own capital ships. He *has* to deal with you quickly."

"He's used this formation before," Kern said. "Remember Gallosect Four? He focused on gunships first so that he could surround the flagship and take it from a distance."

"He had two-to-one advantage at Gallosect," Dennison said. "He could afford to expend fighters keeping the flagship busy. He's too thinly extended to try that here—by pressing to the east, he's going to expose himself to your batteries. He'll lose capital ships that way."

Silence.

"You wearing your visor, Dennison?" Kern asked.

"No."

"I thought not," Kern said. "Put one on."

Dennison didn't argue. The same aide walked back, proffering the equipment. Dennison slipped it on and saw a view from his fighter commander's cockpit.

"Here," Kern said, through the earpiece, no longer using an open channel. "Look at this."

The right half of Dennison's visor changed, showing a smaller version of the battle map. It was covered with arrows indicating attack vectors, and there were annotations around most of the vessels.

"What is this?" Dennison asked.

"Speak quietly," Kern said in a whisper. "Not even my bridge officers know about this feed."

"But what is it?"

"Intercepted *klage* communications," Kern said softly. "This image is being sent from Varion to his commanders here. It's how he commands—not verbally, but with battle maps outlining what he wants done."

"You can intercept *klage* communications!" Dennison said quietly, turning away to muffle his voice. "How?"

"Varion wasn't the only one who spent these last few decades working on technology," Kern said. "We focused on communications and may have gotten the better end of the bargain, since it appears his shields are only effective on a personal scale. Our scientists developed a special bug that can work on a *klage* transmitter. The bug in Varion's ready room, the one he thinks he's so clever to have found, is just a red herring."

"Can you intercept the responses from Varion's commanders?"

"Yes," Kern said. "But only if they come through the *klage* transceiver on the *Voidhawk*."

"And could we change the orders he sends?" Dennison asked.

"The techs say they might be able to," Kern said. "But if we do, we give away that we've been listening in. This gives us an edge. Read that map and tell me what you think."

Dennison zoomed his visor in on Varion's orders. They were succinct and clear. And brilliant. As the fighters engaged, he saw patterns emerge and interact. His brother made brave moves—daring, almost ridiculous moves. Here, a squadron of fighters was lured too close to another group. There, a gunship used its opponents as screens, keeping their cannons silent lest they destroy their own forces.

And he continued to push east. Varion didn't explain himself in his transmissions, but after just a few minutes of watching, Dennison had confirmed his suspicions. "Kern," he said quietly, drawing the admiral's attention back from his command. "He's coming for me."

"What?" Kern asked.

"He's coming for me," Dennison replied. "He's defeated every commander he's ever gone up against—and now he has a chance for what he sees as the ultimate battle. He wants to fight himself. He wants to fight me."

"Nonsense," Kern said. "How would he know where you are? He doesn't have our *klage* interception capability—of that, we're as certain as we can be."

"There are other ways to get information," Dennison said.

He stood quietly for a moment. And then he felt a chill.

"Kern," he snapped, "we need to retreat."

"What?" the admiral said with frustration. He obviously didn't like being distracted.

"This whole battle is wrong," Dennison said. "He's planning something."

"He's *always* planning something."

"This time it's different. Kern, he wouldn't expose himself to the *Stormwind* like that. Not even to get to me. We need to—"

A blast—sharp, shockingly loud—sounded in Dennison's ear. He jumped, crying out.

"Kern!" Dennison yelled.

Chaos. Screaming. And then static. Dennison whipped off his visor, looking at his startled crew. "Raise the admiral!"

"Nobody's responding," said the comm officer. "Wait—"

"... Lord Canton from the *Stormwind* reserve bridge," a voice feed crackled to life. "There has been an explosion on the main bridge. I am assuming command of the ship. Repeat. I am assuming command."

Kern! Dennison thought. He spun, looking at the holographic projection of the *Stormwind*. An explosion on the bridge—sabotage? An assassin?

A shot sounded. Several of Dennison's crew jumped—but this too had come over the comm.

"Lord Canton!" Dennison shouted.

Screams. Weapons fire.

He scanned the battle map. Kern's forces were in chaos. Even within the careful structure of the Imperial Fleet, the loss of an admiral was devastating. Varion's forces pressed on, fighters darting, gunships firing. Pressing toward Dennison.

Kern might still be alive ...

No. Varion's assassin wouldn't fail. Varion wouldn't fail.

"This is Lord Haltep of the *Farmight*," a voice crackled over the comm. "I am assuming command of this battle. All commanders secure bridges! Squadrons Six through Seventeen, press toward the *Stormwind*. Don't let the flagship fall!"

That's what Varion wants, Dennison thought. *He presses east, creates a disaster on the flagship, then cuts us in two.*

This battle could not be won. It was hard to see—technically, they still outnumbered Varion's forces. But Dennison could see the death of Kern's fleet in the chaos of the battle space. Varion was control. Varion was order. Where there was chaos, he would prevail.

But what could Dennison do about it? Nothing. He was useless.

Except . . .

I can't let Kern's fleet be destroyed. These men trusted him.

"Open a channel to the commanders of every capital ship," Dennison said quietly to his crew.

They complied.

"This is Duke Dennison Crestmar," Dennison said, feeling a bit surreal as holographic ships burst and died around him. "I am invoking Article One Hundred Seventeen and taking command of this fleet."

Silence.

"What are your orders, my lord?" a stiff voice eventually asked. It was Lord Haltep, the one who had only just assumed command.

These are *good soldiers,* Dennison thought. *How did Kern, who seemed so relaxed about military protocol, command such respect from his men?*

Perhaps that was what Dennison should have been studying these last two years. Regardless, he had command. Now, what did he do with it? He stood for a moment, watching the battlefield in its chaos, and felt a twinge of excitement. This was no simulation. That was Varion, the real man, on the other side. This was what Dennison had been created to do: to fight Varion, to defend the empire. Why else had he studied all those months?

Why else did I study? So I could know that this battle was unwinnable. Our admiral dead, our forces divided. Varion would easily beat me in a fair battle.

And this one is far from fair.

"All fighter squadrons to the eastern flank," Dennison said.

"But the flagship!" Haltep said. "Our forces have regained control inside. They're on the third bridge!"

"You heard my orders, Lord Haltep," Dennison said quietly. "I want the fighters back, arranged in a tight aegis pattern."

"Yes, my lord," a dozen voices came through the comm. Their fighters and gunships complied, pulling back into what was known as an aegis pattern—the fighters defending the larger ships at very close ranges.

Dennison lost some fighters as they broke off from the enemy. *Come on,* he thought. *I know what you want to do. Do it!*

Varion's ships swarmed the *Stormwind*. It began to fire back, displaying awesome power, but without its own fighters, it was at a distinct disadvantage. Explosions flashed on Dennison's hologram.

"All ships to dock," Dennison said.

"What?" Haltep's voice demanded.

"Varion's fighters are busy," Dennison said. "I want all fighters to dock in the closest command ship. The gunships can even take a few, if necessary. We only have a few minutes."

"Retreat," Haltep spat over the comm.

"Yes," Dennison replied. *I've certainly had a lot of practice.*

It worked. Varion realized too late what Dennison was doing—he'd already committed to taking down the *Stormwind*. It wasn't a mistake, but it was as near to one as Dennison had ever seen from his brother. Obviously he hadn't expected Dennison to concede and run so quickly.

As the larger ships began to *klage* away, Dennison watched the *Stormwind* finally break, its massive hull blowing outward from a ruptured core. Debris sprayed through his hologram as the mighty ship died.

And so, I fail again, Dennison thought as his own ship *klaged* away.

Dennison strode down the walkway, clothed in a crisp white uniform. It bore no ornamentation—no awards, no badges of service, no indications of commissions fulfilled. His speeder sat cooling in the dock; he'd spent nearly a week in transit back to the Point, thinking about Kern's death and the loss of the *Stormwind*. Why did the admiral's death bother him even more than his father's had?

A squad of six armed MPs met him at the foot of the ramp. *Six?* Dennison thought. *Did they really think I'd be that much trouble?*

"Lord Crestmar," one of them said. "We're here to escort you."

"Of course," Dennison said. He walked, surrounded by soldiers, still lost in thought.

What would have happened if he'd fought his brother? He couldn't have won, but Kern likely hadn't believed he'd beat Varion either. Kern had fought, rather than giving up. Rather than running. Now he was honorably dead, while Dennison still lived.

Lived after invoking a near-forbidden article and forcing an embarrassing retreat. Men had been executed for less. Men had deserved execution for less.

The guards led him through four separate checkpoints. Dennison's trip home had been spent in near silence, with sparse communications, so Dennison knew little of Varion's conquests during the last week. However, considering the events aboard the *Stormwind*, the extra security made sense.

His escort led him into a section of the imperial complex filled with bustling aides and officers. It was a testament to their worried state that not a single one paused to notice him, despite the color of his uniform and the crests that declared him to be an Imperial Duke. Crests that he probably wouldn't hold for much longer. After a few turns down hallways, the guards led Dennison to the emperor's command center. They walked apart from him, so they didn't tread on the crimson carpet reserved for High Officers.

The soldiers at the door saluted, and Dennison's escort halted. "The emperor is inside, my lord," the lead MP said.

Dennison paused. This was looking less and less like an execution. Ignoring his pounding heart, Dennison walked into the command center. None of the guards went with him.

The first thing that struck him was the room's busyness. Ten huge viewscreens had been erected all around the chamber, and high-ranking officers stood before these, calling out orders. Aides and junior officers scurried about, and armed soldiers, their weapons drawn, stood in every corner of the room, watching the occupants with suspicion. Nearly everyone—guards and commanders alike—seemed haggard, their faces wan, their eyes red from stress and fatigue. The room was kept dim to make the glowing icons that represented ships more easily visible.

The viewscreens depicted ten different battles in ten different systems. Dennison caught a young officer's arm. "What is going on here?"

"The Silvermane," the woman said. "He's attacking."

"Where?"

"Everywhere!"

Dennison let the woman go. *Everywhere?* he thought, stepping forward. He recognized a few of the men giving orders. High Admirals, like his father. Scanning the screens, Dennison was able to piece together their situation. New Seele. Highwall. Tightendow Prime. These were important core worlds, each home to an imperial fleet.

The emperor had moved his other fleets out to protect his borders. Dennison knew the numbers; he knew how many ships the Fleet had. If Varion took these worlds, there would be nothing left to resist him. The empire would be his.

"And he's fighting them all at once," Dennison said aloud, looking up at the screens. "He's controlling all ten battles at the same time."

An aging admiral—one Dennison recognized from his Academy days—sat in an exhausted posture in one of the room's many chairs. "Yes," the man said. "It's like we're a game to him. Defeating us one at a time isn't enough of a challenge. He planned it like this—he wants to destroy us all at once—to show us just how good he is. By the Seal, we never should have let him leave the Academy. We've doomed ourselves."

Dennison turned away from the screens. At the center of the room, on a platform elevated a few steps above the floor, the emperor sat in a large command chair surrounded by ten smaller viewscreens showing the same ten battles. He was obviously making an effort to maintain an erect, confident posture—but somehow that only made him look wearier, like a warrior straining to bear armor that was too heavy for him.

Dennison stepped up to the chair.

"Dennison," the emperor said, looking at him with tired eyes, but smiling slightly. "You arrived just in time to watch your empire fall."

"I suppose executing me now would be pointless."

"Executing?" the emperor asked, frowning.

"For invoking Article One Hundred Seventeen and losing a flagship."

The emperor sat for a moment, blinking. "Dennison, I was actually thinking of giving you a medal."

"For what, Your Majesty? Most flamboyant waste of half a fleet?"

"For *saving* half a fleet," the emperor said. "Lad, you have always been too hard on yourself. Varion was an optimist all through the Academy; he believed that he could do anything. Why do you always assume that you are a failure?"

"I—"

"Varion struck six separate fleets the same day he attacked Kern's," the emperor said. "In each battle, he managed to assassinate the fleet admiral—and in four of the six cases, he killed the next man who took command as well. We still don't know how he got so many assassins onto our bridges—you can see that we've had to take a number of precautions here on the Point.

"Regardless, of those six fleets, only *yours* escaped. Three of the fleets managed to disengage, but Varion chased them down and destroyed them. If you hadn't abandoned the flagship as you did, you never would have been fast enough to get away."

Dennison regarded the emperor, then looked down.

"Even in victory, you doubt yourself," the emperor said quietly.

"It's no victory with Kern dead, Your Majesty."

"Ah," the emperor said, rubbing his forehead. He looked so exhausted. So worried. "Do you know what happens when a conqueror runs out of people to fight, Dennison?"

Dennison hesitated, then shook his head.

"It's always the same," the emperor mused. "Men like Varion cannot be content with peaceful rule. They make brilliant commanders, but terrible kings. His reign will be filled with unrest, rebellion, oppression, and slaughter."

"You speak as if his victory were inevitable," Dennison said.

"Do you honestly believe otherwise?" the emperor asked.

Dennison glanced back at the big screens. He could easily see why the emperor had set up this room. The threat from Varion's assassins had required a single secure command post—likely with backups, should this one be destroyed—away from the ships themselves. The men here would be blood loyalists of the emperor's household. From this room, the Imperial High Admirals could command the ten separate battles and work for victory right under the emperor's eyes. Unfortunately, they were losing. All of them.

Such brilliance, Dennison thought. *Like a master of games, sitting before his boards, playing ten opponents simultaneously.* Varion seemed to be most brilliant when he was stretched, and these ten battles must have stretched him greatly, because he was in rare form. He pressed his advantage on all ten fronts, and while the battles were by no means over, Dennison could see where they were headed.

"I can't let you take command," the emperor said.

Dennison looked back.

"If that's why you came back to the Point," the emperor said, "then I must disappoint you. I read our almost inevitable doom in these battles, and the men who fight them are good tacticians. Our best. I realize you must want to fight your brother, but we both know you don't have the skill for it. I'm sorry."

Dennison turned back toward the viewscreens. "I didn't come to fight him, Your Majesty. I fled that opportunity."

"Ah. Well, perhaps you will survive his attack, lad. In a way, you are his family. He might let you live."

"As he let his father live?" Dennison replied.

The emperor did not respond. Dennison turned to watch the screens, staring at Varion in his power, his perfection. "If he comes, I don't want to live," Dennison whispered. "He's taken everything from me."

"Your father and Kern."

Dennison shook his head. "Not just that. He's stolen my purpose. I was created to defeat him, and yet I am just as powerless as the rest of you. Nobody can face Varion. For the others, there is no shame in this—but *my* inability is a profound failure. I could have been him."

"You don't want to be that creature, Dennison," the emperor said, shaking a weary head, leaning back. "What has his life been? Nothing but success after success. That has bred an arrogance that will kill him someday. Better to be the failure who nobly strived than the success who never really had to."

Dennison closed his eyes. The words seemed foolish. Better to be Dennison the failure than Varion the genius?

What could I possibly have that Varion does not?

Dennison hesitated. Around him there were sounds—breathing, grumbling, called commands. One of the admirals cursed loudly.

Dennison didn't open his eyes. That admiral's curses—he knew what had caused them. "The battle for Tightendow Prime," Dennison said. "Varion just took the eastern fighter flank, didn't he?"

"Actually, yes," the emperor said.

Dennison stood with eyes closed. "On the fifth screen. He is pressing toward the gunships in the western screen-sector. He is taking them now, though moments ago they seemed safe. On the first monitor, he is pushing toward the flagship. It will fall within ten minutes. On the ninth screen, Taurtan, he is leading your fighters into a trap. They are being cut off somehow—I don't know how, but I know he is doing it. They are lost."

Silence.

"On the eighth screen, the planet Falna, he is collapsing the front line. After that, he will find a way to push the gunships into retreat, breaking their firing lines and opening the way for his fighters."

"Yes," the emperor whispered.

Dennison opened his eyes. "I don't know *how* he will do these things, Your Majesty. That is the difference between him and me. Somehow, he can make his dreams into realities." Dennison turned toward the emperor. "Do we still have the bug in Varion's *klage* transmitter?"

"For all the good it does," the emperor said. "We discover his orders only a few moments before they are carried out. Perhaps that has allowed us to survive this long."

"Just before he died," Dennison said, "Kern told me that you might have found a way to fake the transmissions coming in and out of Varion's ship."

"The long-distance ones, yes," the emperor said, frowning. "But it's far better just to spy on him. If we started fabricating messages, it wouldn't take long for Varion and his men to discover the trick. We'd trade a long-term tactical advantage for a few minutes of confusion."

"Your Majesty," Dennison said, "there *is* no more long-term. If Varion wins this day, then we are all dead."

The emperor's frown deepened. He sat in thought for a moment, rubbing his chin. "What do you propose?" he finally asked.

What am *I proposing?* Dennison thought. *I've failed enough. Why pull the entire empire down with me?*

He started to tell the emperor he'd meant nothing by the comments, but something made him stop. Optimism and pessimism. He'd learned many things from watching Varion—tactics, strategy, how to manipulate a squadron. But it seemed he'd never learned the one thing that was most important.

Confidence.

"I'll need a crew of technicians and aides," Dennison said, "and these ten monitors beside your throne. Oh, and a tech who is familiar with that bugging system we have on Varion's *klage.*"

The emperor continued to sit in his command chair for a moment, looking up at Dennison appraisingly. Then, surprisingly, he stood, calling to one of the admirals. A few moments later a young technician was ushered into the command center.

"You can hack the traitor's *klage* data lines?" Dennison asked the thin man. "Sending false information to Varion's ship?"

The technician nodded.

"How long can you keep it up?" Dennison asked.

"It depends," the technician said. "He has no reason to suspect a bug in his transmitter—he doesn't know about the technology. But changing his information will create some interference that his technicians should notice and pick apart. If I have to guess, I'd say maybe a half hour or so."

Dennison nodded thoughtfully.

"My lord," the tech continued. "It won't be a very useful half hour. We can send false messages in, and we can block the real transmissions from his admirals. But we can't stop orders going *out* from the *Voidhawk*, so the nine other battle groups will soon realize Varion no longer knows what is truly happening, and is relying on bad information."

"No matter," Dennison said. "Prepare to hack the line. I want you to make it seem that the fleets in the other nine battles are doing exactly as I say. Instead of the real reports Varion's commanders are sending, give him the fabrications I describe."

The technician nodded, gathering a small crew and moving to a set of consoles at the side of the room.

"What good will this do us, Dennison?" the emperor asked quietly. "Buy us a little time, perhaps? Sow a little confusion?"

"Yes," Dennison said. "Make certain your admirals make good use of it."

"What of the tenth battle?" the emperor asked. "That's the one where Varion himself commands in person. We can't fool his own eyes—and that battle is happening the closest to the Point. If he wins there, he comes here, and none of our fleets will be able to stop him."

Dennison turned, glancing at the tenth map. The *Voidhawk*, Varion's own flagship, flew there in its glory. Dennison looked away from the ship, scanning the screen, searching for a particular squadron of fighters. They were always at the forefront of the battles where Varion himself was present. It was led by a particular pilot: the woman who had walked beside Varion on Kress.

Dennison walked over to the admiral who was contending with Varion in this tenth battle. "My lord, I need you to do something for me. Take five squadrons of fighters, and make certain to destroy *every single fighter* in that unit at mark five-six-six."

"Five squadrons?" the admiral asked with surprise.

Dennison nodded. "Nothing else is as important as destroying those fighters."

The admiral looked questioningly over at the emperor, who nodded. The admiral turned to obey the order, and the aging monarch looked uncertainly at Dennison, who returned to his side. Then the emperor stepped aside, gesturing toward his command seat, which sat before the ten smaller screens. "You'll need this."

Dennison paused, then quietly sat down.

"I'm ready," the technician said.

"Interrupt the feed," Dennison said, taking a deep breath, "and show Varion exactly what I tell you."

The man did so, and Dennison took control of nine battles. Or, at least, he took *fake* control of them. The blips on his screens became lies. Fabrications, sent to Varion as a poisoned gift of knowledge.

The knowledge of what it was like to be Dennison.

Varion swung his fighters toward the gunship position on the planet Falna, intending to push back the imperial line. In real life, that's exactly what happened. However, in the simulation, Dennison made a few changes. One of the imperial ships got in a lucky shot, and Varion's fighter line took a hit in just the wrong place. The fake imperial line rallied, destroying Varion's ships in a way that was unlikely, but not unreasonable.

Dennison made such changes to each of the nine battles. Here, a squadron attacked at the wrong angle. There, a command ship's engines failed at precisely the wrong moment. Individually, they were the kinds of small problems that happened in every battle. Nothing ever went *exactly* to plan. Yet all of these small bits of luck added up. As the nine conflicts raged in real life, Dennison sent Varion an increasingly invalid picture of his battle spaces.

Whatever Silvermane tried, it failed. Fighter squadrons collapsed. Gunships missed their targets and then were destroyed by a random stray missile. Command ships fell, and sectors were lost—all in a matter of minutes, and across all nine battles.

In Varion's own vicinity, the five squadrons of imperial fighters did their job. The ships Dennison had targeted were gone in under a minute, though the major redirection of firepower left a hole in the central imperial line, making it collapse. Dennison paid no attention to that losing battle, or to the reports that the others were really faring far worse than his simulated victories. He even ignored the emperor, who called for a chair, then sat quietly beside him, watching his empire tumbling down around him.

Dennison ignored all of this. For a moment, he was perfect. He was Varion, his every effort rewarded. His hopes were truth. His commands matched his dreams. He was a *god*.

So this is what it is like to win, Dennison thought as his crew fabricated a victory for one of his squadrons, then sent it to Varion. *This is what it is like to expect to win. Is this really what he feels all the time? Is he so sure of himself that he sees his entire life as merely a simulation, played out exactly as he desires?*

Well, for a few moments, he'll have to live with being Dennison instead.

Dennison made the tactical fabric of the conflicts collapse, caused Varion's forces to be routed. The only battle Dennison couldn't control was the one at which Varion himself was present. However, once the Silvermane was convinced he was losing in other parts of the galaxy, he began to make mistakes on his own front. He took more and more risks, struggling against the omnipotent force that was Dennison.

"Revenge," the emperor whispered. "Is this what you wanted, Dennison? Is all of this about playing a last cruel trick on your brother before he takes our empire from us?"

Yes, Dennison thought. *This* was his victory—his victory over Varion, his victory over a failed life. *This* was his moment: a perfect crescendo of battle, the entire universe bending to his will.

Then it ended.

"Someone must have noticed the bug!" the technician shouted as the viewscreens suddenly snapped back to the real battles. "The *klage* vibrations were a little irregular. I warned you!"

Dennison sat back in the emperor's command chair, releasing the breath he'd been holding. The room was growing quieter—the ten admirals hadn't gained much during their respite. *I've failed,* Dennison thought. The deception hadn't lasted long enough—Varion would now know he'd been duped. His communications now secure, he would easily retake command of the other battles.

"What have you done?" the emperor asked Dennison with a haunted voice.

Dennison didn't respond. He sat motionless, staring at the ten screens. For a moment he'd almost been able to convince himself that he *was* Varion. A victor.

"Your Majesty!" a surprised voice called from the back of the room. It was the aging admiral, pointing at the screen. "Look! Look at the Silvermane's forces . . ."

In the tenth battle, the one that Dennison hadn't been able to falsify, several of Varion's fighter squadrons had turned away from their assault. Then the *Voidhawk* itself broke off its attack.

"Your Majesty, they're retreating!" another admiral said with amazement.

The emperor stood, turning toward Dennison. "What . . . ?"

Dennison stood as well, stepping forward, toward the viewscreen. *Could it be* . . . If Varion's technicians had found the discrepancy and fixed it on their own before telling Varion what was happening . . . extending for just a few moments the time in which Varion believed he was being defeated . . .

Dennison watched Varion's forces retreat, and in that moment he knew the truth. He could see it in the organization of the ships.

He had won. His trick had worked. "In all the things Varion discovered or was taught," Dennison said, a little stunned himself as he sat back in the chair, "for all his success, for all his genius, there was *one* thing he never learned . . ."

Dennison paused, reaching over to his datapad and looking for a specific data feed. He clicked the button, bringing up an image on the main viewscreen: the image that showed Varion's ready room via the bug that Varion had always known about. The bug that he had allowed to remain because it amused him. It showed exactly what Dennison had hoped to see.

There, presented on the enormous screen, was an image of the High Admiral. Lord Varion Crestmar the Silvermane, greatest military genius of the age, sat behind his desk in the *Voidhawk*. In his limp fingers he held a gun, a smoking hole blown through his own forehead.

"He never learned how to lose," Dennison whispered.

POSTSCRIPT

This is the second of the "early Brandon" stories in this collection—and is actually my first published piece of short fiction, though it was written after "Defending Elysium."

"Firstborn" has a quirky publication story. I sold it to *Tor.com*, right when *Tor.com* (now called *Reactor*) was new. They were exploring the idea of doing free fiction for publicity, and bought this story outright to put on their website. On a lark, they put it on Amazon a few years later for one dollar, even though it was free on their website.

This was my first experience with how powerful indie publishing could become, as I ended up earning more money on that story through Amazon than I did in the initial sale. The story was free elsewhere, and was only one dollar even on Amazon, *and* I got only a tiny fraction of the money (since Amazon and Tor both took their chunks first). Even with all of that, the earnings on the story blew away the pay of any other short story market—going on to earn me many multiples of what I could have earned selling it to an anthology or any of the major magazines. (*Tor.com*, it should be noted, had paid quite well for the story, so I'd considered the story as having done its job.) It was eye-opening to get a taste of what ebooks could be.

As for the text, this story is quite obviously a nature-versus-nurture story. I've often said it was a response to *Ender's Game* and the trope of a hypercompetent youth. (In *Ender's Game*, the protagonist's parents are allowed to have a third child because their first two had *almost* been perfect candidates for commanders in the space force, and the government wanted to roll the dice on a third child.)

Here, a direct clone of a genius military commander grows up to be . . . an ordinary guy. I don't know the actual balance between nature and nurture, but exploring such things is one of the reasons we write fiction, and I enjoyed this exploration.

I will note, somewhat critically, how often storytellers of this era (myself obviously included) liked to use suicide as a plot device. It's something that I suspect many of us are more conscious about these days. (In my case, I know that I am.)

MITOSIS

1

The day had finally arrived, a day I'd been awaiting for ten years. A glorious day, a momentous day, a day of import and distinction.

It was time to buy a hot dog.

Someone was in line when we arrived, but I didn't cut in front of her. She would have let me. I was one of the Reckoners—leaders of the rebellion, defenders of the city of Newcago, slayers of Steelheart himself. But standing in line was part of the experience, and I didn't want to skip a moment.

Newcago extended around me, a city of skyscrapers, underpasses, shops, and streets all frozen permanently in steel. Recently, Tia had started an initiative to paint some of those surfaces. Now that the city's perpetual gloom had been dispelled, it turned out all those reflective surfaces could make things *really* bright. With some work, instead of looking the same everywhere, the city would eventually become a patchwork of reds, oranges, greens, whites, and purples.

Abraham—my companion for this hot dog excursion—followed my gaze, then grimaced. "It would be nice if when we painted a wall, we would take a little more concern for colors that matched those of their neighbors."

Tall and dark-skinned, Abraham spoke with a light French accent. As he talked, he scanned the people walking nearby, studying each one in his trademark relaxed yet discerning way. The butt of a handgun poked from his hip holster. We Reckoners weren't *technically* police. I wasn't sure what we were. But whatever it was, it involved weapons, and I had my rifle over my shoulder. Newcago was almost kind of peaceful, now that we'd dealt with the rioters, but you couldn't count on peace lasting long. Not with Epics out there.

"We have to use the paint we can find," I said.

"It's garish."

I shrugged. "I like it. The colors are different. Not like the city was before Calamity, but also a big change from how it was under Steelheart. They make the city look like a big . . . chessboard. Um, one painted a lot of colors."

"Or perhaps a quilt?" Abraham asked, sounding amused.

"Sure, I suppose. If you want to use a boring metaphor."

A quilt. Why hadn't I thought of that?

The woman in front of us wandered off with her hot dog, and I stepped up to the stand—a small metal cart with a transformed steel umbrella permanently frozen open. The vendor, Sam, was an elderly, bearded man who wore a small red-and-white hat. He grinned at us. "For you, half price," he said, whipping up two hot dogs. Chicago style, of course.

"Half price?" Abraham said. "Saving the world does not inspire the gratitude it once did."

"A man has to make a living," Sam said, slathering on the condiments. Like . . . a lot of them. Yellow mustard, onions, chunked tomatoes, sweet pickle relish, peppers—whole, of course, and pickled—a dill pickle slice, and a pinch of celery salt. Just like I remembered. A true Chicago dog looks like someone fired a bazooka at a vegetable stand, then scraped the remnants off the wall and slathered it on a tube of meat.

I took mine greedily. Abraham was more skeptical.

"Ketchup?" Abraham asked.

The vendor's eyes opened wide.

"He's not from around here," I said quickly. "No ketchup, Abraham. Aren't you French? You people are supposed to have good taste in food."

"French *Canadians* do have good taste in food," Abraham said, inspecting the hot dog. "But I am not convinced that this is actually food."

"Just try it." I bit into my dog.

Bliss.

For a moment, it was as if no time had passed. I was back with my father, before everything went bad. I could hear him laughing, could smell the city as it had been back then—rank at times, yes, but also *alive*. Full of people talking and laughing and yelling. Asphalt streets, hot in the summer as we walked together. People in hockey jerseys. The Blackhawks had just won the Cup . . .

It faded around me, and I was back in Newcago, a steel city. But that moment of tasting it all again . . . sparks, that was wonderful. I looked up at Sam, and he grinned at me. We couldn't recapture it all. The world was a different place now.

But damn it, we *could* have proper hot dogs again.

I turned to look around the city. Nobody else had gotten in line, and people passed with eyes cast down. We were at First Union Square, a holy place where a certain bank had once stood. It was also the center of the new city's crossroads. It was a busy location, a prime spot for a hot dog vendor.

I set my jaw, then slapped some coins down on Sam's cart. "Free hot dogs for the first ten who want them!" I shouted.

People looked at us, but nobody came over. When some of them saw me watching, they lowered their eyes and continued on.

Sam sighed, crossing his arms on top of his cart. "Sorry, Steelslayer. They're too afraid."

"Afraid of hot dogs?" I said.

"Afraid to get comfortable with freedom," Sam said, watching a woman rush past and head into the understreets, where most people still lived. Even with sunlight up here now, and no Epics to torment them . . . even with painted walls and colors . . . they still hid below.

"They think the Epics will return," Abraham said with a nod. "They are waiting for the other shoe to drop, so to speak."

"They'll change," I said, stubbornly stuffing more of my hot dog into my mouth. I talked around the bite. "They'll see."

That was what this had all been about, right? Killing Steelheart? It had been to show that we *could* fight back. Everyone else would understand, eventually. They had to. The Reckoners couldn't fight every Epic in the country on our own.

I nodded to Sam. "Thanks. For what you do."

He nodded. It might seem silly, but Sam opening his hot dog stand was one of the most important events this city had seen in ten years. Some of us fought back with guns and assassinations. Others fought back with a little hot dog stand on the corner.

"We'll see," Sam said, pushing away the coins I'd set down, all but two nickels to pay for our hot dogs. We'd gone back to using American money, though only the coins, and we valued them much higher. The city government backed them with food stores, at Tia's suggestion.

"Keep it all," I said. "Give free hot dogs to the first ten who come today. We'll change them, Sam. One bite at a time."

He smiled, but pocketed the money. As Abraham and I walked off, Tia's voice, terse and distracted, came in over my earpiece. "Do you two have a report?"

"The dogs are awesome," I said.

"Dogs?" she said. "Watchdogs? You've been checking on the city kennels?"

"Young David," Abraham said around a mouthful, "has been instructing me on the local cuisine. They *are* called 'hot dogs' because they're only good for feeding to animals, yes?"

"You took him to that *hot dog* stand?" Tia asked. "Weren't you two supposed to be doing greetings?"

"Philistines, both of you," I said, cramming the rest of my hot dog into my mouth.

"We are on our way, Tia," Abraham said.

Abraham and I hiked toward the city gates. The new city government had decided to section off the downtown, and had done so by creating barricades out of steel furniture to block some of the streets. It created a decent perimeter of control that helped us keep tabs on who was entering our city.

We passed people scuttling about on their business, heads down. Sam was right. Most of the population seemed to think the Epics were going to descend upon the city any moment, exacting retribution. In fact, after we'd overthrown Steelheart, a shocking number of people had *left* the city.

That was unfortunate, as we now had a provisional government in place. We had farmers to work the fields outside, and Edmund using his Epic abilities to provide free power for the whole place. We even had a large number of former members of Steelheart's Enforcement troops recruited to police the city.

Newcago was working as well now as it had under Steelheart. We'd tried to replicate his organization, only without that whole "indiscriminate murder of innocents" thing. Life was good here. Better than anything else in the remnants of the Fractured States, for certain.

Still, people hid, waited for a disaster. "They *will* see," I muttered.

"Perhaps," Abraham said, eyeing me.

"Just wait."

He shrugged and chewed his last bit of hot dog. He grimaced. "I do not think I can forgive you for that, David. It was terrible. Tastes should complement one another, not hold all-out war with one another."

"You finished it."

"I did not wish to be impolite." He grimaced again. "Truly awful."

We walked in silence until we arrived at the first unbarricaded roadway. Here, members of Enforcement processed a line of people wanting to enter. People with Newcago passports—farmers or scavengers who worked outside of the downtown—went right through. Newcomers, however, were stopped and told to wait for orientation.

"Good crowd today," I noted. Some forty or fifty people waited in the newcomer line.

Abraham grunted. The two of us walked up to where a man in black Enforcement armor was explaining the city rules to a group in worn, dirty clothing. Most of these people would have spent recent years outside of civilization, dodging Epics, surviving as best they could in a land ruled by nested levels of tyrants, like Russian dolls with evil little faces painted on them.

Two families among the newcomers, I thought, noting the men and women with children. That encouraged me.

As several of the soldiers continued orientation, one of them—Roy—strolled over to me. Like the other soldiers, he wore black armor but no helmet. Enforcement members were intimidating enough without covering their faces.

"Hey," Roy said. He was a lanky redhead I'd grown up with. I still hadn't figured out whether he bore a grudge for that time I'd shot him in the leg.

"How's this batch?" I asked softly.

"Better than yesterday," Roy said with a grunt. "Fewer opportunists, more genuine immigrants. You can tell the difference when you explain the jobs we need done."

"The opportunists refuse the work?"

"No," Roy said. "They're just too excited, all smiles and eagerness. It's a sham. They plan to get put onto a work detail, then ditch it first chance to see what they can steal. We'll weed them out."

"Be careful," I said. "Don't blacklist someone just because they're optimistic."

Roy shrugged. Enforcement was on our side—we controlled the power that ran their weapons and armor—but they too seemed on edge. Steelheart had occasionally used them to fight lesser Epics. From what I'd heard, it hadn't gone well for the ordinary humans on either side of such a conflict.

These men knew firsthand what it was like to face down Epics. If a powerful one decided to step into Steelheart's place, the police force would be worth less than a bagful of snakes at a dance competition.

I gave Roy an encouraging slap on the shoulder. The officers finished their orientation, and I joined Abraham, who began introducing himself to the newcomers one at a time. We'd figured out that after Enforcement's cheerful welcome of stern gazes, strict rules, and suspicious glances, a little friendly chatting with someone more normal went a long way.

I welcomed one of the families, telling them how wonderful Newcago was and how glad I was they'd come. I didn't tell them specifically who I was, though I implied that I was a liaison between the city's people and the Reckoners. I had the speech down pat by now.

As we talked, I saw someone pass to the side.

That hair. That figure.

I turned immediately, stuttering the last words of my greeting. My heart thundered inside my chest. But it wasn't her.

Of course it wasn't her. *You're a fool, David Charleston,* I told myself, turning back to my duties. How long was I going to keep jumping every time I spotted someone who looked vaguely like Megan?

The answer seemed simple. I'd keep doing it until I found her.

This group took well to my introduction, relaxing visibly. A few even asked me questions. Turned out that the family in my group had fled Newcago years before, deciding that the convenience wasn't worth the tyranny. Now they were willing to give it another go.

I told the group about a few jobs in particular I thought they should consider, then suggested they get mobiles as soon as possible. A lot of our city administration happened through those, and the fact that we had electricity to power them was a highlight of Newcago. I wanted people to stop thinking of themselves as refugees. They belonged to a community now.

Introductions done, I stepped back and let the people enter the city. They started forward, trepidatious, looking at the towering buildings ahead. It seemed Roy had been right. This group was more promising than ones who had come before. We *were* accomplishing something. And . . .

I frowned.

"Did you talk to that one?" I asked Abraham, nodding to a man toward the rear of the departing group. He wore simple clothing, jeans and a faded T-shirt, and no socks with his sneakers. Tattoos ringed his forearm, and he wore an earring in one ear. He was muscular, with distinctively knobbed features, and was perhaps in his late thirties. There was something about him . . .

"He didn't say much," Abraham said. "Do you know him?"

"No." I narrowed my eyes. "Wait here."

I followed the group, pulling out my mobile and looking at it as I walked, feigning distraction. They continued on as we'd instructed them, making for the offices at First Union Square.

Maybe I was jumping at nothing. I usually got a little paranoid when the Professor wasn't in town. He and Cody had supposedly gone out east to check in with another cell of the Reckoners. Babilar or someplace.

Prof had been acting weird lately—at least, that was how we phrased it. "Weird" was actually a euphemism for "Prof is secretly an Epic, and he's trying hard not to go evil and kill us all, so sometimes he gets antisocial."

I now knew three Epics. After a lifetime of hating them, of planning how to kill them, I knew *three*. I'd chatted with them, eaten meals with them, fought beside them. I was fond of them. Well, more than fond, in Megan's case.

I checked on the walking group, then glanced at my mobile again. Life was annoyingly complicated now. Back when Steelheart had been around, I had only needed to worry about—

Wait.

I stopped, looking back up at the group I was following. *He* wasn't there. The man I'd been tailing.

Sparks! I pulled up against a steel wall, slapping my mobile into its place on the upper-left front of my jacket and unslinging my rifle. Where had the man gone?

Must have ducked into one of the side streets. I edged up to the one we'd just passed and peeked in. A shadow moved down it, away from me. I waited until it moved around the next corner, then followed at a dash. At the corner, I crouched and peeked in the direction the shadow had gone.

The man from before, in the jeans and wearing no socks, stood there looking back and forth.

Then there were *two* of him.

The twin figures pulled away, each heading in a different direction. They wore the same clothing, had the same gait, the same tattoos and jewelry. It was like two shadows that had overlapped had broken apart.

Oh, *sparks.* I pulled back around the corner, muted my mobile so the only sound it made would come through my earpiece, then held it up.

"Tia, Abraham," I whispered. "We have a *big* problem."

2

A h," Tia said in my ear, "I've found it."

I nodded. I was trailing one of the copies of the man. He'd already split twice more, sending clones in different directions. I didn't think he'd spotted me yet.

"Mitosis," Tia said, reading from my notes. "Originally named Lawrence Robert—an unusual Epic with, so far as has been identified, a unique power: He can split into an unknown number of copies of himself. You say here he was once a guitarist in an old rock band."

"Yeah," I said. "He still has the same look."

"Is that how you spotted him?" Abraham said in my ear.

"Maybe." I wasn't certain. For the longest time, I'd been sure I could identify an Epic, even when they hadn't manifested any powers. There was something about the way they walked, the way they carried themselves.

That had been before I'd failed to spot not only Megan, but Prof as well.

"You categorize him as a High Epic?" Tia asked.

"Yeah," I said softly, watching a version of Mitosis idle on the street corner, inspecting the people who passed. "I remember some of this. He's going to be tough to kill, guys. If even one of his clones survives, he survives."

"The clones can split as well?" Abraham asked.

"They aren't really clones," Tia said. I heard papers shuffling on her line as she looked through my notes. "They're all versions of him, but there's no 'prime' individual. David, are you sure about this information?"

"Most of my information is partially hearsay," I admitted. "I've tried to be certain where I can, but anything I write should be at least a little suspect."

"Well, it says here that the clones are all connected. If one is killed, the others will know it. They have to recombine to gain one another's memories, though, so that's something. And what's this? The more copies he makes . . ."

"The dumber they all get," I finished, remembering now. "When he's one individual, he's pretty smart, but each clone he adds brings down the IQ of all of them."

"Sounds like a weakness," Abraham said over the line.

"He also hates music," I said. "Just after becoming an Epic, he went around destroying the music departments of stores. He's known to immediately kill anyone he sees walking around wearing headphones or earbuds."

"Another potential weakness?" Abraham said over the line.

"Yeah," I said, "but even if one of those works, we still have to get each and every copy. That's the big problem. Even if we manage to kill every Mitosis we can find, he's bound to have a few versions of himself scattered out there, in hiding."

"Sparks," Tia said. "Like rats on a ship."

"Yeah," I said. "Or glitter in soup."

Tia and Abraham fell silent.

"Have you ever *tried* to get all of the glitter out of your soup?" I demanded. "It's really, really hard."

"Why would there be glitter in my soup in the first place?" Abraham asked.

"I don't know," I said. "Maybe the other boys dumped it in there. Does it matter? Look, Tia, is there anything else in the notes?"

"That's all you have," Tia said. "I'll contact the other lorists and see if anyone has anything more. David, continue observation. Abraham, make your way back to the government offices and quietly put them on lockdown. Get the mayor and her cabinet into the safe cells."

"You going to call Prof?" I asked softly.

"I'll let him know," she replied, "but he's hours away, even if we send a copter for him. David. Don't do anything stupid."

"When have I done anything stupid?" I demanded.

The other two grew silent again.

"Just try to curb your natural eagerness," Tia said. "At least until we have a plan."

A plan. The Reckoners loved to plan. They'd spend months setting up the perfect trap for an Epic. It had worked just fine when they'd been a shadowy force of aggressors, striking, then fading away.

But that wasn't the case anymore. We had something we had to defend now.

"Tia," I said, "we might not have time for that. Mitosis is here today; we can't spend months deciding how to bring him down."

"Jon isn't near," Tia said. "That means no jackets, no tensors, no harmsway."

That was the truth. Prof's Epic powers were the source of those abilities, which had saved my life many times in the past. But if he got too far away, the powers stopped working for those he'd gifted them to.

"Maybe he won't attack," Abraham said, puffing slightly as he spoke into the line. He was probably jogging as he made for the government building. "He could just be scouting. Or perhaps he is not antagonistic. It is possible that an Epic merely wants a nice place to live and will not cause problems."

"He's been using his powers," I said. "You know what that means."

We all did, now. Prof and Megan had proven it. If Epics used their powers, it corrupted them. The only reason Prof and Edmund didn't go evil was because they didn't use their powers directly. Giving them away filtered the ability somehow, purified it. At least, that was what we thought.

"Well," Abraham said, "maybe—"

"Wait," I said.

Down the way, Mitosis strode out onto the steel street, then reached back to take out a handgun he'd had tucked into the waistband of his jeans. Large-caliber magnum—far from the best of guns. It was a weapon for someone who had seen too many old movies about cops with big egos.

It could still kill, of course. A magnum could do to a person's head what a street could do to a watermelon dropped from a helicopter. My breath caught.

"I'm here," Mitosis shouted, "for the one they call Steelslayer, the *child* who supposedly killed Steelheart. For every five minutes it takes him to reveal himself, I will execute a member of this population."

3

W ell," Abraham said over the line, "guess that answers that."

"His clones are saying it all over the city," Tia said. "The same words from all of them."

I cursed, ducking back into my alley, gripping my rifle tight and sweating.

Me. He'd come for *me*.

All my life, I'd been nobody. I didn't mind that. I'd worked hard, actually, to be precisely mediocre in all my classes. I'd joined the Reckoners in part because nobody knew who they were. I didn't want fame. I wanted revenge against the Epics. The more of them dead, the better.

Sweat trickled down the sides of my face.

"One minute has passed!" Mitosis yelled. "Where are you? I would see you with my own eyes, Steelslayer."

"Damn," Tia said in my ear. "Don't panic, David. Music . . . music . . . There has to be a clue to his weakness here. What was his band again?"

"Weaponized Cupcake," I said.

"Charming," Tia said. "Their music should be on the lore archive; we've got copies of most everything in the Library of Congress."

"Two minutes!" Mitosis shouted. "Your people run from me, Steelslayer, but I am like God himself. I am everywhere. Do not think I won't be able to find some-one to kill."

Images flashed in my mind. A busy bank lobby. Bones falling to the ground. A woman clutching a baby. I hadn't been able to do anything back then.

"This is what we get," Abraham said, "for coming out into the open. It is why Jon always wanted to remain hidden."

"We can't stand for something if we only move in shadows, Abraham," I said.

"Three minutes!" Mitosis shouted. "I know you have this city under surveil-lance. I know you can hear me."

"David . . ." Tia said.

"It appears you are a coward!" Mitosis said. "Perhaps if I shoot someone, you—"

I stepped out, lined up a shot, and delivered a bullet into Mitosis's forehead.

Tia sighed. "I've got reports of at least thirty-seven distinct copies of him yelling in the city. What good does it do to kill one of them?"

"Yes," Abraham said, "and now he knows where you are."

"I'm counting on it," I said, dashing away. "Tia?"

"Sparks," she said. "I'm pulling up camera feeds all over the city. David, they're all running for you. Dozens of them."

"Good," I said. "As long as they're chasing me, they aren't shooting anyone else."

"You can't fight them all, you slontze," Tia said.

"Don't intend to," I said, grunting as I turned a corner. "You're going to work out his weakness and figure out how to beat him, Tia. I'm just going to distract him."

"I've arrived," Abraham said. "They're already on alert at the government office. I'll get the mayor and council to safety. But if I might suggest, this is probably a good time to activate the emergency message system."

"Yeah," Tia said, "on it."

The mobiles of everyone in the city were connected, and Tia could dial them all up collectively to send instructions—in this case, an order to empty the streets and get indoors.

I dodged around another corner and came almost face-to-face with one of Mitosis's clones. We surprised each other. He got his gun out first and fired, a deafening crack, like he was shooting a sparking *cannon*.

He also missed me. He wasn't even close. Big handguns look impressive, and they have excellent knockdown force. Assuming you can hit your target.

I lined up my rifle sights, ignored his next shot, and squeezed the trigger. Just as I did, he thrashed, and a duplicate of him stepped away. It was like he was suddenly made of dough and the other self *pushed* out of his side.

It was nauseating. My shot took the first Mitosis, dropping him with a hole in the chest. He tried to duplicate again as he died, but the duplicate came out with a hole in its chest too, and fell forward, dying almost immediately.

The other clone, though, was also duplicating. I cursed, shooting it, but not before another version came out, and that one was already trying to clone itself *again*. I brought this one down just before it split.

I breathed in and out, my hands trembling as I lowered the rifle. Five corpses lay slumped on the ground. My rifle magazine held thirty rounds. I'd never considered that insufficient, but a minute of Mitosis cloning himself could run me out with ease.

"David?" Tia asked in my ear. "You all right?" She'd have me on camera, using Steelheart's surveillance network.

"I'm all right," I said, still shaking. "I just haven't gotten used to people shooting at me."

I took a few deep breaths, forced down my anxiety, and walked up to the Mitosis clones. They'd begun to melt.

I watched with disturbed fascination as the corpses decomposed, flesh turning to a pale tan goo. The bones melted after, and then the clothing. In seconds, each corpse was just a pile of colored gunk, and even that seemed to be evaporating.

Where did the mass for each of these new bodies come from? It seemed impossible. But then, Epics have this habit of treating physics like something that happens to *other* people, like acne and debt.

"David?" Tia said in my ear. "Why are you still standing there? Sparks, boy! The others are coming."

Right. Dozens of evil Epic clones. On a mission to kill me.

I took off in a random direction; where I was going didn't matter so much as staying ahead of the clones. "Do you have that music yet?" I asked Tia.

"Working on it."

I dashed up onto the bridge, crossing the river. That river would have made a great natural barrier for sectioning off the downtown, except for the fact that Steelheart had turned the thing into steel—effectively making it into an enormous highway, though one with a rippled surface. The river that had once flowed here had diverted to the Calumet River channel.

I reached the other side of the bridge and glanced over my shoulder. A scattering of figures in identical clothing had broken out of side streets and were running toward me, some pulling handguns from the small of their backs. They seemed to recognize me, and a few took shots.

I cursed, ducking to the side, heading past an old hotel with steel windows and a trio of flagpoles extending into the sky, flags frozen mid-flap. I almost passed it, then hesitated. One of the main doors had been frozen open.

I made a split-second decision and ran for that opening. I squeezed between door and doorway and entered the hotel lobby.

It wasn't as dark inside as I'd anticipated. I inched through a lobby with furniture like statues. Once-plush seats were now hard metal. A sofa had a depression in it where someone had been sitting when the transfersion took place.

The light came from a series of fist-size holes cut into the front windows, which were also steel now. Though empty, the lobby didn't seem dusty or derelict. I quickly realized what this was—one of the buildings that Steelheart's favored people had inhabited during the years of his rule.

I stepped on a bench by a window, leaning against it and peering through one of the holes. Outside, on the daylit street, the clones slowed in their chase, lowering weapons, looking about. It appeared that I'd managed to lose them.

"I would have the truth!" the clones suddenly shouted in unison. The effect was even eerier than seeing them all together. "You did not kill Steelheart. You did not slay a god. What *really* happened?"

I didn't reply, of course.

"Your rumors are spreading," Mitosis continued. "People want to believe your fantasy. I will show them reality. Your head, David Charleston, and my empire in Newcago. I don't know how Steelheart truly fell, but he was weak. He needed men to administrate for him, to act as his army."

The clones continued to stroll, spreading out. Several shook, splitting into multiples.

"I am my own army," Mitosis said. "And I shall reign."

"You watching this?" I whispered.

"Yeah," Tia said. "I've got the city cameras, and I've dialed into the video feed from your earpiece. Shouldn't he be sounding dumber the more clones he makes?"

"I think something must be wrong in my notes," I said. I'd been forced to burn many of my notebooks and keep only the most important ones. I'd lost many of my primary sources and speculations, and I could have easily gotten some details wrong.

Outside, Mitosis continued to duplicate himself. Twice, three times, a half dozen. Soon there were *hundreds* of him. They spaced themselves apart with careful steps, then, one by one, stopped in place. They closed their eyes, looking toward the sky.

What is he doing? I thought, clutching my rifle. I shifted on the bench, my foot scraping the wall.

Outside, some of the clones nearest the hotel snapped their eyes open and turned toward me. Sparks! He'd created his own sensor network, using hundreds of copies of his own ears. It was clear to me now that the clones had more coordination to them than I had assumed. I slipped away from the wall, trying to step quietly. There might be a back way out of this building.

"Got it," Tia said. "Archive of pre-Calamity alternative metal albums in digital format."

Her voice through the earpiece was incredibly soft. Still, outside, there was a sudden scrambling of footsteps. They'd heard.

They were coming.

I cursed and ran, leaping over a couch and scrambling toward the back hallways of the hotel. There had to be a way out somewhere.

I passed through streams of light, holes cut like spigots into the ceiling. The hotel had this flat building in the center and a tower to the side, many stories high. I didn't want to get trapped in the tower, so instead I turned down another hallway, passing a door that had been destroyed long ago. That light ahead was probably an exit for—

Shadows moved in through the exit. Clones, around a dozen of them, one after another. One pulled out a gun and leveled it at me, but when he squeezed the trigger, the entire thing shattered and turned to dust. The clone cursed, charging.

Huh? I thought.

There wasn't time for me to wonder. I threw myself to the side, entering another hallway. These were the administrative rooms of the hotel, behind the lobby.

"I'm trying to get you a map," Tia said.

"No," I said, sweating, "the music."

"Right."

More clones that way. I was cornered.

I ducked into a room. It had once been some kind of clerical office, judging by the desk and frozen chairs, but someone had turned the desk into a bed with cushions, and there was even a wooden door affixed by new hinges attached to the steel ones on the doorway. Impressive.

I grabbed that door and slammed it closed. An arm got in the way at the last moment.

The clone grunted on the other side as I shoved, but other hands scraped around the doorway, grabbing for me. Each had an old wristwatch on it, and those snapped and broke as they rubbed on the door or wall. When the watches hit the ground, they shattered to dust.

"They're unstable," Tia said—she was still watching via my video feed. "The more clones he makes, the worse their molecular structure holds together."

The clones forced the door open, throwing me backward. I whipped my rifle from my shoulder and got off one shot as a dozen of them fought into the room, heedless of the danger. Their clothing ripped easily, and when fragments fell off, they disintegrated immediately.

"'Albums by Weaponized Cupcake,'" Tia read.

The clones piled on top of me, hands gripping my throat, others pulling my gun away from me.

"Which one?" Tia asked. "*Appetite for Tuberculosis? The Blacker Album? Ride the Lightrail?*"

"Kind of getting murdered here, Tia!" I said, struggling to keep the hands from my neck.

There were too many. Hands pressed in closer, cutting off my air. Clones continued to clog the room, and those nearby began to split, making it difficult to move. They wanted to trap me in here. Even if I got these fingers off my neck, I wouldn't be able to run.

Darkness grew at the edges of my vision, like a creeping mold. I struggled to pull the hands from my throat.

"David?" Tia's voice in my ear. "David, you need to turn on your mobile speaker! I can't do anything. David, can you hear me? David!"

I closed my eyes. Then I let go of the hands holding my neck and forced my fingers through the press of arms. Choking, feeling as if my windpipe would collapse at any moment, I strained and got my fingers to my shoulder, where my mobile was attached. I flipped the switch on the side.

Music blared into the cramped, suffocating room.

The clone directly on top of me started to shake and vibrate, like he was going to split—but instead, he began to melt, the flesh coming off the bones. The others nearby backed away in a hurry, smashing identical versions of themselves up against the walls.

I gasped in air. For a moment, all I could do was lie there, clone flesh and bones melting to goo around me.

Air. Air is really, *really* awesome.

The music continued unabated, a thrashing metal riff moving from chord to chord with the quality, almost, of a beating heart. The clones near me vibrated in time with it, their skin shaking like ripples in water, but they did not melt.

"So *awful*," one of them said, a sneer on his lips. "Jason couldn't write a riff to save his life. The same four chords, over and over and over."

I frowned, then scrambled for my gun. I sat in the middle of the group of clones. Some had moved out of the room.

"That's odd," Tia said.

I need a way out, I thought.

"Even the ones outside are vibrating a little bit, David. I can see it on the cameras. Surely they can't hear the music."

"They're connected," I said, coughing. I stumbled to my feet, holding my rifle in one hand, ripping the mobile from my shoulder with the other. I flashed it about, trying to ward the clones off. "We need more music," I said. "A lot of it, loud as we can get it. That—"

The clones charged me. Ignoring the danger, they piled on top of me, reaching for my mobile, trying to rip it out of my fingers. Those nearest to me started to melt, but they still grabbed at my arm, fighting even as the flesh sloughed off their bones.

I backed into a corner, then noticed a sliver of light coming from above. A window, covered with a board.

To the sound of thumping rock music, I held the clones at bay, leaving a half dozen of them melting on the floor. Others gathered opposite me in the room, faces shadowed in the dim lighting.

"How did it really happen?" they asked in unison. "Which Epic killed Steelheart, and how did you take the credit?"

"It's not like Steelheart was immortal," I said.

"He was a god."

"He was a cursed man," I said, inching my way toward the window. The gooey remnants of bone and flesh steamed off me, evaporating, leaving my clothing as dry as if nothing had happened. "Just like you are. I'm sorry."

The clones stepped forward. I used the music to melt those who drew close, but they didn't seem to care. They marched on, falling to the ground, dissolving to nothing. They kept coming at me until only one stood in the doorway, though I could see shadows of a few more waiting outside. Why were they killing themselves?

One toward the back took out his handgun. It didn't break as he raised it. Sparks. Mitosis had just been trying to reduce his numbers to make the copies more stable.

I cried out, jumping onto the desk. I had to drop my rifle to rip the board off the window.

A large crack sounded from behind. I felt an immediate thump in my right side, just under my arm—like someone had punched me.

Back in the factory, we would watch old movies every night, after work was done. They'd played on an old television hung from the cafeteria wall. Getting shot didn't feel like it looked in those shows. I didn't gasp and collapse to the ground. I didn't even realize I'd been shot at first. I thought the clones had thrown something at me.

No pain. Just heat on my side.

That was the blood.

I stared down at the wound. The bullet had ripped out a chunk of flesh just beneath my armpit before cutting through my upper arm. It was messy, all warm and wet. My hand didn't work right, wouldn't grip.

I'd been shot. Calamity . . . I'd been *shot*.

For a terrifying moment, that was all I could think about. People died when they got shot. I started to shake; the room seemed to be trembling. I was going to die.

Another shot bounced off the wall beside my head.

You'll die way sooner if you don't move! a piece of me thought. *Now!*

I spun and threw my mobile at Mitosis. That worked; when the music got close, his clone wavered and melted. The mobile came to rest in the doorway, warding off those outside. I still had in my earpiece, though, which was connected wirelessly.

Somehow, I gathered the presence of mind to haul myself by one arm up and out the window. I tumbled into sunlight and collapsed to the ground outside.

I'd often heard that it wasn't the bullet wound that killed you—it was the shock. The horror of being hit, the panicked sense of terror, prevented you from getting out of danger and seeking help.

I slammed one hand over the hole in my side, which was worse than the hit in my arm, and squeezed the wound shut as I pressed my back against the wall.

"Tia?" I said. I figured I was still close enough to the mobile for the earpiece to work. I wasn't sure how far I'd have to go before I lost reception.

"David!" Her voice came into my ear. "Sparks! Sit tight. Abraham is on his way."

"Can't sit," I said with a grunt, climbing to my feet. "Clones are coming."

"You've been shot!"

"In the side. Legs still work." I stumbled away, toward the river. I remembered there being some inlets to the understreets there.

Tia cursed on the line, her voice starting to fuzz as I hobbled away from the hotel. Fortunately, it seemed that Mitosis hadn't anticipated my actually escaping this way. Otherwise, he'd already have clones back here.

"Calamity!" Tia said. "David, he's multiplying. There are hundreds of him, running for you."

"It's okay. I'm a rhinoceros astronaut."

She was silent a moment. "Oh, sparks. You're going delusional."

"No, no. I mean, I'm surprising. I'll surprise him. What's the most surprising thing you can think of? Bet it's a rhinoceros astronaut." The connection was fading. "I can hold out, Tia. You just find the answer to this. Get some music playing across the city, maybe on some copters. Play it loud. You'll figure it out."

"David—"

"I'll distract him, Tia," I said. "That's my job." I hesitated. "How am I doing?"

No reply. I was too far from the hotel.

Sparks. I was going to have to do this last part alone. I hobbled toward the river.

4

tore off part of my shirt, wrapping it around my arm as I stumbled along; then I put my hand back to the side wound. I reached the stairs to the river and looked over my shoulder.

They came like a wave, a surge of identical figures scrambling along the street.

I cursed, then hobbled down the steps. Still, this was good. A terrible kind of good. So long as Mitosis was chasing me, he wasn't hurting anyone or trying to take over the city.

I reached the bottom of the staircase as the flood of figures arrived, some jumping over the sides of the rail to skip a few stairs, others scrambling down each step.

I pushed myself faster toward a set of holes drilled into the wall just above the river. Air vents for the understreets; they'd be big enough to crawl in, but not by much. I reached one just before the clones and clambered inside, kicking away a hand that tried to grab my ankle. I managed to spin around, facing the opening, and backed away into the darkness.

Figures crowded around the tunnel opening, cutting off my light. One of them squatted down, looking at me. "Clever," he said. "Going where only one of me can reach you at a time. Unfortunately, it also leaves you cornered."

I continued to back away. I was losing strength, and my blood made my hands slippery on the steel.

Mitosis crawled into the tunnel, prowling forward.

A lot of Epics liked to think of themselves as predators, the step beyond humans. The apex of evolution. Well, that was idiocy. The Epics weren't above humans. If anything, they were less civilized—more instinctual. A step backward.

That didn't mean I wasn't terrified to see that dark figure stalking me—to be confined in an endless tunnel with the thing as I slowly bled out.

"You'll tell me the truth," Mitosis said, getting closer. "I'll wring it from you, little human. I'll know how Steelheart *really* died."

I met his gaze in the darkness.

"I wanna kiss you!" I shouted. "Like the wind kisses the ra-i-ain!"

I belted out the song as loudly as I could. Tia had played it earlier, and I knew the words, though I'd been too distracted by the whole getting-strangled-then-getting-shot thing to listen closely. I'd heard it as a child, played time and time again on the radio until I and pretty much everyone else got sick of it.

Mitosis melted in front of me. I stopped, breathing deeply, as a second clone crawled over the melting form of the first.

"Cute," he growled. "How long can you sing, little human? How are you feeling? I smell your blood. It—"

"I'm gonna miss you," I shouted, "like the sun misses the ra-i-ain!"

He melted.

"You realize," the next one said, "that now I'm going to have to kill everyone in the city. Can't risk them having heard these songs. I—"

Melt.

"Stop *doing* that!" the next one snapped. "You—"

Melt.

I kept at it, though my singing grew softer and softer with each clone I killed. One of them found a knife and passed it up the line. That didn't melt; it just fell to the floor of the pipe each time one of them died. The next one picked it up and kept crawling.

Each clone got closer. I moved back farther in the tunnel until I felt a ledge behind me. The pipe turned down toward the understreets—and an assuredly fatal drop.

"I could shoot you, I suppose," the next Mitosis said. "Well, shoot you *again*. But then I wouldn't get the pleasure of cutting off pieces of you as you scream out the truth to me."

I screamed out the next lyric, which proved to be a bad idea, because once I'd melted that Mitosis, I found myself slumping against the rounded wall of the small tunnel. I was close to blacking out.

The next Mitosis plucked the knife from the goo, holding it up and letting bits of his other self run down the blade and drip to the floor.

He shook his head. "I was trained classically, you know," he said.

I frowned. This was a change from the talk of torture, murder, and other sunny topics. "What?"

"Trained classically," Mitosis said. "I was the only one in that band who knew his way around an instrument. I wrote song after song, and what did we play? Those stupid, *stupid* riffs. The same chords. Every *damn* song."

Something about this tweaked a part of my brain, like a piece of popcorn on fire because it cooked too long. But I couldn't focus on it now; his talking had almost let him reach me. I sang.

Weakly.

I didn't have a lot of energy left. How long had it been? How much blood had I lost?

This Mitosis wavered, but as my voice faltered, he came back.

"I am beyond you, little human," Mitosis said, and I could hear the smirk in his voice. "Now, let's get on with my questions."

He reached me, took me by the arm, and yanked.

That *hurt*. Somehow, during all the running and scrambling, I'd never noticed the pain. Shock. I'd been in shock.

Now that pain came crashing down on me, an entire detonated building of agony. I found my voice and screamed.

"How did Steelheart die?" Mitosis asked.

"He died at the hands of an Epic," I said, groaning.

"I thought so. Who did it?"

"He did it himself," I whispered. "After I tricked him. He killed himself, but I caused it. He was brought down by a common man, Lawrence."

"Lies!"

"Common people," I whispered, "will bring you all down."

He yanked my arm again, delivering pain in a spike of agony. What did it matter what I said? He wasn't going to believe me. I closed my eyes and started to feel numb. It felt nice. Too nice.

Distantly, I heard music.

Singing?

A hundred voices. No, more. Singing in unison, the song that had blared earlier from my mobile. Their singing was far from perfect, but there was a *force* to it.

"No. What are you doing? Stay back!" Mitosis roared.

All those voices, singing. I could barely make out the words, but I could hear the progression of chords. It actually sounded pretty, since I could ignore the awful lyrics.

"I am an army unto myself! Stay back! I am the new emperor of this city! You are *mine*!"

I forced my eyes open. Mitosis, in front of me, shook and vibrated, though the song was distant. The clones were all connected—and if enough of them were hearing the song, the effect transferred even to the ones who weren't.

In a moment, the line of clones in the pipe screamed, holding their heads.

"Common people," I whispered. "Who have had enough."

Mitosis exploded, each clone popping in a sudden burst. Their deaths opened up a passage to the light outside. I blinked against the abrupt sunshine, and despite the confines, I could see what was out there. People, standing on the frozen steel river, in a mass. Thousands of them, dressed in suits, work clothing, uniforms. They sang together, almost more of a chant.

The people of Newcago had come.

5

"You're unreasonably lucky, son," Prof said, settling onto the stool beside my hospital bed. He was a solid man with greying hair, goggles tucked into the pocket of his shirt.

I flexed my hand. Prof's healing powers—gifted to me under the guise of a piece of technology—had mended my wounds. I didn't remember much about the last few hours. I'd lain in a daze, several city doctors working to keep me alive long enough for Prof to arrive.

I sat back against the headboard, breathing deeply, remembering the final moments with Mitosis. They came to me clearly, though the time after that was muddy.

"How did she get them all there?" I asked. "The people?"

"The Emergency Message System," Prof said. "Tia sent out a plea to everyone near the river, begging them to go to you and to sing along to the music she sent through their mobiles. They could easily have remained in hiding. Ordinary people have no business fighting Epics."

"I'm an ordinary person."

"Hardly. But it doesn't matter."

"It *does*, Prof." I looked at him. "This will never work if they don't start fighting."

"Last time the people fought," Prof said, "the Epics slaughtered millions and the country collapsed."

"That's because we didn't know how to defeat them," I said. "Now we do."

Prof sighed and stood up. "I've been told not to antagonize you, to let you rest. We'll talk about this later. You did well against Mitosis. He . . ." He hesitated.

"What?" I asked.

"Recently, Mitosis has been staying in Babylon Restored. Manhattan, as it used to be called."

"That's where you just visited."

Prof nodded. "That he should come here when I went to scout Babilar . . . it smacks of him coming intentionally while I was gone. That couldn't have happened, unless . . ."

"What?"

Prof shook his head. "We'll talk later. Rest now. I need to think. And son, as well as you did, I want you to do some thinking too. What you did was risky. You can't just keep rushing in, making snap decisions. You are *not* the leader of this team."

"Yes, sir."

"We have an entire city's worth of people to worry about now," he said, walking toward the door to the small room, which was warmed by sunlight through an open window. "Sparks. That's the one thing I never wanted." His face seemed shadowed in that moment. Grim, along with something else. Something . . . darker.

"Prof," I said, "how do Epics get their weaknesses?"

"It's random," he said immediately. "Epics' weaknesses can be anything. They make about as much sense as the powers themselves—which is to say, none." He frowned, looking at me. "You know that better than anyone, son. You're the one who has studied them."

"Yeah," I said, looking out the window. "Mitosis's weakness was his own music."

"Coincidence."

"Hell of a coincidence."

"Well, maybe the weakness wasn't really the music," Prof said. "Maybe it was performance anxiety, or insecurity or the like. The music just reminded him of that."

That was probably right. Still . . .

"He loathed the music," I said. "His own art. There's something here, Prof. Something we haven't noticed yet."

"Perhaps." Prof lingered in the doorway. "Abraham sent me with a message."

"Which is?" I vaguely remembered Abraham pulling me out of the tunnel and carrying me to the hospital.

Prof frowned. "His exact words were 'Tell him he was right about this city . . . so I'll forgive him about the hot dog. Just this once.'"

POSTSCRIPT

This fun story came about because my publisher for the Reckoners series wanted a short story tie-in. I loved the voice of David, the protagonist, so they didn't have to push me much to do a short piece with him as the star. It also let me play with one of the more interesting superhero powers that, I think, hasn't been explored in media outside of comics as well as I think it could be.

We did a short graphic novel (graphic short story?) adaptation of this as well, which you can find floating around on the internet here and there. It was actually our first graphic novel adaptation of anything I'd ever done, I believe, so it's a fun relic.

I don't have as much to say here as for some of the other stories, but to those who love the Reckoners—well, now your collection can be complete.

MOMENT ZERO

One

This is it, Lisa thought, standing up from her chair. *I've got him!*

She forced her hands flat against her desk and took a few calming breaths while rereading the open file in front of her. After so many years of preparation . . . it was time. She scooped up the folder, then snatched her blazer off the hook by her door and threw it on as she pushed out of her office into the main room of 1PT—the nickname for the metropolitan police headquarters.

Things were always in motion at 1PT. Uniformed officers moved between desks, while others worked phones. Lisa's assistant, Rowna, bobbed up from her own seat—a firecracker in a blue uniform, just waiting for an ember to set her off. Lisa provided it in the form of the folder, raised triumphantly.

"We," Lisa said, "are a *go*. Gather the troops."

—

Dane counted off the seconds, a single line of sweat streaking the side of his face, his back against the cold concrete wall. One hand traced the badge on his belt, the other held the holstered handgun at his side.

As usual, he counted his heartbeats to calm himself.

Go.

He ducked around the corner, pulling his sidearm and flicking off the safety in one smooth motion. He sighted, red dot lined up, and squeezed off three shots— one in each chest. He sighted the head of the next and fired. Those shots—though muffled by his ear protection—seemed a second heartbeat to his own as he advanced, counting his bullets as he fired at more targets, then reloading while taking cover behind a pillar.

Calming heartbeats. Reminding him he was in control.

He popped out and fired eight more times as he proceeded through the wide covered room, reminiscent of a parking garage. Cool air, hard floor, the kind you didn't want to have to hit—but he did anyway as he took cover behind a large concrete wedge. He ducked to the side, pulling an AR-15 from the box on a table set up to simulate retrieving it from the back of a car, then came around for the next segment, firing.

Two in the chest. One in the head.

Two in the chest. One in the head.

Advance around the barricade. Turn right.

Two in the chest. One in the head.

Two in the chest . . .

Damn.

He slipped around the last corner, sweat streaming from his brow, as Perez clicked his stopwatch and whistled softly. The range master turned it around to show the time. "That was under one minute, Dane."

"Missed the last shot," Dane said, then did his safety check on the AR: removing the magazine, clearing and visually inspecting the chamber, putting on the safety. He handed that to Perez, then checked his sidearm—1911, standard issue. He nodded to Perez and holstered.

"Range is cold!" Perez shouted. "All firearms down!"

Together, he and Perez walked past the dummy stands scattered through the course, Perez marking that each of Dane's shots had landed within the target spot. His aim had been dead-on . . . except for that last shot.

"Fifty-seven point three," Perez said as they reached the front of the course.

"Missed the last."

"You clipped the target," he said. "So it's only half a second deduction. Dane . . . that score would have placed top three in last month's competition."

"I don't shoot in competitions," Dane said. "Will this get me into SWAT?"

"Should do so." Perez hesitated. "Dane, do you want to talk about this?"

"This?" Dane asked.

"You're a full detective, and with your work on the Goffrey case . . ." Perez left the last part off. *You're successful where you are, Dane. You going to throw that away?* He'd worked for a good decade as a detective, and while SWAT wouldn't be a complete step backward, it was an odd move for someone in his position.

Dane's phone beeped. He checked the text, from Lisa.

Going to the DA. Want to be there?

She would like that—as her partner, she'd want him to take some of the glory too. He shot back, *I've done my part. This can be yours.*

You sure?

Was he? *Yes,* he typed.

"What's that?" Perez asked, glancing over his shoulder. "You're not going? What if she needs you?"

"Lisa hasn't needed me since the mayor learned her name, Perez. Set up the course again. Let's see if I can do it without missing a shot this time."

———

Lisa slammed the folder down on the DA's desk, surrounded by her team: a full contingent of officers who worked the white-collar crime division.

"We have it," Lisa said. "Everything you need to bring down Goffrey."

Angela Pines, the district attorney, picked up the folder. "Paper, Lisa? You could have emailed me."

"Hard to do a dramatic slam on the desk that way, Pines." Lisa leaned forward. "You told me to get you more evidence. I got it. You told me you needed witnesses. I found them. You told me the case had to be *rock solid* to bring down a billionaire. That folder is granite. We have him."

Pines started reading. And kept reading. They'd been working together for months now, as this wasn't the sort of case you investigated without involving the DA—but Pines was meticulous. She'd want to go over every piece again, including the bits added today.

Lisa glanced at her team, who gathered around, excited. She probably shouldn't have brought them all traipsing in here, but they'd worked on this case for years. And now . . .

She turned back, holding her breath.

Pines met her eyes, then nodded. "Time for an arrest warrant. Nice work." She paused. "The mayor is going to be pleased about this, Lisa. I'll make sure he knows it was you."

"Thank you," Lisa said. "But he already knows. You think I didn't email him first?"

Pines hesitated, realizing that there would be no hogging this particular spotlight. Then she smiled—the smile of one working professional to an equal.

"I think," Pines said, standing, "we'll be seeing a lot of one another in the near future. Let's go grab that warrant."

———

Eight hours later, Dane strolled the quiet confines of 1PT after almost everyone had gone home. He always found an empty police building to be unsettling. Back in his twenties—when he'd been a beat cop—he'd worked some of the smaller stations. In those places, there was never any quiet—particularly not at night. The streets didn't sleep, so neither did the force.

But this was department headquarters, a place that emphasized the "office" part of police office. Here you'd find paper pushers, not drug pushers. Here the lights did go out at night—because if people kept working, it was the type of work they could carry home in a laptop bag.

So he strolled past rows of empty cubicles. White-collar division. He'd never thought it would happen to him, but either you died a hero or you lived to become management.

Though it was approaching eleven, one light was on, as he'd suspected it would be. He passed his own office—neat and orderly inside, which was an obvious sign to anyone who knew him that he rarely used it. Instead, he leaned against the doorway of the lit one beside it, where Lisa was—of course—still working. Even after taking down one of the biggest names in the state, here she was. Lisa Sterling: tall, with long black hair, white blouse, no-nonsense brown slacks, and an intense stare that could pound nails through concrete. She was on track to be the first Black woman in the city to be appointed police chief.

Judging by the text message chains, which she'd included him on, the team had gone out for drinks in celebration. Not Lisa. She always had more time for work, but friends? Well, she could always find new friends, couldn't she?

"So," Dane said, "you got him."

Lisa didn't look up. "*We* got him. You did excellent work on this case, Dane. The brothers eventually broke and took a deal to testify. Like you said they would."

"Same old story," he said. "Just need to follow the money . . ." He continued to idle in the doorway. "Think it'll be enough to get a conviction?"

"Trial will probably go on for years. But I'm confident." She moved a few more pages, scanning them with her eyes. "We should have grabbed Harmon first though. Small oversight . . . He'll go to ground now that his boss is down."

She loved to work with actual paper; the keys on her keyboard weren't worn, not even the A or S. He'd always liked that—Lisa's determined fondness for the analog felt genuine. One of the few things about her that did, these days.

"You should have come," she noted, writing down a few things. "DA asked after you."

"No she didn't."

"She noticed you weren't there."

"I'm not interested in political games, Lisa. I don't care if she wondered where I was."

Lisa finally sighed, then set her papers down. She looked at him, noting the sidearm, then focused on his face. "Dane," she said. "This is the sort of case that makes careers. The mayor is paying attention."

Dane folded his arms. "Of course he is. And we both know why."

Lisa put a hand to her head, and Dane felt bad for raising the point on what should have been a victorious day. It was just that . . . halfway into the investigation, he'd learned that the man they were chasing—Goffrey—was backing the mayor's opponent in the election.

"You doubt Goffrey is guilty?" Lisa asked.

"No. But it's awfully convenient timing, is all. The opposition's biggest backer, implicated in a huge embezzlement scheme? No wonder we got extra resources to chase it down."

She turned back to her papers. "This is how you play at our level, Dane. The mayor gets a boost to his campaign; I get to put someone legitimately despicable behind bars. Stealing from his own people's pension fund?"

"Scumbag, through and through," Dane agreed. "I just hate the game."

"You didn't hate it so much four years ago."

Dane winced, but she did have him there. Without her help calling in some favors . . . well, he wouldn't be here—he'd be writing traffic tickets, if he was even still a cop.

He turned away. "Don't you ever miss it?" he asked softly. "Going out there. Making a difference. Saving lives."

"You think this doesn't save lives? He's been *embezzling* from his *own employees*."

Dane shrugged and looked around the too-quiet room, with its empty cubicles full of the kinds of cases that could always wait for another day to be solved. "I feel like I did more on the street. One person matters there, Li. In the way they never can in this room, where you convict by committee and jump for a tissue whenever a politician sneezes."

She drew in a sharp breath. Damn. He'd gone too far that time, hadn't he? If Chief Bront was retiring like everyone said, the department could do worse than Lisa. He just . . . he could never tell anymore what she did for the common good, and what she did for her career.

"You realize," she said coolly, "nobody needs another overarmed cop with a hero complex. You're not some supersoldier, Dane. You're a police detective in the *white-collar* division. You're never going to need to fire an assault rifle in the line of duty, and you look more and more ridiculous the longer you pretend otherwise."

She affixed him with one of her glares. The kind that could have made a boulder wilt. He held it, because he was feeling stubborn. But at times like this . . . well, he wondered if he remembered earlier days right. When Lisa hadn't needed a warm cup of antifreeze before she'd manifest a pulse.

He sighed finally, and broke first. "I'm putting in for a transfer to SWAT. I've been training; think I can hit the benchmarks."

She grew still, and he could see the surprise in her posture. They'd worked together for years, and he could guess that she'd assumed he would still be with her for years to come.

"At forty, Dane?" she said. "Really? You'd throw away years of work as a detective—the boost to your career this case will give you?"

He shrugged.

"Dane, you are at the age when most people are looking to move *into* management. Not starting all over with a new career path that is *more* physically demanding."

All valid complaints. But after years following her along and through to white collar . . . something simply wasn't right. She couldn't see it. He could.

"I'd have done it earlier," he admitted. "I probably should have. I just . . . I like to see things through. Chief Bront retires . . . when?"

"I've been told, confidentially, he's been waiting for this case to break before he goes to the mayor."

"Not long then."

"If I get the job, I suppose I could see you get whatever post you want."

"Figured," he said, then met her eyes. "Maybe that's why I've been waiting. Guess I play the game too, don't I?"

"I wouldn't have asked you to be my partner all those years ago if I hadn't suspected."

He stifled a sigh. Why didn't he tell her the whole thing? Why did he linger, wishing not to say it? Was it because of them?

People grew apart, careers changed. Natural progression of life. Still, instead of continuing this conversation, he slipped a folded sheet out of his pocket and tossed it onto her desk.

"What's this?" she asked.

"A lead on a case I've been working. Thought maybe we could chase it down. We're still partners, after all. For a few more months."

She unfolded the page, looking curious—he expected she'd appreciate holding actual paper. Soon, she sighed. "The missing scientist again?"

"They wear white collars," he noted. "On their lab coats."

"You know that's not what it means, Dane. This case should be with missing persons—and I believe they said it looked like she wasn't even missing. She'd just refused contact with family."

"They're wrong."

"I read the briefs. Her disappearance *truly* looks voluntary."

"Then no harm in confirming, right?" He nodded toward the paper. "Make sure she's really okay. Chase a lead. Hit the street. One last time."

She considered. She was getting important enough that the little cases, even in white collar, weren't her duty any longer. She spent way more time in management, being primed to take the chief's job, since both he and the deputy chief were getting on in years. The Goffrey case had been a special situation, their first real detective work in far too long—and Dane had spent most of the case sitting around reading other people's reports.

She let him play with little things like this missing scientist now and then because . . . well, they both knew he'd go insane otherwise. Regardless, he expected her to say no tonight. Instead, she packed her papers away, leaving the desk neat and tidy—just a jar of pens, her name plaque, and the picture of her and Nova at the girl's elementary school graduation two years ago.

"Well then, let's go," Lisa said, standing.

"What, *now*?"

"You're the one always saying cops here should be more busy at night. Your tip says that missing scientist was spotted around midnight, so we can assume she keeps hours like you."

"Yeah," Dane said. "All right. Hell, why not? Your car or mine?" He hesitated. "Mine."

"Because of the guns in the trunk, I assume?"

He shrugged.

"It's a simple missing person case," Lisa replied, pulling on her blazer. "What? You think we're going to run into terrorists?"

"Don't get my hopes up. Besides, my car has Bluetooth. While yours has . . . what is that abomination called?"

"An eight-track. And they're *very* hip these days."

"Li, you're forty-three. You can't be hip anymore. It's in the handbook." He paused as they walked out toward the parking lot. "Actually, I'm pretty sure the word 'hip' isn't even hip anymore . . . We'll have to ask Nova."

Lisa smiled. For the briefest moment, it was just like old times. And who knew? The missing scientist was honestly a long shot—but maybe they'd still find something interesting.

Two

90 Minutes from Moment Zero

Dane, of course, couldn't get his phone to work, and so got them lost halfway to the location.

Lisa sighed, tipping her head back in the passenger seat of his enormous SUV. While he was trying, and failing, to navigate, she pulled out the tip he'd gotten—a voice log, from a phone at a convenience store, to emergency.

Log Date 5-15-24, 13:42

Operator: 911, where is your emergency?

Caller: I . . . I don't know. Not really.

Operator: What is your location?

Caller: Look, there's this home. 1103 South Maple Court. And some freaky stuff is happening there, man.

Operator: Are you there now? Is anyone injured?

Caller: No. I did a delivery there. Last night. Late, like midnight. And . . . Freaky stuff. Just . . . check it out, okay? I've got to go.

Operator: Can you tell me more about the nature of the problem there? Is someone in danger?

Caller: I think so. I don't know. Look, there's this woman, and she seemed strange. Nazeem. Uh, yeah. Her name was Nazeem.

Operator: Can you describe her?

Caller: Short and thin. Red hair. Something's wrong, man. Just . . . go look. Okay?

[Caller hung up. Officers dispatched to the source of the call uncovered no leads. Description and name of the woman mentioned match that of a missing person. Escalating to open cases.]

Dane shouldn't have been working this case, but missing persons was overloaded. Plus, Chief allowed Dane a few . . . hobby projects to keep him occupied.

The scientist's disappearance still seemed voluntary from Lisa's standpoint. It wasn't illegal to ignore your family, wasn't even illegal to leave your home behind and not come back. Scummy? Potentially. Illegal? No. Usually in situations like this, police followed up and made sure the person was all right. Afterward, they weren't allowed to say anything to the family other than to promise their loved one was safe.

This kind of case wasn't a terribly high priority, but Dane did see the work . . . and well, everything . . . in his own special light. She read the tip over again, then sent a text to Nova in case she woke up wondering where her mom was. Fortunately, Lisa's parents lived three doors down, and Nova was unreasonably sharp for a fourteen-year-old. Lisa would trust her to take care of herself almost more than she trusted Dane. At least Nova could work her GPS.

Dane cursed softly beside her, shaking his phone.

"Bluetooth, eh?" Lisa asked. "Super useful."

"Helps when I remember to charge the phone . . ." Dane held up the device, which displayed a dead battery symbol on the screen—and nothing else.

"Again? Didn't I tell you to buy an adapter?"

"I did! It's . . . on my desk."

"Yeah. Out of curiosity, how many guns did you pack?"

"No comment."

She held up her phone, a "dumb" phone. "Five days on one charge."

"Yeah? How's the GPS?"

". . . Nonexistent."

"And if you have to look up something on the fly . . ." He glanced at her with a smile as they turned down a dark side road. "Text Nova?"

"Text Nova," she admitted. "Honestly, I'd check out a smartphone if I was on important fieldwork—rather than being bullied into a random chase at midnight by a man who really should have better things to do."

He smiled, as he could tell there were no teeth to that barb. She winced at the memory of what she'd said earlier though. *Why'd you say things like that to him, Li? You know how much he wants to help people.* Was that how she was going to lead the department? By pushing down eager officers?

She'd have to learn to do better. She wanted Dane to be happy, even after all of it. The idea of him moving to SWAT, nearby but in another building, intrigued her. Maybe if there were some distance between them, things could get less heated. She could fix this, with time. It was what she did.

"Hey," he said as he turned another corner. "Did you get someone to record Nova's recital today?"

"I didn't have to. I was there."

"But the bust—"

"There was no need for me to be the one to cuff Goffrey," she said. "I was going to let you do it, but because you didn't come, I let John have the honor. He likes that sort of thing."

"You did? Huh." He eyed her. "That's why you were working late? Felt guilty for skipping the bust?"

"Maybe," she conceded.

"It's okay to take time for your kid."

"I know, Dane. Please don't patronize me."

"Sorry," he said, and seemed to mean it. Plus, maybe she was a little sensitive to the topic—but the number of lectures, side-eyes, and assumptions she'd had to fight from others . . . It was hard for people, even him, to recognize that a woman could both be a good mom and have a serious career. They always assumed Nova was getting the short end of the stick.

"You should have come," she said. "To the recital, I mean. Nova missed you."

"Last year . . ." he said.

"Chris wasn't even there today."

"Bastard missed his daughter's recital?"

"Bastard got punched and booked by you last time he attended. Can you blame him?"

Dane got a crook of a smile on his lips. But . . . well, Chris *had* asked for it, coming drunk to the recital. Nova had been mortified at the continual outbursts until Dane, ever the white knight, had done something about the problem the only way he ever seemed to understand.

Lisa had never admitted—and never *would* admit—how satisfying it had been to see Chris go down with one good hook to the jaw—after stupidly trying to throw the first punch. Dane had hauled him out immediately and arrested him for disorderly conduct. Nova had been able to finish the recital in peace, and she still talked about Dane's actions with glee in her eyes. A little too much. That girl . . .

But, well, there was no getting around it. Nova would find out if Lisa didn't make good, so she reluctantly pulled something from her pocket and dropped it onto the dash. "She sent you this."

Dane pulled into parking along the street, then picked up the item: a charm bracelet, with real coral and a small silver heart. Well, half a heart. He looked from it to the similar one Lisa was wearing.

"Jewelry-making class," Lisa said. "After-school program."

"You've told her that you and I . . ." he said. "I mean . . ."

"She's not blind, Dane," Lisa said. "But she's also an optimist." She looked to him.

"Yeah," he said. "Good that someone in the family is." He grabbed the bracelet, then pushed open his door. "We're here."

"I thought we were lost."

"We were. Now we're here. General area at least."

"Define 'general area,'" she said, climbing out of the car. It was late, but this was a fairly nice neighborhood—the sort of place they'd find her type of criminals, not his.

"This is the right street, I'm pretty sure." He went to the trunk of his car, and she leaned against the side as he opened it and rooted around. "Hey, if you make chief, does that mean I'll have to salute you?"

"It would be protocol in a formal setting," she said. "Promotions and the like. Have you . . . ever saluted any superiors? I honestly can't remember you doing so."

"I only do it to the ones I respect."

"Dane . . . you really should think about your career *once* in a while."

"And you really should think about standing up to those overstuffed idiots once in a while. But I guess we'll both do what we'll do, eh?"

She fell silent, not wanting another argument.

"Ah," he finally said. "Here we go."

She held out her hand sufferingly right before he pulled out a handgun and a shoulder holster for her. Both knew she hadn't brought one. And both knew he'd insist she carry. It *was* protocol, so she wasn't going to complain. Instead, she checked the safety and chamber, then slipped it on under her blazer.

He turned longingly toward the rest of his equipment. Assault rifle. Flashbangs.

"Dane . . ." she said.

"I know," he said, closing the trunk. "I'm not bringing it tonight."

"You don't need all of that."

"You don't need it," he said, "until you suddenly do."

They started off, her checking a few texts on her phone as he counted house numbers. Near a streetlight, they spotted a man getting mail from his box, despite the late hour. The man looked up, friendly, as Dane approached—but the moment the man caught Dane's badge flashing in the streetlight, his disposition changed.

"A cop?" the man said, instantly hostile. "What do you want?"

"Hey, nothing's wrong," Dane said. "I just need directions."

The man pointed the proper way, and Lisa pretended not to hear what he called Dane under his breath as he walked off.

Dane wilted. And . . . well, it did hurt to see how one casual interaction stole the zip from his posture. As they walked, she caught him glancing backward, lingering on the light near the mailboxes. Though she wouldn't say such interactions were common in neighborhoods like this, they weren't uncommon in general. Dane was always so *surprised* when someone treated him with contempt, even after all these years.

Eventually, he led her down a side street that ended at a large gate. She couldn't see into the grounds beyond because of several thick walls, with various types of brush growing in front of them to make the fortification seem less out of place. She'd recognized this was a nice neighborhood, but not "private driveway with its own security" nice.

Here, he let her lead. Lisa strolled up to the intercom and pushed the call button.

She got a gruff voice on the other end. "Yes?"

"Police," Lisa said, showing her badge to the associated camera. "We're working a case about a missing person, and would like to ask you a few questions."

Silence.

"Who is missing?" the voice eventually asked.

"Caroline Nazeem," Lisa said. "Short, Caucasian, red hair. She's not wanted for any sort of crime—but her family is worried."

More silence.

"We haven't ever heard of that person," the voice said.

"Can we come in and ask some questions anyway?" Lisa asked.

"Do you have a warrant?"

"Like I said," she replied, doing her best to sound amiable, "we don't suspect any wrongdoing. We're only trying to confirm for our records that Nazeem is fine. No need for a warrant." Now the stinger. "Yet."

Silence.

"This is Caroline Nazeem," a voice finally said on the line. There was a different tenor to the background—some kind of thrumming, like machinery. It seemed the line had been sent to someone's mobile phone. "My security guard says you needed to talk to me?"

"Just want to confirm your whereabouts, Ms. Nazeem," Lisa said. "Your family is worried."

"You've been had, Detective," the woman's voice said. "My siblings are well aware of my location—they're simply angry I have justifiably cut off contact with them, including removing their stipends."

"Can we at least see you with our own eyes, to confirm—"

"Tell my siblings I'm done with them. Good night."

The intercom went dead. Lisa got no reply to the follow-up. So, together with Dane, she retreated down the sidewalk—hopefully away from cameras and microphones.

"Come on," Dane said, taking her arm once they were around the corner. "You've got to admit that was suspicious."

"Suspicious how? Woman doesn't want contact with her family. They try to get the police involved to intimidate her—you know how often that sort of thing happens."

"And those odd sounds?" Dane said, waving.

"Odd sounds aren't probable cause."

"The note says 'freaky stuff' is happening inside. We should sneak in."

"A claim of 'freaky stuff' *also* isn't probable cause." She sighed. "Dane, we can't afford to escalate here. We should log what we discovered, then send a team during daylight to try again. Heck, if you're *really* worried, we can post a plainclothes to get a visual on the scientist when she next leaves. Either way, she sounds safe."

"If that *was* her on the line," he said. "They materialized a woman to be Nazeem the moment you threatened a warrant. Who knows if it's actually her? And if the real Nazeem *is* in trouble in there—or if she was coerced into talking to us—we *just escalated* by tipping off everyone inside."

"You're jumping to conclusions."

He looked back. "It's called a hunch. My gut wants us to push a little more."

"All your gut wants is chips and Heineken, Dane."

"Let's at least do a walk-around of the premises. After such a disturbing tip, nobody could fault us for walking around to see if we could get a visual of anyone in distress."

She considered, eyeing him. Damn. He was getting that look about him. He was going to—

"You *owe* me this," he said.

"Owe it?" she snapped. "How do I owe you anything, Dane?"

"You know."

"I legitimately don't. So why don't you tell me?"

He stood there, more stubborn than a boulder, and glared at her. So she sighed and turned toward the car.

"I'm not moving within the department, Li," he said from behind. "When I apply to SWAT, it won't be here in the city. It will be in another state."

She hesitated, then turned back.

"I have the paperwork ready," he explained. "Applying in California, several places." He met her eyes. "I figured . . . clean break. You know."

Those words struck something inside her. A bullet, with Dane's impeccable aim, bearing a simple message. *I'm giving up on us.*

Damn. Still, she didn't give voice to her hurt. "That's probably a good idea," she said instead. "You'll have to find a way to tell Nova."

"I know. That's the hardest part."

That was the hardest part?

I can fix this, Lisa thought firmly to herself. *I'll find a way to fix this.*

He nodded back toward the house. "Come on, Li. It's our last case, maybe our last night, as actual partners. If Chief has been waiting . . . well, we'll probably get news of his retirement before the week is out. This is it. Tonight."

"Dane," she said, "we can't go trespassing because you want a last hurrah."

"I'm not saying we trespass! Do you even listen? I want to do a walk-around. We'll play it by the book, do a visual through those woods, not entering the grounds." He eyed her. "That should be fine, even for someone who needs her record as clean as possible, to keep her career looking bright."

Lisa took a deep breath, and found herself of two minds. On one hand, this was typical Dane immaturity. Insisting they do things his way, because he had a hunch? He wanted to pretend, one last time, to be the cowboy—and for some reason he always wanted her there to be his sidekick. But she couldn't afford to go off half-cocked like he did. She'd tried to explain before how everyone watched her, in particular, for mistakes and missteps—how she was always both a target and an example—and how it had forced her to learn to navigate a world he chose to simply ignore. She'd never found the words that wouldn't make it sound as if she was acting like a victim. Another thing people watched for in her with annoying hypervigilance.

She was inclined to let him go on his own. He almost certainly would, if she walked away.

"Please," he said. "Just this last time."

On the other hand, this was obviously important to him. Silly, yes, but people were like that. You could appreciate something was important to a person without seeing the importance yourself. Lisa wavered, and then felt Nova's bracelet—suddenly seeming heavy and noticeable on her wrist. A walk-around *was* within protocol.

If she went, would it encourage him to stay in the city? Did she want him to? She checked her watch—just after eleven thirty. She considered, she wavered, and eventually she made her decision.

Three

5 Minutes from Moment Zero

Dane pushed through the woods surrounding the mansion, with Lisa reluctantly following him.

She had come. He hadn't been certain she would, but she had. That meant something, didn't it? That she still wanted to try? Or was he reading too much into a simple decision?

I can make this work, he thought. *I can fix it. With more time.* If . . . there was more time to give.

Regardless, his excuse for why he wanted to do this walk-around was flimsy. The grounds had an enormous wall, offering almost zero opportunities for them to see anything relevant. Plus they had phone recordings of the missing woman, and that *had* sounded like her voice on the intercom.

It wasn't adding up though. Her siblings had seemed legitimately worried. He'd listened to the recording of the call from the man who'd given the tip, and there was an uneasy tone to his voice that the log couldn't convey. Something strange was happening here.

Or maybe Dane only wanted to pretend there was. He glanced back at Lisa, and couldn't help feeling unsettled by how easily she'd taken the news that he was leaving. He'd struggled for weeks deciding how to tell her. When it just gushed out, she told him to talk to Nova? Had she ever legitimately cared?

He gritted his teeth and continued on, growing more and more upset. Like so often lately, the most annoying part was that he *knew* he didn't have good reason for that feeling. Life *was* good. He *should* have been satisfied with his job—or if not, he *should* have done something different. Rather than waiting for answers to come to him.

But those were old problems, well trodden by his worried mental pacing. For now, he tried to focus on the surroundings. As he'd noticed earlier, the land outside the mansion wall was largely an uncultivated snarl—the kind of hollow (scrub trees, rocky earth, steep banks) that had probably been a riverbed before the area's development. His uncle had considered doing construction in such a place, then had learned how much it would cost to level it all out. He'd eventually sold the land to the neighbors so they could leave it as a patch of scenic wooded wetland in an otherwise manicured suburban environment. Maybe this was the same.

These woods went all around the property, which wasn't as enormous as it had seemed from the front. Maybe four acres—a large plot, yes, but not the expansive grounds he'd imagined. His reassessment was validated by that wall, eight feet tall, with no wires or barbs on the top. That was—as he also knew from his uncle—per city code, though the truly rich had ways around such restrictions.

Whoever owned this place, either they weren't important enough to get an exemption, or they didn't care. Or . . . he supposed, maybe they didn't want to draw attention by asking for an exemption. Instead they put up a maximum-height wall and used security cameras rather than barbs or spikes.

He and Lisa picked their way through the underbrush in the darkness, passing stubby trees that looked like hands with an unnatural number of broken fingers.

"You think," Lisa said softly as they rounded to the back side of the property, "you'll really find what you're looking for in another city, Dane?"

"Won't know unless I try."

"A fresh start . . ." she said. "But Dane—and I'm not trying to start a fight—but do you *really* know what you're looking for? I fully support you trying something new—even out of state. But tell me you actually *know* what you want. That you won't end up floating through life in any new department, like you have here."

He didn't reply. A lot of people would have assumed he wanted glory—Perez laughed about it when he didn't think Dane was listening. The cop who thought he would end up a hero because he knew his way around an assault rifle.

"I want to make a difference," he whispered.

"If that were true, you'd be more excited by the white-collar cases you've helped crack."

Damn her, she was right. Why *did* these kinds of cases, then, feel so . . . removed? It was too difficult for him to feel relevant when he couldn't take someone by the hand and pull them out of a tough spot. Marks on a whiteboard weren't the same.

And will it be different in another department? He'd considered joining a homicide division, but he knew that was actually very similar to what he and Lisa did now, despite what the shows liked to depict. Take testimonies. Interview suspects. Sit in a cubicle and build a case. SWAT would be thrilling, but if anyone ever got ahold of the blots on his record that Lisa had helped tuck away four years ago . . .

If he was perfectly honest with himself, the idea of moving made his stomach somersault. Was this really done? Everything? His life here?

Such musings were interrupted as he heard something. He stopped in the darkness, hand toward Lisa, who'd been pushing some branches out of her way. Was that . . .

Muffled groans.

"Shit," Lisa said. "You hear that?"

"Coming from beyond the wall," he said, as he heard thumping and rattling as well.

"Give me a boost."

Dane smiled. In a second, Lisa the cop emerged—and she'd been a damn good one. She scrambled over to the wall and waved for his help. He gave her a boost with his hands under her foot, letting her grab the top of the wall and haul herself up.

"Storm cellar," she said. "Locked with a chain on this side. Someone's trapped in there—I can hear them moaning as they try to push through." She glanced down at him, and moonlight caught her eyes. "You and your stupid gut."

"Just got to keep it well bribed," he said. "Chips and Heineken."

He took a running jump to grab the top, then she pulled him up. Together they landed on the other side, feet thumping against manicured grass.

Lisa called dispatch as they crossed the grounds. "10-67, person in distress under suspicious circumstances," she said. "We've breached a potentially hostile compound with personal security on site. I want some uniformed officers here immediately. Address is . . ."

Lisa looked to him, then held out the phone.

"I logged it, Marci," Dane said, leaning in to the microphone. "Right before we left. Make sure they look for the court, not the street—they're off one another."

"We've got it," dispatch said. "Commander, are you . . . on beat yourself?"

"Affirmative," Lisa said. "Dane and I are rendering assistance now. Get those cars here, Marci. ASAP."

They reached the cellar doors, which were set into the ground beside the house's wall and sounded with rattles and muffled groans. Lisa crouched down to talk through the doors, telling the person help had arrived.

They needed something to get through that chain . . . Dane sprinted to a groundskeeper's shack nearby. Less than a minute later, he arrived back at the cellar doors with a crowbar.

"We're police," Lisa was saying. "Can you confirm you are in distress?"

The muffled reply sounded like a yes.

"You need confirmation?" Dane said, getting the crowbar in place.

"Always good to check," she said, glancing behind them. "We'll have company soon—they were probably watching while we prowled out there."

"Yeah, okay," he said, grunting as the crowbar slipped. But the metal rings the lock was on were affixed to old worn wood that he thought he could . . .

Crack. He pried the entire mechanism off, splintering the wood.

"Nice work," she said, throwing open the cellar doors. He went for his phone to provide a flashlight, then remembered the damn battery was dead. Fortunately, the moon was bright enough to reveal someone on the steps below, gagged, hands bound. (Asian male in his fifties or young sixties, red tearstained eyes.) He'd climbed the steps and had obviously been slamming his shoulder against the door.

"Who the hell is that?" Dane asked.

Lisa helped the man up and began working on his gag. "Watch for security," she said. "Do *not* escalate this unless they pull weapons, Dane."

"You kidding me?" he said. "There's a man tied up in—"

"We don't have all the information," she said. "This doesn't have to end with a shootout. We'll get this man to safety, wait for backup, then sort through the facts."

He eyed her. That wasn't protocol—there was *clearly* proof here that the people in this compound posed a threat. She likely wouldn't have demanded this of common beat cops . . . but common beat cops weren't political landmines like she was these days. Couldn't have Commander Lisa Sterling being part of a deadly shootout that was spun wrong in the press.

He sighed, and although he kept his hand on his sidearm, he didn't draw it as the expected guards—three men built like linebackers—came running across the lawn from the front of the building. They saw him, and their hands dropped to their sides as well.

"Police," Dane shouted. "You know we are. Don't play stupid, and don't *be* stupid."

He waited as, behind, Lisa finally got the gag off.

"You have to stop her!" the captive man said. "There's no time! Don't bother with me! *Stop Nazeem!*"

Dane felt calm silence surrounding him as he watched those hands on guns. Yes, his pulse increased. Yes, sweat began to bead on his forehead. But he was calm.

He'd trained for this, but he didn't draw.

The security guards raised their hands to the sides, away from their weapons. "We don't want trouble, Officer!" one called. "This is all a big misunderstanding."

"Why do you have a bound captive in your cellar?" Dane shouted.

"He took too much, and went paranoid. He does that sometimes—it's always fine in the morning. We're happy to chat about it. I assume you've got back-up coming—we'll just wait here, then explain."

"They're stalling," the captive man said. "You *have* to listen to me. She's going to activate the device, but her *math is wrong*. She's going to destabilize reality."

"Slow down," Lisa said, awkwardly loosening the ropes from his hands. "Device? What device?"

"There *isn't time!*" the man exclaimed. "Please. Leave me and go *stop her!*"

Regardless of what the guards said, the captive wasn't strung out on some-thing. Dane had seen enough of that during his beat cop days to tell. He eyed the security guards, who had inviting postures and hands raised unthreateningly.

Yeah. They were *absolutely* stalling.

He grabbed Lisa, towing her with the now-unbound prisoner back into the cellar.

"Dane?" she said.

"Gut!" he shouted, pulling the doors shut—then he rammed the crowbar through the door handles on the inside. Cursing outside indicated the guards were approaching.

He spun the former captive in the near darkness of the cellar stairs, lit only by a single emergency light. "Look, you're too important a resource for us to leave behind. We'll do what you say, but we can't rush in without intel. Can you show us what you want us to stop?"

"I . . . Yes! All right," the man said, and there was something familiar about his voice. "Yes, we need to get through the doors down here, into the main facility."

The two doors above them rattled while the former captive scrambled down the steps, pointing at a different closed door below.

"Great," Lisa said, following as Dane rushed down the stairs—though he noticed she'd pulled her sidearm. "You realize you might have locked us in here."

"Did you see how panicked that fellow is?"

"My name is Yung," the man said as he reached the door out of the cellar, into the house proper. "Professor Yung, theoretical physics . . . at TYCC."

"A community college?" Lisa said.

"Fewer positions for us than you'd think," he said. "Sometimes makes us a little desperate. I'm sorry. I should never have let this go so far. When I realized she wouldn't listen to me, I left the project—but returned today to try to talk her out of proceeding. They tossed me in here."

"Wait," Dane said. "Your voice. You're the delivery guy who called 911!"

"A subterfuge, trying to get someone to check on this facility!" Yung said. "I'm sorry for the lie. But there isn't time now! Please, I can show you, but hurry!"

Fortunately, this second door was nothing too worrisome. Three solid kicks and Dane got it open—then checked the hallway (white walls, sterile lights, no carpet) outside.

"The device," Yung said at Lisa's prompting. "Have you heard of a wormhole? We found one. The thing is, the math says the equipment can't handle the power outflow, so . . ." He took a deep breath. "What we've built is a bomb, Officers. Whatever she *thinks* we've done, it *ended up* being a bomb. If Nazeem activates it relying on her flawed calculations . . . it will detonate. I'm sure of it."

Behind, the guards continued to pound on the doors to the cellar. Yung led the way, turning left at the hall.

Lisa, being Lisa, wanted more information. "How big a bomb?" she hissed as they reached the next intersection, and Dane halted them—despite Yung's urgency—to check corners. This long hallway led straight toward a room with glimmering lights. Voices echoed from that direction.

"I can't say," Yung replied. "Because I don't know which figures she's using, and therefore how much power it will pull from beyond. Could be enough to destroy the building. Could be enough to . . ."

"Destroy the block?"

"Um . . . more, Officer. Far, far more."

"Hell."

"Please," Yung said. "We *must* hurry. It's just up there."

Sidearm out, Dane glanced to Lisa, who nodded. Lethal force it was; heaven send Yung wasn't lying, confused, or crazy. Dane led the way down the hall. Lisa slipped ahead of Yung, telling him to stay back, and followed.

Dane hugged the wall to give himself some semblance of cover, but this approach was a nightmare. Brighter lights behind than ahead, and a long hallway that spilled into a large room with blind corners. Plus, shouting from those guards . . .

Well, it was no wonder he was on edge as he reached the end of the hallway and peeked into the room beyond. It was empty, though much of the far wall was glass. Like . . . he was in a recording studio, and there was a control booth on the other side. That had a group of people in it, including three more guards with guns out.

Dane stopped at the doorway, sweating, staring down those guards in the control booth beyond the glass. With them, he could see a few tech types and Nazeem herself. She stood with her hands laced before her, wearing jeans and a button-down shirt. Lisa pulled up beside him. Crossing this empty room would leave them completely open, but staying here wasn't any better. In this hallway, they were two large fish in a very narrow barrel.

"Now, now," Nazeem said, her voice projected into the larger room. "No need for weapons, is there, Officers? Perhaps we should all just calm down a little."

Dane scanned the corners. Yes, the room (twenty-five feet wide, square, dim lighting) was empty. The control booth had computers and desks. But . . . what were those sparks at the edges of the room? Like glitter in the air. As he noticed them, he picked up on something else unusual. A black dot at the center of test chamber, easily lost in the low lighting. This point, however, was somehow darker . . . and once he saw it, he couldn't look away. It was small, smaller than a pencil's eraser, but *magnetic* to his attention.

"Tell your guards to stand down," Lisa said, seeming as if she hadn't seen the dot. "And everyone step away from those computers. Nobody push a *single* button."

He finally tore his eyes away from the dot. Nazeem smiled and nodded. She had a narrow face, framed by red bangs with highlights. Strangely, Dane's tension *increased* as she had her guards lower their weapons.

Yung inched up and peeked around Lisa. "Oh no. Those lights at the corners of the room. You've opened it already, Nazeem?"

Nazeem's eyes found him, and her smile faded to an angry line. It was back a moment later. "Yes. In preparation for a test. The one you kept refusing."

"You can't send a person, Nazeem!" Yung cried. "Listen, your calculations are wrong!"

"Oh, Yung," she replied. "That's not what *they* say."

". . . They?" Yung asked.

"The voices," she said. "From the hole."

Dane clenched his gun in a sweaty grip, trying to decide his next move. Though her techs had backed away from the computers in the booth, she remained within reach of those computers, clearly visible through the mostly glass wall.

"Away," Lisa said, gun up, "from the machines."

"Of course, Officer," Nazeem said. But didn't move.

Dane trained his gun on Nazeem. And finally, she did back away from the console. Though . . . that control room was set up to look in on this larger one, as if to shield those inside. The glass would be bulletproof, he thought. Rather, it would be built to withstand an explosion, and therefore his gunshots.

So why had she backed away?

"Does this feel wrong to you?" Lisa hissed.

"Yeah," he said. "Yung, what was that she said earlier? About voices?"

"I don't know," Yung said. "I never . . . I mean . . . if something is *speaking* from the wormhole . . . Nazeem! It's too dangerous. You *cannot* send a person through that hole!"

"A person, Yung?" she replied from the control room. "So small-minded. I'm not sending a person. I'm sending the entire house."

A glow appeared beneath the dot, mechanical equipment on the floor powering up. The truth hit Dane like a brick dropped from a thousand feet: they were *still* stalling.

"The device is on a timer!" he yelled, dashing into the room, heedless of the danger. Gunshots sounded ahead as a guard peeked out of the control room. Dane wasn't hit; he had to reach the controls before—

All became white as something exploded up from beneath him.

Four

Lisa started awake.

In bed. Her bed. Alone.

Had it . . . been a dream? Hand to her head, she sat up, then glanced through gossamer drapes at the rising sun. Clock on the nightstand said 6:37. Three minutes before her alarm was to go off.

She flipped off the alarm and meandered toward the bathroom, amid memories of . . . one last investigation with Dane before he got a job in another city. *The device is on a timer!* Gunshots, and a grunt from Dane, as if he'd been hit. A white light.

She waited for it to fade as dreams always did. She'd fallen asleep in her clothes . . . because of the long night spent working? How had she gotten home? She didn't remember, but in her morning daze, that didn't bother her.

She showered and got ready. By the sounds of the plates clattering below, Nova was already up and making breakfast. That was odd, as Nova was *not* a morning person, but maybe that was changing now that she was fourteen and heading to high school. She'd gotten up on her own a few days ago too.

Lisa walked down the steps, feeling an ethereal sense of . . . displacement. That dream hadn't faded. She remembered it as if it were real. She emerged into the kitchen, where Nova was scrambling eggs at the stove, dressed in her plaid school uniform. The girl wore her black hair straight and long, like her mother. She had a ready, dimpled grin for Lisa—though she turned too quickly to show off the eggs still in their pan. Her elbow knocked a box of cereal off the counter.

Just like she had a few days ago.

Puff cereal scattered across the floor, and some rolled up to Lisa's feet. She stared at it, dumbfounded, remembering . . .

Oh! Shi—I mean, shoot! Sorry, Mom!

"Oh! Shi—" Nova said. "I mean, shoot! Sorry, Mom!" She put down the pan and scrambled for the broom.

This had happened already. On Monday. "Nova," Lisa said, "is this some kind of prank?"

"Didn't mean to! I'm nervous about practice. Sorry, sorry!" She moved to clean up, but Lisa took her by the shoulders, looking her in the eyes.

The girl tugged against the grip, eyes to the side, fingers twitching—as if trying to go through sweeping motions.

"Nova?" Lisa asked, feeling legitimate horror. That look on her daughter's face was so unnatural, like she didn't even *see* Lisa. "Nova!"

Nova focused on her, then cocked her head, as if seeing her for the first time. As soon as Lisa released Nova though, the girl jumped to clean in a flurry before gobbling up the eggs.

"Sorry, Mom!" Nova said. "Early morning practice for the recital, remember?" She beamed, back to her normal self, then took Lisa's hands. "You're going to come, right? Even if work is busy?"

"Coming . . . I already went . . ." It was distinct in Lisa's mind. The sounds, sights, scents of the auditorium. Jazz piano echoing in the hall, fading to applause.

Could she have dreamed that?

"Not just to practices," Nova said. "The actual recital!"

"Which is . . ."

"On Wednesday."

"And today is . . ."

"Monday." Nova rolled her eyes. "As if you don't have every minute of your life scheduled."

"You flub the ending of 'A Night in Tunisia' . . ."

"I won't flub *anything*," Nova said, letting go and grabbing her backpack. Then she paused, before digging in her pocket and pulling out a red-coral bracelet.

Lisa's hand went to her wrist, and the identical one she was *already wearing.*

"Here!" Nova said, giving the new one to her. "I made this for you." Then she bit her lip, getting out a second. "I made one for Dane too. Will you . . . give it to him? To help him think about us." Nova glanced down, holding them both out.

"Nova," Lisa said, holding up her hand with the bracelet she was already wearing. "*Nova.*"

"I know, Mom," the girl said with a sigh. "I know that you two . . . But please give it to him. It's important I try."

"Nova, look at my arm." She tapped the bracelet, and Nova stared at it for a moment. Again, she cocked her head.

"How . . . did you get one already?"

"Something is going on, Nova," Lisa said, lowering her arm. "Something very strange."

Nova looked away. "Well, I think Dane will like one. Can you please give it to him?" She set both on the table. Then she turned back. "You don't think . . . Dad will come this year . . . will he?"

"Nova, does it matter?" Lisa asked. "I'm telling you, something is *wrong*."

"Yeah. If he comes, it would be wrong." Nova heaved a sigh, but then perked up. As if . . . she'd completely forgotten the oddity about the bracelets, or she didn't want to confront it. "But I suppose Dane will deal with him again! I should get going! Bye!" She scampered out.

Lisa sank into the chair, feet disturbing cereal puffs that Nova hadn't fully cleaned up. That conversation had felt so strange, and . . . how . . . how *had* Lisa gotten home last night? With a frown, she called Dane, but it immediately went to voicemail because of his stupid smartphone with its anorexic battery. She started a text, but as she did, one came in from Nova's father.

I suppose, it said, *I'll live with that.*

She frowned, until she remembered texting him a few days ago, promising to record the recital for him—but suggesting it would be a bad idea for him to come in person. She scrolled up, and found the exact same text he'd just sent. Dated Monday, 6:52 AM. Just like this one was. Same date. Same time.

Heart beating more rapidly, she ran upstairs and checked the bed, then the floor next to it. There. Dane's gun, on the floor. The one he'd given her out of the back of his car—she'd been holding it during the explosion. Shaking, she scrambled downstairs and made a furious drive to headquarters, arriving around seven thirty, having beaten most of the traffic.

She burst in and hurried to her office, rushing up to Rowna—who was in early. Something she never did on Tuesdays or Thursdays, when she drove carpool for her kids. If she was here . . .

"Rowna," Lisa said.

Rowna kept typing.

"Rowna?" Lisa said, feeling something in her beginning to crack. "Please?"

The woman shook, then glanced at Lisa and started. "Commander! You should know better than to sneak up on an armed woman like that." She said it with a smile, but Lisa's nerves were fraying . . . and Rowna frowned soon after. "Commander?"

"The Goffrey case."

"We're close," Rowna said. "Just need one of the Kim brothers to break. I'll have a testimony on your desk the moment it happens. But you'll have to persuade the DA this is enough. Good luck with *that*, Commander."

Lisa stood, feeling a chill down to her bones. Nearby, none of the passing officers even looked at her—it was as if she were invisible. Rowna went back to her typing, and started again when she turned and saw Lisa there. Like she'd forgotten.

Davis walked in with coffee for his team. Monday was his day. The whiteboard had a perfect replica of Lisa's notes from Saturday, the ones she'd erased on Tuesday night to outline their battle plan for the actual arrest. She glanced at her office. Glass was cracked in the door. They'd replaced that . . . on Wednesday . . .

Oh, heck . . .

"Dane," she whispered. She put a hand on Rowna's shoulder, which startled her *again*.

"Commander?" Rowna said. "Still worried about the case?"

"Dane," Lisa said. "Is he in?"

"Commander . . . it's before noon. What do you think?"

Lisa turned and walked out, faster with each step, until something even *more* unnerving happened. People started noticing her and turning toward her, smiling and waving, saying good morning. Because . . .

Because it was 7:48—around when she normally arrived at the office. Probably the exact time she'd arrived on Monday. The . . . other Monday. Now that she was *supposed* to be here, people suddenly began interacting with her like normal.

But this was anything but normal. She fled.

Back in her car, she drove to Dane's apartment, which wasn't too far—but there was more traffic on the road now, and people kept *almost hitting* her. It happened five times. After the fifth car swerved away and honked, Lisa parked and walked the last three blocks.

She had to try twice to get Tim, the beanpole of a doorman, to notice her. "Ah, Miss Lisa," he eventually said.

"Dane," she said, sweating. "Has he come out today?"

"Nope, Miss Lisa," Tim said. "After all, it's—"

"—Before noon. Yes, I know."

She rushed past the broken elevator—the thing had been out of service for years—and bounded up the steps to the second floor. Breathing deeply, she forced herself to adopt a semblance of calm. Something had happened at that house, with the "device." What was it the woman had said at the end? That they were going to send the entire *building* through . . . what? A hole of some sort?

Activating it hadn't destroyed the city, fortunately, but something *had* happened. Something incredible, something mind-breakingly strange. Either that, or Lisa was going insane.

She used the spare key—she kept meaning to give it back—to get in. The place had a distinct scent; call it *l'eau d'bachelor*. Mingling odors of leftover Chinese, beer cans in the recycling, and dirty clothing piled in the tiny laundry room.

Dane wasn't slovenly—in her beat days, she'd *seen* slovenly, and beyond. He was average, at least for people who lived on their own and didn't often have visitors.

She pushed open the bedroom door, and . . . he wasn't there. Bed was messy, but that didn't mean much. His phone was gone though, not in its charging stand—and more importantly, his gun was missing. He normally hung his sidearm in a holster from a peg by his bed. He only locked it away when someone was staying over, so if it was gone, it meant something.

Either he had come back and was having the same odd experiences as Lisa, but hadn't gone into the office or tried to call her. Or . . . or he *hadn't* arrived back here as she had.

Feeling confused, exhausted, and overwhelmed, Lisa sat quietly on the corner of his bed. Somehow, impossibly, that white light had sent her to her home three days into the past.

But where . . . or . . . or *when* . . . had it sent Dane?

Five

Sometime After Moment Zero

Dane groaned, feeling like the bits of gravel that got stuck between the grooves in the soles of combat boots. Blinking, he found himself on the hard floor, covered in dust. He sat up and sent it streaming off him, puffing up, floating lazily through afternoon light from a single dirty window.

. . . *His* window?

This was his bedroom, except the bookshelves had fallen from the walls, and their contents lay on the floor, where they seemed to be *decomposing*. Books half crumbled. A vase broken from the fall—but some pieces of it having become granulated.

He scrambled to his feet. That . . . seemed to be the remnants of his *bed*. Chunks of broken wood, sheets that tore like spiderwebs. He brushed off the dust, utterly dumbfounded, then spotted something in the debris at his feet. He fished out his gun, which was solid, and held the grip for support.

It was so *quiet*. Life downtown was *never* quiet. Occasional shouting was a sign all was well, and sirens were his nightly serenade. He stumbled to the window and leaned against the sill, and the wood there *cracked* beneath his left hand.

. . . *The hell?* he thought, raising his hand, and looked at the impressions he'd made in the sill. Then, he holstered his weapon and carefully used his sleeve to wipe the glass—which fell out of the window at his touch. Dane winced at the stark sound of it shattering below, like a gunshot in a quiet theater.

He didn't dwell on that long, however, as . . .

Damn . . .

Along his street, the buildings were mostly still standing, but the cars lay in rusted heaps. Some in the center of the road, others parked, frozen as if they'd all stopped working at the same moment—then had been left for centuries to decay. Hollow windows. Stumps instead of trees. Fallen streetlights, leaving rust-red lines on the ground. And silence.

So much silence.

"What," he whispered, "did that bomb *do*?"

He suddenly didn't feel very safe on the second story of a building. Fortunately, his apartment was basically a concrete box—and though his carpet was tatters and dust, the floor was more solid. He walked to his door, tried to open it—but just pulled the doorknob off, the mechanism inside crumbling. Even the doorknob, which was brass, flaked a little—and he could scrape it with his fingernail.

That wasn't normal decay. Brass lasted, like, forever, right? They still had Roman armor made from the stuff, didn't they? He put his hand to his head, and pushed through the door—breaking it to splinters—then walked through his kitchen toward the door into the hallway. That one was already gone—blown inward, judging by the remains.

The lights weren't working, of course, but unfortunately—after some rummaging in his rooms—he found that his flashlight was rusted out and no use. He crept back to the hallway outside, which was dark save for sunlight drilling through holes in the far wall. Like a shotgun pattern. He turned right and walked toward the stairs, the floor strong underfoot. Good old concrete and rebar. At the stairwell, he edged down a few steps, but the darkness here was absolute. He slipped his phone out of his cargo pocket . . . only to find a black screen with a blinking dead-battery sign.

Right. He zipped it back in, then—with a deep breath—carefully felt his way down, worried that at any moment he was going to step onto a patch of stairs that had crumbled away. *Only one story,* he told himself. *Even if you fall, it won't be that far.* Besides, he had no other choice. The fire escape seemed to have rusted away, and the elevator never *had* worked, not that he'd trust it in this situation anyway.

Pulse pounding, he traversed the blackness, each step feeling like it was into some infinite pool of nothing. The only sound his frantically beating heart. He had trouble using his pulse to find the calm of a firing range—at least there, he could see his targets and execute on his training. Here . . . he just had to take step after step, hand flat against the concrete wall, tapping down with a toe. Each time, he felt he had to stretch too far before finally finding the next step.

It was pure relief when he spotted a sliver of light, and he probably took the last few steps too quickly in his haste to reach it. He emerged into the lobby, which was dim—but lit by sunlight from out front.

Hell, he thought. *That was way,* way *too disturbing.* He was in some kind of strange futuristic hellscape . . . and walking down a stairwell was what frightened him? He hurried through the dust-strewn lobby, then froze. Footprints. All over the floor here. For that much dust to gather . . . it felt like the lobby had been left desolate for . . . centuries?

Damn. Could it have been *centuries*?

Uneasy that someone had been here recently enough to leave those footprints, he slid his sidearm out, inspecting the shadowed lumps of furniture and the fallen front desk. Then, one of those lumps opened glowing white eyes.

Dane's heart tried to extract itself from his chest as he backed up, cursing softly, and brought his gun to bear on the shadow, which stood up. It became an emaciated man in tattered remnants of clothing. Tall, with a comb-over . . .

"Tim?" Dane whispered, naming the doorman. "Hell, Tim. What happened to you? Why do you . . ."

Why do you have glowing eyes?

Tim focused on him, then whispered six chilling words. "I can feel your warmth, Dane."

Dane took another step backward, but his heel hit the wall—the only thing behind him was that hollow stairwell. He kept his gun on Tim, who advanced.

"You're still warm," Tim rasped. "Share your heat. I need it."

"Stop, Tim. Don't move. Show me your hands."

"I *need* it."

"DON'T TAKE ANOTHER STEP!"

Those glowing eyes fixed on him, and something *stretched* out of Tim's side: a shimmering figure, a screaming face and torso, transparent and white—as if trying to rip free. That . . . that was *Mrs. Banler.* The woman from three doors down.

Tim surged forward.

Dane fired, two shots, right at the man's core—as per training.

They didn't do anything.

Tim hit a moment later, slapping aside Dane's gun with a strength those twigs of arms shouldn't have been able to produce. Dane was shoved back against the wall, scrambling to reposition his gun with one hand while holding off Tim with the other. That . . . spirit . . . of Mrs. Banler kept trying to pull free, face a howling mask of pain, as Tim planted a hand around Dane's neck.

The touch pulled something from Dane, sending a chill through his body. Like the same emotion of extreme alarm he'd felt *jolt* through him when he'd heard his mother was in the hospital, but magnified to the square. Dane grunted, and Tim's eyes widened, glowing brighter.

Fortunately, that style of hold wasn't a particularly effective one. Despite the mounting enervation, Dane found his MMA training. Holster the gun, grab under the arm, shift his weight, and . . .

Dane executed a throw, tossing Tim into the remnants of the front desk. The man rolled through splinters, grunting. Dane stumbled, breathing deeply. He reached for his gun again, but . . .

Damn. Two shots directly to the core hadn't done a *thing.*

Tim screamed and scrambled to his feet. Dane went against training and grabbed Tim in hand-to-hand again, trying to put the man into a hold—which proved difficult. Not only did touching the man's skin provoke that same terrible chilling sensation, but Tim was *strong*. Stronger than any of Dane's instructors.

Tim broke the grip and shoved Dane against the wall. A kick to the chest at least sent Tim backward. He was strong, but he had the body weight of a scarecrow.

Not going to win a long fight against him regardless, Dane thought, noting how easily Tim jumped back up, while Dane already felt worn out. Dane glanced to the side, then grunted, pushed off the wall, and met Tim in the middle of the room, delivering a punch to his face. That last part had been mostly instinct, as Tim was open and the boxing part of Dane's training wanted to punish—but it *worked*.

Two bullets hadn't done a thing, but fist-to-face seemed to daze Tim. So Dane followed with two more, wishing he had gear, feeling cold at each touch. With a final move, Dane grabbed the doorman by one arm, then turned and heaved—tossing him straight through the wooden panel that blocked the elevator shaft. It had been left there by the people working on it, but was as frail as anything else, and Tim smashed right through it.

He howled and plunged into the basement, where the sound cut off abruptly.

Dane fell to his knees, puffing, feeling worse than any sparring match had left him. He was exposed kneeling there though, and there *were* stairs up from below. So he heaved to his feet and checked the elevator shaft.

Tim's body lay twisted and broken at the bottom, visible by the cool white light coming off it, vaporizing slowly—the image of the screaming woman vanishing. Tim looked like . . . like he'd fallen straight on his head. Importantly, he didn't get up.

"Well," Dane said, hands on his knees, breathing deeply. "Finally got to use that elevator for something . . ." He turned about, checking the other shadows—but no white-eyed monstrosities waited for him. He looked down at Tim again, feeling sick. Not just from the touch and the fight, but . . . that was *Tim*, or some remnant of him. They'd gone out drinking together. Now . . .

Now the final bits of light faded from the man, the corpse succumbing completely to the darkness.

Fortunately, Dane felt his strength return—his body warming up. Whatever that touch had done to him didn't seem permanent, and he felt almost normal—save for his tension from the fight—as he inched out of the building and checked the street in both directions. His car wasn't in its parking spot. Hell, it was probably decomposing on the street near the house with the explosion.

None of this made any sense, but he didn't need *sense* at the moment. He needed to find a safe place to think, and he certainly didn't feel safe in this building. Whatever had happened to Tim could have happened to others inside—and judging by the sun it was nearly evening already; Dane did *not* want to get trapped here at night.

Maybe he'd be safer out in the countryside where there were fewer people? How to get there without a car, though? Every vehicle on the street looked like it had been left to rust for generations.

Whatever it was that happened, he thought, *it had to do with that experiment. The device, the white light.* So . . . should he move out to the west, since the house had been in the eastern suburbs? That was his best guess, so he acted, slipping onto the street—sidearm held in a sweaty grip.

He moved down the dilapidated sidewalk, scanning each cross street, craving a sight other than decaying buildings and abandoned roads. If there were survivors who weren't . . . whatever Tim was . . . they'd have left some trace, right? He turned down Rosemary, and *swore* he felt something watching him from a building along the way.

Dane picked up his pace, running around a corner—where he spotted figures hiding beside a broken-down truck. He hesitated and considered turning back, but . . .

He had to check. Those could be people, not monsters. Nervous but determined, he jogged that direction with his sidearm out in front of him, pointed down. Soon, one of the figures turned his way and proved to be an ordinary person, with clothing that wasn't falling apart and eyes that—while wide and terrified—didn't glow.

Still, Dane closed the last distance carefully. Two people, maybe in their twenties. One woman (Hispanic, short hair, thick leather jacket) and one man (Caucasian, mullet, freckles). As Dane approached the truck, they spotted him and jumped. The man's eyes flashed to Dane's badge, worn—as always—on his belt.

"A cop?" the woman asked.

Because of old habits, Dane braced himself.

"Thank *God*," the woman said, reaching to a cross around her neck. She waved Dane toward them urgently with the other hand, and . . .

Well, his gut said these weren't monsters. Not with those nervous postures and relieved expressions. Plus, his own relief at seeing someone who *didn't* seem to want to kill him was nearly overwhelming. He hurried over and knelt with them, gun pointed safely to the side.

"We need to get away!" the man hissed. "Now!"

"But the others—" the woman began.

"They're dead! We need to *move*."

"Others," Dane asked. "Where?"

The woman hesitantly pointed around the rusted truck, which had dust for tires. In the near distance, Dane spotted other figures that the bend of the street had hidden from him: a group of three people in tattered clothing, two emaciated, but one man showing an impressive musculature. Like a bodybuilder.

As Dane watched, glowing shadows tried to pull out of the biggest one, their faces twised in agony. All three figures had the same luminous eyes as Tim, and they prowled into a specific building through a ground-floor window. A bank he'd often passed on the way to work.

"There's a whole *pack* of revenants in there," the woman whispered. "We split up in a panic. We two ended up here, while Terri and the others . . . they ran for the bank."

"How many?" Dane said. "How many friends are in there, and how many of those monsters did you see?"

"There's four more of us," the woman said. "The revenants . . . there must have been . . . more than a dozen. Plus those three stragglers who came just now, probably because of the screams."

"We have to go," the man insisted. "Terri and the others are *dead*."

Go.

"Yeah," Dane said, "not on my beat. You two stay hidden here, though shout and move to the open if you need help."

"But—"

Dane unzipped his left cargo pocket and pulled out two extra mags to tuck into his belt. He refilled his current one with two bullets from one of these. Then, as the survivors huddled and watched with terror, he moved out from behind the truck, standing tall, sidearm in hand.

He approached the front of the building and called: "This is Detective Andrew Dane. I want you three out here with your hands up, *now*. Slow movements. No running. I am not going to ask a second time, and I am *not* going to hold back if I have to breach that room. Ten seconds for you to come out slowly, or I come in shooting."

Hands trembling, Dane counted in his head, remembering. For the first time in years, he was in this situation again. He . . .

A figure leaped from the window, eyes glowing.

Dane found his calm.

He delivered a shot straight to the being's forehead. She crashed to the concrete, rolling to a stop as the second emaciated being followed her out, yelling about Dane's "heat."

He fired a second time, and that man fell like the woman had. Both stopped moving, the light dissipating from them. They . . . they really could be killed.

But only two had come out. From the second story, Dane heard shouting—the sounds of living humans in trouble. So, hating the idea, he breached the building, checking the corners. His training saved him, as the final of the three creatures he'd spotted earlier—the one who wasn't emaciated—tried to grab him from the left.

Dane dodged backward and the beast followed him, glowing spirits trying to rip out of it—a new one each time. As if, unlike Tim, this thing had absorbed dozens of people. That might explain the well-fed look.

Dane scrambled out of the building as the thing swiped for him. It followed, and Dane delivered a bullet straight to the creature's head.

It kept coming.

The thing seized Dane—whose next shot went wild—and tossed him to the side, sending him rolling. The creature followed with incredible speed, leaping on top of Dane and slamming him down a second time with enough force to knock his breath away. There, Dane felt himself begin to be drained, that cold washing through him.

"Your heat," the creature said, leaning low, "tastes wonderful, Detective. Andrew Dane. You know, I like the idea of hearing the name of one of my meals?"

Dane blinked, bleary-eyed, through tears and pain—and saw where he'd hit the creature in the head. The bullet had been deflected, cutting skin but not penetrating the skull.

Pinned down, his very life being consumed . . . Dane made a decision. Maybe a stupid one.

He headbutted the thing.

Dane saw stars as pain broke through the cold, but the beast released him. Though it immediately grunted and grabbed him again, Dane was able to bring his sidearm up. Seeing only shadows, he managed to set the gun against the monster's chin right as it slammed him back down.

Dane emptied the entire rest of the magazine into the thing's jaw. The creature jerked, then exploded with light as ghostly forms ripped from it. Its scream waned, then it collapsed.

With a grunt, Dane heaved the corpse aside—it fell onto its back, eyes dead and staring upward—then found his feet. "That last bullet's name was Nancy," he muttered, kicking the thing in the head. "You're welcome."

He speed-loaded a mag, then stumbled toward the building, gun at low ready, counting on his strength to return, though his numb fingers felt like they'd been holding chunks of ice for an hour. Inside, he was confronted with another of those dark stairwells. He gritted his teeth, then followed the sounds upward. He soon saw light: one of the creatures, those eyes shining on the walls as it turned.

One to the head.

Gunshot still ringing in his unprotected ears, Dane leapt over the corpse, blessing his hours on the course. His strength returning, his heartbeat strong, he let his years of practice take over.

He entered a room and checked for enemies. Two figures. Glowing eyes.

One to the head.

One to the head.

He dashed past the two trembling bodies, light fading from their eyes. Out into the hallway. Check the room to the right.

Something burst out from the left.

Turn, aim.

One to the head.

Step aside as the body fell.

Follow the shouts. Find a broken vault door, torn apart by clawlike hands. Into the chaos. Assess quickly. Three enemies.

One.

Two.

Three.

Dane lowered his sidearm. That was seven he'd killed. The people outside had mentioned a dozen—but eyewitnesses tended to overestimate these things. He stood in the vault room, surrounded by decomposed bills, facing four terrified people who had been struggling against the monsters. He watched their faces change from terror to confusion, to stunned relief.

"Any other enemies?" he asked.

"Who . . ." one of them (male, bald, glasses) said.

"Any other enemies?"

They shook their heads, so Dane knelt by the one who looked the worst off—scratches along her face and throat, bleeding. Her breathing was shallow.

"How do we help her?" he asked.

"Heat," a woman said, gathering the fallen woman into her arms. The two others huddled around, so Dane stepped out to check each enemy he'd shot. *Always double-check the ones you think you've killed.* Taylor—his firearms instructor—was an ex-Marine, and when he'd given that advice there'd been an edge to it. As if he'd been speaking from haunting personal experience.

The things did all appear to be dead, so Dane checked out the window and waved to the two people watching from the street below. He gestured them forward, then went down to meet them in the small bank lobby.

"Three of the others seem all right," he said, leading them up the steps. "Though one woman is in worse shape."

Back on the second floor, they passed the revenants he'd killed. The woman rushed into the vault, but the man with the mullet lingered in the hallway outside, staring at the dead monsters.

"How . . ." the man said. "I mean . . . *Damn.*"

Dane quietly changed magazines in his gun, counting the remaining bullets. And feeling . . .

Feeling *alive*. His warmth had returned, and had brought something with it. An excitement, a thrill, a sense of *purpose*. He holstered and nodded toward the vault, where the woman who had been down was starting to stir—still held close by the group.

"Are there other survivors like you all?" Dane asked. "Do you know of a safe place?"

"Yeah, we're a scavenging crew," the man said. "We were sent to search a hardware store for some gear. Got cut off, then panicked and ran. Never should have entered a Dead Zone . . ."

"How many survivors are there, that you know of?"

"Couple hundred," the man replied. "Holed up at the country club, over by Seventeenth."

Dane nodded. Lots of open space there; easy to tell if someone was trying to approach. Not the best location to hide out, but by far not the worst.

"Are you . . ." the man said. "I mean . . . you special forces or something? Is the military coming? Are we saved?"

They were still expecting the military to come? "How long has it been?" Dane asked. "Since . . . I don't know . . . whatever started this?"

"We call it Lightbreak," the man said. "You know, when the . . . eruption of . . . How can you not know how long it's been?"

"I got knocked out somehow. Woke up just a little bit ago to all of this. How long has it been? Twenty years? Thirty?"

"Three days," the man said, sounding numb. "Officer, it happened . . . it happened *three days ago.*"

Six

63 Hours Before Moment Zero

Lisa paced Dane's bedroom, resisting the urge to clean up the pile of socks. He always forgot to take them off before climbing into bed, so kicked them off then, amassing an incredible collection. How often had he shrugged and just bought more? She was pretty sure an archaeologist could dig down through the layers and find socks from his junior prom.

Focus. She'd found a pocket-sized notepad and a pencil in his bedside table. She scribbled what she knew.

1. I'm in the past, somehow. I remember the next three days, but nobody else does.
2. In approximately sixty-three hours, at midnight on Wednesday, a scientist will conduct an experiment that will warp time itself.
3. Everyone I meet treats me strangely, as if they can barely see me. Like I'm not truly here.
4. Dane's stupid phone probably isn't charged yet. Either that, or he's in a time or place I can't reach. So I don't know if I should look for him here, or not.

Worry for him churned inside her. She'd heard gunshots before the explosion, and she thought she'd seen him get hit, but in the chaos she wasn't certain. She wished she knew whether he had been returned to her time, and working under the hope that he had, she sent him another text. He'd see them if he charged his phone. That done, she then tried to figure out a course of action. Go to 1PT and gather her analysts? Or should she get a team and go raid the site of the explosion? Nazeem's guards wouldn't be expecting anything; they wouldn't actually "meet" Lisa for another two and a half days.

Except . . . could Lisa even find the site? Dane had gotten lost on the way, and as she thought about it, she hadn't been paying much attention to their surroundings—she'd been answering emails during the drive. She could probably find the general area, but felt uncertain about that plan for other reasons as well. If she tried to gather a team to raid the place, would they even listen to her? Would half of them wander off in the middle of the strike?

She didn't like the idea of depending on a squad she couldn't trust. What she needed was an expert . . .

She stopped, lowering the pad of paper.

"The scientist," she whispered. Yung, the man they'd found tied up. What had he said? That he'd left the project for moral reasons, only to return on the day of the experiment? That meant in her present timeline, he was probably living his ordinary life. He not only knew the location of the explosion, he understood what the group was trying to do.

He was at TYCC. Tyson Yards Community College. *Fewer places for us than you'd think . . .*

It was a plan, a real way to wrestle some control—or at least some answers—out of this situation. She practically ran down the stairs, passing Tim—who didn't look up from his magazine. She thought she saw him jump as the door slammed.

On the road, she got out her maps. It wasn't far. She admittedly drove faster than she should—she'd always kept strictly to the speed limit, to be a good example, and was stern with other cops who pretended their jobs gave them license to go as fast as they wanted in nonemergency situations. When she was chief, she'd—

The accident happened so quickly, she barely had time to respond. A car slammed into her from behind as Lisa rolled to a stop at a light, shoving her out into the intersection. She got a face full of airbag. Right as—

CRASH.

Something else plowed into her from the passenger side, spinning her car in a loop.

Lisa came to rest seconds later. She gasped belatedly, full of adrenaline, heart thundering, stunned. But for all the crash's suddenness, these weren't large streets, and the speed of the side impact hadn't been immense. She was shaken, and she'd hit the airbag with enough force to put a kink in her neck . . . but nothing felt broken.

Trembling, she fought her door open and got out of the vehicle, eyes wide, terrified she'd get hit again. She needn't have worried, as her car was up on the sidewalk, the passenger side pressed against the wall of a convenience store. In the intersection, the two other drivers were checking on each other, and they seemed baffled.

"Hey!" Lisa shouted. "Idiots!"

They looked over at her, and both jumped, shocked to see her. Dang . . . She'd noticed earlier that cars were aggressive with her. *I shouldn't have been driving,* she thought. *This was my own stupid fault.* Her mind still had trouble accepting what was happening. That had nearly gotten her killed. *So, do I call this in . . .* They were supposed to when an officer was involved, even for a wreck much smaller than this. She debated it, then decided against it for now, considering that she'd likely be ignored. She wasn't even certain how she'd get the car towed. *Save the city first. Then worry about lesser matters.*

The two drivers exchanged information, and other cars stopped for them, not creating a bigger pileup. But as she sat on the sidewalk recovering, neither driver came to talk to her, and she thought their exchange of notes went too fast. Moreover, once they finished, they both got into their cars and drove away—with wobbling wheels in one case—as if returning to their routine.

Right, Lisa thought, leaning on the wall of the convenience store. *Okay. Only use the subway from now on . . .*

It took far longer, as she had to change lines twice. Plus, people kept bumping into her, or trying to sit in the seat she had taken. Still, it wasn't nearly as dangerous. So, eventually, she stood in front of TYCC—a three-story building with an inviting number of windows for its age.

Inside, she found you needed a key card to get beyond the lobby. This wasn't the roughest area, but neither was it ritzy. Pretty standard security protocol. Some high schools around here had similar protections.

She flashed her badge at the front desk. "Detective Lisa Sterling. I'm here to speak with Professor Yung."

"Yung . . ." the woman said, typing on her computer. "I'll send for him. If you'll wait a moment."

Lisa paced. A moment became two, then three. Finally, she stalked back to the desk. "Is he coming?"

The woman there blinked. "And you are . . ."

Lisa flashed her badge again. "I asked you to call Professor Yung."

"Yung . . ." the woman said, typing on her computer. "I'll send for him. If you'll wait a moment."

Lisa sighed, right hand to her forehead, still trembling from the car wreck. So, when the next student opened the inner door, Lisa just followed—and nobody called her out on it. It wasn't protocol, but protocol didn't really cover what to do when a freak accident turned you basically invisible.

She found her way to the faculty offices, and each—helpfully—had office hours posted. Yung's said he was supposed to arrive in ten minutes. Lisa knocked anyway, got no response, then stood there wondering if he *was* inside but couldn't hear her. It was locked, so waiting seemed like the best course, frustrating though it was.

She waited.

And waited.

He didn't show, but eventually something encouraging happened. Her phone buzzed. She pulled it out, then nearly dropped it in her excitement.

Dane was finally calling her.

Seven

67 Hours After Moment Zero

'm Charles, though everyone calls me Chip," the guy with the mullet said, then pointed to the Hispanic woman who had insisted they not leave the others. "And that's Adriana."

One at a time, the members of the group introduced themselves while Dane watched the hallway outside to be certain no more revenants came prowling up the stairs. So far, so good. Everyone needed time to recover, but it would be dark before too long—and he wanted to get moving soon.

First, more information.

"So these things," he said, gesturing toward the dead, "they were ordinary people, until . . ."

"Until three days ago," Adriana said. "Yeah. Whatever it was that escaped at Lightbreak, it slammed down through big swaths of the city."

"Escaped?" Dane said. "What do you mean, *escaped*?"

Several people in the group shared glances.

"There were these big glowing columns of light," Chip finally said, "that came from a point in the city, over in the eastern suburbs. Those who were watching say they looked a little like enormous, shining, transparent tentacles. They burst out, rose into the air, then slammed down like spokes on a wheel."

"They *weren't* tentacles," Adriana said. "They were more like huge writhing beams of light. More eruption than monster."

"Well, whatever they were," Chip continued, "everything they touched . . . became a Dead Zone."

"People there became revenants," Adriana whispered. "And the Dead Zones immediately started to decay. Wood splintered, iron rusted, even some other metals became brittle. It gets worse and worse each day . . . It's the eschaton. It—"

"These 'revenants,'" Dane interrupted. "Everyone in the Dead Zones changed into one?"

"Unfortunately," Chip said. "Only the people, we think—no animals—and it took longer for some than others. Those who'd been indoors changed faster than those who were outside."

"That seems backward, doesn't it?" Dane said. "Why would it take longer for those who were directly exposed to the light?"

The others shrugged. "Nothing makes sense anymore," one whispered. "Why search for reason in . . . in all of this . . ."

"Anyway," Chip said, "by the end of the first day, everyone who had been touched by those things—"

"It was the light of God's judgment," Adriana said.

"—had changed."

"And the revenants feed on regular people?" Dane asked.

"Yeah," Chip said. "Those of us not in the path of the Lightbreak—we're food to them." He shivered. "They sense our warmth. Come hunting. It's worst at night."

Of course it was. Well, Dane had thirteen bullets left, all in one mag. He might be able to handle another pack of the things, but after that . . . he didn't fancy fighting them with fists or a rock. Fortunately, the wounded woman—Felicia— had recovered a little. Time to be moving.

"Let's see what you have in those supplies," he said, nodding to the backpack of scavenged equipment someone was carrying. "Any radios in there?"

"Radio doesn't work anymore," Chip said.

"What do you mean, *radio doesn't work*?"

"Like, radios . . . don't work," he said with a shrug, looking to everyone else. They nodded. "Even a few feet apart, with non-rusted equipment, they don't . . . well, work."

"You all find that as unnerving as I do?" Dane asked.

"Yeah," Chip said. "Officer, the world just . . . isn't the same. Don't know what it means, but some back at HQ are working on it. Might want to talk to them."

"I'd love to. So if you weren't grabbing radios, what did you find?"

"Mostly power tools," one explained. "And other stuff from the electronics section. Portable lights, cords, rope, some headphones, a couple of power banks . . ."

"Power banks?" Dane said, taking a small, palm-sized one as it was handed over. "Any juice in these?"

"They often come with some charge," Chip said. "Depends on how long they've been on the shelf."

With a grin, Dane pulled a USB cord from another pack and plugged his phone into the power bank.

"Phones don't work either," Felicia whispered. "Towers are all down, and even if they weren't, the electrical grid passes through Dead Zones. All the wires have degraded."

"Well, at the very least, a phone is a backup flashlight," Dane said. "And plus, someone might get a network up and running somewhere. Other cities might find it odd we've gone silent, and broadcast somehow. Assuming something weird isn't happening with them too."

He checked whether they'd found any guns on their scavenging mission, and they hadn't, but there was an impressive bowie knife in one of the packs. He appropriated that, then got them moving, sneaking down the steps and through the street. Outside, he checked again on the big revenant he'd killed—the smart one. Still dead; still missing a chunk of skull.

"How many are big like this?" Dane asked.

"Never seen one before today," Chip said.

The others agreed one at a time.

Dane frowned, looking down. Damn. He cocked his head. Was there . . . something familiar about that face? "It had way more . . . ghosts . . ."

"The souls of the people it killed," Adriana said, holding her cross necklace. "You freed them, Officer Dane."

"Maybe it ate so many," he said, "it . . . um . . . got stronger?"

They shrugged, and he was reminded again that it had only been *three days*. Less, considering Lightbreak had happened at midnight, and it was now evening on the third day.

The country club—HQ—was only a half-hour walk away, but much of that was through the Dead Zone. Dane led the way, gun out and ready, and kept them to the center of the street. Yes, that left them in the open, but he didn't want one of his team grabbed through a doorway or window.

He passed shops that had been ripped open; even the metal bars or mesh—pulled down at night to protect the merchandise—had been shredded. Most buildings felt like pits, with an intimidating darkness beyond their doors. He hadn't realized how quickly, without modern lights, a city street would become like a row of tombs.

"Do cars still work?" Dane whispered, snapping to sights as something moved ahead, but it was just a forlorn cat that took one glance at them and disappeared into a building.

"The ones that weren't caught in a Dead Zone, yeah," Adriana said. "But the roads are full of broken-down vehicles, so it's impossible to get anywhere. We've had a little luck with motorcycles, but . . ."

"But?"

"Whatever happened to the Dead Zones seems to be spreading," she whispered. "Bikes we found at a shop near one, but *not* actually in the zone, were starting to corrode. If you carry equipment through a Dead Zone, it eventually suffers. It's like . . . the areas that were touched . . . are radioactive, but with a new kind of radioactivity we can't measure."

Well, hell. That made him want to be away from this region even faster. Unfortunately, Felicia was still weak from nearly being eaten by a revenant—and had to walk slowly, with help.

"She'll be like that for a while," Adriana whispered. "We don't know how long—we have no idea if people who were touched, but not killed, will ever recover fully."

"Is there a chance she . . ."

"Will turn into one?" Adriana whispered. "It hasn't happened so far, thank God. Best we can tell, if you get completely drained by a revenant, you stay dead. More of them aren't being made. But the Lightbreak eruption . . . those beams grew thicker as they moved away from the epicenter, big enough they hit over half the city, so . . ."

So there were more than enough revenants to worry about. Still, it eased his mind to know that other people weren't turning. "She'll recover," he said. "I did, after all."

"You . . . what?" Adriana asked.

He called a halt with a raised fist as he heard something down a side street. Soon, two revenants—the normal emaciated kind—loped toward them, picking up speed. Dane took a deep breath and sighted, waiting. The closer they were, the better his aim. Just a few more heartbeats . . .

Bang!

Breathe. Wait for his handgun to steady.

Bang!

The second one tumbled to a stop on the pavement, the bullet hole straight through its head.

"Damn, you're good," Chip whispered.

"Helps that they don't dodge," Dane said. Eleven bullets left. "Let's keep moving."

The others had said that sound could draw revenants, but not as well as it might draw conventional predators. They could be distracted briefly by heat. A bonfire, for example. Difficult to manage, with how much wood was decomposed in the city, but HQ had two nearby buildings piled with wood and oil, and a sport archer ready with a flaming brand. In the event of a large-scale attack, they hoped to be able to divert and distract the revenants long enough to fight back or escape.

The more Dane heard about their preparation, the more impressed he became. Considering how short a time it had been, he'd have expected most people to still be confused and panicked—but someone obviously had their wits about them. Unlit bonfires primed for distraction, watchposts to spy on large groups of enemies, strategic scavenging missions? Not bad for three days into the apocalypse.

"How big do the packs get?" he asked softly.

"They seem to be getting bigger," Adriana said. "First day, there was a big wave of them as people changed. Second day, we saw mostly solitary ones. Third . . ." She shivered. "With telescopes, we've seen bands of thirty and forty roving within Dead Zones. Maybe more . . ."

Damn. If they hit a pack of thirty . . .

He moved them faster, instructing two of the men in how to hold Felicia in a fireman's carry. They entered a wider street, and then . . .

Ahead, buildings that didn't look dilapidated. Trees that were still growing and not rotted stumps. He got his team almost there before the ground gave way beneath his foot.

Crack.

Darkness.

Dane hit hard with a grunt, barely managing to stay on his feet as he landed. Cursing, he looked upward to a glowing disc of light . . . a manhole. He'd stepped on a *manhole* cover that hadn't fully degraded. The iron had given beneath his weight, and he'd dropped some thirty feet into a subway access tunnel.

He blinked, gauging the distance again as heads gathered around the circle of light up above. Yeah that had . . . that had to be thirty feet. Or more. He looked down at the concrete he'd landed on. Had he really just . . . fallen thirty feet, and landed *upright*? His legs smarted from the fall, but that faded.

People didn't fall three stories and walk it off, did they?

"Officer Dane?" Chip called from above, panicked.

"I'm fine," Dane yelled back. "Throw me a rope."

They did, then had to lower it farther after they—rightly—assumed he couldn't have fallen more than ten feet or so without hurting himself. Then they lowered more. He was able to climb up and pull himself out of the manhole.

"Stupid mistake," he said to them. "Sorry. I should have watched my feet."

"How far was that?" Chip asked.

"Let's keep moving," Dane said, ushering them forward. "I want to be out of this Dead Zone."

They seemed to feel the same way, though they'd warned him that it wasn't *safe* outside a Dead Zone. Merely *safer*. Revenants roamed outward, but they returned regularly to these swaths of broken city, as if they needed something within the Dead Zones—perhaps that undetectable radiation.

Regardless, Dane felt a whole lot better when they crossed that line, leaving behind buildings that looked a hundred years old for ones much more like the city he remembered. There were some broken windows and signs of disrepair, as everyone living in this area had . . .

Well, either they'd been contacted by the survivors and moved to the country club, they'd fled the city, or they'd been taken by the revenants. The buildings here—mostly homes rather than shops—were as empty as the ones they'd left, but the scattered corpses were more fresh. And, as he'd been warned, the trees nearest the Dead Zone were starting to rot away on one side. Spots of rust were appearing on cars.

Dane urged his team forward, as it seemed the borderlands would be where revenants tended to hunt. He pulled ahead in his eagerness, and Adriana joined him, whispering—once they were out of earshot, "How did you survive that drop?"

"No idea," he admitted.

"What aren't you telling us?" she demanded. "You said you got touched by a revenant?"

"Yeah. Doorman to my building, after I woke up and went downstairs. He got me pretty good, drained me to the point I had trouble standing. But I threw him down a hole, and then I was back to normal in maybe a minute or two."

"That hasn't happened to anyone else," she said. "Those who get so much as a *single brush* from a revenant are worn out for days. None of them have recovered fully, and those that were partially drained? They're all still in their sickbeds. Yet here you are, not just walking, but falling *three stories*?"

He kept moving, turning to wave the others forward.

"You say you woke up in your apartment," she said. "But that was in a Dead Zone, so you couldn't have been asleep there three days. Besides, you have a working gun. What *are* you?"

"I'm a friend."

She looked to him, and her eyes widened. She grabbed her cross again and nodded, seeming . . . encouraged.

Well, hell. She thought he was an angel or something, didn't she? Maybe he should have explained. He didn't think he'd been in bed for those three days—he was increasingly sure that the explosion had made him slip through time, arriving after it all had gone down. But why his bedroom? And how did he explain surviving that fall?

She didn't ask more questions, which was fortunate, because he didn't have answers.

As he was urging everyone along he felt something buzz in his pocket. His phone, charged, had booted up again. Good. He unzipped his pocket and pulled it out. Now he could see if . . .

He blinked at the screen.

Three new messages.

"What?" Chip said, as the group crowded around. "A signal?"

"Kind of," Dane said. "Lisa. Lisa texted me."

Dane. Call me once you charge your damn phone.

That one had been sent fifteen minutes ago . . . or actually, that was probably when his phone had turned on in his pocket, and he hadn't noticed. Same for the second one.

I just left your apartment after looking for you there. Heading to TYCC to chase down that professor. Please CALL ME.

But there was a third. Which had come mere moments ago, making his pocket buzz.

When this is done, I'm BUYING you a new battery.

"That timestamp . . ." Chip said. "That's impossible. Phones don't work. Look, you have no service."

Dane glanced at him, then the others. He hit the call button.

It rang.

Then *Lisa answered.*

Eight

Dane," Lisa said, raising the phone to her ear as she paced outside Yung's office. "Finally. You're all right? You didn't get shot?"

"Lisa?" his voice said on the other end, distorted for some reason, but audible. "Hell, Lisa! No, I'm well enough. Except . . ."

"It happened to you too?" she asked.

"Yeah. Just a minute. Let me get away from the others." The line cut out, then there was a muffled scratching sound. "Okay, I put one of my earbuds in so I can be hands free, then stepped away to talk in private. Li, I think we must have slipped through time somehow."

Lisa took in, then released, a long breath. She hadn't realized how eager she'd been to hear that response. It wasn't just her. She wasn't crazy.

"Dane," she said. "You all right? I heard gunfire before the explosion, and those guards were facing you."

"They didn't hit me. What about you? You safe?"

"I am. I've got a tip, if you haven't figured it out yet. Don't drive."

"No issues with that here. Where are you?"

"Trying to track down the captive you found. Yung, that scientist from a local community college. He might have answers for me, I figure. You?"

"I'm a few minutes out from the old country club," he said. "Fairgreen, the one near downtown. There are some survivors holed up there."

Survivors? Lisa froze in the center of the community college hallway. "What do you mean, survivors?"

"You haven't encountered any? What about revenants? You need to be careful, Lisa. They can sense heat."

The way he said it with such urgent tension put a chill through her. "Dane, everyone I've met seems normal, except for the way they treat me. It's like they can't see me at first, and even when we interact, people keep ignoring me if they can. You?"

"I *wish* I were being ignored," he said. "I've put down almost a dozen of the things so far. They're dangerous. Stay away from the parts of the city that are decaying, but the revenants can be anywhere. If you see someone with glowing eyes, that was caused by the explosion three days ago, when—"

"Three days ago?" she whispered.

"Yeah."

"Dane. What day and time is it where you are?"

"Evening," he said. "Saturday the eighteenth."

The eighteenth.

Oh, *flip* . . .

"Wait," he said over the line. "What about you?"

"It's the thirteenth here," she said. "Still before noon. I woke up this morning remembering everything we went through—the missing scientist, following after you, untying Yung, the explosion . . . But I'm back to Monday. I *literally* relived the exact same morning. I'm in the past."

"I'm in the future, Li," he said.

He couldn't . . . It . . .

Was he lying?

What a stupid thing to even question. That wasn't Dane's joking voice. That was his "I just had to kill several people" voice. She'd only heard it once, but it still haunted her.

"It's bad?" she asked.

"Whatever that explosion was," he explained, "it messed things up *good*. Just a sec. Hell."

Gunfire followed. Then shouts, grunts. Lisa listened, feeling helpless, each shot making her jump.

More gunfire—distant. Silence. Then Dane . . . laughing? She relaxed.

"A patrol," he said. "Some of the monsters found us, but then we ran into one of the country club patrols. They're barely armed—only two fellows with hunting rifles—but it was enough. I think we're going to make it. Country club isn't far now."

"Dane," she said, pacing in the narrow hallway, watching each person who passed—though they didn't so much as glance at her. "How are we talking? We're almost six days apart."

"I have no idea. But you said things were weird for you there?"

"Super weird. Though nobody's trying to kill *me*."

"Revenants. Kind of like . . . I don't know. Vampires? That suck out your heat? Don't need to bite you though, so maybe they're more like ghosts? They have bodies and we can shoot them, but they keep coming unless you hit them in the head."

It sounded outlandish, but after what was happening to her . . . "Dane," she whispered, "please tell me you're exaggerating or being metaphorical or something."

"No," he whispered back. "Li...it's terrifying. Whole city has fallen apart. Buildings are decaying at incredible speed. Cars rusted out, though it's only been three days. I told you, that explosion . . ." He paused. "Hell. You're in the past. You can *stop* it!"

"Will that work?" she asked, watching a student pass—suddenly terrified that their eyes would start glowing and they'd attack her.

"How should I know?" Dane said.

"Well, I've got a lead. Professor Yung. Like I said, I'm trying to chase him down."

"Mister community college theoretical physics?"

"Exactly. Unfortunately, I've passed the time for his office hours, and he hasn't shown up yet. I'm beginning to worry he isn't here on campus. I might need to go raid the site with the explosion instead—so now that I think of it, give me the exact address of that place."

She wrote it down on the pad she'd taken from his room. Though . . . as she wrote, she noticed something bizarre. The notes she'd taken earlier *rubbed free* as her hand brushed them, coming straight off the pad—the graphite crumbling and smearing beneath her fingers.

"Li?" Dane said. "What is it?"

"Some notes I took earlier in this notebook . . . they're vanishing." She ran her thumb across them, and again the graphite wiped off in an unnatural way. She could see the indentation her pencil had made when she'd originally written, but it was like . . .

Was it insane to think this? It was as if reality was *resisting* her. Rejecting anything she did.

"Huh," Dane said, though he seemed distracted. "Well, that's interesting."

"Disturbing is more like it."

"I wasn't talking about your notes, Li. Sorry. Um, I have news. It might be good, might be bad."

"What?" she said, feeling cold.

"That professor you're looking for? Well, I might know why you can't find him; he's standing right in front of me."

Nine

Dane, with the patrol and his survivor group, had reached the perimeter of the country club. And there—standing on an improvised watchpost made from a cherry picker and a ladder, about ten feet up—was Professor Yung.

Holding a shotgun, his chest strapped with twin bandoliers full of cartridges, the professor looked a world different from when Dane had found him tied up. It felt odd to reconcile that captive with this capable-looking man with sleeves rolled up, gun at his shoulder, and confident attitude. Yung looked him over, then slid down the ladder. He nodded to the leaders of the patrol. Then, grinning, held out his hand to Dane. "Officer. You are a sight for sore eyes."

"You remember, then?" Dane asked, taking his hand. "The explosion, everything? Were you sent forward in time too?"

"Forward in . . ." Yung trailed off, then hurriedly grabbed Dane by the arm. "We need to talk."

—

"I don't know how I survived," Yung explained a short time later as he and Dane settled into comfortable seats in the country club's smoking room. Yung had appropriated it for his office, as he was the leader of this cell of survivors, and the origin of terms like "Lightbreak" and "revenant."

Yung had plastered the wall with notepads—the big kind with sticky backs— and had pulled in a large whiteboard. Even with that, he hadn't been able to *completely* nerdify the place. It was still marked by hardwoods and fine furniture; it felt distinctly strange for Dane to go from fighting for his life in a decaying apocalypse to sitting in an overstuffed leather chair beside a fireplace, sipping bottled water with a bowl of expensive olives on the side table. They were working their way through the food that had been opened already.

Dane's phone sat on the table, still plugged in, on speaker with Lisa listening.

"I crawled from the wreckage of the site, largely unharmed," Yung explained. "Perhaps . . . unnaturally so. I can now take a punch like I never could before. Lift like I've been working out all my life. My hand-eye coordination seems better as well, and it's improved my aim. Only Doug and Carlos are better shots among us here. You met them, both hunters."

Dane grunted. "You fall down any holes?"

"No. Why?"

"I survived a drop that should have broken bones. I also recovered within minutes after a revenant touched me."

Yung nodded. But Lisa's voice piped up from the phone. "Wait. What are you saying, Dane?"

"Whatever happened at Lightbreak," Yung said, "exposed the world to a new kind of energy—and, best I can determine, to new laws of physics. Radio no longer works, no matter what part of the city you try it in. Maybe the Dead Zones are causing interference. Or maybe . . . it's something else."

"What kind of something else?" Lisa said.

"I have theories, Officer," Yung said. "But before we go further, you are at my place of work in the past?"

"Your office at the college, yes. I was hoping to find you—the past you."

"Well, I was there at work six days ago—and you not finding me is evidence of something."

"Maybe we three only exist once in time," Dane said. "I mean, Lisa went to my apartment and didn't find me there."

"Perhaps," Yung said. "I have reason to believe otherwise, but that isn't relevant for the moment. Officer Sterling? My apartment is only three blocks from campus, and should contain all of my notes on the project. The apartment is in a Dead Zone in our timeline, so everything there is dust. But during your time . . ."

"I'm on it," Lisa said. "Just give me the address."

He did so, explaining the best way to get there—and giving her the door code to the building. Dane sat back, worried about the implications of what Yung had said. Was there another Dane out there somewhere in Lisa's timeline?

"Now," Yung said, standing from his seat, "let's test my professorial skills and see if I can explain. I believe Nazeem's experiment ripped a hole in reality and opened a portal to another dimension—a dimension where the rules of physics are different."

"How can physics be different though?" Dane said.

"Why not?" Yung said, stepping up to one of the papers he'd stuck to a hardwood panel on the wall. He pointed at a list of observations he'd made about the Dead Zones, many of which Dane had experienced firsthand. "In my classes, I talk about the 'simple why' of how things work, and the 'deeper why.' We can explain the simple why of something like subatomic particles—we can say how they behave, and how they interact. But the deeper why . . . well, we've been searching for a unifying theory for almost a century now.

"Why can't we go faster than light? It's due to the relationship between mass and energy, as explained by the famous equation. But the deeper why can be confounding—in this case, *why* is the speed of light that specific number? Likewise, why is gravity's range infinite? We can plot out mathematics that explain the implications; we can find the constants . . . but at their fundamental roots . . . well, many things we take for granted in science just *are*. We don't know the deeper why yet, so we have to discover the constants and use them. We've had to assume they will never change. Until now."

"Until . . . now?" Dane asked.

"I believe that the speed of light has changed, Officer," Yung explained, gesturing to a different pad. "That opening the wormhole to the size we did, letting through whatever was beyond . . . it shifted at least one fundamental law of the universe. That explains radio not working, for technical reasons having to do with our digital receivers. I'd hoped to find an old analog one where you can shift the dial manually, in order to test my hypothesis, though I have some evidence . . ."

Dane listened, feeling lost. Yung stopped by one of his papers stuck to the wall and tapped it with his fingernail.

"So . . ." Lisa's voice said. "You think the portal let some . . . other dimension's ways of working . . . into ours?"

"Basically, yes," Yung said, and seemed *excited*. "But, I suppose I should explain what Nazeem was *trying* to do."

"Yes, please!" Lisa said. "Also, you said your apartment was on Third . . ."

"Indeed. Large blue building."

"Got it," she said, puffing slightly. "Please keep going."

Dane sat quietly, drinking his water, munching olives, trying not to feel overwhelmed.

"Nazeem and I discovered a small wormhole," Yung said, walking to another giant Post-it with some sort of schematics on it, this one covering up a nice painted portion of the wall. "I noticed strange readings in one of my experiments some years ago, and she was the only one I could talk into funding me. When you work for a community college and have few papers in respectable publications, you take what is available. I originally moved here to study the readings, and met her through local fundraising work.

"She took me seriously, and I was able to find this pinprick of a wormhole, then so small it was basically microscopic. With my efforts, we found we could shrink or grow it. You . . . do know what a wormhole is?"

"A, like, teleportation tube?" Dane said, trying to remember some things he'd seen in movies. "They fly ships through them in science fiction shows."

Yung nodded. "Yes, well, a lot of the early material and hypotheses talked about them on the extremely small scale. Quantum level. So a pinprick-size one is actually enormous by comparison. Regardless, it was one of *three* I eventually found in the city, tiny little holes in reality. None anywhere else, but these seemed *stable*, and . . ." He took a deep breath. "And with power hookups, we stabilized them more, so they didn't vanish. We kept the secret, wanting to study them on our own until we had something we could present, well documented. It was supposed to make both of our careers. For me, it would lead to respect. Meaning. For her, it would take a small fortune and make it large. She bought up the three locations, and we built facilities there, hoping we could use them to teleport matter across distances."

". . . This doesn't seem like the result of teleportation, Professor," Lisa said. "She ripped apart reality!"

"Well, to teleport, that's what you'd have to do," Yung said. "Our physics says it can't happen, but the laws in another reality? We did experiments with these wormholes, and had success sending data through one hole to the others. It's all very technical, but you put in some energy, feed it into the wormhole to initiate the transfer. We started with digital signals, like . . ." He paused, looking back toward Dane.

"Like cell phone communication?" Dane asked.

"Yes," Yung said. "Like that. I don't know why this is working for you two—cell phones use radio waves. But this is the problem with *everything* we're trying to understand in the new world—the rules, the very laws, have changed. In ancient times, people didn't know why lightning struck, only that it did. Suddenly we're back in that world. It's all *new*. And we have no explanations for why yet, merely inklings."

Again, he seemed far too excited by the whole thing, but that did make some amount of sense. If you'd spent your entire life studying this, the appearance of something new to research had to be amazing.

"Perhaps you two are entangled in some way," Yung said. "Regardless, Nazeem wasn't satisfied with communication alone. She worried that once we revealed the wormholes, someone else would come in and do all the important work and get all the credit." He rested his hand back on the Post-it with the schematics. "No danger of that anymore now, is there?"

"So," Dane said, "the experiment we interrupted. She was going to do more than send data through?"

"Yes. I left the project over this, assuming that without me, they wouldn't be able to proceed. Too much energy was coming through during the experiments. A kind of energy that didn't fully register on my instruments, but which I could *feel* somehow. My calculations were off. I kept getting the wrong numbers from experiments. We'd send something through, and it would arrive some days later, as expected, but magnified . . . and the numbers never matched my projections.

"Something was very wrong, and I worried that if we forged ahead, we'd . . . well, release something huge. Unfortunately, I heard from a friend on the project that Nazeem had continued without me, and made her own *even more flawed* calculations. I knew *she* was going to feed in far too much energy. My leaving the project didn't work. It only made things worse."

"So you called in a fake 911," Lisa said over the line. "And when that didn't work, you returned and tried to stop it in person."

"Yes. You know the rest." He let his hand slip from the paper. "Except . . . do you remember what she said before it all went wrong?"

"That she'd been communicating," Dane said, feeling cold, "with something *inside* the wormhole."

"Maybe even I have no idea what was really happening all along," Yung said. "I've always found it odd how quickly and easily she accepted my theories, when other potential investors walked away. How quickly she purchased the locations, particularly that mansion, as if she'd already known . . ."

He fell silent, and Dane gave him a moment. Over the line he heard a ding— probably an elevator.

"So how did we end up where we are?" Dane asked. "Teleportation did happen, but not to the other two facilities you noted. I went to my home, and Lisa to hers. But in different *times.*"

"It is difficult to say anything with confidence," Yung replied. "Not yet. Not without more data. I have the same questions about you two. Why you were sent forward, Officer Dane, and your partner sent backward . . . that doesn't make sense."

"And time travel *does* make sense?" Lisa asked, her voice echoing in a hallway.

"It explains the problems with my calculations," Yung said. "That's what we were missing . . . It's why the initial tests for matter were off. We weren't sending to other locations, but other *times.* Yes . . . that's why it took so long for communications to arrive . . ." He began scribbling on a notepad.

"So, um . . ." Dane said. "I know I'm the dummy in this conversation, but . . ."

"Questions are never to be disrespected, Officer," Yung said. "And no one who is confident enough to ask them is a dummy."

"Right," he said. "So the communications you sent through . . ."

"Even some bits of matter," Yung said. "The wormhole didn't need to be big enough to squeeze them through; it was the rip we needed, the seed. We could send small things through with energy, making the hole large enough temporarily. But even after shrinking down again, its size would have increased from its previous state. Regardless, your question?"

"You said they arrived some days later. But isn't teleportation instantaneous? Isn't that the point?"

"No," Yung said. "The point was to go from point A to point B without traversing the space between them. Certainly, instantaneous teleportation would be remarkable—and I do know that Nazeem wanted to get there. At first, we were content with time gaps between transportation and arrival."

"How long a gap are we talking?" Dane asked, feeling like . . . something was close to clicking.

"Depends on your frame of reference," Yung said, "and on how traveling in the other dimension affects the perception of time. To the transportee, we had no idea how long it might feel. But to us, the initial test was . . ." He trailed off, then turned back. "Officer Sterling . . . how many hours were you sent back in time?"

"Sixty-something," she said. "Between two and three days."

"Could it have been exactly sixty-five hours?" Yung asked softly.

"I woke up between six and seven," she said. "And the explosion was at midnight, so . . ."

"So yes," Yung said. "Sixty-five hours. Or close to it. Why only close to it though?"

"Let me guess," Dane said. "That's the time it was supposed to take to teleport?"

"Yes," Yung said. "Though the numbers aren't quite right. Perhaps they changed some of my calculations. Officer Sterling, have you reached my apartment?"

"I have," Lisa said.

"There's a spare key in the possession of my neighbor, Sunny," Yung said. "Knock, and I'll tell him over the phone to give it to you."

"Right," Lisa said, and did as he asked. Knocking.

She had to do it way too long, but someone eventually answered. "Excuse me?" they said, sounding dazed. "But—"

"Sunny," Yung said over the line. "It's me. Could you please lend this woman my spare key? She's a police officer."

"Um, sure . . ."

"I thought you said they couldn't see you," Dane said to Lisa.

"They *can*," Lisa replied, "but it's . . . hard for them. Like, I have to get their attention. Here, I slipped into the room after Sunny—and he just went back to watching TV. Yung, where is the key?"

"Usually keeps it in a chest of drawers beside the door," Yung said. "Upper right. It has a blue top."

"Got it," Lisa said. "Heading to your apartment now."

"Good," Yung said. "Look and see if there are signs of me having been there recently. It would help if we could find my past self to aid you."

"Okay," Lisa said. "But I thought we decided that the three of us only existed in one time frame."

"No," Dane said, looking toward Yung. "He said he thought it was the opposite. Why?"

Yung glanced at him, then away. Finally he sighed. "Because . . . when I woke from the wreckage of the facility, there was a corpse near me, beneath a fallen wall. It was . . . Officer Sterling. I assumed you, Officer Dane, were dead as well. That's why I was so shocked to see you earlier."

Lisa's line had gone silent. "What did you say?"

"I'm sorry, Officer," Yung said. "But I saw it very clearly with my own eyes. You'd been crushed when the ceiling fell in. I could lead Officer Dane to your corpse now, if we had time to spare. I'm sorry . . . but unless we change things, at midnight the day after tomorrow, you are going to die in that explosion."

Ten

D ie.

On one hand, Lisa knew she shouldn't be intimidated by that word. The city was facing an apocalypse—and if she didn't stop it, a *huge number* of people would die. Those stakes were far greater than her own life.

Yet . . . knowing Yung had seen her corpse . . .

That rattled her. More than anything else had. She steeled herself, however, as she moved into his apartment and locked the door from the inside.

"I'm sorry to say it so bluntly," Yung said over the line—she had her phone in her pocket and a Bluetooth headphone in one ear, the kind the force used that had a microphone. She *could* work technology, no matter how much both Dane and Nova liked to joke.

Nova. *Oh . . . Nova!* Was her daughter alive in the apocalypse? It was all happening so fast, and the existence of Dane's timeline so academic until that moment, that she hadn't thought through the natural progression of what would happen to the people she loved who lived in that world.

"I put off explaining," Yung continued, "as I didn't know how to say it in a considerate manner. Then I just blurted it out anyway."

"It's . . . I'm all right. Thank you for telling me. But if there's an alternate me"—*Dead. Bloody. A corpse.*—"in the future, then there should be an alternate Yung and an alternate Dane in the past with me. And an alternate Nova, Dane, in yours."

"Yeah," he said, his voice grim. "Li . . . I'm looking at the map of the city. Your place is right in one of the Dead Zones. I'm sorry."

She shivered, sick. *Don't think about it. Don't think about her, that other little girl, alone when the disaster arrived. It hasn't actually happened yet, even if Dane is living it. Your Nova is still alive; you can save her. And yourself. You have to stop it.*

"We should find the past you, Yung," Lisa said, relieved that she managed to sound confident. "I can use him to help me."

"Like I said," Yung replied. "But I'm not at my apartment?"

She did a quick sweep of the three-room place. "No," she said. "But someone *was* here."

"How can you know that?" Yung asked.

"Wet toothbrush. Remnants of breakfast dishes in the sink. Corn flakes. Didn't look too old."

"Probably me," he agreed. "That was a quick read, Officer."

"Lisa's one of the best," Dane said on the other end of the line. "Or . . . she was."

Still am, Dane, she thought with annoyance. *Just because I set my sights higher doesn't mean I've lost my edge.*

She didn't say it, as she tried not to squabble in front of civilians. Plus, the thought of Nova in the future . . . the thought of her own body lying beneath a chunk of concrete . . . it left her wondering. She was a good detective, yes, but this? Was she up to *this*?

"We need my notes," Yung said. "It would take me years to re-create them— even the calculations I brought in to try to stop Nazeem three days ago took *weeks* of effort."

"Those notes . . ." Lisa said, stopping beside a conspicuously open wall safe.

"In a safe behind some books in the bookcase. The code is—"

"No need. It's open already, and empty."

"Empty? Of . . . everything?"

"What else was inside?" Dane asked.

"Cash," he said. "Prepaid credit cards. Burner phone. Fake passport."

"Your laptop is gone too," Lisa said, walking to his desk. "You left the cord though."

"I have a spare cord in my bag." A deep sigh sounded over the line. "Is my actual phone in the trash?"

She checked. "Yes," she said, holding it up.

"It will be wiped," Yung said. "And I don't remember the number of the burner. It appears, Detectives, that something spooked my past self quite seriously."

"You have a burner phone and panic money?" Dane asked. "What kind of scientist has those sorts of things lying around?"

"The kind," Yung said, "who dabbles in dubiously legal projects funded by eccentric millionaires. I believe I told you three days ago—I recognize that the activities I was participating in were questionable."

"You blew up the city, Yung," Lisa said. "Questionable doesn't cover it."

He fell silent. "I recognize that, Officer," he finally said. "At least I tried to stop it . . ."

"Try harder," Lisa said. "Your past self has bolted. Where?"

"I would run for a hotel," Yung explained. "But I purposely didn't pick one ahead of time, as I wanted to inject randomness into a potential flight, so as not to be anticipated. I could be one of a hundred places. Searching them would take weeks, not days, by design."

"Which means this lead is a dead end," Lisa said. "I'm going to have to raid Nazeem's facility and shut it down. Tell me everything you know about the place."

"I am fully willing to lend whatsoever aid I can, Officer," Yung replied. "But I fear that may not be enough."

"Why not? If I jail Nazeem, there will be no explosion. No explosion, no apocalypse. Right?"

"Well, let's test something," Yung said. "You're in the office room of my apartment, correct?"

"Yes," she said, turning and surveying the small room, with thick carpet and one of those plastic roller pads covering half of it.

"On my desk," Yung said, "there should be a mug with some pens. Does one say 'Fan-Con 2009'?"

She searched through them, then eventually pulled out a blue pen—the cheap kind given out for promotions. White lettering on the side fit his description. "I have it."

"I have been wearing, in my pocket, the same pen," Yung explained. "I took it when I went to confront Nazeem, and have been using it to take notes in your future. It's the only pen of that description in my possession, perhaps one of the last remaining in the world, as Fan-Con was poorly attended that year. I want you to take that pen and break off part of it, then replace both in the mug."

She nodded slowly, following him. She easily pulled off the clip, then dropped the pen and clip back in the mug.

"Any change?" she asked him over the line.

"None," Yung said.

"Wait," Dane said—his mouth sounding full of food. "What are we doing?"

"Testing," Lisa said, sinking into Yung's chair, suddenly exhausted, "if what I do will change things for you in the future. And . . . it doesn't seem that it will."

"Alas," Yung said. "This pen is completely unaltered in my time."

"Which means . . ." Dane said around bites of food.

"It means we've branched apart," Lisa said. "Something happened during the explosion."

"A Moment Zero," Yung said. "A point which caused our two timelines to diverge."

"Which means we're completely separate," Lisa said. "I can influence my own future, but not yours."

Their Nova isn't mine. She *had* to think of it that way. She couldn't do anything for that little girl.

"Indeed," Yung said. "A depressing outcome, but not unexpected. Branching is one of the only reasonable ways this could work. Unless . . . well, unless you come back and the pen has somehow repaired itself."

Lisa felt a sudden spike of alarm, like cold water to the face. "What would that mean?"

"First," Yung continued, "I have to make it clear *again* that we are in completely uncharted territory. We don't know the rules anymore—and theories are basically meaningless without more data. Working from ideas about time travel from the days when it was pure speculation will be like guessing the identity of an object in the dark with only the faintest contextual clues. But it's all that we have for now."

"Okay, fine," she said, sitting up, fixating on that pen. Which was still broken. "But tell me what it would mean, say, if I were writing things in a notepad—only to find that the graphite has been rubbing off, like it refuses to stick."

"Ah . . ." Yung said. "I see. And people almost exclusively refuse to acknowledge you . . . unless you're doing what you were *supposed* to be doing on the day in question, correct?"

"It's like they can't see me," she said. "As if . . . the universe itself is trying to ignore me."

"Hm. Yes." Yung took a deep breath. "Look at the pen again, Officer."

Hesitant, Lisa pulled the pen out of the mug. And . . . and the clip she'd broken off was attached back on. "Oh, heck."

"I assume it reconnected?" Yung asked.

"Yeah."

"It seems the past might not be as elastic as we would want it to be."

"Which means what?" Dane asked.

Lisa, though, already knew. She wasn't a theoretical physicist, but she'd lived this day—and she had seen how people responded to her.

"It means," Yung said, "Officer Sterling can't stop the apocalypse. As far as the universe is concerned . . . it has already happened. And so must happen again."

Eleven

Dane pushed himself up out of the overly plush chair. "No. I don't accept that."

Professor Yung turned away from his wall full of notes. "Officer Dane? I'm sorry. The reports from your partner indicate her timeline is *highly* inelastic. Here, look."

He drew a line on a sheet, then made a big mark in the center, which he labeled "Moment Zero." He then made another mark to the left, which he labeled "Past Timeline."

"This," Yung said, pointing, "is your partner's timeline. She branched off from the main timeline three days ago—but she can't change much. When she tries, the universe refuses. Not that it's *aware*, mind you, although we use phrases like that. But it *resists* change, like gravitational forces resist us escaping Earth's atmosphere."

He drew a line deviating off the main one from where Lisa went back in time—but then as he spoke, he pulled it back to the main one, arcing it to meet again at Moment Zero.

"I'd guess that an infinite multiverse does not exist," he continued. "I've read a great deal about this possibility, and evidence seems to support that there is just one primary timeline, at least for our universe. When Nazeem used so much power in her experiment, she destabilized that timeline, and two possible sequences of events opened up—but the deviation will likely be brief. Many have theorized that our universe is self-correcting in these situations, and will enforce this future. By the time Officer Sterling reaches Moment Zero, everything will be aligned."

"I'm alive for a reason, Doc," Dane said, striding up to him and pointing. "*We're* alive for a reason. To stop this."

"We're alive," Yung said, "because—best I can tell—we were close to the epicenter of the explosion. The rules were different inside that little bubble of altered space-time. You, who were right at the very point of the wormhole, were drawn through and teleported."

"That's the 'simple why,'" Dane said. "Not—what did you say earlier?—the 'deeper why'?" He pointed at the sheet, directly at Moment Zero. "I'm here to stop this."

"You don't know that."

"You don't know I'm not," Dane said. "You *just* said that you don't know the rules anymore. That any theories from before will be like guessing in the dark. So how can you be so certain the past is unchangeable?"

They stood, facing off, until Lisa spoke. "I agree with Dane," she said. Though her voice had been trembling before, it grew stronger. "You used gravity as an example, Professor. Well, humankind eventually *did* overcome that force and escape into space. In the same way, maybe we simply need some manner to escape the momentum of my timeline. After all, I *can* make people see me if I try. The past I'm living is not *completely* rigid."

Yung drew his lips to a line. He seemed . . . harder than he had been back when they'd saved him. More pragmatic. Could three days make that much of a difference?

Perhaps if those three days were spent living through the end of the world.

"I must admit," Yung finally said, "that I can't discount the *possibility* that we could change all this. I do not see a method of doing so."

"I've got an idea," Lisa's voice said from the table beside Dane's half-eaten sandwich. "Wait for a second."

"All right," Dane said. "Professor, the way I see it, the universe has decided this timeline is the real one. Can we invert that somehow? Make *Lisa's* the real one?"

"I don't see how," Yung said. "Look, here are some numbers on what is happening." He pulled a pen from his pocket, but in his haste accidentally dropped it, sending it clattering to the floor. He glanced to it, then froze in amazement.

Dane was confused until he saw it. The clip had broken off the dropped pen, and lay in two pieces.

"What's happening?" Lisa asked.

"The pen just broke," Dane said.

"Ha!" she said. "Look, a second ago I broke my pen's clip off and snapped it in half, then tossed both pieces out the window."

"This could be coincidental," Yung said, holding up the pen. "Or . . . or it could be an indication of the universe trying to align our timelines. Since repairing what happened to the pen in Officer Sterling's timeline was the more difficult option, it made my clip snap . . ." He shook his head. "Could still be a coincidence."

"Or it could not be," Dane said, feeling a surge of confidence. "What do your books say?"

"That . . . with this evidence . . ." Yung took a deep breath. "All right, I don't completely believe, but the only way we *could* fix this is if the elastic theory is correct. That the universe will try to merge the timelines, and will take the path of least resistance in doing so.

"We have a problem, however. This timeline, Officers, has the most *momentum*. It's the real one because so much energy is invested into it going forward—which is why it resists Officer Sterling. It's like . . . a boulder rolling down a hill. So much has changed. So many have died."

He began writing, doing calculations on one of his wall notepads. "Officer Sterling will have trouble changing what happened from her timeline because of this inertia—it won't be like altering a pen. She could raid Nazeem's offices, and that might stop it for a short time—but I suspect in that case, someone would click the button accidentally during cleanup. Or it will short-circuit and go off. Any number of things, because the universe will push toward the timeline with more momentum."

"You've got to have something for us, Doc," Dane said.

Yung looked back at the branching diagram he'd drawn. "I have one idea."

"Anything," Lisa said. "Please."

"What we need to do," Yung explained, "is make it so that the timeline where this didn't happen is the most reasonable, most plausible. I *think* . . . and this is just a guess . . . that if *you* were to stop it, Officer Dane, we might have something."

"I'm not following," Dane said.

"We send you back, Officer, to when the explosion happened. And you stop it here in this timeline." He drew a loop, going back from the main timeline to the starting point.

"Wouldn't that fragment the timeline further?" Lisa asked.

"Not necessarily," Yung said. "I think part of the chaos of all of this is directly related to Nazeem's failed calculations—there was so much energy, it *blasted* the timelines apart. When we did our experiments before? There were no branching timelines, as far as I can tell, because I was careful with the energy usage. This is all very technical, but I think . . . I think I can send you back to Moment Zero in *this same timeline*. You stop the explosion there. That should free Officer Sterling to do the same in her timeline, as Lightbreak is no longer happening here. Then the two timelines should snap together, because they are so similar."

"So, to be clear," Lisa said, asking for more information and clarification as she always did—something Dane was glad for in this case. "You think he can stop Lightbreak, but I can't?"

"Exactly," Yung said. "At least, you can't stop yours until it's been stopped in this one. Yes . . . yes, that would work, I think. It's like . . . digging a trench for a rushing river. Let the flow of time take the path of least resistance. But *can* I send you back in *this* timeline, Officer? If I did, it would be the ultimate proof that my calculations were correct . . ." He started scribbling on the notepad again.

"Assuming you could do it," Dane said, "how would we get the machinery? Wasn't the mansion completely destroyed in the Lightbreak?"

"There were two other facilities, right?" Lisa asked.

"Indeed," Yung said, pointing to the map of the city tacked to the wall. On it, Yung had greyed out enormous radiating lines, growing wider as they left the place the experiment had started. Two other sites were marked on the map, forming a triangle. Those two facilities were outside the Dead Zones, though both were pretty far away. Even the closer one would require crossing multiple Dead Zones to reach. But if it was the only option . . . hell, they needed to try.

"How do we power it?" Dane asked.

"Each of the facilities has backup generators," Yung said. "That should be good enough to get the machinery running. But now that I think about it, I might be able to get the equipment started with a few good batteries. The question is, as I said before, can I send you back, and to a specific point? The numbers could make sense . . ." He rested his hand on the map, with those large sections greyed out. Two-thirds of the population—gone. "I think I could do it, if we can get my notes in Officer Sterling's timeline, but let me make this clear. This is a wild guess. A gamble. One chance to stop this, yes, but also a chance that I'm wrong. That I'll display the same hubris as Nazeem, and all we'll do in activating the machines again is destroy more of the city. Let more of . . . whatever has already occurred . . . into the world."

Dane fell silent, considering the implications. Damn. He . . . wasn't sure he could answer.

"Do we have to make the decision now?" Lisa said, using her "manage the situation" voice. "And if we do, what do you think our odds are, if you can even calculate them?"

"The longer this timeline goes unchecked, Officer Sterling, the harder it will be to change. So in answer to the first question, then, I do think that if we are seeking to change events, we need to be quick. We can probably spend a couple of days, but we shouldn't wait longer." He glanced at the phone. "As for the second question . . . I find myself encouraged by meeting you two this way, in a manner I might not have been earlier. That phone, the way you—Officer Sterling—can go about in the past making legitimate changes . . . What you have isn't traditional entanglement as it exists in my understanding of quantum physics, but there's something here. Something about you two is a kind of tether holding the timelines together.

"I believe it would be best if you both arrive at Moment Zero, and you both prevent the device from activating—it should work either way. Officer Sterling can get there using the slow method, moving through her three days naturally. We can get the machinery up and running, and then send Officer Dane once we're ready. If we have to send him earlier, so he can prevent Lightbreak in this timeline first, days before you do in yours . . . it should still work. I hope. But my instinct says we should try it regardless. We are the only ones who have a chance at stopping this."

"Then I agree," Lisa said. "We should at least set things up so we have the option."

"Yes!" Dane said, growing excited. "Yes. I agree. That's our plan! I go back three days and stop the device from being activated. Timelines stick together again. Everybody is saved."

"Assuming we can find my notes," Yung said.

"I'll do it," Lisa said over the line. "Yung, I'll find the past you."

"Missing scientist case . . ." Dane said, smiling. "Just a different scientist, with different stakes. Lisa *is* one of the best, Yung. She'll find those notes."

"It helps that I have access to a version of you," she added.

"That won't help as much as you think," Yung said. "Protocol, as I indicated, was for me to pick a random hotel, then pay cash and use a brand-new prepaid card if I need one for check-in, and hide. Even I don't know where I'd be going. Plus, we don't know *why* I started running in the first place."

"More proof though," Lisa said, "that the timelines aren't set. I'm not the only one acting out of sync—your past self is too."

"Admittedly, that's a good point," he said. "You might have provoked a butterfly effect the universe can't contain. Good news for us, who are going to try to shift it."

"You should try to find past me to help too," Dane said.

"Any idea where you'd be? I looked at your apartment."

"Yeah. Monday morning . . . I didn't sleep at home that night."

"Oh." Lisa paused. "Do you remember her name?"

Of course she'd gone there immediately. Dane rolled his eyes. "I watched the game with some of the guys at Perez's house on Sunday night. Had a few beers, decided to be a good example—even though I was almost certainly below the legal limit—like you're always saying. I crashed at his house. You might still find me there, if for some reason everyone is ignoring me too. I mean, when I sleep in . . . I can *really* sleep in."

"Got it," Lisa said. "I'll try to find my timeline's Yung first though. You get to the teleportation facility. We'll feed the relevant calculations to your Yung via the phone line, then unless by that point we have a reason not to, we activate the device again and try to send you to the past. Easy. Insane, mind you, but easy."

"Easy?" Yung pointed at the map—at the second facility. "To reach this, we'll have to pass through *three* Dead Zones. Worse, by our scout reports, hundreds of revenants have been congregating around the three facilities. Perhaps they can sense the energy coming from the wormholes. How much ammunition do you have in that sidearm of yours?"

"Eleven bullets," Dane admitted. "You have any 9mm?"

"Two boxes," he said. "We found them here at the country club, along with one handgun and a shotgun. But most of what we have for the shotgun is birdshot— which has proven useless against the revenants. I have one small box of slugs, half gone. Beyond that, we have a total of four hunting rifles, which I generally leave behind to protect HQ. How are we going to get through revenant-infested lands, and fight our way into the facility, with such uninspiring arms?"

Dane turned, scanning the map. He snapped his finger down on an address that was barely outside the nearest Dead Zone, maybe ten miles away. "SWAT is housed at this station," he said. "There's an armory in the basement. I assume, regardless of what happens with the time machines, your survivors could use some more firepower?"

For the first time, Yung smiled. "I doubt that would be a difficult mission to persuade my people to undertake."

"Ten miles is a long hike," Dane said, thoughtful. "But didn't Chip say something about motorcycles?"

Twelve

Lisa could hear in one ear as Dane and Yung prepped for their mission, grabbing more food and organizing a team to head for the SWAT armory. They left the line open—with Dane apparently finding some Velcro to stick the phone and power bank to his chest, like an officer's body radio. No one wanted to end the call, just in case it wouldn't connect again.

She turned the sound down and settled at Yung's desk, trying to think through what to do. She'd confidently proclaimed she could find her timeline's Yung, because that was what you did when people were worried and there was a problem to solve. Now that she confronted it though . . . three days? To find a capable quarry who had gone to ground? Without support from other officers?

It seemed a tall order. She couldn't even take notes. Or could she? She glanced at the phone, still transmitting. It was a little brick of a device, but it did have a note-taking function. She checked through it, and the texts she'd sent Dane hadn't vanished.

Whatever I was carrying with me when I was teleported back, she guessed, *is being treated the same as I am. Or maybe electronic signals are harder to wipe?* She took a few notes to herself, and was pleased when—a few minutes later—she looked back and they hadn't vanished. It was a small thing, but it boosted her confidence. She *could* exert some control over her situation.

Now . . . how to start this case? She doubted there was a money trail to follow. Yung—she dubbed him Past Yung in her notes—was using cash. She did a more thorough search through his rooms for anything that might be relevant, but unlike in the detective novels, there wasn't a conspicuous matchbook to be found to lead her to the right hotel. Who even used matchbooks anymore, anyway?

Modern trails were almost all digital. He'd wiped his phone, and had taken his laptop. But . . .

"Hey, Yung," she said. "You have any old computers lying around?"

"Hmm?" he asked. "Oh. Under the bed. Bunch of old electronics in there. Why?"

She smiled, fishing under the bed and pulling out a box. People regularly upgraded their tech, and always seemed to forget to clear their old devices. Indeed, Past Yung had left in a rush, and hadn't considered any of this. She got out the newest-looking laptop. Same model as his newer one, she suspected, from the power supply on the wall. She plugged this one in, and as she hoped, it powered on.

"When did you upgrade?" she asked. "I found an old laptop; looks only a few years old."

"Yes, I cracked the screen three . . . four years ago, and got a new one. Password is 1f2g3h4j5k. But Officer, that isn't going to have any pertinent data on it. I mostly used that one for my college courses, and even if I did jot something down about the device, those notes would be too old to be useful."

"Yes," she said, "but it connected to your apartment's Wi-Fi automatically, and it's still logged in to your email address." She checked the pull-down. "All of them, actually."

He fell silent. "Well, that was an oversight on my part, wasn't it?"

"A shockingly common one," she said. "Do you know how many people we catch who destroy their phone to hide their data from the police, only to leave an old model iPhone back at the house? One that auto-syncs to the cloud, to give us everything that was on the new phone?"

"Anything useful?" Yung asked as right next to the phone, Dane was trying out one of the motorcycles. It revved a few times.

"Emails from the community college administration," she said, scanning. "A bunch of them. Huh. Give me a few minutes . . ."

This was interesting, because each email was almost identical—sent five minutes apart. Yung had been missed at a staff meeting, and the dean had fired off an email to find out what was wrong. Then another. Then another. They weren't follow-ups; they were virtually the same email, with a few variations. As if . . .

As if the dean kept noticing Yung wasn't there, then forgetting.

Could it be?

"Yung, it looks like the universe hasn't wiped emails that were created due to you going off-script, so to speak."

"It seems to be using natural processes. When you broke off the clip from the pen the second time, was it easier?"

"Much."

"Like it reattached not through magical force, but by the happenstance of it getting jammed back together. Graphite flakes off your notepad because it rubs free. Those records would probably get expunged eventually, but during the next outage, or purge or the like on the cloud."

She moved to Past Yung's sent emails. And there found her confirmation: an email he'd sent earlier that morning.

> Mom,
>
> Please tell me you get this. Please tell me you know I'm still alive. Something is very wrong, and . . . and I worry I'm going crazy. Students stare at where I'm not standing, and answer questions I haven't asked. People collide with me in the halls. Everyone acts as if I don't exist.
>
> Please. You aren't answering your phone. I need to hear a familiar voice. Please.
>
> Albert

"Your first name is Albert?" Lisa asked over the line.

"Yes. Why?"

"Looks like you and I are in the same predicament, Professor," Lisa said, turning up her volume. "Take the phone from Dane for a moment. You have to hear what I found."

He pulled the phone off Dane's chest, and then she read the email.

He whistled softly. "I guess we know what spooked me into running. I've got the same affliction you have. We . . . probably should have seen this. I was close to that blast myself."

"So Past Yung goes to class this morning," Lisa said. "Like me, he assumes that the events at the facility were a nightmare. After all, he's woken up in bed, and everything seems normal. At first.

"But he gets off schedule a little, maybe arriving to class late, and is out of sync with what the universe wants him to be doing. He tries to play along, but it eventually gets to him and he runs home. He writes this email, but things are so strange, he ends up bolting."

"I'll bet he put together that something *did* happen at the facility," Yung said. "He realizes he's messed up the timeline somehow. I . . . had a similar sense when I woke up in that wreckage. Yes, I can understand—but by deliberate choice, I can't tell you where I'd have gone."

She glanced at a notepad by the table. There were lots of scribbles and notes, but she looked for one that had scraped free. One he'd written today, which the universe tried to erase. She found a number via the indentations that hadn't faded yet—same as the notepad she'd brought. 237.

"Yung," she said, "how would you have chosen a random hotel?"

"Well, there are a lot of them in the city."

Lisa checked his browser history, which had been cleared. Suspicious. "There are two hundred and thirty-seven," she said. "First Google result for a list of hotels in the metro area gives me that number—same one you wrote on a notepad here before leaving. Again, how would you choose among them?"

"Huh. Well, I suppose I'd have asked my phone's AI chatting app to pick a random number between one and two-thirty-seven. That might not be truly random, but it's arguable whether anything ever is, and it's my habit to use the device."

"AI chatting app, you say? You have a specific service you like?"

"I do."

"Website and login?" she asked. "They keep logs of all questions asked, don't they, so you can scroll back and see your previous interactions?"

He swore under his breath, then gave her the information. There, after she logged in, was a generation request for a number between 1 and 237—along with the number it had returned. Number 19.

"You're at the nineteenth hotel on this list," she said, scanning through them. "One of the downtown Marriotts."

"Damn," Future Yung said. "I'm not very good at this whole hiding thing, am I?"

"You're actually doing pretty well," she said. "Better than most who try to cover their tracks—but you're not a career criminal, Yung, and I *am* a career detective. Does that fake passport have a name on it?"

"Theodore Shanxia." He paused. "That's not a real name, but a joke. Chinese for 'under a hill' . . ."

"Cute," she said. "Looks like I need to go to this Marriott and see if they've got you registered." She considered. "Ordinarily, I'd flash a badge and make them tell me, but with how things are? Lobby staff probably won't even notice if I start typing on their computers."

Over the line, the motorcycle revved again, louder. Lisa sat back in Yung's seat, imagining Dane preparing to ride through a future hellscape . . . and absolutely loving his life.

He was built for that sort of thing, and had always felt like a man out of time. Perhaps that was why the universe had sent him forward, and her back. She always liked everything so stable, so carefully planned out. What could be more stable and planned out than a past she'd already lived?

Thinking that left her feeling cold again. It was terrifying to consider that there was possibly nothing she could do about her situation. That Nova was in danger, her parents and sister . . . that they were all on a proverbial train ride straight toward death, and she could not stop it.

Please, she thought. Prayed. *Let that not be true. Let me at least have a chance to change things.*

It had been a while since she'd gone to church with her parents. Maybe that was one of the habits she shouldn't have let lapse in her newer busier life . . .

The revving grew louder as Yung apparently gave back the phone. Shortly after that, Dane's voice came on. "And you said I'd never get on a bike again after buying my truck. How are you holding up?"

"Well enough," she said. "Just sitting and worrying that suddenly I might have absolutely no control over my life."

Dane fell silent on the other side of the line.

"It's just . . ." Lisa said, standing and tucking Yung's apartment key in her pocket. Best to get moving toward that hotel. But she paused by the door, voicing something that had been looming—and building—ever since Dane's Yung had said she was dead in their timeline. "It's so *unnerving.* The mere concept that maybe I can't do anything relevant to change my situation. Have you ever felt so completely impotent, Dane?"

"Yeah," he said softly. "Every day of my life since we moved to white collar, Li."

"You could have left, swapped jobs. It's not the same."

"I suppose it's not," he said, suddenly subdued. "But in some ways, knowing that I could change—that I should have—made it worse. Made it more humiliating that every day, I simply kept going. Doing the same things. Hating them. Locked in, like a bullet in a magazine on the shelf that never gets fired."

"I still don't understand *why,* though. Why not come to me earlier? Why not put in for a change?"

"Momentum is a hell of a motivator. Besides, there was . . . well . . ."

"Don't say you stayed for me."

"I didn't. But for *us* . . . maybe. I don't know, Li. You ever feel like you're in the right *place,* but you're the wrong *person*?"

"Never," she said. "Not until today."

She stood in silence a moment.

"That event four years ago—" Dane started.

"You don't have to talk about it," she said, perhaps too quickly. "It wasn't your fault."

He took an audible breath. "Four years ago," he continued, "after the shootout with those dealers . . . I realized something. Politics *would* get me, even if I ignored it. That in the end, the world didn't care if I did the right thing—some days it just needed someone to hang, and it looked for the unprotected necks. You had my back. Thank you."

"You're my partner, Dane. And my friend."

"Yeah," he said, and she heard him slide a magazine into his sidearm with a distinctive click. "Today, Li, I've got your back. I'm not letting this city go down." He paused, and she could hear the smile returning to his voice. "Guess there's still a need for a man to be a cowboy now and then."

"Please. You've never ridden a horse in your life."

"There was that one time at the kids' farm when I was six," he said. The motorcycle engine revved to life, and a group of others followed. "I'm better with a hog than a horse anyway. I'll mute this to spare you the noise. Look for a text when I have the guns."

"Affirmative." She took a deep breath, then strode out again into a world determined to ignore her, chasing a man who had the ability to hide even from reality itself.

Thirteen

Dane's motorcycle ride through the apocalypse wasn't as hectic as he'd imagined. They wove among lines of stalled cars, a sickening number of which had corpses in them. He'd gotten an explanation from Cal (bearded, baseball cap, Metallica tee), who rode his own bike nearby, hunting rifle slung across his back. The larger streets had become magnets for the first revenants who had poured out of the Dead Zones. The combination of hot engines, hot bodies, and people stuck in a panicked gridlock had been like a buffet. While the monsters consumed heat and . . . well, souls . . . they left behind corpses.

So many dead in such a short time. Dane stopped looking through windows and joined the other four survivors as they kept moving at a steady pace along the road. Yung led the way, along with Adriana—who was a former cab driver, and one of their chief scouts. Cal and his sister Sissy (cowboy hat, forearm flag tattoo, ripped jeans) were self-proclaimed rednecks, and kept to the rear. They were the sharpshooters—which for this team meant they'd gone deer hunting every season.

All five of them stayed to the center of the road, along the space between columns of cars. As he'd guessed, entering buildings—even outside the Dead Zones—could be dangerous. Each gaping doorway could hold packs of the creatures, waiting for unwitting prey to wander past. For every living human, there once had been three to four revenants—but three days in, nobody knew how many survivors remained. Neither did they know how many revenants were still in the city—packs had been spotted moving out across the countryside, seeking prey in unsuspecting towns beyond.

Dane leaned low on his cycle, sunglasses holding back the wind, and honestly couldn't decide which would have been more horrifying. Sitting in one of these cars, trapped on the street as the things closed in, or sitting at home in the countryside, oblivious to what had happened in the city, until something came crawling in through your window . . .

We're going to stop it, he thought, forcefully banishing the images. *When we're done, this will never have happened.*

For how complicated and technical it had been, he was able to follow the general idea of the plan. The universe wanted one timeline, and had chosen this one to be the "real" one. It was pulling Lisa's timeline toward the explosion, resisting her attempts to change it. But if Dane could somehow get back to Moment Zero, he could make *this* timeline the one that got abandoned, and *her* timeline the "real" one.

No more dead. No more revenants.

The front door of a minivan slammed open in front of him.

Though it had been a few years since he'd been on a bike, his reflexes were on point. He swerved dangerously to the side, but managed to dodge the open door without crashing into it or the car to his left. He picked up speed, leveling out, and checked his mirror to see a revenant scrambling out of the car behind. Too slow to catch up, fortunately, but it seemed to have been lying in wait.

Doors began to fly open all around them, creatures with glowing eyes and captive souls tearing out of cars. A door hit Yung square on, smashing him into the car beside him, sending him sprawling. As a revenant leapt for him, however, a shotgun slug tore half its head off.

Yung was up a second later as Dane pulled to a stop beside him. "Go on," Yung said. "It's an ambush! Everyone keep moving!"

Hell. He was right. Dozens of revenants were crawling out of cars, making for the five humans. The other three survivors had slowed, but at Yung's order they revved and shot forward. Dane waited until Yung was moving before joining him. More car doors were opening ahead, so the group rode up onto the sidewalk—Adriana in the lead, the rednecks next, Yung and Dane in the rear.

Unfortunately, the sidewalks were less even, and cluttered with paraphernalia. Book carts on wheels outside the bookstore. Chairs and tables with an awning for the café, with only a narrow aisle to ride through. Mailboxes, signs. The survivors kept barely dodging, until . . .

Cal hit a curb wrong. At these speeds, he was down in the blink of an eye. The others—Dane included—were past him in a flash. They slowed, but damn. There were revenants everywhere, pouring out of buildings and cars like from a hundred hornet nests. A group of them was on Cal even as Dane pulled his sidearm.

"Go!" Yung shouted. "The mission is more important! We can't fight them; we have to outrun them!"

He was right. Dammit. But . . .

This is my beat.

Dane spun around and headed back, wind against his face. The others shouted, but his focus was on Cal—a struggling figure lost in a pile of ravenous monsters. Working on instinct, Dane slid his bike to the left and swung off it, letting it crash sideways into a different group of approaching revenants.

Dane *should* have fallen; he'd been going thirty miles an hour. Yet as he leapt free, he leaned into a skid, somehow keeping his balance. He took aim, even while in motion, at the pack attacking Cal.

Dane delivered six shots straight into the pack—though he counted four enemies, he couldn't afford to miss one, and doubled up on shots he felt unsure about. As his feet ground to a stop on the sidewalk right by them all, he reached into the pile and pulled free a dazed Cal—leaving four dead revenants. Dane spun, hoping they hadn't had too long with Cal, and tossed the man toward his bike lying nearby. Then Dane leveled his gun and shot the leading revenants one by one as they scrambled out from among the nearby cars.

Bang.

Calm.

Bang.

Focus on those in front.

Bang. Bang.

Focus on the heartbeat as you swap mags.

Bang. Bang. Bang.

A bike revved beside him. Dane spun and found Cal—white in the face but strong enough to have gotten his bike up and running—in the seat. Cal slid back, making room as Dane dashed over and settled in the driving spot. He shot one final revenant ahead of them to clear the way before holstering the gun and hitting the throttle, tires squealing with a protest of smoking rubber as they took off just ahead of the arriving pack.

Cal held on, barely, and Dane heard him from behind. "Thanks. I . . . just . . . thanks, Dane."

The others had slowed, and it seemed they'd gotten past the ambush. Only a few straggling revenants were climbing over cars nearby. Dane shared a look with Yung as he caught up, but neither said anything yet. They picked up speed, leaving the terrifying pack of creatures behind.

Before too long—but long enough that they didn't have to worry about those revenants catching up—Dane spotted the weathering along the walls of buildings that marked the presence of a nearby Dead Zone. One turn later, there it was: the 18th, SWAT headquarters. A tall, narrow building in a long row of old-school, Main Street–type structures. Once a town of its own, this area had been absorbed by the city decades ago, though the touches of its individuality remained. They weren't in the Dead Zone yet, but they were dangerously close. Hopefully the decay hadn't reached the guns in the basement.

The bikers pulled to a stop, looking at the police station. The front doors had been ripped open, the windows shattered, but there was no hint of any officers—

alive or dead. Dane realized he had hoped against hope that he'd find another cell of survivors here—but no such luck. Instead, he thought he caught sight of a single pair of glowing eyes in that darkened foyer. A second later they vanished.

"Well," Dane said, glancing over his shoulder, "this is obviously a trap. They set up an ambush; now this place sits with doors open and shadows inside. How did they know we were coming?"

"Know?" Adriana asked. "It was just bad luck on our part. A large pack of them was sleeping there on the road, and we stumbled into them."

Sissy helped Cal sit down and got him something to drink, then she stood with her rifle at the ready to watch for revenants.

Yung folded his arms. "Revenants we've encountered so far don't appear to make plans, Officer Dane. My interviews with survivors indicate that the revenants remember their old lives, but those seem like . . . faint memories to them. They have become more animal than person."

"That holds for most of them I've seen," Dane said. "But there was one. Adriana, you remember it? Bigger, looked well fed. Hid and tried to ambush me."

"He's right, Doc," she said to Yung. "I saw it. That devil didn't act anything like the others."

Yung grunted. "If you say they can plan and think, I have no real basis to contradict you. Three days . . . not enough time for true science. Only enough to jump to bad conclusions. But how would they even know we were coming this direction?"

They shared glances. Upon consideration, that was the truly disturbing part of this. Dane looked back at the foyer of the police office, peering into the darkness, and knew. Knew they'd be there lying in wait for him specifically. Somehow.

"What do we do?" Adriana said. "There could be an army of them waiting inside."

Dane flipped mute off on his phone. "Give me a minute to plan."

Fourteen

61 Hours Before Moment Zero

The subway could actually be convenient now and then, when you didn't have to change lines. Lisa could probably have reached the Marriott faster driving at this hour, as the morning rush was over, but she had more time to think on the subway. More time to decompress.

She was feeling better about everything when she arrived. The hotel was of that "cheaply rich-looking" style you found in a lot of downtown places: elevated enough that you wouldn't feel bad having business dinners there, not so ritzy that your corporate accountants would think you were being frivolous.

It wasn't too busy; she seemed to have arrived at a lull. She inspected the long front desk—with six different stations for clerks—and was planning her approach when Dane came back on the line.

"Hey," he said in her ear. "Do you know the Eighteenth station very well?"

"Not terribly. Why?"

"I've got a feeling I shouldn't go in the front door," he said. "Think you could call dispatch and see if they can pull me a layout?"

"Dispatch is likely to ignore me," she said.

"Right. Damn, I keep forgetting."

She considered, leaning on the wall in the lobby, arms folded—watching people pass, being ignored. What was it that Yung had said? The universe wanted things simple—the path of least resistance. Could she use that?

"Give me a second," she said, and muted him. She knew how to do two calls at once on her phone—dumb though it was, you sometimes needed to conference call, so she'd learned. She had to try three times before she managed to get Rowna on the line.

"Boss?" her assistant said. "It says I missed two calls from you. How . . . I don't know how that happened. I'm sorry. I thought you were in your office working on the case . . ."

"Never mind that," Lisa replied. "I need someone to pull the specs for the Eighteenth Precinct building for me."

"Sure. I'll transfer you to—"

"No," Lisa said, imagining spending hours on hold for someone who never noticed she was there. "I need you to do it."

"Right, right," Rowna said, and her voice started to grow distant. "What was it you needed . . ."

"Eighteenth Precinct building specs. The one with SWAT headquarters."

"Sure. I'll transfer you—"

"Rowna, *no*," Lisa said. "Listen to me. *You do it.*"

Silence.

"Do . . . what, boss?"

Dang. How could Lisa make it easier for the universe to go along with what she wanted, rather than resist her? Like Yung had said: digging a ditch for the water to flow. Monday . . . what had she been doing on Monday, other than working on the big case?

Inventory reports. Since the chief was grooming her to take his spot, he'd been offloading some work to her. Including that stack of inventory reports, which she'd looked through for him on Monday.

"Inventory," Lisa spurted out. "I've got to do inventory for Chief."

"Oh!" Rowna said, and seemed to snap back to the conversation. "Yeah, that's right. You need to get that done, don't you?"

"Yes," Lisa said. "I'm going to send someone to do a count of the SWAT munitions—but I don't want them to know it's coming. I suspect they haven't been accounting correctly."

It was close enough to being true, from those inventories. SWAT liked to spend time on the firing range, and they didn't always check things in and out properly.

"Okay, pulling the Eighteenth building specs . . ." Rowna said. "What is it specifically that you want?"

"A way in that isn't the front. What are my options?"

"Hmm . . . Three entrances, each with a booth and security. Unless you wanted to come in from the roof, of course, and go down the sniper climb."

"Sniper climb."

"Sure," Rowna said with a laugh. "They insisted on a closed stairwell to put an officer on the roof. It's nothing special, but they like to call it that. You know how they are."

It took only a second to realize what Dane would choose. Lisa got the details for each entrance, and images of the building layout, sent to her phone. "Thanks, Rowna." She cut the line, forwarded the schematics via text to Dane, and switched back to his line. "Dane, still there?"

"Yup."

"You're going to enjoy this next part: rooftop entrance."

"Rooftop? Awesome." He spent a minute scanning the schematics before continuing. "Though I'll have to watch out for sections of the building that aren't made of concrete. Structure is more modern, and not just a simple concrete block, with lots of holes in the ceilings and floors that might have rusted away."

"That's a problem?"

"Depends on proximity to the Dead Zones. We're close here, but the building is still standing, so it might not have been too affected. Still, I worry I could take a wrong step and fall through the floor."

Well, she was glad she'd gotten him so much detail, then. The fact that his phone could receive pictures from her was also a nice thing to verify—it indicated she'd be able to send Yung photos of his notes. Assuming she could find them.

She had Dane mute again, but both knew to watch for texts. Now, her part. She took a deep breath, then walked through the tall-ceilinged hotel lobby toward the front desk. She didn't make any moves to draw attention, and then when a desk clerk came out through a side door, she slipped in and walked around behind the others.

Feeling as conspicuous as a junkie shooting up on the corner outside 1PT, she watched the clerks from behind, learning what she could of the system. Nobody even glanced at her, though she had to step out of the way as several moved about. After spending her entire life fighting to make sure people didn't dismiss her and took her seriously, counting on people to ignore her now was unsettling. When one clerk went on break, Lisa stepped to his terminal and did a quick search. And . . . there Yung was, under the false name, in room 1412. With a note underneath: *Stop trying to put other people in this room. It's occupied! —Kathy.*

She made herself a key, following the motions of the clerks, and slipped out, breathing a sigh of relief. She knew she was basically invisible, but it still felt strange to be acting in the open. In a way, it cheapened the detective side of her work—but she supposed if she'd been visible, she'd have just gotten answers via the badge anyway.

As she made her way to the elevators, she felt a traitorous thrill at being in the field again. Chasing a lead that was more than numbers in a spreadsheet. Heck . . . was Dane right? *Was* this more fun? It felt more real. She was able to forget, a little, about the idea of her possibly inevitable death.

She got in the elevator—electronics, it seemed, were far less likely to ignore her—and tapped the fourteenth floor. As she did, she caught a glimpse across the lobby to where a muscular man was leaning against a pillar.

He looked right at her.

The way he focused on her and cocked his head gave her a chill. It was the first time since she'd left 1PT that someone had noticed her. The glimpse was cut off as the doors closed, but as the elevator started to move, she realized something.

She knew that man. He was a security guard from the facility—one of the three who had gotten into a confrontation with Dane, then followed him into the building through the cellar.

From the look he'd given her, she was absolutely certain that—unlike everyone else she'd met—he could instantly see her.

Fifteen

70 Hours After Moment Zero

Dane surveyed the 18th, SWAT headquarters, from a hidden spot atop a nearby apartment structure. And . . . yup, a portion of the rooftop was sagging right where the specs had made him think it would be. The proximity to the Dead Zone *was* making this place start to degrade.

Those guns had better be all right. They were locked in large safes, and Yung thought they'd be fine—the corrosion seemed to work from the outside in—but that rooftop had him worried. By the schematics, the weaker section was where the original builders had left room for a skylight—something the police hadn't implemented.

The climb up to this other roof, where he surveyed from, had involved scaling a brick pattern at the back. His days at the rock wall had proven helpful; he hadn't needed to go through the cavernous interior. Maybe he shouldn't have been so proud though, because Yung had followed him easily.

As Dane inspected the target through binoculars, he couldn't discount that he felt . . . energized being this close to the Dead Zone. He could feel it to the right, like a second sun—a powerful font of invisible warmth. He'd been able to scale the outside of this building at record speeds. He felt in control, *strong.*

Focus, he thought. *You have a job to do.* He handed the binoculars to Yung, who—crouched beside the chimney with him—took them and looked over the SWAT building two structures away.

"You can make those jumps?" Yung asked.

"I could have made them before, no problem. So now it will be even easier."

"Yeah. I feel it too." Yung handed back the binoculars. "We'll draw their attention, but I don't like this, Dane. If you're right, and they *are* waiting for us, it speaks to us not having all the information we thought we did."

"I'll handle it, whatever it is."

Yung rested his hand on Dane's shoulder. "Don't assume you're invincible. You can take a fall like a champ, yes, and climb a building with minimal handholds—but whatever is happening to us *does* have limits. I'm still smarting from getting slammed into that car; might have cracked a bone."

Dane took a deep breath, but nodded. It was a legitimately good reminder. Some expanded capacity had him feeling like he could do anything, but he remembered that deep, soul-cutting chill. Tim *had* come close to killing him.

However, the sun had just set, and he wanted to be in and out of the armory before it got too dark. "I'll be careful," he promised. "You should get into position."

"One last thing," Yung said. "Try this phone number."

Dane frowned, but switched to a different line from Lisa's call—currently muted as she searched the Marriott—and dialed.

Yung's phone rang.

"But—" Dane said.

"I was there too," Yung said. "I didn't get flung through time like you did—I must not have been close enough. The light hit you first, then Officer Sterling, then me. We know my past self is experiencing some of the same effects that she is, and I'm feeling some of the same physical augmentations that you are. So I thought perhaps this would work too." He answered the phone, walked a short distance on the rooftop, and spoke into it. "Can you hear me?"

"Barely," Dane said, having to concentrate to pick out the faint words over the line. "You sound distant."

"You too," Yung said. "Like the . . . connection isn't as strong. How *fascinating*. Well, at least this will let us communicate if we get separated. Good luck, Officer."

"Same. Though I'm muting you for now."

They parted, and Dane strapped his phone to his chest, then pulled out his side-arm. Three mags, all reloaded. Forty-five shots. Hopefully he wouldn't need any of them. Still, he would have killed for some proper gear—he didn't even have hearing protection. Though, considering how little his ears had been bothered by the previous indoor firefight . . . maybe he was tough enough to not need it anymore.

He gritted his teeth, crouched in place, and waited for the signal. A single gunshot. Followed by others. That would be Yung's group of four survivors firing on the front doors. This distraction had better work, because they were going to waste a lot of their ammo on it.

Blessedly, he soon heard the screams of revenants as they began to pour out of the building, realizing their trap had been sprung. More gunfire sounded, and then . . . what absolutely seemed like *return fire*. The revenants were armed.

Lovely.

At the count of a hundred, Dane took off running. He leaped, then hit the next rooftop at a dead run, not even needing to roll. The next leap took him soaring across the gap onto the rooftop of the police station, where he deliberately landed away from the sagging section. From there it would be a quick dash down several flights of—

The door to the stairwell slammed open. And there was a hulking figure with glowing eyes, wearing . . .

Damn. That was a guard uniform. Private security. Seeing him, Dane finally realized where he'd seen the *other* large revenant. Yung and Dane hadn't been the only people near that explosion—there had been six security guards. Three following through the cellar doors, three others inside the room behind the blast shield.

Seemed the epicenter had done something to him, Lisa, and Yung, while those just outside of it . . .

Revenants.

The creature leveled an assault rifle in Dane's direction. Making a snap decision, Dane chose to go the quick way. He leaped for the sagging portion of the roof as the bullets started flying. A second later, he crashed down through dust and chunks of corroded metal, landing on the fifth floor of the building.

The interior office space had few windows, and those had apparently been boarded up by the revenants. So Dane entered a strange realm of blackness and dust particles glowing from the light streaming through the open hole in the ceiling. Around him, eyes opened—haunting white eyes.

Each was, fortunately, a convenient target.

Dane started firing, gun flashing in the darkness as he moved out of the light, leaping over desks and through cubicle walls, both of which had begun to degrade from the ghost radiation. SWAT officers, in his experience, loved to leave things lying around, and so he knocked mags, knives, even bullets off breaking tables to scatter and clatter to the floor. He felt as if he were fighting in some child's diorama made from paper and glue—he could tear through walls at a whim. Furniture was just solid enough for him to kick into enemies, sending it splintering in the blackness.

For a second he was a tempest of gunfire, and he used the dying revenants—who glowed briefly as their life faded—to get his bearings. He'd repositioned by the time the large revenant with the assault rifle dropped through the ceiling. The former security guard scanned the room, and he was fully decked out: body armor across his broad chest, SWAT helmet on to protect his most vulnerable weakness. And . . . were those *grenades* on his bandolier? Where had he gotten those? They were *not* allowed, even for SWAT, though they were occasionally confiscated in drug busts.

Dane got off a shot on him, but the helmet deflected it—and then the beast began laying down fire, not worrying who he hit. Dane ducked under it, hiding in the remnants of a cubicle, but the revenants could feel his heat; the darkness wasn't as much of a cover as he'd hoped. Two normal-sized revenants prowled around behind him, and even the big one soon zeroed in on him, ignoring the gunfire from below and outside.

Damn. Dane grabbed one of the smaller revenants as it came for him, seizing the thing by its scraps of clothing and using it as a shield as he ran for a part of the room he'd spotted earlier, where chairs were pulled together as the floor bowed. Bullets grazed him—and the revenant in his hands scrambled and howled, clawing at Dane's head, causing his skin to go cold. Dane reached the sunken section and—throwing the revenant aside—leaped up and came down with both feet together, crashing through and landing hard in the break room on the fourth floor.

Above, revenants howled—and worse, on this floor, new pairs of eyes opened around him. How many of these things were *in* here? Swapping mags at speed, Dane shot two, then smashed through the wall into the hallway, trailing dust and smoke through increasingly darkened chambers. The only light came between boards on windows and filtered through the hole above.

A hole that was soon filled with revenants dropping down. But Dane . . . Dane felt something *pulsing* through him from the east. The Dead Zone, and its invigorating warmth, drove him to move by instincts he'd cultivated for years and rarely let loose. Gunfire was his battle cry and the glowing bodies of the dead his flashlight. He pushed down the hallway, trailing dust, his shots downing the demons that emerged.

He reached the conference room, where he knew from the schematics to expect a sagging floor. Instead he found a hole, the ground here already collapsed. He leapt for it as the wall ripped open to his right, the large revenant having taken a more direct route.

The beast lunged for Dane, dropping the assault rifle to hang on its straps. They collided, falling into the hole, and Dane scrambled with his free hand to push the monster off him.

As they hit the third floor below, Dane got a grip on something metal that he thought—in the flurry—might be part of the enemy gun. He grabbed it, but it pulled free. He managed to kick off the brute, rolling across the floor of the office building and coming up in a crouch—his handgun in his right hand, and what he'd grabbed in his left.

Grenade. No pin. Lever held down.

Hell.

He nearly tossed the thing, but in such cramped confines—locked mostly in shadows—he was likely to blow himself up. Instead, he spun with his handgun—holding tight to that grenade with his left hand—and started firing. Bullets glanced off the brute's helmet, and though one tore through his arm, he just smiled. White teeth and a triumphant expression behind the helmet and cracked eyepiece where the bulletproof plastic had done its job.

Dane tried some more shots anyway, but on the second the gun locked back: out of ammo. With a curse, he shoved shoulder-first through the nearest wall—semiautomatic fire chasing him. He ducked for cover behind a large filing cabinet that he hoped was more hardy than everything else, and in the darkness struggled to strip the empty mag and load a new one without letting go of that grenade. He considered scuttling it around the corner, but maybe . . .

Wait. Was that blood?

He rested the fingers of his right hand against his side, and they came back wet. He'd been hit, straight through the lower abdomen. He . . . he didn't even feel it. Hell. A part of him had realized he'd been too lucky to survive all those shots without one landing.

First aid gear will be in the basement, he thought, *inside the armory.* He stanched the wound as best he could with his hand; there wasn't time to apply a tourniquet, and that wasn't a place on his body where one would work anyway. The room he wanted in the basement had a steel roof. More secure in the real world, but here . . . without a concrete shell, he could hopefully bust through.

He wiped the blood on his jeans, chambered a round from his final mag, then fell still. The gunfire out front had trailed off; his people might be out of ammo. No other revenants had appeared on this level. Just dust, light held back by boards, and shadows.

"I feel your heat, Officer," a voice said from the darkness. "You blaze like a bonfire, hotter than any other meal. How did you hide from us for three days?"

The different floors were a jumble in his head, though he'd tried hard to memorize the layouts. Weak floor here would be . . . east corner? Or west corner?

"Are you the one who killed Adam?" the voice asked, and he saw a shadow moving through the darkness, eyes glowing. No figures trying to rip out of this man though. "He was a friend for a great long time. Reborn to be a king in this new world. You cut that short."

The ground creaked as the creature moved across it to Dane's right, passing slivers of light, as if daring Dane to take a shot.

"Come out," the creature said. "I'll give you one free shot. Try to take me down."

Instead, Dane ran. East corner. A muzzle flash lit up the room as Dane slid into a small office. Which had no sunken floor. *Damn.* He'd been sure. With a growl, he leaped up and slammed himself onto the floor.

Which, blessedly, broke. He hadn't been wrong; this one had merely been a little more sturdy. The ground splintered around him, sending him down in a shower of debris. Below, revenants howled, and dozens of eyes opened in the darkness. Without firing, Dane ran, bounding over—and through—desks as the large revenant crashed down behind him.

Dane reached the center of the chamber.

Slam.

Down to the first floor, on top of the basement room—and the floor here held his weight; the metal hadn't lost its structural integrity. Well, there was another way. He scrambled to the rear stairwell, reaching it after gunning down two revenants. There, he plunged into the darkness, bleeding, trailed by haunting scraping noises and terrible glowing eyes. As he reached the basement armory, he turned and fired—using the light of his muzzle flash to get a glimpse of the room's layout.

In those brief flashes, he caught sight of the armory door—ripped off its hinges. He backed into the room—firing twice more—and saw that the revenants had been working on the safes with tools. One was broken open; two still stood, the rusted outsides scarred and dented.

Those were just what he needed.

The large revenant roared as he came shoving after Dane. Repeated flashes lit the room as the beast fired quickly, which merely meant he ran out in seconds. You had to be careful about firing like that. Bullets never lasted as long as you wanted.

Plus, if your quarry was behind a giant steel safe, it wasn't terribly effective. A second later, Dane's thrown grenade shook the room, releasing a terrible burst of light and sound, spraying the place with debris.

Then silence and darkness. Pitch-black save for blinking, glowing eyes recovering from the daze of the explosion. The larger monster cursed, and Dane heard him reload with a few clicks. Spirits began to pull out of the beast as he did so, lighting the room. Showing him dominating the center of it, smaller revenants cowering behind. Maybe he'd been holding the spirits back until now.

The beast raised his assault rifle, but right before he chambered the first round, Dane came running—fists out. Hitting a man in the face when he was wearing eye gear wasn't the most pleasant experience, but Dane's knuckles withstood it. He punched again and again, causing the creature to lower the gun to its strap and reach for him.

Dane ducked backward. "You know," he said, "some on the force make fun of private security guards?"

The thing lunged for him. Too fast. Dane barely dodged.

"I don't," Dane said. "A lot of those guys are former military. Not smart to make fun of that type. But there *are* some who get into the business without any real experience."

The thing growled, backing Dane toward a corner, then lunged again. This time Dane wasn't fast enough. They locked into a grapple, Dane grunting as he focused mostly on breaking the hold. He strained, pushing against the grip with one arm, reaching with his left hand.

"You know how you tell the bad ones?" Dane asked with a hiss.

The beast tried to go for Dane's head, to lock him, and Dane twisted and pulled free.

"The bad ones wear grenades on their chests," he said, "like freaking hood ornaments." He tossed a pin at the fellow's face, then dove behind the safes again.

The blast that followed wasn't as shocking as the first. Dane let it blow over, then scrambled around, finding the beast with a hole in his chest, lying on the floor dazed—somehow still alive, a dozen souls trying to escape him. His glow lit the room like a fireplace.

Dane scooped something up, then approached the fallen creature. The beast met his eyes, then—with arms that didn't quite work right—reached for his gun, but that had been blown free in the explosion, as had the monster's helmet. The thing about grenades was, though, they didn't do that much damage to the non-squishy bits. A gun could survive some shrapnel.

"I'll take that free shot now," Dane said, chambering the first round into the assault rifle, and delivered a point-blank bullet to the eye.

Several minutes later, Dane stepped out of the front of the SWAT building, leaving dozens of dead revenants behind him. His crew peeked out from their cover, and he guessed—from their amazed expressions—how he must have looked: wound bandaged, clothing covered in dust, assault rifle at his shoulder.

Revenant bodies littered the ground in front of them, though it seemed most of the creatures had pulled back into the building to try to stop Dane. Even as the team stumbled out, one of the "dead" revenants suddenly leapt to its feet and attacked.

Dane shot it right before it got to Yung.

"Always double-check the ones you drop," Dane said, moving among them, kicking each one. "Half of you stay here on watch. The rest, head down below and start packing. I got the safes open. We need to loot this place, then get out of here."

Sixteen

60 Hours Before Moment Zero

Lisa reached the fourteenth floor of the hotel, still disturbed by that man who had definitely been able to see her. It should have been a relief, but instead it put her on edge—to the point where, when she located Yung's room, she didn't knock or burst in. She put her ear against the wood.

Voices on the other side. The door was too thick to tell what they were saying, but would Yung have company? He was paranoid—having destroyed his phone and gone to ground. Lisa made a quick decision, then hid around the corner down a side hallway, waiting. Her caution was rewarded a few minutes later as the door opened and the voices emerged.

". . . Don't have any idea where he went, boss," a masculine voice said. "We got the computer though, and a pile of notebooks. Everything that looked relevant."

Sweating, Lisa pressed herself against a door, hoping the contour of the doorway might shelter her. Three men crossed the hallway beyond, heading toward the elevator. In the distance, an ice machine buzzed loudly, but blessedly the men didn't look her direction.

"Yeah," one of the men said, on the phone. "Adam thought he spotted someone odd. Black woman, long hair. No idea who she could be, but he *swears* she could *see him.* Don't know how he could tell that . . ."

Two of the men wore security guard uniforms, while the one on the phone was in plain clothing. Maybe one of the scientists? One guard had his gun out, and was looking around suspiciously. The other carried a box of what she assumed were Yung's notes, with his laptop peeking out over the top.

Lisa leaned forward, itching to arrest them . . . but that would show her hand. That guard looked ready to shoot. If they had her same affliction, she could imagine they'd be on edge. Dangerous.

Don't rush into anything, her instincts said.

She could hear the one on the phone keep talking as they waited for the elevator. She inched forward, slipping her gun out and holding it at low ready, waiting by the corner.

"No idea how Yung evaded us," the scientist said. "Must not have been gone long. Yeah, Hamilton did a good job bugging the laptop; we'll bring the whole thing to you. You were right to be worried about Yung. He's involved somehow in why everyone ignores us. Perhaps he created his own teleportation device. Maybe that would explain all of this."

The elevator dinged, and Lisa peeked around the corner. The man from the lobby, gun out, was waiting there. Adam, they'd called him, a brute of a man with beady eyes and an angry attitude. If she popped around the corner now, there would absolutely be a shootout. And if she'd gone for the arrest earlier, this guy would have surprised her.

Maybe she was too timid these days, as Dane claimed, but she couldn't afford to get shot. Three against one, even if she had the upper hand, would risk her death—and if that happened, nobody would remain to stop the end of the world. Better to be careful, especially since she knew where those notes were going: straight to the facility. If she could manipulate the other officers into helping her, like she'd done with Rowna earlier, a raid on the place was her best bet. A way to get the notes *and* access to Nazeem's scientists.

But where was Yung?

That question helped her make the final decision not to intervene as the three joined Adam in the elevator, which then closed and carried them away. Praying that she hadn't doomed the city, she hurried back to Yung's room and let herself in.

They'd ransacked the small chamber, which would make it hard to find clues. If he'd left his things, he had to be nearby, but the bed had been sliced open, the suitcase ripped apart and clothing scattered. The carpet was even cut in places to make sure nothing had somehow been hidden beneath it.

She idly played with her bracelet, thinking about a time she and Dane had investigated a similar apartment. Maybe trying to determine anything from this was backward. The security guards hadn't found Yung, so searching in here might not be relevant anyway. What had tipped him off, letting him know to escape? She checked the window to see if she could spot any conspicuous car wrecks. If Nazeem's people had been hit on the street, maybe that had spooked Yung. She saw nothing, and . . .

No, that wouldn't explain it. He left his laptop.

He wouldn't have done that unless . . . unless he was just stepping out. She glanced toward the room's small fridge. On top of it were some cups, ignored by the thugs, as what was there to see from a collection of clean cups?

Only the obvious clue: the large spot in the middle where an ice bucket had once been. Yung hadn't gone running. It was pure happenstance he'd been out when Nazeem's people arrived. Lisa checked her theory by leaving the room and hunting out the ice machine. There she found the smoking gun . . . in the form of a spilled bucket of ice, likely dropped as Yung spotted the thugs approaching. She knelt, noting that the ice was largely unmelted. This *had* been recent. She turned, and saw the emergency stairwell just across the hall.

Lisa slipped down multiple flights, around and around in an unornamented concrete stairwell, until she heard sniffling. She paused, then rounded the last flight to find a door with the words EMERGENCY EXIT: ALARM WILL SOUND emblazoned on it. Yung sat on the ground here, his back against the wall. Eyes closed, tears leaking down his cheeks.

"I didn't know which was more likely—" he whispered, "that you'd chase me down the stairwell, or that I'd alert you by sounding the alarm. I chose poorly, I suppose."

"Depends," Lisa said, "on who you think I am."

Yung opened his eyes, blinking. He studied her, then shook his head. "Are you from one of the other two facilities?"

"No," she said, offering a hand. "I'm Detective Lisa Sterling. In about two days' time, I'll save you from being tied up in a cellar—and together we'll fail to stop Nazeem from blowing up the city. I'm hoping to change that second part."

His eyes went wide. "Two days' time . . ."

"You don't remember?"

He frowned. "Why would I?"

"I thought you might since *I* remember it, and so does your future self. But I suppose he would, wouldn't he?"

"My future self . . ." Past Yung seized her hand and let her pull him to his feet. "Nazeem activated the device? It warped reality. That's why no one seems to be able to see me! It's not because of something that has happened, but because of something that *will* happen!"

"*Might* happen," she corrected. "My partner and I are doing everything we can to stop it." She pushed open the door with the alarm sign on it—and no sound went off. At Yung's confusion, she shrugged. "These things never actually have an alarm on them, at least not in the city. It's too easy for people to cause a general panic at the noise, thinking there's a fire. Code forbids it. Come on. There's a lot I need to fill you in on."

Seventeen

Dane winced as he poured antiseptic on his wound (low on the torso, right side, above the hip, didn't hit the bone). It had started hurting something awful, but strangely didn't slow him down. He'd thought that a bullet wound would lay him flat, but he felt he could keep going without much trouble.

Yung handed him a roll of gauze as he walked past. The two of them were back in the smoking room at the country club. A variety of guns lay on the nearby counter; both seemed to find it comforting to have them nearby.

"I believe I warned you," Yung said as Dane rewrapped the wound, "that we weren't immortal."

"I'm doing well, all things considered," Dane said, though he failed to cover a wince. "It's barely even bleeding. Odd, for a shot that went straight through me."

"You need to be careful," Yung said. "It's possible that our enhanced sense of strength is merely that—a *sense*. The damage to your body is extensive. You might be able to ignore it better, but it could very well still be killing you just as an ordinary wound might."

"I feel like I'm healing faster."

"We don't know that for sure. Please be careful."

"It's the apocalypse, Doc. There isn't time for careful." He checked his phone after that, thinking of Lisa. And then the bracelet—the one from Nova—shook a little on its own, then rotated on his wrist.

Huh. That was odd. It stopped a second later. Lisa had given that to him. It had half a flat metal heart on it, the type that was normally prefabricated—but it looked like Nova had made this one herself and snipped it in half. One half on each bracelet.

Yung stepped up to the map on the wall. "You're still sure you want to try this tonight? In the dark?"

"I did fine in the SWAT HQ in the dark."

Yung glanced at the bandage. "Fine, eh?"

"If you're right," Dane said, "and this wound is worse than I'm pretending, then we're in trouble. There are no hospitals, and we have barely any medicine. So we need to try to reach the teleporter while I'm feeling up to it." He pulled on a shirt.

"A fair enough point, but I'm not going to risk any of my people on a trip through three Dead Zones. I'll go with you. No one else."

"Fine," Dane said. "But in that case, you have to stop complaining about me taking risks."

Yung smiled. "Feels good, doesn't it?"

"Being shot?"

"Making a difference. Meaning something."

Dane crossed to the table, where he began picking through equipment, including a ballistic vest with MOLLE straps for his magazines. He glanced over his shoulder at the professor, then nodded. "It does." An overqualified scientist relegated to teaching introductory physics classes at a small-time college, and an expert marksman who spent his days at a desk job.

Neither had been something the world needed. Until suddenly it did.

Dane's phone buzzed.

I have Past Yung, Lisa wrote. *Nazeem has his notes. I'm working on a plan to get them back.*

He forwarded the text to Future Yung, then flipped off the mute. "Nice work."

"Eh," she said. "I let Nazeem's people slip away from me. You'd probably have gone after them, shooting."

"Depends on if you were there to talk sense into me or not. Raid on the SWAT headquarters went well, but they *were* waiting for us, as I worried."

"That's troubling," Lisa said.

He had his theories on what was up with that, but he didn't want to voice them yet. Yung walked over, eyeing Dane's torso—although the bandage was hidden—and cocking an eyebrow. Dane shook his head. No, he wasn't going to tell her. Lisa had enough to worry about already.

"Yung, meet yourself," Lisa said over the line.

"Hello, Albert," Dane's version said.

"Hello . . . Albert," the same voice said from Lisa's end. "I must admit, I find most of Detective Sterling's story to be . . . outlandish."

"You know it's true anyway, don't you?" Dane's Yung said. "It's the only explanation."

"Yes," Lisa's Yung said. "'Outlandish' is apparently not a synonym for 'impossible.'"

"We need to wait for me to put a squad together," Lisa said, "and raid Nazeem's main facility. Then we'll have the notes."

"Not sure if we can afford to wait that long," Dane said.

"Why?"

"Call it my gut," Dane said softly. "But more than that, the revenants were waiting for us. They knew what we were doing, and they must know we're trying to prevent Lightbreak. I suspect if we wait for you to put together a raid, in my timeline this building will be flooded with enemies. We can't give them time to plan or respond."

"But we don't have the notes."

"We have two Yungs though," Dane said. "Maybe that will be enough?"

"I . . ." Lisa's Yung said. "I spent all day reviewing my notes before they were taken, looking for an explanation of what happened to me. Now that I know the details of what went wrong . . . that you were sent through time, not through space . . ."

"Too much power," Dane's Yung said. "Nazeem drew way too much power. I'm convinced the overage is what caused problems in my timeline."

"Yes . . ." Lisa's Yung continued. "The calculations are fresh in my memory. With an hour or two, perhaps I can reconstruct the relevant parts, find a way to activate the device without causing a similar disaster. It would be far better if we had the notes, obviously, but if that's not possible . . . I can remember enough, I think."

"Better than I can, certainly," Dane's Yung said, with a grunt. "It's been a long three days for me."

"Yes," Lisa's Yung said. "But um . . . I realize I'm not up to speed on all this. I just . . . There's a question."

"What?" Dane asked.

"Does anyone have a theory," her Yung asked, "on why one of you went forward in time and the other backward?"

"I don't think that's what happened," Dane's Yung said. "Officer Sterling might have forgotten to mention that there's a dead version of her in this timeline. So . . ."

"So you both got sent both directions?" Lisa's Yung asked.

"Except not," Dane said, frowning. "Because you found her corpse at the site—it hadn't traveled in time."

"You were closest to the wormhole though, right?" Lisa's Yung said. "That's likely the explanation. You got completely sucked through. Officer Sterling, standing close to you, ended up in the past—but with memories of the future. Myself, Nazeem, the guards hunting me, we are aware something is wrong, but don't have the actual memories. Proximity to the wormhole, I think. I need time to work with the numbers . . ."

"Unfortunately," Dane said, strapping on the body armor, "I can't give you that time, Doc. My Yung and I are leaving for one of the facilities now—it will likely take us an hour or so, considering we have to get through several Dead Zones. When we get there, we're going to need calculations. Can you do it?"

"One hour?" Lisa's Yung said. "I'll spend most of that writing out what I remember from my notes. But . . . um . . . maybe? If all we're doing is changing the device settings to not draw so much power . . . Maybe?"

Dane looked to his Yung, who nodded. They couldn't wait, not with Dane wounded. Today, "maybe" would have to be enough.

Eighteen

59 Hours Before Moment Zero

Lisa led Past Yung into the subway. He'd apparently walked to the hotel.

"I like walking," he explained as they used her subway card to pass the turnstile. "It gives me time to think."

He'd calmed down in the short while they'd been together. It seemed that having answers helped his anxiety—and she could relate. Knowing that she wasn't crazy, that someone else had been through what she had, meant a great deal.

"Well, whatever you do," she said as they walked down the steps, "don't drive until this is all done. In fact, in the subway, watch out for people trying to sit on you."

He nodded, joining her as they entered a subway car. It wasn't terribly crowded though, so he did sit—where he began typing on his phone, trying to remember and recalculate the relevant parts of his notes. She left him to it, stepping to the side, and flipped her phone off speaker before raising it to her head.

"Dane, you there?" she said.

"Yeah," he replied, and she was surprised by how muffled the motorcycle sounded.

"You driving? I can barely hear anything."

"They found me a helmet with Bluetooth."

"Well," she said, "Past Yung and I are on the way to the same facility that you are. He thinks maybe we should sneak into this one, with lesser security, and find the numbers they've inputted in their controls. That will help with his calculations."

"How dangerous will it be?"

"Shouldn't be too bad," she said. "None of the guards or scientists at this smaller facility would have been at the explosion—so they shouldn't be able to notice us."

"Sounds good."

Lisa hesitated for a moment, but decided to push forward. "Now that the Yungs aren't listening, Dane, what happened? There's something you aren't telling me. I can hear it in your voice."

"I got hit," he admitted. "Bullet wound. Not debilitating, but not pretty either."

"Aren't you a superhero or something in that timeline?"

"That's the strange part. I feel like I can shrug it off, but Yung worries the wound is worse than I'm acting. That it will catch up to me. I don't know. But Li . . . I do feel an urgency. I'd *much* rather have this wound cared for in a timeline with real hospitals."

"You . . . going to be able to do the mission?"

"Should be."

She paced back and forth in the subway car. This line was a straight shot to their goal. No transfers. "You're worrying me, Dane."

"Trying not to. I just have to keep moving. Like I said, I feel urgent—and not only because of the wound. I don't like the enemy having too much time to plan."

"Yes, but you always feel urgent," she said, pacing back the other way. "You always have to solve problems *right now*."

"Not always. I waited on us. Maybe too long."

She bit her lip. "That . . . wasn't just you, Dane. I kept telling myself I'd fix it. Eventually. Kept believing that it was possible. Still . . . still believe it, if I'm being honest."

He laughed. "If we both want to fix it, why can't we?"

"I worry we have different definitions of what a fix involves."

"Yeah." He fell silent. "Do you think . . . the real problem with us was what happened? Four years ago? With me, during that emergency call?"

She . . . didn't know. That had been right when she'd decided to actively pursue a political career. Chief had told her he might retire soon, and the deputy chief had decided not to follow him into the position. Lisa's record was stellar. She'd met the mayor, and . . .

And then the emergency call had come in—a woman, frantic, saying that her boyfriend was involved in a drug deal gone wrong. That men were pulling guns, and she was afraid for her life. Technically, all officers in the region—detective or beat cop—were to respond to emergencies of this level. Dane had been closest, so respond he had.

When he'd arrived, he'd gone in without waiting for backup or confirmation from other officers. The situation had escalated as he'd breached, and Dane had been forced to take cover. He'd tried to bring the main shooter down, but hadn't been able to get him before the dealer had shot three other people. Including the woman who had made the call.

That left the question. Should he have tried to de-escalate? And if afterward he *had* decided to go in, bringing down the shooter would have been the best result. Dane hadn't done anything wrong, specifically. He'd used his judgment, tried to help, and hadn't shot first. The department had backed him up, but it had taken work to make certain he hadn't become a sacrifice in the heated political climate. Plus . . . Lisa couldn't say, 100 percent, that she ever wanted Dane in another situation like that again. When hostages were involved, and innocents might be in the crossfire.

On the line, Dane's motor cut out.

"Dane?" she asked.

"We've crossed out of a Dead Zone," he said, then she heard what she thought was him taking a drink from a water bottle. "Two more to cross. We're waiting while Yung scouts the next street with his binoculars."

We need to talk about it, don't we? Lisa thought. *I have to push. I can't keep putting this off.*

Perhaps this wasn't the time to distract him, but . . . the way things were going . . . there might not *be* another chance.

"Dane," she said, "what happened four years ago isn't relevant. I trust you. I always have."

"You insisted I spend more time at the desk," he said, then took another drink. "And . . . I agreed. I was shaken."

"You did great work in white collar."

"Miserable work."

"For your own good. Do you know what it took to keep you out of the news? It happened *right* after that exposé on our failures to de-escalate."

"And did you do that for my good or for yours, Li?"

"For yours, obviously."

"I . . . Li, I don't believe you. I want to, but deep down I don't. That's the problem, isn't it?"

"One of them," she said, still pacing, walking by Past Yung, who continued typing away on his phone. The car shook as it took a curve at speed. "Dane . . . I trust you to do what you see is right."

"But you don't trust my judgment," he said. "You know I'll do what I see as right, but you don't trust that I *can* see what is right. At least not by the department's definitions."

She winced, hating that he said it. Or rather, hating what saying that might do to him.

"Yeah," he said, surprising her. "Okay. I can accept that feeling from you. I'm not sure I trust my judgment all the time either. That day four years ago . . . I could have waited for backup. I *should* have waited. I ran in without a plan, and threw away my training. When they started firing, I wasn't in a position to know where everyone was, and worst of all I didn't have the skill to bring down the guy that needed to be taken out. It . . . Li, it was my fault twice over those people died. I didn't pull the trigger, but my judgment got them killed."

Hell. He'd never admitted that before.

"The shooter had his gun out," she said, "and was threatening everyone. You said he'd put a shot in the floor."

"He did," Dane said. "In the moment, it really felt like if I didn't get in there, they'd be dead. But we can't know, Lisa, and the honest truth is that I didn't consider if I should wait. I just went straight in. I should have at least wondered, asked where other officers were. Assessed whether a negotiator should have approached first, instead of me."

That . . . that was all she had *ever* wanted him to admit.

"And . . ." Lisa took a deep breath. "Dane, I have to be honest. I . . . probably did bury you in paperwork because I was worried about my career. I honestly didn't think of it that way, but looking back . . . well, it's a mess. But . . . what you accuse me of . . . *was* there. It was, and it is."

Oddly, he chuckled. And the bracelet on her wrist moved of its own accord, as if he were fingering it in his timeline. Were they paired like the phone signal?

"Is that you?" she said. "With the bracelet?"

"Yeah. You feel it with yours?"

"I do."

"A sign the universe thinks we belong together?"

"At least one little girl does, Dane."

"And the adult one I'm talking to?"

"She doesn't know." Lisa paced back the other way.

"Same here. You know why I rushed in? I've thought about it, now and then. It's the same reason I stayed in white collar, when I should have put in for a transfer."

"Why?"

"I was always just looking for a chance," he said, "to show you what I could do. Maybe because, like an idiot, I wanted to be right. Maybe . . ."

". . . maybe you wanted me to be proud of you."

"You said something like that to me once," he told her, his voice wistful over the line. "Right before we became partners. Before . . . any of this. Said you'd read my record and were impressed. Guess I wanted to hear it again, now that you knew me." He sighed. "Sorry. Shouldn't put that on you. Makes it sound like you did something wrong."

"Maybe I did."

"Maybe we both did."

"Probably we both did."

"Li ... you ever considered that we want to fix our relationship because that's what we do? Never admit defeat? Keep working on a problem until it cracks?"

She breathed out, and ... and ...

And he was right. Because the moment he said it, she understood why she held on. Not because she wanted to be with him, but because letting go felt like failure. "Oh. Oh *hell*, Dane."

"Strong words from you," he said with a chuckle. "Li, I wanted you to respect me ... but that's different from wanting you to love me. And the more I think about it, the more I worry I conflated the two, thinking that wanting one meant I also wanted the other. Now, looking at it all, I ... I think I want to let go. It's not bad to acknowledge that we were never *actually* good together, is it? As partners, yes. But us? In a relationship?"

"It was terrible!" she said, strangely excited. "We spent most of the time pushing each other's buttons!"

"It was *awful*," he said with a laugh. "Remember the last Christmas, with your parents?"

"Please don't remind me." She paused. "Nova sees you like a father figure."

"I can be that as your partner and friend."

"Hell yes you can," she said. "You'll stay in the city, then? Transfer to SWAT, with my recommendation?"

"You trust me in situations like that?"

"Dane," she said—meaning it, feeling it—"I trust you with the fate of the world. Yes, I trust you. Doesn't mean we have to be together though. It ... it really doesn't, does it?"

"Nope. Takes the end of the world for us to admit these things?" He laughed. "We're *both* stubborn as boulders, aren't we?"

"Neither of us are the type, as you said, to admit defeat."

"Not a defeat, then," he said. "The relationship was a total success—it taught us both what we're *not* looking for."

She found herself grinning. On the line, his motorcycle revved up again, the sounds muffled by his helmet. In the following quiet as he drove, she felt ... a catharsis. A long-standing flaw, like mold in the walls of a building, had been uncovered and the work begun to right it.

"Feels good to finally have that out," Dane said. "And if it matters, Li, I still care. About my friend, who will be the best damn police chief the city has ever had."

She smiled. "Well, I'm glad if I had to be caught in the end of the world, it was with the best partner in the world, Dane. I'm relieved that I went in to find you, before the explosion. Even with everything that has happened."

"Went in?"

"At the house, with Nazeem," she said, glancing at the readout that listed the next stop. "You made me decide either to go with you, or leave and let you do your walk-around alone. I decided to leave . . . but if I'd kept going, instead of turning back . . . who knows what would have happened. Would I even remember the explosion? Would we be entwined? Would we have a chance to stop this?"

"Huh," he said. "I didn't realize you'd turned to walk away. Guess I was being extra stubborn. Very unlike me."

Her train pulled into the proper stop, and she nodded to Past Yung, who quickly stood up.

"We're near the second facility," she said over the line. "You?"

"Half hour out, maybe? It's eerie. We're in the second Dead Zone, but haven't seen a single revenant."

"I'll try to sneak into the place," she said. "Yung says it's an old trailer park, where they found a wormhole. They bought one of the double-wides and turned it into a lab. I'll scout the premises so you'll know what you're going into. I'll grab the data Past Yung wants, then wait on you to get in. Theoretically, all you'll need to do is type in what Yung tells you, then activate the device."

"Affirmative," he said. "Don't get shot, Li. It's legitimately awful."

"I'll do my best. In turn, please don't get eaten. That would be *super* awkward to explain to the rest of the department at your posthumous medal ceremony."

"Here lies Dane," he said. "May he give those zombies indigestion. Amen." He revved his engine. "You should hang on the line; I'll merge your call with my Yung's so you can both listen. I'm going to explain the plan to him, and I might be jumping in a little too quickly on this one as usual . . ."

Nineteen

72 Hours After Moment Zero

In conclusion," Dane said as they rode through the second Dead Zone, headlights illuminating the way, "you and I both go in guns blazing, fast and hard, and count on superior firepower and speed to tear through their ranks and get to the teleporter."

"Straight in from the east," Yung said over Dane's in-helmet earpiece. "Bold. Maybe insane."

"That's your plan?" Lisa said. "Like, seriously, Dane? You told me to stay on the line to hear it, and it equates to, 'We shoot everything. The end.'"

"Well, I mean," he said, "I doubt we can shoot *everything* . . ."

She sighed over the line. "I guess I did specifically say that in this situation, subtlety goes out the window. Plus, I don't know if you're equipped for anything else. So, guns blazing it is. At least you'll have me on this side, scouting sans zombies."

"Probably the best we can manage," Dane's Yung agreed. "Unsubtle though it is. How confident is my counterpart in his ability to get us the right calculations?"

"Moderately?" Lisa said, sounding uncertain. "He's confident we won't blow up the city again, and he thinks he knows how to pinpoint a specific time to send Dane—though I have no idea why. You didn't even know time travel was possible."

"We knew *something* odd was happening," Dane's Yung said. "And the numbers kept being off. Sometimes all it takes is the disclosure of what one is doing wrong. Occasionally we'd send an object through, and nothing would happen. We were baffled. Where did the energy go? Why didn't it change? Now I can see; through some process, we were sending it back in time."

"You didn't notice objects teleporting into the past?" Dane said.

"Ah, but where did you wake, Dane?" his Yung asked.

"In my bedroom."

"As did Detective Sterling. When you were sent back, you appeared not where you left *from*, but where you were during that timeline. The universe was trying not to disrupt the flow. Inanimate objects, as we attempted to send . . . well, they couldn't say anything, or change the timeline. So they appeared overlapping—taking the place of—their past self, and the timelines didn't diverge. Except there was the one time when we sent a chronometer, and the readings were odd."

"Indicative of time travel," Lisa said.

"Yes. That is now clear; when we picked up the chronometer to send it, it already had a reading on it. We assumed that was some kind of mistake—but actually it had been counting since it had arrived days before, and then the timelines had aligned and snapped back together, leaving it with its reading."

"Well," Lisa said, "my timeline's Yung says he doesn't remember all the proper variables."

"I can re-create most of my work," her Yung said, jumping onto the line, "but I will need to grab some data from one of the machines at the facility to get the last part. We have to make sure not to send Officer Dane into the *future* again. At least we have the frame of reference of Moment Zero. That should be the most relevant piece for him—midnight Thursday morning. We can use that as a baseline for our target."

"Just make sure I arrive *before* that explosion," Dane said. "Doesn't do us a lot of good if I show up right as everything is going to hell."

"Right, right," that Yung said, then evidently handed the phone back to Lisa.

She added, "So long as we are absolutely certain not to keep splitting the timeline. Not sure if I'll know how to deal with two Danes, if the other one ever shows up. Four would be *completely* unbearable."

Dane grinned, though his Yung took the comment seriously.

"My pen proves that the timelines are trying to reconcile," he said. "I even . . . now have glimmers of a memory of meeting you, Officer Sterling, before you and Officer Dane rescued me. Emerging in my mind, as the timelines try to reconnect. If we're careful about energy expenditure, I think instead of splitting and fragmenting our futures, we can pull them together in one."

"Your best guess will have to do," Dane said. "We'll hit the enemy hard, straight from the east. It's a direct line from here to there."

They muted the line—as Lisa was scouting the location, and didn't want a sudden voice over her phone drawing attention. Dane and his Yung rode a little farther, out of the second Dead Zone and across the narrower strip of unaffected city. As they entered the third and final Dead Zone—the trailer park with the lab was just on the other side, to the west—Dane waved to his Yung, then took off down a side street.

Yung, after a moment of confusion, followed. He gestured for an explanation, pointing at his helmet—which was connected to his own phone. Dane shook his head, then continued leading them in an arc so they could come in from the north, in direct violation of the plan he'd explained earlier. Soon he spotted a big open park, where he was confident he'd be able to see a revenant coming if it tried to sneak up on them. There, near the rusted remnants of a jungle gym, he brought them to a halt.

"What is going on?" Yung asked, pulling off his helmet. "Why aren't we making straight for the facility?"

"We're going to walk the rest of the way," Dane said, swinging from the motorcycle, turning it off, and sending them into gloom as his headlight was extinguished. "We'll come in from the north—there's a sewer line under the road here. I was down there for a case a few years back. I should be able to slip into it through a manhole, approach underground, then come up right next to the trailer park."

"What happened to going in with guns blazing, quickly and powerfully?"

"That's what I wanted the enemy to hear," Dane said, setting his helmet on the motorcycle. "They've tapped our phone line somehow."

"What?" Yung said, visible by the dim light still on the horizon. He grabbed his assault rifle, scanning the area. "How can you know that?"

"I . . . don't, not completely," Dane said, pulling his backpack from the motorcycle's storage box. He slung it on, though he had extra magazines strapped to his vest, and an AR-15 along with his normal sidearm. He carried some flares and flash-bangs, carefully zipped in a cargo pocket. Last was a SWAT helmet, matching his body armor.

"Explain, if you would, Officer," Yung said.

"They set up that ambush on the street."

"Which could have been a coincidence."

"There was a revenant waiting for me on the rooftop of the Eighteenth. There's no way you position your biggest, most dangerous enemy all the way up there unless you *know* someone is going to try to sneak in that direction. And the roof was the first thing Lisa mentioned to me over the line."

Yung nodded slowly.

"I worried," Dane said, affixing a flashlight to the front of his AR, "about there being a mole among your organization. Only that wouldn't have worked."

"Yes," Yung agreed. "How would they have gotten the information to the enemy fast enough for them to set up that ambush? Unless we assume they have access to our phones . . ."

"Your phone can call mine, just like mine and Lisa's can connect. Well, Nazeem and a bunch of her cronies were there, close by during that blast."

"You . . . might be right."

"There's an easy way to test," Dane said. "If they've got their forces sitting at the trailer park, pointed east, waiting for us to arrive . . . well, we'll know they were listening in." He slung on his rifle. "Either way, we can hope they won't expect a quiet assault underground, from the north."

"Fair enough," Yung said. They turned to watch the last of the twilight fade, giving Lisa a little more time to get into position. "Dane . . . tell me honestly. Are you . . . going to miss this?"

"Miss the *apocalypse*?"

"No, not that, obviously. But . . . this sense of doing something, of being relevant."

Dane glanced to the side, but didn't speak.

"I spent my life dreaming of making great discoveries," Yung whispered, "only to end up teaching bored freshmen about waveforms. Suddenly, these last few days, I'm a *leader*. I'm the one who *knows*, and people *listen*. I've built something. It took terrible circumstances, and I would not wish these deaths to have happened. Yet a part of me . . . will miss this."

"You'll still be important on the other side, Doc," Dane said. "You'll be the one who discovered *time travel*. And you'll be a hero for saving the world."

In the fading light, Yung nodded, seeming reassured. He looked ashamed to have even said anything—and perhaps someone else would have condemned him for it. What kind of monster would be sad about trying to stop the end of the world? Yet Dane had to admit he felt it too, that same faint melancholy. The world finally needed him; here he was the man with the skill to survive and protect people. And all that training following a job he'd botched . . . years on the range, trying to be certain that if he ever got into a firefight again, he'd at *least* have the skill to put his bullets where he wanted them . . .

Here, it was that training, and not the hours spent behind a desk, that finally meant something. If he returned to the other timeline . . . even if he moved to SWAT, he'd never again be needed so desperately as he was here. Despite what he'd said to Yung, he wasn't certain anyone in the main timeline would celebrate them—or even know what they'd done. He waited, and felt his bracelet tremble as Lisa played with hers, maybe while thinking about him.

The thing was, he realized as he thought it over, he *hadn't* done all his training for the sake of recognition. He really hadn't. Not even from Lisa—despite what he'd assumed. He wanted her respect as a partner, but he didn't need her to think of him as a hero. He didn't need that from anyone. He decided he was fine if nobody knew what he'd done. That wasn't why he'd prepared.

It was so that this time, he'd be able to do things right.

Dane wrote a few things on a pad of paper he'd taken from the country club, and as the time to move arrived, he double-checked the straps on his extra magazines, then turned to Yung. "Do you think you could talk me through working the machinery of the teleporter?"

"Why?"

"There's a building at Seventeenth and Arbor that should give you a good view of my approach," Dane said. "The old fire station, which will have roof access along the east wall. I've been up there. Sure would make me feel easier if someone were spotting for me."

Yung considered. "The device is quite delicate, but we will likely need to change only two of the inputs. You'll have to log in to the device's controls, but I was the one who supervised the building of this equipment before I left. I installed backdoors for myself. So . . . yes, I can talk you through it. Assuming you don't care if they overhear."

"By then they'll know what's up, so I don't mind. I don't want us both in there possibly being caught or killed; one of us should remain outside and offer fire support. If I go down, you'll need to make your way to the third facility and see if you can send yourself back instead. Understood?"

Yung nodded.

"Great. If we need to communicate, let's do it via text—and use these signals." He handed Yung a paper he'd written some code words on. "Let's get moving."

"Very well," Yung said. "I do have to say . . . I find this plan a *great deal* more encouraging."

"I'm not always an idiot," Dane said, leading the way to a manhole. "Once in a while, a good idea falls on me. Or in this case, I fall into it." He nodded to Yung, then kicked the rusted manhole cover so it shattered, the pieces dropping into the darkness. He shined his light down, checked the distance, then leaped in.

Once down, he moved with efficient speed, rifle up and flashlight pointed forward. He had to hope the enemy had enough control over the local revenants to have pulled any out of places like the sewers to set up for the attack, because he did *not* fancy the idea of needing to fire his weapon down here, which would obviously alert the enemy to his approach.

But he had also promised Lisa—at least implicitly—that he'd try to do better than going head-on into problems without support. In this case, he hoped to surprise even her.

Twenty

58 Hours Before Moment Zero

Lisa shook her head as she approached the facility. It was the most Dane thing in the entire world to apologize for going into a situation guns blazing, then in the very next conversation explain his plan for going into another situation guns blazing.

At the same time, he was the one living in the apocalypse, not her. If she had learned one thing about leadership in her years being groomed to lead the department, it was to not second-guess the officers on the ground. She could offer advice and suggestions, but at the end of the day, the people actually involved in a situation were going to have the best read on what to do. Assuming they were trained properly.

He'd just better not get shot. Well, again.

"So," she said as she walked up, Past Yung at her side, "a trailer park?"

"We couldn't choose the locations," he reminded her, "but this was actually a good place for a facility. These are often poorly regulated, without landlords who ask too many questions. They probably figured we were setting up another meth lab. I only visited a few times, mostly when I brought in the equipment meant to expand and feed power into the wormhole. I spent most of my time at the first facility."

Lisa snapped a few photos of the entrance and sent them to Dane. The place was poorly regulated indeed—the gate was wide open, and there didn't seem to be an attendant. Acting casual, she walked in, though the place appeared largely unoccupied. Many homes looked to be sitting empty, which wasn't uncommon in the city. It had negative growth these days—though you'd never know it on the freeway at rush hour. Apparently, you could get an abandoned mobile home for free, if you were willing to pay the lease on the land it sat on. A lot of mobile home parks were essentially ghost towns.

Thinking that made her shiver and check the sun. Afternoon here—and later during Dane's timeline. He'd be arriving in the dark. She kept moving, and was surprised by a sound behind her.

"Yung?" she said, glancing back at him. "You should wait out front, just in case."

"I don't like the idea of being alone again," he said, huddling up next to her. "I . . . It was . . . not a fun morning, Detective. What if you vanish, or forget me?"

"We both know it doesn't work that way."

"We both know," he replied, "that we don't completely understand the rules. Regardless, what if you need help? Um, backup? I know I'm not much, but . . ." He shrugged.

Bringing a civilian into a potentially dangerous situation? Broke all kinds of rules, but—as she'd indicated earlier—the prime rule was to trust the officer in the situation. And with the fate of the city, maybe more, at stake . . .

"Stay close," she whispered. "If anyone seems to notice us, don't look at them. We can't say for certain nobody at this second facility was at the first one the night of the blast, and I think making eye contact with that guard was what got me into trouble."

"Right. You don't . . . have an extra gun, do you?"

"No, but we shouldn't need to use force."

"Right, right," he said, glancing about. "No zombies in our timeline. We think."

She led the way, counting off rows to the proper location. She took photos at each intersection and sent them to Dane. She'd seen her share of trailer parks during her beat days, and some didn't deserve their reputation. In many, you'd find trees, playgrounds, rows of buildings that—while small—were homey and well maintained.

This wasn't one of those. Barely any yard per home, more weeds than grass, no trees. Like a parking lot where you stuck your unwanted, and left them.

It wasn't difficult to pick out the facility: a double-wide with two men sitting out front. They didn't wear uniforms, and were sipping drinks in their lawn chairs, but were obviously security. The trim haircuts alone were a giveaway, and polos? In a trailer park?

Lisa idled on one corner, pretending to play with her phone as she covertly took some photos. She had Yung remain behind as she walked past. She felt dangerously exposed, but these weren't any of the guards she'd seen at the hotel—and they knew only six had been involved in the blast. These men were highly unlikely to have been among the remaining three.

She did a test anyway, calling and waving at a random stranger as if she knew them. The sharp outcry should have drawn the guards' attention, but neither paused in their conversation. Either they weren't very good at their jobs, or she was invisible to them. Good enough. She circled back, collected Yung, and then—with a deep breath—led him right past the guards to the mobile home. Yung inputted the code on the door, and they slipped through while the two guards—sitting not five feet away—were still discussing last night's game.

They'd gutted the entire double-wide, creating a large open space—with a few structural pillars through the middle—for all kinds of mechanical equipment. The back right corner held a plexiglass blast shield, like a clear box, and inside was a pinprick of blackness.

The wormhole.

A half dozen scientists worked in here on computer gear, though three were gathered around one specific computer, chatting. Lisa and Yung had entered a little alcove in the center of one wall, where they crouched down to move through the room while she took some photos and texted them to Dane.

"... Don't like these readings," one of the scientists was saying. "We haven't initiated the test, yet the readings have already gone haywire."

"We haven't, but we *will*," a voice said from the computer. On a video call, it seemed.

"That's Nazeem's voice," Yung whispered to Lisa.

"Yes," the scientist near Lisa said, "which is what gives me concern. If what we *will* do is showing up in our measurements of the anomaly ..."

"... Then it means we're on the right track," Nazeem said. "The readings are proof that we'll be successful. Your concerns are completely unfounded."

"I still think we should ask Yung," a man at the computer said. "What you're planning, Nazeem ... The *moment* you begin feeding power into the wormhole, I feel like it's going to destabilize. Yung would know how to stop that." The two scientists with him nodded.

"Do *not* bring Yung into this," Nazeem's voice said. "We proceed as planned. Hell, you'll all probably forget me as soon as I get off the line."

The three scientists regarded one another, while three others continued their work nearby, hunkered down—as if pointedly ignoring the conversation. Or maybe forced to do so by temporal inertia.

Lisa nodded to Yung, and they crept forward. He needed access to one of those computers—and she found herself glad he'd asked to come. Her earlier plan, of stealing one of the computers and hiking out with it, seemed far less efficient than plopping him down in a seat here to gather the information he needed. Though admittedly, doing so while literally surrounded by the enemy felt unsettling.

"Just continue whatever you were doing," Nazeem said from the computer with the three people around it. "I suppose you can't help it. Either way, stop bothering me."

The call ended, and the others stepped back. Lisa froze, mere feet away, directly in their line of sight.

Not a one looked at her.

"I hate this," a female scientist said, folding her arms. "Do you think there's anything to her insistence that we're . . . caught in some kind of . . . I don't know, ripple in time?"

"Oh!" one of the men said. "Maybe we're in a loop, like that movie. Over and over and over . . ."

"*Something* is going on," the third said. "I . . . don't want to admit it, but I keep not noticing her calls. I get fuzzy in the brain every time we converse. I tried writing it down, but last time—after the call—I got distracted and apparently stopped writing *midsentence.* It's eerie."

"We should do something about this," the first woman said, arms still folded. "Stop the experiment. Maybe this is proof that it will work, as Nazeem says. Maybe not. Who knows? We should do more testing before we proceed."

They agreed. Then the three of them stood there for a while. Finally, unnervingly, they wandered back to their posts and presumably started working on whatever they'd been doing before the call. Lisa crouched with Yung beside a desk, teeth gritted. They'd just decided to stop the experiment—but now appeared to not even remember. Time was shoving them forward, toward the explosion.

"Fascinating," Yung whispered. "They can notice something is wrong, but seem incapable of doing anything about it . . ."

"Focus, Professor," Lisa whispered. "Can you use that empty computer station there?"

"I don't have a backdoor to these—only the one attached directly to the machine, which is where we input parameters for the transfers. Unfortunately, someone is working that one." He paused. "Why are we whispering and crouching, by the way?"

"Feels right," Lisa said, watching each of the scientists in turn. Nothing she saw gave her cause for specific concern, though getting Yung access to a workstation was going to be more difficult than she'd assumed. People did leave theirs now and then, but came back soon. If they walked up and collided with him, they'd notice him for certain.

What she needed was . . . a fire alarm.

Hell, was she really considering that? An old Dane staple for clearing a room? She'd chided him on that sort of stunt more than once, but it *was* usually effective.

"Hey, Yung," she hissed. "Do these labs have some kind of alarm system that will make everyone evacuate?"

He cocked his head, then got a wicked-looking grin. He waved her to follow him to the right side of the chamber, where he fiddled with a device plugged into an outlet on the wall. "Just have to set it to test mode . . . Best back off, Officer, in case they come to investigate it."

She did, and seconds later an alarm started blaring through the room. The scientists didn't notice. Lisa closed her eyes, annoyed, trying not to let the sound get under her skin.

A good thirty seconds into the alarm, finally one of the scientists looked up. "Hell!" he said. "Is that the radiation alarm?"

The other five froze. Then, blessedly, what followed was a mad scramble from the building, the scientists carrying only essentials. Yung followed them to the exit, then threw the security door's manual override, whispering that with that done, the keypad was deactivated. He quickly locked the other door, showing initiative that hinted at the man he'd end up becoming during the end of the world.

"Think that will work?" Lisa asked.

"It had better," he said, killing the alarm. "Because there's no way I can function with that noise." He settled down at a station. "They left this computer unlocked."

"Can you get the data you need?"

"It is here," he said, typing. "All of our previous tests—most importantly, the data on the ones where I'm sure we actually sent an object back in time and didn't realize it. With this, I might be able to get the right inputs to Officer Dane when he enters the facility in his timeline. And they *might* work. But I'm going to need a few minutes."

Lisa went to the window, which had frosted glass—but a peep section she could pull back and look through. Outside, the scientists and two security guards were standing around looking confused, perhaps wondering—now that the alarm was no longer sounding—what had happened. One tried the door and was perplexed to find it locked, their code not working to undo the deadbolt.

We're in, she texted to Dane, *and Past Yung is working to get you numbers. But our time in here might be limited.*

She waited, anxious. Was he in the middle of an assault? Was he even alive?

We're still not in position, his reply came. *Sorry. I unexpectedly stopped for a meal.*

Stopped for a meal? You make it sound like you hit a drive-through for burgers.

I'd kill for a burger, honestly. But it has been good to relax a little without having someone at my throat. Give me a sec. I need to wash up. Then we'll move.

Twenty-One

73 Hours After Moment Zero

Dane lowered the phone, then leaned back against the sewer wall, his heart pounding. At his feet, a dead revenant—with a knife through the side of her skull—stopped twitching. He rubbed his forehead, feeling her chill touch begin to fade.

His phone buzzed. *Well,* Lisa texted, *aren't we feeling proper today.* A response to him saying he needed to wash up.

He forced out a smile, then braced his foot against the corpse and pulled the knife free. Sloppy, letting this one get a jump on him. He didn't think it was some kind of scout for the larger force of revenants—just a lone straggler making her way through the sewers, where she'd found a potential snack. A snack who couldn't afford to fire his weapons, lest he bring down the wrath of hundreds more.

He cleaned the knife and slid it back in the sheath at his belt, then picked up his phone and typed. *You know me,* he said. *Always so proper. I know where to put every dining utensil. Anyway, Yung and I are gearing up again. Should reach the facility in about twenty minutes.*

Hopefully, if the enemy was monitoring his phone, that would explain why it had taken him longer to arrive than expected. He wasn't certain they'd be able to intercept texts; he wasn't even completely certain they were listening in. This seemed his best course anyway.

Dane hauled himself to his feet, and found that the effects of the revenant draining him were nearly gone. He approached a nearby ladder, tried a few of the rungs—and they were solid. He'd jogged out of the Dead Zone into the center of the living zone; there was barely any rust on this ladder at all.

At the top, he lifted a manhole cover and peeked out. The moonlight filtering through the clouds was his only guide, though he figured he'd be able to see the glow of the revenants regardless. The way was clear to the facility a few blocks ahead. He dropped and jogged the rest of the distance. At the base of another ladder, he put his hand to his bandaged wound. He still felt odd, how little it bothered him. Instead of worrying, he went over the images Lisa had sent him, memorizing the path to—and layout of—the proper building.

He sent a final text to Yung, a simple question mark. He got back, *Wait*. Which was their signal that he was actually in position. Dane replied with an arrow, another sign they'd agreed on, indicating he was on the move.

That done, he flipped off his flashlight, climbed one last ladder, and slipped into the darkness of night outside the trailer park. It hadn't been too bad a place, once. His grandmother had lived in a park like this, a few blocks away. He had fond memories of playing there among the rows of homes. Nighttime in the apocalypse transformed pastoral into predatory. He inched forward, worried that each lump of shrubbery was a crouching revenant with their eyes closed.

It was difficult to gauge how fast to move. Certainly a slow advance would give more time for them to find him—but in the darkness, he couldn't persuade himself to go at speed. Tripping over a toy—as he nearly did just after slipping inside the gate—and making a ruckus would *also* get him noticed. So he kept it calm and steady, using his old habit of listening to his heartbeat to soothe his nerves.

It worked. Because he was watching when some of those shadows finally started moving, charging toward him from hollow trailer homes, eyes glowing with the softer light he'd come to associate with the weaker revenants that hadn't fed on many souls. Six of them. He couldn't fight them all with a knife. He caught flashes of wide, hungry eyes in the darkness, then gritted his teeth, flipped on his flashlight, and started shooting.

His shots broke the air, as grating as firecrackers in a library. Worse, in this darkness, he couldn't be sure he was hitting all of his targets. Bodies moved, emaciated faces showing in the beam of his light, as he drilled enemy after enemy in the head.

Something tackled him from the side. He went down, scrambling for his knife, until a more distant *bang* sounded, and the thing fell off him.

Dane leapt to his feet, then unmuted his phone, which was stuck to his chest, opening the party line that had both his Yung and Lisa on it.

"Nice shot," he said to Yung before dashing toward the facility—all need for stealth abandoned. Fortunately, he'd crossed half the distance easily.

"Two more trailing you," Yung said. "Maybe more. I'm having trouble telling. Shame about the night-vision gear."

They'd recovered night-vision equipment from SWAT headquarters, but the wiring inside had begun to decay. The guns that had been inside the safes, fortunately, were proving more resilient.

"Dane?" Lisa's voice. "Are you in trouble? I thought you wouldn't get to the facility for another fifteen minutes."

"I'm actually almost in," he said to her. "I'll explain later. Please get your Yung ready."

A shot sounded. "Got him," Yung said.

"Be sure your muzzle flashes don't lead them to you," Dane said, skidding around a corner. The mobile home he wanted should be right ahead. He threw a flare, then dropped another as he ran. Two more distant cracks in the air announced Yung putting down the revenants on his tail.

"I'm more worried about how many will come for you," Yung said. "I think the plan was a success, as they're mostly gathered at the other entrance, but you'll have hundreds on you in minutes."

"Then we'd better work fast," Dane said. "Li, I'm going to need those calculations."

"I'll push Past Yung," she said.

"Great," he said, shooting down the five revenants he spotted in the yard of the facility. The flares were distracting others nearby, though those reportedly wouldn't work for long. Better than nothing, so he threw another one of them through the window of a nearby motor home. Then he burst into the facility, blessing Lisa for her photographs that had led him here so quickly.

He inspected the surroundings using his gun-flashlight. No revenants inside that he could see.

The machine itself was . . .

Was destroyed.

He froze in place, blinking as he looked at the wreckage before him. The small dot of a wormhole was there, but the machinery that fed it power and made the actual teleportation work . . . had been destroyed. Not rusted away; it had been deliberately hammered to pieces.

"Why are you so eager," a feminine voice said, "to stop our rebirths, Officer Dane? Isn't the new world so much more interesting than the old one?"

He spun, searching the darkness, heart thundering as he put his back to a wall and tried to pinpoint the speaker. That voice . . . it was Nazeem.

"You destroyed the machine," he said, mostly for Yung and Lisa's sake. Indeed, he heard both of them curse. "Why?"

"Can't have you undoing all my hard work," she replied from somewhere inside. "Officer. I've learned so much from those who live beyond the darkness. The old world was stagnant, declining. Exploration, achievement, initiative . . . all dying off, like flowers with no sunlight."

"You killed hundreds of thousands of people."

"Maybe millions," she said. "The Dead Zones, as you call them, should extend for hundreds of miles. The changes to reality extend even farther. But Officer Dane, you know as well as I do that this is what we needed. I understand . . . so well . . . from those who speak from the darkness. Whenever life stagnates, it needs a reset. A challenge."

He continued looking around for her. Hell. Was she stalling, waiting for her hordes to arrive and kill him? Should he run? He at least had to try to get out of here with the broken pieces of the machine, didn't he? Maybe Yung could science them back together.

It seemed a . . . a frail hope. It was all he had. He inched toward the broken device.

"I know you've discovered my eavesdropping," Nazeem said. "The voices hear your communications, sent through that place beyond the darkness. I know from them that the past is resisting change. Officer, the universe *demands* this. Heroes and monsters have returned to the Earth. Do you really want to go back to a life without either?"

A glow came from the far wall, to his right. White light, surrounding a black void six feet across. Despite himself, he lowered his gun, gaping. The voice came from within that circular void, which looked like nothing more than . . . a small black hole, light *curving* around the perimeter.

Whatever Nazeem had become . . . it wasn't just a revenant. She'd gone further, with the help of something else. Something whispering from that distant place.

"We will be enemies," Nazeem said softly. "You fighting for the survivors, me fighting for the reborn. Our clashes will improve us both, force us to grow. And when we are finished, they . . . they will accept me . . . as an *equal*."

"Dane," Lisa's voice said in his ear. "Stall!"

"What?" he hissed.

"We have a plan!"

Bless her. And maybe, if Nazeem had to get her information about the communications from the wormhole, he might have time before she realized that Lisa had a plan.

But . . . stall the glowing black-hole entity that had once been a scientist? Easy. Ummm . . .

"What the hell happened to you?" he blurted out.

"I communed with them. The darkness beyond light."

"Any chance the darkness makes more sense than you do? I'd love to ask it a few questions."

She laughed. Through the window, Dane saw shadows. The frosted glass didn't let him see details, but there had to be hundreds of revenants gathering, pulling in, judging by the glow of those eyes. A haunting sea of shining eyes and hollow faces. Whatever Lisa's plan was . . . it would need to be pretty incredible, because his opportunity to run had passed.

"Officer, Officer," Nazeem said, "why must we insult one another? We want the same thing."

"Which is?"

"A better world."

"Dane," Lisa hissed in his ear. "Listen." A muffled scratching indicated her phone being moved.

"Um . . . all right . . ." her Yung said. "Your phone line exists in both time periods. I think . . . I think any portal we open will behave the same way. The original one affected both of you after all. It opened into both timelines."

"What are you saying?" Dane's Yung demanded. "Get to the point."

"We don't need you to activate the device, Officer Dane," Lisa's Yung said. "Because if *we* activate it in *our* timeline, a portal should open in *yours* as well. It is the thing that transcends and connects the worlds."

Well, damn. Maybe Dane wasn't dead. He glanced at the light-surrounding-dark that was Nazeem, and her glow intensified. She seemed to have just learned they were planning something—so he stalled some more by unloading a full magazine into her. You didn't get to do that often, and there was something satisfying about it, even if his bullets ended up getting pulled into the corona of light, where they zipped around in a circle.

Revenants began to burst in through windows and doors, but as they did, Lisa's Yung delivered the goods—for a glow appeared on the floor beneath the wormhole, which started to vibrate and change. Dane scrambled that direction, leaping over the broken remnants of the machine, the flashlight on the end of his gun tracing a zigzag on the ceiling.

"Officer!" Nazeem shouted. "Don't ruin this! Don't take from us the rebirth we've earned!"

"Lady," he said, ducking into the glow on the floor, "the only thing you've earned is a swift elbow to the . . . um . . . event horizon. Yung, this will take me back to before the explosion happened?"

"I . . ." he said. "Um. There wasn't time for enough calculations! I—"

He was cut off as the light completely consumed Dane.

Twenty-Two

Light.

Lisa saw Dane. Standing on a street at night. The one outside the mansion.

Please. Just this last time . . .

She walked away, toward the car.

Then . . . she shifted, and was suddenly in the hallways of the mansion, chasing after him, Yung at her side.

Gunshots. Dane, she thought, was hit twice. But everything went white . . . fuzzy . . .

Only a memory. It faded as the light did. Leaving her standing in a doorway, looking in at rows of seats arranged before a small stage with a piano on it. Mrs. Dougall was handing out programs, with each child listed in turn. Behind, someone cleared their throat, trying to prompt Lisa to move.

The recital. She was at Nova's recital.

Numb, Lisa sidestepped Mrs. Dougall, not taking a program. She'd been at the facility with Yung, and he'd opened a portal for Dane. Now, suddenly she was here?

She spun until she saw a wall clock. Half past six. "Wednesday? It's Wednesday?"

Mrs. Dougall had turned back to giving out programs, and nobody in the seats Lisa had passed so much as glanced at her. It was still happening. She had to work to get the attention of a man in the back row.

He shook his head as he finally saw her hand on his shoulder. "Um . . . can I help you?"

"Wednesday," she said. "Is it Wednesday?"

"Yes." He held up a program with the date on it.

Lisa turned away from him, looking for the exit. Then she froze. If it was still happening . . . if she'd lost *days* and was now mere hours from Moment Zero . . .

Her job had just gotten far more urgent, but she couldn't get to it yet. She instead rushed through the doors into the preparation room, where she found Nova—in her black recital dress—pacing nervously.

Lisa took her in an embrace, and the girl finally noticed her. ". . . Mom?"

"I'm here, Nova," Lisa whispered, tears in her eyes. "I'm going to fix this. This one . . . this one I can fix. I have to."

"Mom, is it Dad? Is he—"

"It's not that," Lisa said. "It's something big. I have to go. I don't think you'll even remember this; I hope you'll simply think I'm there watching, as that's what the universe wishes. But if you remember anything . . . remember that I love you."

Some moms got eye rolls in response to professions like that, but Nova had always been one for hugs. She embraced Lisa back, obviously still confused. Then her eyes fixed on the bracelet.

"You're wearing it!" Nova said.

"Yes," Lisa said, then noticed it move on its own. Dane. Whatever had happened, Dane was still there, and he wanted her to know it. "And it's helping."

She put her hand to Nova's cheek, then wiped her own tears and forced herself away. It was the day of the explosion, and she was there much earlier in the day. What about Dane? Did this mean he'd arrived on time?

As she ducked out of the room, she quickly dialed his number, but got sent straight to voicemail. But she had the bracelet. She spun it on her arm, and it spun back the other way a moment later. He was likely having problems with his phone again.

She composed a brief text and sent it—before thinking of another number. She looked where she'd put it—the number to Yung's burner—in the notes on her phone. Blessedly, the number hadn't vanished. She dialed, pacing.

He answered. "Officer Sterling?"

"Yes."

"Oh, thank God. What took you so long? It's been days!"

"Not for me, Professor," she said. "I was with you minutes ago—now I've appeared at my daughter's recital. Roughly five hours before the explosion."

"Oh . . . Oh! It's the same time for me, but I got here by waiting out the days. When Officer Dane stepped into the portal, you were pulled through time by whatever tethers you together. Have you contacted him?"

"No reply. Maybe he's on target, as it's always been later in the day for him."

"I'm just . . . I'm just relieved to hear you. Two days . . . felt like years, hiding from Nazeem's people . . ."

"Tell me what happened," she said, pushing out into the light of early evening. It would be two hours until sunset.

"The machine overloaded," he said. "Not as cataclysmically as when Nazeem tried to teleport her entire facility, but my numbers were still off somehow. I've spent two days going over and over the calculations, and I'm baffled. I don't know what went wrong—everything seems like it *should* be right."

"Okay," she said, processing that. "But what's your situation?"

"I ran from the machine as it blew up—then snuck back that night. I couldn't find you anywhere. Nazeem was there, with guards who could see me, so I ran. I'm staying at— Oh, I shouldn't tell you in case they're listening . . ."

"It's all right," she said, taking a deep breath. "It's possible that Dane arrived as planned in time to stop things in his timeline. We won't know until we can contact him. For now, we should prepare for tonight. We'll want to be at the primary facility to stop Nazeem from activating the device."

"Yes . . . Okay, yes. I can . . . I can be there."

"For now, stay wherever you are," Lisa said. "I'm going to do something I've been trying to do since this all began."

"Which is?"

"I'm going to find our timeline's Dane," she said, heading with purposeful steps toward the subway station. "Call me if anything changes."

"Okay. I will."

She hung up and hurried down the steps. Fortunately, she was pretty sure she knew where she'd locate her Dane. He hadn't gone with the others on the case to bust Goffrey in his office, nor had he joined Lisa at the DA's. His excuse for those absences had been the same: he needed to get some training in at the range beneath 1PT.

So, Lisa soon went striding up the steps to headquarters. She passed plenty of people on their way home after the day's work, though most everyone in white collar had gone on the bust. At least Lisa didn't have to face the indignity of Rowna ignoring her.

In the basement, her keycard got her into the firing range. Jeri, at the desk, didn't even look up from her phone. The range itself was in two parts: firing stalls to her right, and the larger obstacle course to her left. Straight ahead, at an equipment table, Perez was inspecting some weapons. Flags were out—indicating the range was cold. Everyone was to have safeties on, weapons holstered, standing away from stalls. She passed a couple of officers who were reloading magazines.

All of them ignored Dane's corpse, which lay in the center of the obstacle course.

Lisa froze as she spotted it slumped behind a concrete barrier. Then, with a silent prayer, she walked up and knelt beside him. Two bullets to the chest . . . as she'd thought she'd seen right before the initial flash of light at the primary facility.

The corpse wasn't fresh, but neither was it that old. Very little blood on the floor. She imagined, though she probably didn't have time to check, that it had been teleported to Perez's couch during the first flash of light and taken the place of Dane in the past, as she'd done when looping through her timeline. There, it had likely bled out all over his furniture. More recently it had teleported here, when the second device had activated.

She was dead in his timeline. And he was dead in hers. Was that what had caused the split? And . . . what did that say for reunifying the timelines?

Or could this be the future him? she thought with a chill. *He said he'd been hit . . .*

No. He'd said that one wasn't life-threatening, and she'd felt the bracelet moving. This must be the him from her timeline; all those hours, he'd been decomposing on Perez's couch.

The shock of it all—the weathering upon her caused by this strange day, or days, or whatever—kept her kneeling there until Perez called the range hot. Dazed, she forced herself to the safety of the corridor between the two halves of the range. There, she wrapped her arms around herself and trembled. If she died, would her corpse just lie there too, ignored? Would they suddenly notice Dane's body once the timelines were fixed? Or . . . or was that version of him always going to be caught in the strange tide of temporal inertia, unseen, until he was a skeleton that people accidentally tripped over while running the course?

A part of her feared she would remain like this forever. Unseen, even by those who loved her. So it took time to pull herself together. Enough time that her phone buzzed with a text from Future Dane—she *had* to think of him as the *real* Dane.

And he was still in trouble.

Twenty-Three

5 Hours After Moment Zero

In the light, Dane saw himself and Lisa working together one last time as they discovered Yung, then approached Nazeem and her scientists. Gunfire. A last-ditch run to try to stop it . . .

He thought that maybe he was in the right place—that the teleport had worked. Then the vision faded, and he found himself in his apartment, in his own bed, at night.

Well, at least he wasn't on the floor this time. His pillow, his covers. He got out of bed, feet brushing his pile of emergency socks. Damn. The whole thing felt like a dream, except . . .

Hand to his side, he prodded tenderly at the bandaged wound beneath his body armor. More, the room felt wrong. It took a moment to realize no light was peeking in from behind the blinds. Nor was his alarm clock on. He unslung his assault rifle, then stumbled to the window. Every streetlight was off, every home light dead.

People clogged the street below, milling about. As he pushed the blinds aside farther, they fell. The rod holding them up had snapped. Hell. He realized his fingers had made impressions in the wood of the windowsill. The carpet was starting to fall apart. It had already begun.

He hadn't reached Moment Zero. He'd gone back, but not far enough. With trembling fingers, he took out his phone—and got a dead battery warning.

"You're kidding me . . ." he said, then pulled out the power bank. Also dead. He'd been using his phone so much, he'd never gotten much of a charge—and when the power bank had run out, the phone had soon followed. Hell. It had probably been running on fumes that entire assault on the second facility.

He leaned back against the wall, feeling the footboard crack. They'd missed Moment Zero. But . . .

But this was a good sign, right? He'd jumped backward, instead of going farther forward. The room wasn't nearly as decayed as last time, and none of those people below had glowing eyes. Lisa's Yung had done *something* right. Maybe not quite *enough* of that something, but Dane wasn't going to complain. He'd been surrounded mere moments ago. Now he had another chance.

He made his way into his closet—where he wasn't worried about the flashlight drawing attention from outside. There, he took stock. Body armor and helmet. Phone, out of battery. Small first aid kit with painkillers. His AR, six fully loaded mags. His sidearm, two spare mags. Two flash-bangs, three flares.

He was well equipped, though he needed to get another power bank. That was his first priority—to establish communication with Lisa and the Yungs. Though, he considered, then turned his bracelet about. A few seconds later, it turned back the other way. He was still bound to Lisa, somewhere.

That gave him the push to get moving. He switched the flashlight to its dimmest setting, hooked it to the front of the AR, then loaded back up and made his way out. In the hallway, he caught Mrs. Banler (Caucasian, muumuu, body shape of a white woman who liked muumuus) peeking through her door with wide eyes.

"Dane?" she said. "What happened?"

"I don't know," he lied. "But best thing you can do is stay put for now. Um, lock your door. Don't let anyone—especially not Tim—in."

"I feel sick," she said, letting the door open farther. "I was out when that explosion happened. The subway and buses stopped running, so I walked back here. But Melissa isn't home, and my phone doesn't work."

Dane stood outside her door, feeling helpless. If she'd been on Fourth . . . she'd been outside the Dead Zones. But now she was in the *center* of a place where *every other person* would soon hunger for her soul . . .

It began with the people inside buildings, for some reason. Those who took a lesser dose changed faster. Yung had told him that the first changes had happened five hours or so after Lightbreak. People who had been indoors first, followed shortly thereafter by people who had been outside.

"Listen to me," he said, taking her by the shoulder. "You need to get moving. Go to the country club. You know the one? Over off Seventeenth?"

She looked at him. And by the light of his flashlight, she seemed to understand. She gave him a nod.

"Good," he said. "Come on. I'll lead you down the stairs."

"Melissa . . ."

"If I see Mel," he said, "I'll send her to the same place. On your way, don't stop or talk to anyone. Just get there as fast as you can and wait. Please . . . trust me."

He got her down the steps and across the lobby, then ran almost face-first into Tim, who was standing outside. Staring up at the stars. He'd always been spindly, but Dane could *swear* he was looking even more gaunt now.

"Dane?" Tim said, dazed.

"Hey, Tim," Dane said, shoving Mrs. Banler to the side, getting her moving the right direction. "How are you feeling?"

"Cold," Tim whispered. "Frighteningly cold. Like I have never . . . never known anything warm . . ." He fixated on Dane. "You're warm though . . ."

Dane ran. As he reached the next intersection, he heard Mrs. Banler scream from the right. He turned and trained his rifle on two people who were holding her against a wall. One woman looked to him, and her eyes began to glow with a phantom white light.

He shot her. And the companion. The sounds drew hundreds of heads—people milling about on the street, suddenly aware of him. Sweating, he reached Mrs. Banler, who was down, trembling, barely able to move.

"D-Dane?" she asked. "W-why . . ."

"Hush," he said, looking up. Other revenants were coming out of buildings nearby, though the people milling on the streets hadn't changed yet.

Too many to shoot. Too many to . . . to . . .

What was he going to do? Run all the way to the country club carrying Mrs. Banler? He popped a flare and threw it into a building with a cry, hoping to divert some revenants—and some did stare that direction.

"You have to get up," he said to Mrs. Banler.

She just lay there.

This is my beat. I have to . . . to . . .

He couldn't help her. He . . . he couldn't. Screams sounded from down another street, then more the other direction. People shouting for help. More and more revenants began appearing out of lobbies, corridors, homes. He realized . . . Mrs. Banler wouldn't be the only person who had come home after Lightbreak. Some of those milling about would themselves change. Others could have been saved . . .

People yelling. And he . . . he couldn't help them. Except by stopping the problem at its source.

Feeling helpless, hating himself, he left Mrs. Banler. She was piled on after he did so, three budding revenants going for her at once. She didn't have the strength to scream.

I can't save them one at a time, he thought. *I have to do something for them all. That starts with finding a battery.*

If things were already degrading here, he'd need to get out of the Dead Zone before locating an electronics store. Trusting his memory, he started running in the general direction of the country club. Fighting soon consumed everything, the revenants from the buildings attacking the soon-to-change ones on the streets, causing mass panic.

He ducked around the side of a building, listening to the fighting, and downed a revenant that came for him. Soon, however, things began to quiet. He peeked out, and saw something terrifying—many of the people who had been running from the revenants were now changing. The second wave, everyone who had been outside during Lightbreak.

Once they started to change, the revenants lost interest in them. All began to focus on the poor people who were unfortunate enough to have made their way home afterward—those who weren't revenants, and weren't going to change.

Dane turned and dashed down the alley. He found this terrible jog worse than the eerie silence of his last time awakening. Now he had to turn away from those calling for help. Had to be chased by their cries of pain, of abandonment, of loss.

He kept going, head lowered. All across the streets, people were changing, running, screaming. The chaos served him, however, as he was able to gun down any revenant who focused on him specifically. It was while he was taking aim at one such that he heard other shots in the near distance.

He pulled the trigger, then ran toward the sounds. Was someone else fighting back? Indeed, as Dane burst onto 17th—which he was certain was just outside the Dead Zone—he saw lights for the first time. A long line of car headlights and brake lights. People trying to get out of the city, but although this was a larger road (four lanes, with stoplights) it ran through a Dead Zone several miles upstream. All the cars in there would have stopped, so this gridlock was a death trap.

Someone had driven a car up on the curb nearby and was hiding behind it, firing down a cross street. Dane caught the man's attention, then got permission to approach with a wave. Soon after, Dane crouched beside the guy (Black, short hair, looked like he lifted) who was firing shotgun slugs at glowing eyes as they approached up a side street.

"Assault rifle?" the guy asked, brightening as he took Dane in. "Hell, you have an extra?"

"Afraid not," Dane said. "That gun of yours will work though, if you shoot for the heads."

"I . . . remember that part."

"Wait. Remember?"

"Yeah," the fellow said. "Like a dream . . . Lots of white . . . These things were everywhere around me. Did I see the future somehow?"

This was new. "I'm Dane," he said, holding out a hand.

"Malik," the man replied, taking it. "You military?"

"Just your friendly neighborhood police officer," Dane said, looking up over the car. White eyes, congregating that direction. And the path he'd come down?

More and more, flooding this way. Looked like they'd finished feeding on the few people inside the Dead Zone who were either from outside or had taken longer to change.

Dane glanced behind him, along 17th, where those cars were stuck. He might be able to charge his phone in one of those. Except he needed a battery he could carry. Plus . . .

"This place," Dane whispered, "is about to become a giant buffet for tens of thousands of revenants, Malik. Our best chance of stopping this is to travel in time and prevent it from ever happening. I can't explain more right now, but are you willing to cover me as I try to find a way to power my phone? With it, I can get us backup."

"My phone has juice," Malik replied, "but I can't get anyone to pick up."

"Towers are all down," Dane said, pulling him by the shoulder as the eyes from the side street started to approach in large groups. Like bobbing fireflies in the darkness.

Malik resisted being pulled away, but Dane got him moving after a moment—he likely realized that there were *dozens* of those sets of eyes. More. He joined Dane in running, while muttering under his breath, "I don't like this. I don't like any of it. It won't happen . . . It can't . . ."

Dane ran toward some people, holding aloft his badge. "Get moving toward the country club up the road!" he shouted. "If you see someone else, tell them! Knock on windows, and get people out of these cars. Pass the word! Anyone with glowing eyes is a danger! Avoid a fight if you can, but if you can't, they're only hurt by shots to the head!"

Most stared at him aghast, but others started running. A couple of people began passing his word. With Malik, he dashed toward a small electronics shop along the street. He saw people inside—normal ones. They'd pulled down the steel mesh over the windows, offering decent protection.

His badge got them to open the door. Malik explained to them about the country club while Dane found the portable power banks on one shelf, then ripped one open. When he plugged his phone in though, the charging indicator didn't appear.

"When did you stock these?" he asked the family who ran the place.

"Sticker on the back says when," the woman said, her accent thick. "Should we stay here in the shop or run?"

Dane recalled the ripped-open shops with rusted fronts that he'd seen on this very street two days from now. That mesh wouldn't hold long. "You should run. I'm sorry. Both options are terrible, but they will break into this shop if you stay."

The family ran. He hoped they'd make it, but once again he felt powerless.

No. His goal was to see that they didn't *have* to make it. He wasn't abandoning these people; he was focused on a better way to help. Like Lisa always said.

The back of the power bank's packaging showed a sticker of when it had been shipped and shelved. A year ago? Hell. He raised others, checking the stickers until at last he found one from another brand that had been shelved only a few weeks ago.

Come on, he thought, ripping open the packaging and plugging in.

The charging indicator came on. He heaved out a sigh, then tucked phone and battery into places in his body armor. Give the phone a few minutes, and it should turn back on.

Screams and shouts outside. This little store was one of many identical downtown shops: the long, narrow type that were sometimes delis, sometimes convenience stores, sometimes electronics stores. Weren't much bigger than long closets. Malik stood by the glass doors while Dane waited for the phone to charge.

"I hate that this happened," Malik said.

"You and me both, buddy," Dane said. "Can you tell me more of what you remember?"

"I remember Nazeem telling us we should search for a cop," Malik said. "I remember . . . the experiment. I should have stopped it. We all knew something was wrong . . ."

Wait.

Oh . . . oh *no.*

"You're one of her guards," Dane whispered. "The ones who were near the explosion. That's why you remember."

"Used my bike, and rode for the police headquarters these last hours, hoping they could stop it. I felt . . . something this direction." He turned toward Dane, his eyes glowing. "Your heat."

Dane whipped out his firearm in a smooth motion, right as Malik raised his shotgun and fired. Dane got two shots in the revenant's head as something struck him hard in the left leg, causing him to fall backward into the shelves.

Malik stumbled. Didn't go down, but also didn't fire again. "It can't be stopped," he whispered. "I'm going to turn into a monster. Took me a few hours longer than most, but it will happen."

Two more shots, fired by Dane where he'd fallen, dropped the man. Dane groaned, left hand to his leg and the fresh wound there. Damn, damn, *damn.* He should have seen something was off with Malik. He tried to stand, but slipped and fell. So instead he crawled to the front of the store, double-checked that Malik was dead, then locked the deadbolt. There he applied a tourniquet to his leg—he'd been shot straight through the left thigh—using his bandages.

Outside, revenants had plenty to distract them; screaming people tried to run as more and more of the monsters poured out of the Dead Zone, howling and hungry for heat. Even with so many people around, some revenants turned toward his little shop, looking at him through the mesh. He thought of those ripped-open buildings. So he forced himself to his feet—foot—and limp-stumbled to the back of the shop, hoping to escape that way.

Something was already pounding on that door. Scratching. Howling. Revenants. Hell. He checked the deadbolt, then backed away, realizing that with that leg wound . . . he couldn't fight his way through to escape.

He sank down beside a wall filled with phone cases, feeling numb. At least . . . at least the leg wound didn't seem to hurt as much as it should have . . .

Dane's phone buzzed. *Alive?* Lisa had sent.

He smiled. *Alive,* he replied. *Though it's not going as well as we hoped on this side.*

Her call came a second later. "Dane," she said, relieved. "When this is done, I am *absolutely* buying you a new phone."

He chuckled. "Yung's calculations were off, Li."

"Let me guess. You're a few hours after Moment Zero?"

"Yeah. It's probably early morning. Sunrise isn't here yet, but it's getting lighter in the east already. Maybe . . . five AM?"

"That matches me," she said. "I'm about five hours before the event. Appeared at the recital. I was hoping you arrived on time. I'm sorry."

He nodded as the banging on the back door grew louder, and revenants at the front began rattling the steel lattice over the windows.

"What's that noise?" Lisa asked.

He winced, then retrieved some more bandages from his pack and—by flashlight—tried to do something more to help his thigh. It looked *horrible.*

"I might have gotten myself into a pickle," he said.

"Oh, *hell.* You only use stupid words like that when it's bad."

"Got hit in the leg. I won't be running anywhere anytime soon. I'm trapped in a store on Seventeenth, with revenants trying to break in both doors. But if I need a new phone case, I've got a *ton* of choices."

She fell silent, though he could hear her breathing on the line. He could practically feel her concern.

"Sorry, Li," he said, closing his eyes to the howling and the pounding. The screams of people dying on the sidewalks or inside their cars. "I . . . don't know how I'm getting out of this one. You might need to find a way to do this on your own."

"We have to stop it in both timelines."

"Maybe my Yung can do it. Find the me from your timeline to help you—"

"He's dead, Dane. I just found the corpse. And Yung specifically mentioned that teleporting *you* was our best shot. I don't know if he can do it."

He breathed in and out, searching for some other solution. "What Yung did was effective. I jumped backward in time—simply not far enough. We need to try again. Get me to a facility, open a portal, with new calculations . . . Surely if Yung knows he was off by a few hours, he'll know how to further change the numbers. Like calibrating a gun's sights."

"I've already talked to Past Yung. He feels like his calculations were correct, but you're right. There has to be something he was missing. We could try again. If . . ."

If Dane could get moving. He managed to stand, with effort—but he could barely put any weight on the leg. Even that much shouldn't have been possible. He grunted in pain, then forced himself to look at the revenants trying to break through the front door.

There were dozens or more piling around outside. He . . . probably wouldn't have made it out there even unwounded. They seemed to think him a finer meal than the others.

"Lisa," he whispered, "I *really* don't think I can get out of here. Even if I fire every bullet I have, I'm going to be overrun. You'll *have* to solve it without me."

"No," she said, adopting that tone of hers. "Dane, I'm going to fix this."

"Not everything can be fixed, Li."

"Listen to me: when *you* stepped into the portal, *I* jumped forward in time. You understand? We're linked. So if I can get a facility working on *my* side, and I send myself exactly five hours into my future . . ."

Then he might be pulled exactly five hours backward. To Moment Zero, appearing where he'd been in the timeline at that hour. It . . . it might work.

"I'll handle this," Lisa promised. "All you need to do, Dane, is survive long enough for me to get another one of the teleporters up and running."

Twenty-Four

5 Hours Before Moment Zero

Lisa strode down the steps of 1PT, a phone line open to Past Yung. "We need to activate one of the devices," she said. "As soon as humanly possible."

"But . . . I don't know what we did wrong!" he exclaimed over the line. "It's dangerous to continue."

"As dangerous as letting the world end in five hours, Yung? Can your future self go back in time and stop it? Can anyone else?"

"I don't know," he admitted. "But it seems the link between the two of you is strongest. When he stepped in, you teleported—but neither I nor my future self appear to have done so at any point. You two almost certainly need to be the ones."

"So if Dane dies, so does our best hope of reconciling the timelines. It's time to be a little reckless. Can you *guess* on calculations that will bring us closer to Moment Zero?"

"I . . . This is hard, because we're working with such limited understanding of what we're doing. We don't even know exactly what caused the timelines to split."

"I'm dead in one, and Dane's dead in the other," she said. "It's related to that, I assume."

"Maybe. The act of pouring so much power into the wormhole . . . well, *that* is the real source. When that happened, decisions nearby had a chance of fragmenting timelines. Choices. I suppose in one, he ran for the guards first, and in the other, you did so."

"I was too far away," she said, "coming up the hallway at a run after untying you. At any rate, Yung, this is it. This is *your* chance. You can save the world—if you can figure out how to get those calculations to work."

"I will try," he said. "But I'm all the way across the city from the main facility, Officer Sterling—out in the suburbs. It will take me at least two hours by subway."

She stopped near the street. Would Dane last two hours?

"And the third facility?" she asked.

"Well, it's closer to me," he admitted. "But Nazeem and her guards . . . they will remember what happened two days ago, when we raided the second facility. From their perspective, we destroyed it. I heard them talking as I hid in the darkness, hoping to be able to find you in the rubble. She'll have both remaining facilities guarded—and with people who can see us, as she knows some of what is happening."

Lisa mulled this over. "Where is the third facility?"

"On Mayflower. Upper side."

"Commerce district?"

"Yes. Fourth floor of an office building."

Commerce district . . . upper side . . .

"Text me the address," she said. "I'll meet you there in thirty minutes."

"And we get in how?"

"I'll have it covered," she promised. "You can get there in time?"

"Probably. Subway stop is on . . . Eighty-Ninth, is it? Yes. Where are you?"

"Downtown."

"Subway lines won't—"

"I'll try a rideshare instead of the subway," she said. "App won't care if the driver doesn't notice me."

"No," he said. "I tried it yesterday. Driver canceled the ride five minutes in, then took another fare."

Damn. She stopped on the sidewalk, then turned, until she saw . . .

Dane's giant SUV. Parked conspicuously on the roadside ahead. She still had his spare key fob.

It was rush hour. And she'd need to take the freeway at high speeds to reach Yung in time.

Oh . . . this was a bad idea, wasn't it?

"I'll meet you there," she promised Yung again. "Thirty minutes. Get moving."

She hung up on him, then approached the monster of a vehicle. Taking a deep breath, she climbed in, then adjusted the seat. She'd always believed in driving defensively, even as a beat cop, but there were times when defense broke down and you had to rely on a little offense. She turned the car on and revved the gas engine, then tore out onto the street with the lights and sirens blaring—hoping that might help keep people from ignoring her.

It didn't. She was nearly sideswiped the moment she pulled out, and she had to drive up onto the sidewalk to avoid it. Then she immediately had to swerve back off so she didn't run into a family that didn't see her car. With a curse, she ran the light—stopping would risk her getting rear-ended—and took a corner at speed, tires screeching.

Sweating, she reached the on-ramp after narrowly avoiding a car that tried to plow into her from the side. It was like . . . like the universe itself considered her a valid target for unrestricted fire, and every layman in a car was a potential bullet. Fortunately, it got better on the freeway, as there weren't stoplights. Plus, traffic was actually moving for once.

She stayed mostly to the shoulder, where she was relatively safe at the moment, and dialed Rowna, who theoretically wouldn't be in the office, but out in the field. Lisa had to call three times before the woman picked up.

"Commander?" Rowna said. "Aren't you at the recital?"

"I got some intel about the Goffrey case," Lisa said. "It's going to make or break the arrest."

"Oh!" Rowna said, coming more alert. "But we're almost ready to grab him!"

"Whole team is there with you?" Lisa said, forced off the shoulder by a bridge, right back into traffic. She veered to the side, almost slamming into another car as someone cut into her lane from behind, then tried to zip straight through her spot.

"Yeah," Rowna said. "Everyone wanted a part of it. And with the search warrant, we'll need a lot of hands."

Ten people would go on this arrest, then. An unusual number, but it was an unusual case. They didn't think Goffrey would resist, as he'd want to play the courts, but he did have bodyguards. So everyone would be armed, just in case.

"I was reviewing reports earlier," Lisa said, "and I spotted something. Goffrey's accountants . . . they'll go to ground once we get him. We need to bust Harmon first."

"Um . . . do we?"

"Yes," Lisa said, hoping it was plausible enough. "Tell the others to hold off on the arrest. We're hitting the commerce district first." She'd realized the Harmon issue later in the night on the real day, when Dane had come to pester her. It was a genuine problem, and one she would reasonably have wanted to tie up. She needed a separate warrant, but she thought she could talk her way past that, at least in the short term.

Did the universe care that it was plausible that the real her would have interrupted the arrest? She still wasn't completely certain that was why Rowna had listened to her before, when she'd asked for the architectural plans.

Indeed, today Rowna just kind of drifted away from the call. Lisa heard some talking, then Rowna hung up. Lisa gritted her teeth and had to focus on driving for a short while, as the traffic slowed and the shoulder was again too narrow to make it past. The slowing proved more dangerous, because everyone saw her spot on the road as deliciously empty: a wonderful place to slide in and get a few car lengths ahead, so they could maybe arrive home a fraction of a second earlier.

She avoided two such cars, but the third—a *very* determined Tesla driver—

boxed her in. Lisa set her jaw, then fought back, slamming the Tesla to the side and sending it into a wreck that she hoped wouldn't be too bad.

She dialed Rowna again with a voice command.

Rowna didn't pick up.

"Come on," Lisa said, wincing as she was forced to slam another car to the side. "I'm trying to make this all plausible for you. Don't you hate that I'm causing wrecks? Doesn't that break the timeline too?"

But as Yung had said, the universe didn't actually *care*. It wasn't actively *trying* to steamroll her, any more than the wildfires last summer had *cared* about the homes they burned. It wasn't volition that resisted her, but inertia.

Inertia.

When Rowna answered, it was because Lisa was persistent. When people noticed her, it was because she kept trying to draw their attention. On the phone call about the SWAT headquarters, she'd refused to let Rowna hand her off. Maybe getting what Lisa needed wasn't about persuading or tricking the universe. Maybe it was just about being so dang annoying, she built up inertia of her own.

She called Rowna three more times. Then, when the woman finally answered, they had the exact same conversation as before—about going after the accountant. But this time Lisa refused to let Rowna drift away.

"Focus!" Lisa exclaimed, grunting as a car hit hers. "Rowna, we need to go after Harmon."

". . . We do?"

"Yes!"

The same conversation happened *again*, before Rowna got called away—and hung up absently, despite Lisa's protests.

So Lisa called again. Same conversation.

Then a fourth time.

Then she dictated a short email and sent it to the whole team. Twenty times. Another call.

"Commander?" Rowna said.

"We need to hit Harmon," Lisa said. "Don't go after—"

"Yeah, yeah," Rowna said. "So you've said, boss. Commerce district. We're moving."

It . . .

It had worked?

It had *worked*!

Maybe. Lisa called dispatch as she off-roaded to get to her exit. She ignored the stoplight and tore onto the street, blessing Dane's beast of a car and its own stupid inertia. She had dispatch redirect the team officially to the commerce district, sending them to the address provided by Yung. Then she did it twice more.

A short time later, when Lisa reached the address in question—going up over the curb for the final approach—she found her team idling there, somewhat conspicuous, on the corner. Ten cops, including Rowna and nine other uniformed officers. They noticed her immediately.

Dang, that felt good.

After Lisa pulled to a stop, she kicked out the broken side window—the door was jammed shut from being hit—and climbed free. The SUV was a mess. Would Dane be mad?

No. He'd think it was badass, wouldn't he?

"Commander?" Ramirez asked. "You sure this is the right place for Harmon?"

"I've got a tip. We're going in. Fourth floor. Half up the east stairwell, half up the west. Assume the location is hostile. Disarm and restrain any security personnel you see, and don't touch anything. Especially not any laboratory equipment."

"Do we . . . have a warrant?" Rowna asked.

"We have probable cause," Lisa said. "If this goes south, I take personal responsibility. You all witness that?"

They nodded.

"Commander," Cason said, waving someone forward. "This man was waiting for us. Says he's expected?"

"Hello, Yung," Lisa said.

"Officer," Yung replied, looking at the car. "Um . . . that was quite an entrance . . ."

"Move, everyone!" Lisa said. "I'm with the western incursion group."

They burst into motion. Heck, if she'd known that all she needed to do was be extra, *extra* stubborn . . .

Well, that was her specialty.

She let Ramirez and his breach team take point. This was the sort of thing SWAT should have done, but she kept them focused by explaining they didn't have time. They rushed up the steps, and while they took positions for breach, she swapped to Dane's line.

"Please still be there," she whispered.

"Still here," he said. But then gunfire sounded. "Most of me. There's a chunk out of my leg that got blown off by a shotgun earlier. Still haven't found it . . ."

More gunfire.

"Dane . . ." she whispered.

"They've ripped a few holes in through the front of the store," he said. "But those aren't quite big enough, and they're so eager, they all try to crawl in at once. Slows them as they have to pull the corpses back. But others keep ripping at the mesh . . ."

Gunfire.

"There were these games," he said, "when I was young. Arcade games. Had a toy gun you could shoot at the screen as enemies popped out. Used to play them a lot."

"I'll bet you were awesome at them," she said, then nodded to Ramirez, who burst through the door onto the fourth floor. Armed security was waiting, as Yung had predicted. She heard them shouting for the officers to keep back.

Dane grunted. "Actually, I sucked at those games. Always felt it was unfair how nothing moved realistically." He paused. "Feel a little vindicated now, to be honest." More gunfire sounded over the line.

"We're almost in position. *Hang on.*" Then she shouldered up through the stairwell to the front of the group of cops.

"You're right," Ramirez hissed at her. "Armed opposition. Won't stand down. Do we wait for a negotiator?"

Well, heck. She thought she heard Dane chuckle on the line.

"No, we don't," she said. His way wasn't always right. But once in a while . . .

This was *not* going to be according to protocol. Lisa ducked out of the stairwell and opened fire, downing both security guards. Ramirez cursed, then his team burst into motion, joining her as they rushed the rooms beyond. They found a large laboratory chamber similar to the others, but with more space and equipment.

There were guards in here too. A good dozen of them—it seemed that Nazeem had figured out how to game the system as well. Though those numbers were far more than Lisa could have taken herself, when they saw armed cops ready to fire . . . blessedly, the guards stood down, dropping guns, putting hands up. Private security, unlike in the movies, didn't often want to tussle with law enforcement. They didn't get paid enough for that.

Her second team burst in from the other doors, and she had them cuffing and separating scientists in seconds—all the while confused by what she was doing, and where Harmon was.

She left them to their confusion. "It's time for a miracle, Professor," she said, setting Yung at a computer. "I need a portal to Moment Zero."

"Give me a second. I'll . . . do my best."

She stood back, waving Rowna—and her questions—away. This was breaking so many rules, so many laws. But . . . she supposed *she* was the officer on the ground at the moment, and needed to trust herself.

"Dane," she said. "How's the shooting gallery?"

"They really up the difficulty on these last levels," he said, breathing hard. "Make you count your bullets."

"Yung is getting the numbers in now," she said, her anxiety spiking at the tone of Dane's voice.

"I got mine on the line," Dane said.

"Hello, Officer," Future Yung said. "I wish I had data to help . . . or that there was anything I could do."

"You remember everything?"

"Indeed," he said. "I wasn't transported in time, Officer Sterling—at least not completely. My link to you both is lesser, as I was farther away from the blast. I do mostly seem to remember what happened with you . . . what will happen with you . . . all in a few days. As if I dreamed it. I didn't believe until I got the call. I've been considering whether I should go help Dane, but . . ."

"It would be suicide, Yung," Dane said, then fired some more. "Besides. We have an answer. Lisa is solving everything. It's what she does. But if I die . . . you're our backup. Okay?"

"I am uncertain if my connection is strong enough, Dane," Future Yung said. "You need to pull through."

She glanced at Past Yung, then told Rowna the team could go grab Goffrey. They took to that eagerly, even with all their confusion at what they'd done here. The timeline wanted them back to the original bust. They should have asked her all kinds of questions, including *why* she'd shot two security guards. But the timeline kept them moving instead, shoving them toward what they should have been doing, now that Lisa was willing to let them go.

"Getting a bit lightheaded," Dane said softly.

Past Yung looked at her, then shook his head. Not yet.

"Dane," she said, "keep fighting."

"They've pulled back," he said. "I think they're preparing for a larger assault. One of the big ones is out there. I just spotted him. I think the next attack will get through. Whatever you're going to do . . . you need to do it now."

Yung held up one finger, typing with the other hand.

"Just a little longer," Lisa said. "You're going to survive, Dane. Listen to me. I'm really looking forward to you being my ex. We'll have *tons* of embarrassing evenings laughing about how bad the relationship was."

He chuckled. "It was terrible, wasn't it?"

"It *was* fun at times. When it worked. Can't believe we actually tried it. Rather, I can't believe I let you talk me into trying it."

"We did have our moments, didn't we?" He laughed. "I wish we'd talked about the problems earlier. Guess that's the sort of conversation I find uniquely terrifying."

"Uniquely terrifying? Aren't you facing down an army of zombies?"

He grunted in pain, but she could hear him smiling.

"Say it," she prompted, with a sigh. "I know you want to."

"An army of zombies, or talking relationships? What do you *think* a guy finds more intimidating?"

"That's sexist. You think *I* wouldn't pick the army of zombies if I had the option?"

He laughed, then coughed from the laughter. "It's been one hell of a last case, eh? Are you still glad you went with me that night?"

"If I hadn't," she said, "all of this would still have happened—but we wouldn't have had a chance to stop it. Heck, I feel foolish for having walked back to the car that night, even if I did eventually chase you down."

"There it is again . . ." he mumbled.

"What?"

"Li . . . when did you walk back to the car? That didn't happen, did it?"

"Of course it did. You insisted on doing a walk-around on Nazeem's property. I didn't want to, so I returned to the car, knowing you'd dang well do whatever you wanted anyway. But then . . . I came back."

"You went with me from the start."

"No I didn't. I—"

"Oh, hell," he interrupted. "They're coming."

"It's ready!" Past Yung said.

"What did you do, Albert?" Future Yung said over the line. "I thought we didn't have the calculations!"

"Sometimes the best you can do is estimate," Past Yung said, turning in his seat toward Lisa. In front of him, beyond the clear blast shield, light began to glow on the floor—directly under a floating dark speck. "Good luck, Officer Sterling."

Lisa approached. Dane had always just jumped in. But, tense though things were, she found herself peering through that widening hole, rather than stepping in entirely. She saw . . .

Glowing light.

Then she saw the original facility. This would take her there. Except . . .

Something was still wrong.

Twenty-Five

Slumped in the corner with his assault rifle at his shoulder, watching an army of glowing eyes begin to rip through the remnants of the front of the shop, Dane felt . . .

Strangely untethered. Only one magazine left. It—

He started to glow.

It was *working*!

In a second, he was consumed by white light. And then, as that light retreated, he found himself standing on a quiet street corner in the suburbs. He leaned immediately against a stone mailbox, leg screaming in pain. But there didn't seem to be any revenants around him.

An explosion of light ripped out of a building in the distance.

Nazeem's lab . . . the primary facility. White liquid light rose from it—a glorious brightness that made . . . the vague shape of a single enormous tentacle, faintly translucent, reaching high into the air.

Light spread across the ground nearby, consuming homes, yards, streets . . .

Lightbreak.

"This is still wrong," Lisa said over the line.

"Li!" he screamed. "We're still too late! I'm seeing Lightbreak." He stumbled back, his leg holding him, pain lost in the panic of the moment.

It was beautiful.

He'd imagined squid tentacles, but these were something more ethereal—quiet, graceful for all their size. More like a sprouting plant than a nameless horror. Eyes wide, Dane tipped his head back as the fountain reached higher and higher, then split into radials and began to fall, like spokes, toward the city.

Wherever they hit would become Dead Zones.

And one was straight above him.

—

Lisa didn't touch the small rift in the air—which had grown to about the size of a baseball—but it had a magnetism to it. She could see her skin fuzzing, stretching toward it, as if she were a painting being smeared. It seemed this proximity was enough to have teleported Dane, but she didn't fully commit, not yet. She remained outside, resisting the last step forward.

Through the tiny hole, Lisa watched Dane climb a tree, then throw himself over the wall. She saw herself chase after, climbing up on her own, then spotting him as he fired a few shots at the guards that came running to investigate.

They immediately turned hostile, firing back, but Dane managed to kick in the cellar door and jump through. Inside, he'd find Yung, then leave him tied up—instead running to stop the device. Lisa would find Yung a few minutes later, coming in after both guards and Dane.

She'd untie Yung, and together they'd run for the room with the device. She'd arrive just in time to see . . .

Dane being shot . . .

An explosion.

The living Dane was shouting at her through the line. She watched his past, transfixed by the light, and realized their mistake.

"Yung!" she shouted, though she was being pulled forward strongly enough she couldn't even turn around. "What if we're wrong about Moment Zero? What if it *didn't* happen when the device activated?"

"That would throw *everything* off!" he shouted back.

"We've been using it as a baseline in the calculations," Future Yung said, his voice distant over his weaker phone line. "A kind of beacon. If it didn't happen at midnight . . ."

"We won't *ever* be accurate," Past Yung finished. "But what else would it be but when the device went off?"

"It was on a timer!" Lisa said. "What if Moment Zero—the moment everything changed—happened when they *set that timer*. Not when the device was activated, but when it was turned on and the power put into the hole. That's what caused the break that shattered the timelines, right?"

"If that's the case," Future Yung said, "we're screwed, as we wouldn't be able to know when that was."

What time had that been? She'd looked at her watch.

"You said that choices made in that moment could have been what diverged us!" she said.

"Yes," Past Yung said. "A choice made close to the epicenter, right when the hole was force-fed that much power."

I looked at my watch . . . just after eleven thirty . . .

"Eleven thirty-seven," Lisa said. "Put that time in!"

"But—" both Yungs said.

"DO IT!"

Past Yung punched in a few numbers. "Done."

As Dane shouted for her to do something, Lisa touched the portal.

Twenty-Six

Moment Zero

Dane appeared on the corner in front of Nazeem's house—far enough away to be out of range of her surveillance equipment.

Suddenly, he understood why Lisa had picked this moment. "The timeline split right here," he whispered. "Not when the device went off... but..."

"But when I made my decision," Lisa said over the phone line. "Whether to follow you or to go back to the car. We remember two different versions of the next twenty-three minutes. In one timeline, you went on ahead—and got shot."

"And in the other, you went with me. Then... you got shot."

"Quite the pair we are," she whispered. "I'm kneeling by your dead body right now."

"I'm not. Why is that?"

"The me from that timeline must have died immediately from the gunfire—that's why Yung found my body in the wreckage. He thought it was due to the explosion, or the collapse. But the you from this timeline got shot, survived long enough to get teleported, then bled out. The body, like the items we're carrying, got entangled with us two."

He nodded, trying not to think about his own corpse lying dead in front of her. "Li? Why *did* you come back, in your timeline? Why walk away, then return?"

The line was silent briefly, then she replied, "When I left, it was because of Dane—the infuriating boyfriend—refusing to see what made sense. When I came back... it was because Dane, my friend and my partner, might end up in danger. I didn't want him to go into it alone."

"Thank you for that," he said. "Even if it wasn't enough to save that version of me. But here we are, still with split timelines. Shouldn't we be able to see each other? We've reached the same moment, when things diverged."

"No," she said. "We also have to synchronize events—both stopping the explosion. If we do, *that* becomes the path of least resistance. The universe will hopefully accept that the non-apocalypse future is the 'real' timeline. At that point, everything should merge."

"That right, Yungs?" Dane asked, standing.

No reply. He checked the phone, and while Lisa was still on the line, his Yung was not. He tried dialing, and got no answer.

"They're probably tied up," Lisa said. "Trapped in the same situation they were in on that night."

"Oh . . . right," Dane said. "So . . . it started right here. With your decision."

"Likely the switching on of the machine," she said, "the dumping of so much power into the wormhole, caused the discordance that allowed the possibility of branching timelines. What happened with us might not be the only difference. But . . . yeah."

"So you're saying," he told her, "there's a *reasonable* way for me to claim you caused the end of the world."

"Only," Lisa said—and she was breathing hard—"if you're an idiot and trying to intentionally misunderstand this entire situation."

"Sounds like me." He turned, and his leg suddenly flared up. It hadn't hurt until just that moment for some reason, but now he winced. "So we're doing this? Assault the place, alone?"

"You're still standing there?" she said, and he realized her puffing was because she was jogging.

"Uh . . . yeah," he admitted.

"Get going! We have twenty minutes to save the world."

He tried, but that pain kept him from moving at more than a limp. He reached the front gate, looked up, and realized he could never climb the wall in his condition. He'd need another way. Maybe . . . something a little more Lisa-esque.

He pushed the call button.

"Yes?" a guard said.

"It's me," Dane said. "Is Malik there?"

"Wait," a new—more familiar—voice said. "How do you know my name?"

"Do you remember?" Dane said softly. "You did in the last jump. Revenants with glowing eyes. The end of the world. Tell me you remember."

The line fell silent. Then a haunted reply, "That's a nightmare."

"It's what will happen if Nazeem activates the device," Dane said, leaning against the gate by the call box, sweating, blood escaping his tourniquet and trickling down his calf. "Look, I'm wounded. You shot me—or will, in about five hours. Thanks for that. You sounded regretful, Malik. You know what she's doing is wrong. Let's stop this."

Dane leaned against the gate, waiting as the call box again went silent. He knew he probably shouldn't even be on his feet, but if he ignored the pain, he found he could stand and limp. He did so, moving back as the gate opened.

Two security guards approached, one being Malik, the other being—he was pretty sure—that overly muscular revenant he'd killed inside the SWAT head-quarters. They stopped in front of Dane.

"We tied up Adam," Malik said. "He always was a little too, um . . . on board with all this."

"What do we do?" the other guy said. "To make sure the nightmares never come true?"

"First," Dane said, limping forward and waving for them to follow, "we get that scientist out of the cellar. Then we turn off the machine." Holding up his phone, he continued, "I'm in, Li. What about you?"

"On my way," she said. "Sorry about your car. Again."

"What?"

———

Lisa smashed through the front gates of the mansion in Dane's SUV, then tore across the grounds—leaving gouged-out tire tracks in the lawn. She pulled to a stop by the cellar, then crawled out the window, carrying Dane's assault rifle from the trunk. Loaded, chambered, and ready. She'd been fast enough breaking in that the guards didn't have time to reach her before she used the car's off-roading winch to rip out the cellar doors.

As she'd hoped, Past Yung was inside, tied up, looking to her with hope. She pulled down his gag.

"Took you long enough," he said. "Um. Thank you for the rescue."

"No problem," she said, cutting his bonds with a swift swipe of the knife.

"The machine will be counting down to activation," he said. "It must have been engaged at the same moment you made an important decision, branching the timelines to—"

"Figured that part out already," she said, giving him a handgun. "Let's move."

He nodded, joining her as they hurried down the steps into the cellar, and across to the door—which she opened with a few swift kicks. "How do we stop the machine? Will enough bullets do it?"

"You're just as likely to set it off early as stop it that way, Officer. Remember, the wormhole is *already* powered."

"Please tell me you programmed in a kill code."

"Do I seem like the type to program in a kill code?"

She froze, looking to him.

"The answer, Officer," he said, raising the gun, "is *of course* I do. And I did."

Lisa smiled, then—after leading him around the corner—pulled something out of her pocket and rolled it down the final hallway.

"Smoke grenade," she explained. "Hold your breath as we breach the room. Dane, what's your end look like?"

———

"Good," Dane replied, helping his Yung stand, then handing him a gun. Together with the two guards, he reached the bottom of the cellar. Malik kicked the door open, and the four of them started toward the room with the machines.

On his way he saw . . .

"Lisa?" he said, freezing. The others bunched up around him, and one of the guards made the sign of the cross.

A phantom version of Lisa and her Yung were in the hallway here, armed, hurrying forward. They were transparent, barely visible.

"The timelines are aligning," Dane's Yung said from beside him. "I . . . can't believe I'm seeing this . . . The implications . . ."

Lisa stopped in the hall and looked back, then her eyes widened. She wore her earpiece, phone in her pocket.

"You see me?" Dane asked.

"Yeah. Transparent."

"The timelines are aligning," he barely heard her Yung say in the background. "I'm so lucky to be here . . . The implications . . ."

"Hurry," Lisa said, turning down the hallway. Dane followed with his team, careful—and when he peeked into the final room, he saw phantoms of guards and Nazeem inside, coughing from the smoke. Those were all from Lisa's timeline—and she and her Yung efficiently cuffed them with flex-cuffs as each of the guards raised their hands.

But in Dane's version of the room . . . nothing. He expected a shootout when he arrived. But it was . . . empty? Nobody here *or* in the viewing room beyond.

"Nazeem?" Dane called, sensing a trap.

We sent her away.

The voice, like a hundred overlapping whispers, forced its way into his mind.

We don't need her right now. Because you're not going to stop this.

In her timeline, a phantom Lisa tackled a phantom Nazeem, who tried to run.

Dane's attention snapped to the wormhole in the room just in front of him. Wavering, having grown larger, full of crackling energy.

You won't stop this, the voice said, *because you know it's needed. All new birth is predicated on death.*

Dane gritted his teeth, then moved into the room, ignoring the voice—though the *force* of it was so strong that he found it difficult to pay attention to anything else. He barely noticed the phantom version of Lisa's Yung—who had started coughing—kicking the smoke grenade back down the hallway in her timeline.

The control room. Dane could reach it . . .

If you stop this, you become nothing again, the overlapping voices said. *We have come to bring change, revolution, and rebirth. You will not stop it, because you know, all along, you've been fighting the wrong fight. Listen to the instinct inside of you. The part of you that understands.*

"All that part of me wants," Dane said from the control room, his team following, "is some chips and Heineken."

In the room, he found the machine preparing to activate—at least, all the lights on the computers here were on. A workstation at the side displayed a countdown timer.

Nine minutes to go.

The phantom Lisa stepped up beside him. "Hold Control," her Yung said over the phone line, "Shift, and F12."

They did so, and a kill screen came up. Fantastic.

"We should try to do it at exactly the same moment," her Yung said. "But . . ."

"But what?" Lisa said.

"Are we sure we want to do this?" said her Yung.

"Why wouldn't we be?" Dane asked.

"Don't you . . . don't you hear it?" her Yung asked.

"Yes."

His Yung.

Gunfire sounded behind Dane. He spun to see the two guards—who had entered the control room with him—on the floor, bleeding. Dane cursed and raised his weapon. Too slowly.

Do it, the voice said. It hadn't been talking to him. It had been talking to the Yungs.

Right as Dane got his gun to his shoulder, Yung—grim-faced—shot Dane in the head.

He dropped.

"Dane?" Lisa said from the phone. "Was that gunfire? Dane?"

His eyes flickered closed. Someone approached and took his assault rifle—then his phone. That was followed by a cracking sound as it was stepped on, and Lisa's voice cut out.

"Well done, Yung," Nazeem said, entering from somewhere behind. "They said you'd listen."

"I . . ." Yung's voice. "I . . . talked about this with Dane. He persuaded me that I'd be a hero if I stopped it. That's not true. That *isn't me* in the other world. It's another version of me. *He* would be a hero. If Lightbreak doesn't happen . . . then I, the me I've become, would just . . . stop existing, like this entire timeline."

"We both get what we want, Yung. A world of heroes and monsters."

"A world . . ." Yung said softly, "where I can mean something . . ."

His breathing labored, Dane tried to find the strength to move. But he felt himself slipping. And then his grand constant—his heartbeat, source of peace and focus—fluttered. And gave out.

Twenty-Seven

Dane!" Lisa screamed into the line, looking at the body on the floor, which—transparent—faded away. Not because it was gone, but because the timelines were falling out of sync again. She called his phone and got no reply. She tried again, then looked to Past Yung, who stood behind her.

He had his gun aimed straight at her.

Lisa felt cold in that instant. Sweating. Staring him down. Oh . . . *hell.*

"Are we . . . we sure," he said, stuttering, "that we want to stop this?"

"The apocalypse? Of course we do!"

"But listen. Just listen." He glanced at Nazeem and her guards, in a cuffed row back in the test room. The smoke was clearing, though some still wafted in around Yung, standing in the doorway of the smaller control room. "I hear . . . whispers. Very distant whispers. They remind me that I don't mean anything in this world. Neither of us do. Officer . . . Lisa. We don't *mean* anything."

"Yes, we do," she said, standing up carefully. She moved her hands away from her gun. "We do, Yung. Our lives matter. Our hopes matter."

"That world we could live in," he said. "Doesn't it at least interest you? Completely new physics to discover? People to protect? A war to fight, against a terrible enemy? We could make sure you don't die, so you could join us. Those kinds of events *make* heroes. The great scientists of the past are great in part because they had something to discover. While we . . . we sit in classrooms . . . and merely teach about them."

"Yung," Lisa said. "Albert. Meet my eyes."

He did so.

"This is the moment," she said, "when you get to mean something. When you choose whether to shoot me, or save the world. *Right now.* The voice told Nazeem to do what she did, and the you in Dane's timeline . . . You don't have to listen to it though. Be the better man of the two."

He held her eyes.

Then dropped the gun.

"The code," he whispered, "is two-seven-four-seven-three."

She turned and started inputting it. Then froze. "You said that it's best if we do it at the same time as Dane."

"Best if you finish at the same moment. To help align the timelines. But . . . Lisa. I think . . . I think Future Yung might have killed him. In a timeline where I'm *not* the better of the two . . ."

She placed her hands on the workstation table, sweating, heart thundering. Dane . . .

Dane couldn't be dead.

She clasped her hand to her bracelet and spun it. Hoping. Praying. Knowing. Andrew Dane was not dead.

Not while there was a beat left to protect.

Twenty-Eight

5 Minutes to Lightbreak

You should get moving." Nazeem's voice. "You won't want to be here when the explosion happens."

"I need to be close enough." Yung's voice. "To be dosed with the radiation. To become all that I can be."

"I need to be closer." Nazeem. "I remember . . . the power. The invincibility. Our clashes will be legendary, Yung."

"Heroes," he said.

"And monsters," she said.

And some who are both.

Dane knew . . . floating in darkness . . . why his wounds hadn't killed him. He knew why he'd been able to tell a revenant was in a dark building those times when nobody else had spotted them. He knew why he could fall thirty feet and not die.

He supposed he'd known it all along. Why the pain had gone away completely when he'd witnessed Lightbreak—and been dosed by its radiation. Why he'd always felt invigorated, stronger, when he was near a Dead Zone.

The more energy you absorbed, the longer it took to transform you. Those indoors went first. Those outdoors next. Then the guards, shielded in their blast room. Then . . .

The ones who had taken the most of it. Him and Yung. Even now, Dane could feel—eyes closed—the heat of the other people in the room. Subtle, but there.

He opened his eyes to find his vision ringed by glowing light. He slipped his sidearm free with a calm, quiet motion. The strong ones . . . it had always taken a few shots, even to the head. The bullet lodged in his forehead hadn't quite been enough.

And so, with no heartbeat to guide him, Officer Andrew Dane rose again, a revenant. He shot Yung three times straight in the head before turning and gunning down the two security guards who had entered with Nazeem.

The woman herself screamed, ducking back into the doorway and firing his assault rifle, the one Yung had taken from him. Dane hadn't noticed her appropriating it. He found cover beside some equipment near the teleporter and pressed himself against the wall, feeling the heat of the fallen. Beside him, Yung's corpse lay with open eyes, a bloody mess.

"I told you, Yung," Dane whispered. "Always double-check that they're dead." He felt so . . . strangely unnerved without that heartbeat to guide him.

"Do you realize what you're doing?" Nazeem shouted from where she crouched in the doorway, just out of sight. "We worked so hard for that world! Don't ruin it!"

He knew his time was running out. But the phone . . . the phone was dead. Cracked and broken on the floor. He . . .

His bracelet quivered. Then moved.

Lisa, you genius, he thought as she carefully spun it a specific number of times. A code. Two. Seven. Four. Six. Three. Then a reset, a pause, and a repeat. Ah, he'd counted that six wrong. It was a seven as well.

"You could be a hero," Nazeem said. "To everyone in this city."

"There's only one person I've ever wanted to be a hero for," he said softly. "And she already knows."

He stepped out from behind the equipment.

Bullets tore through Dane's body as he calmly sighted, and—to an imagined heartbeat—fired three shots straight into Nazeem's head. She collapsed.

He slumped against the computer desk. Damn. Looked like his body could indeed only take so much punishment. That would have been useful to know.

With bloodied fingers, he typed. One number at a time.

2.

Lisa started to fade in beside him.

7.

He couldn't hear her gasp as she saw him, but he could imagine it.

4.

She became more solid. And mouthed, "I knew. Because you are incredible."

7.

He smiled and raised his bloodied finger, limp as he struggled to hold himself in place, to the 3.

She mimicked his motion. The countdown was under a minute. But . . . with his free hand, he gave her a deliberate salute.

It was good that she was crying. He'd have hated to be the only one.

He hit the key right as she did. And in so doing, Officer Andrew Dane gave up a world that needed him, to preserve a better one that did not.

The room went white one last time.

Epilogue

Lisa sat in the mayor's office as he reread her report. He was a brute of a man, former firefighter, with a delicate side he used to enhance his image. He did have three daughters, but the photo of him wearing pink and celebrating with his youngest at her ballet class had been carefully planned.

That was true political shrewdness. Taking who you really were, then presenting a . . . version of that. With an eye toward plausibility.

"I find this quite difficult to swallow, Sterling," he said.

The report contained only the half of it. The parts she'd decided that someone in his position *might* accept.

"I have the press hounding me," the mayor continued, "calling for answers. I can't give them *this*."

"We have all the testimonies of the officers I involved, the scientist, and the guards. You've read it. You know they can't all be lying."

"You were still reckless," he said. "Moved without authorization, warrants, or backup. I have a dead officer and two dead civilian security guards, along with a ton of property damage, cars run off the road, buildings destroyed. Not to mention Nazeem herself—she'll bring lawsuits . . ."

Lisa nodded. That was all true. The report indicated the explosion they'd prevented, mentioning nothing about an apocalypse. Instead, she'd used some technobabble from Yung about the devices causing memory loss and erratic behavior. That explained why her people, who were tracked by body cams and GPS to her break-in at the lab, were completely unable to remember being there. It explained why she hadn't been able to get help.

A version of the truth. Taken and presented with an eye toward plausibility.

She was nervous. She'd grown strangely used to knowing the future these last few days; now she didn't know what would happen. He might fire her. Her career might be over. But . . . did that matter? She'd always said she was doing something better, and the good of the city came before anything else. Sitting in that chair, she found she was confident—for the first time in years—that she actually *meant* that.

She and Dane had saved the city.

Granted, she still wanted her career. If she couldn't have it . . . she'd made her decision. And heaven help her if the mayor, or anyone else, discovered that she and Yung had gone to each facility during that night after Moment Zero to completely destroy the wormholes. Yung was the one who had initially stabilized and grown them with power inputs—and as he'd once told her, he knew how to shrink them too. They'd collapsed all three, then destroyed what notes, equipment, and computer files they could.

"We'll pin the wrecks and deaths on Dane," the mayor finally said. "You'll be presented as the level head who got the job done and kept him from going too far. They'll buy it, after we unlock his records."

"No," Lisa found herself saying.

The mayor looked up, surprised. "No" wasn't a word he liked to hear.

"Detective Andrew Dane," Lisa said, her voice firm, "was a *hero*. He gave his life for this city. He will be known for that, or you can have my badge. It's non-negotiable."

The mayor glared at her long and hard. She glared back. She'd bullied the timeline itself. She could handle him.

"You know," he eventually said, "I was worried you would say or do anything to please me and get that promotion. Good to know there are lines you won't cross. Infuriating too, mind you, though I've learned it's what I need."

He stood.

She did likewise.

"It will have to be a commendation for Dane, then," he said. "This is the harder road. If it goes poorly with the press this next month, I might be forced to roll back your promotion. Hell, might have to give you up for prosecution, if we can't spin this right."

"I'll take that risk," she said. "And I can handle the press. After all if I can't, would I be worth giving the job to anyway?"

He smiled, then held out his hand. She took it.

"I think," he said, "that I'm going to enjoy working with you, Chief Sterling."

"Likewise, Mister Mayor."

"Now," he said, with a wave, "go fix this mess."

"It is what I do," Lisa replied. "Whenever it's appropriate."

POSTSCRIPT

Here we hit the cornerstone of this book, the big new story I wanted to do so there was a brand-new centerpiece to this collection, other than simply having all these stories in one location.

This is an idea story. The pitch of "cops try to stop the apocalypse from either side of it in the time stream" was too engaging not to try to write. I loved the structure of one person going forward in time a few days, and the other going backward a few days, then both of them moving through the story closer and closer to the central moment when it all went wrong.

The real key to this story came when I discovered the twist—that of the reader (and the characters) not knowing when Moment Zero actually was.

This is a story where I have in my notes a ton of the mechanics for what is happening rules-wise, but I decided not to put most of it in. (Though the final draft does have a lot more of this sort of thing, at the request of my editorial team.) The idea was that I didn't want the focus to be on the mechanics, but on the flow through time of the characters and their interactions.

The other distinctive thing about this story was writing a relationship that is on its way out rather than on its way in, so to speak. A relationship that is over, and the characters need to come to terms with that. My agents in Hollywood wish that they'd just gotten back together at the end, but I think that would undermine the story too much. We have tons of stories about people hooking back up after a failed relationship, but not many (action stories, at least) about the very natural last days of a relationship that didn't quite get there. This proved too integral to the narrative for me to pull out during revisions, so I've gone with it, and I hope it works.

Anyway, that's *Tailored Realities*! Twenty-five years (whew) of Brandon Sanderson fiction packed into one volume. I recognize that the Cosmere stories tend to be more popular, but these kinds of pieces are often where I explore new ways of telling stories that eventually end up informing how I write in the Cosmere. Outside the Cosmere, I often have a little more freedom than I do inside it—and

I tend to do things more outside my wheelhouse, so the stories can be a bit all over the place. (I'm looking at you, "Probability Approaching Zero.")

I hope you enjoyed this book in part as a historical look at my development as a writer over the years, but also as . . . well, a collection of really fun tales.

Hopefully I'll have another one of these for you in . . . oh, another quarter of a century.

—*Brandon Sanderson*

ACKNOWLEDGMENTS

Although the stories contained in this tome are mine, getting this book into your hands is an incredible group effort. The following paragraphs contain the names of the many people I have to thank for bringing these tales to readers.

At Tor: Stephanie Stein, the in-house editor for the book, and an excellent team of editors, designers, publicists, marketers and more, including Heather Saunders, Julianna Kim, Peter Lutjen, Rafal Gibek, Emily Mlynek, Eileen Lawrence, Steven Bucsok, Aelxis Saarela, Sarah Reidy, Steve Wagner, Terry McGarry, Christina MacDonald, Hayley Jozwiak, Devi Pillai, Lucille Rettino, Claire Eddy, and Will Hinton.

At JABberwocky Literary Agency: Joshua Bilmes, Susan Velasquez, Christina Zobel, Valentina Sainato, and Brady McReynolds. At Zeno Literary Agency: John Berlyne.

At Dragonsteel: COO, Queen, and Co-President Emily Sanderson

Creative Development: Vice President Isaac Stewart, Art Director Shawn Boyles, Art Director Ben McSweeney, Rachael Lynn Buchanan, Jennifer Neal, Hayley Lazo, Priscilla Spencer, and Anna Earley.

Editorial: The Inductive Peter Ahlstrom as VP, Editorial Director Kristy S. Gilbert, Continuity Director Karen Ahlstrom, Jennie Stevens, Betsey Ahlstrom, Emily Shaw-Higham, and Jack Rose.

Publicity & Marketing: VP Adam Horne (a.k.a. the Godzilla Expert), Octavia Escamilla, Tayan Hatch, Taylor Hatch, and Donald Mustard III.

Operations & HR: Operations & HR: VP Matt "the HRinator" Hatch, Operations Director Jane Horne, Lex Willhite, Jerrod Walker, Kathleen Dorsey Sanderson, Ethan Skarstedt, Becky Wilson, Christian Fairbanks, and Makena Saluone.

Merchandise & Events: Kara Stewart (VP of Merchandising, Events, and Writing Big Checks), Merchandise Director Christi Jacobsen, Events & Support Director Kellyn Neumann, Finance Director Emma Tan-Stoker, Richard Rubert, Dallin Holden, Matt Hampton, Ally Reep, Brett Moore, Joy Allen, Katy Ives, Daniel Phipps, Braydonn Moore, Mem Grange, Michael Bateman, Alex

Lyon, Jacob Chrisman, Camilla Waite, Quinton Martin, Hollie Rubert, Gwen Hickman, Amanda Butterfield, Logan Reep, Pablo Mooney, Rachel Jacobsen, Zoe Hatch, Owen Knowlton, Laura Loveridge, Jake Dellamas, and Mary Nolivos.

Narrative: VP Dan Wells, still the only member of the Narrative Department, because with his One Direction fan fictions being so good, why would we need another?

Arists: Bryan Mark Taylor with the cover art and Jessi Ochse and Ben McSweeney with the interior illustrations.

Law enforcement experts consulting on "Moment Zero": Troy S. Thurston, Zachary Zavala, Moises Mascorro, and Tiffany Kalinowski.

Beta readers: Kendra Alexander, Jessica Ashcraft, Rahkeem Ball, Joe Deardeuff, Ted Herman, Jana King, Lyndsey Luther, Suzanne Musin, Kalyani Poluri, Billy Todd, Paige Vest, Glen Vogelaar, and Rob West.

Gamma readers included many of the beta readers as well as Amir Kasra Arman, Siena "Lotus" Buchanan, Tim Challener, Taylor Cole, Violette Colla, Dariyan Edsinger, David Fallon, Aaron Ford, Craig Hanks, Joshua Harkey, Brian T. Hill, Alexis "Lex" Horizon, Sarah Kane, Jayden King, Bob Kluttz, Ashley Kowalczyk, Ari Kufer, Valencia Kumley, Erika Kuta Marler, Eliyahu Berelowitz Levin, Mark Lindberg, Brian Magnant, Karen Marks, Chris McGrath, TJ McGrath, Seth "Forger" Mosey, Aerin Pham, Bao Pham, Jennifer Pugh, Rachel Rada, Becca Reppert, Britton Roney, Nisarg "Strifelover" Shah, Amit Shteinheart, Gary Singer, Lauren "Biz's Mom" Strach, Philip Vorwaller, Spencer White, Deana Covel Whitney, Dale Wiens, Rosemary Williams, Kendra Wilson, Kyle "Dorksider" Wilson, and Lingting "Botanica" Xu.

—*Brandon Sanderson*

ABOUT THE AUTHOR

Brandon Sanderson grew up in Lincoln, Nebraska. He lives in Utah with his wife and children and teaches creative writing at Brigham Young University. His bestsellers have sold 40 million copies worldwide and include the Mistborn saga; the Stormlight Archive novels; and other novels, including *Tress of the Emerald Sea*, *The Rithmatist*, *Steelheart*, and *Skyward*. He won a Hugo Award for *The Emperor's Soul*, a novella set in the world of his acclaimed first novel, *Elantris*. Additionally, he completed Robert Jordan's The Wheel of Time®. Visit his website for behind-the-scenes information on all his books.